THE WARRIOR

Wanda Ann Thomas

CHAPTER 1

Upper Galilee 48 BC

The first scream tore away the blanket of quiet covering the rolling hills. Nathan of Rumah's donkey brayed and kicked up dust. By the second scream, Nathan was halfway up the hill, running toward the trouble. Habits from his days fighting in the Jewish army kicked in. He slowed, pulled a hunting knife from his belt, and crept forward.

Cresting the knoll, he ducked behind a thorn bush. Willing his breathing to slow, he scanned the rocky terrain. The autumn sun shone down on a bald man standing guard over a family. An older man, a boy, and a young woman knelt in the dirt, clinging to each other. Blood stained their clothing.

Movement on the opposite hill caught his eye. A small band of men and donkeys were making a hasty retreat.

Beelzebub, take them! Judas and Hezekiah were at it again. Why wouldn't his friends listen? Attacking Roman sympathizers wasn't going to convince the Romans to go home. Nathan had marched beside the armies of Rome and seen firsthand how they dealt with sedition. Death on a cross was a drawn out and excruciatingly painful affair.

Though he'd dearly love to give chase and take a piece out of someone's hide, it would have to wait. He sheathed his knife and headed toward the injured travelers.

The bald-headed man, a slave, stepped aside. "My master is Simeon Onias. You know him, I imagine?"

Simeon was a priest and one of the richest men in Judea. He wore the austere robes of a Pharisee. What was the religious man doing in one of the most remote stretches of Galilee? Pharisees lived almost exclusively in Jerusalem, never traveling far from the holy city due to their zealous devotion to the Temple and the sacrifices.

Nathan knelt beside Simeon. The frightened man cringed. His son, a youth of about fourteen, wept loudly. The daughter, a young woman of marriageable age, patted her brother's back. Trepidation filled her eyes.

The air smelled of blood and fear. Though a common outcome of battles big or small, he never learned to like the smell as many soldiers did. During a fight, he'd been as brutal and senseless to the violence as any of them. Afterward, without fail, he was sickened by what he'd done.

He put his hands up to show them he meant no harm. "*Shalom.* My name is Nathan of Rumah. I am a farmer. I was on my way south when I heard your screams. You're safe now. I'll protect you from any further harm."

The woman sat up straighter. "They took Lydia." Blood speckled the heavy white veil covering her face.

"Is Lydia your mother?" Nathan asked.

She shook her head. "No, my sister." She gestured in the direction the rebels had gone. "Please, Lydia needs your help."

"Silence, Alexandra," Simeon Onias said. The Pharisee's face and neck were covered with large, red welts and his eyes were nearly swollen shut. Yet he still managed to scowl at Nathan. "Forget Lydia. Help my son."

The boy held his face. Blood streamed down his cheek from a long, horizontal cut.

Nathan was having a hard time accepting what he was seeing—the maiming of the boy, the abduction of a young woman, the pummeling of the religious man. This was no ordinary attack. His friends *couldn't* have had a part in this.

"Father," the young woman protested. "James's injury will heal. Lydia needs help now."

Simeon's lips pursed with distaste. "Cease your clamoring, Daughter."

The young woman winced, but her eyes stayed on Nathan, begging him to do as she'd asked.

"Don't play the whore," Simeon accused.

Alexandra ducked her head.

Nathan interceded. "Who attacked you?"

"The leader is called Judas the Zealot," Simeon said. "Do you know him?"

I thought I did, Nathan's mind protested. Sickened to his core, he managed a nod.

The Pharisee waved a dismissive hand. "That whoreson is welcome to keep the girl. No self-respecting man will want to marry her now."

Nathan glared at Simeon. He would love to go after Lydia just to spite the mean-spirited man, but the family's donkeys had been stolen, and it was a long walk to the next town. They'd do well to reach shelter before dark. Plus, the boy needed to be stitched up. A line of sweat rolled down Nathan's back. He exhaled heavily. "Get them up, and I'll go retrieve my donkey," he told the slave.

The young woman rose to her feet. Despair clung to her like grave clothes.

Nathan's chest tightened. He was partly to blame for what had happened here. He should have put a stop to the raids.

He took a step toward Alexandra. "I will find your sister and bring her home to you. You have my solemn promise."

A tremble shook her. Beautiful gray eyes met his. "Bless you," she whispered.

He admired her quiet bravery. She'd make some man a fine wife. His hand moved to smooth the soft, brown wisps of hair floating about her face.

She tensed.

His fingers curled. The heat must have turned his brain to mush. She wasn't his to touch. He moved off. Halfway up the rocky incline, he glanced back. Today's ordeal would leave scars on the battered family deeper than the one on the boy's face. Putting a stop to raids was the right thing to do. He scrubbed his face. His friends and neighbors were not going be happy with him when they learned he'd finally chosen a side in their damnable rebellion, and it wasn't with them.

He hated the whole business. Hated it down to his last fiber.

◆ ◆ ◆

Alexandra watched the broad back of the stranger who had come to their aid disappear over the hill. Strong and handsome, Nathan exuded confidence and vitality. His presence was a great comfort. No more harm would come to them while they were under his care.

But what of Lydia? The sour smell of alcohol from the outlaw's breath lingered in Alexandra's nostrils. She gagged and clutched her stomach. Dear Lord in heaven, how much more evil would her sister have to endure?

Why, why, why had Father brought them to this remote wilderness? Her father believed a woman's place was in the home, a principle he normally followed to the strictest degree. Father's announcement that he was journeying to Galilee and taking them with him had come as a complete surprise. Her sister had been delighted with the adventure, though. From her constant smile, you'd have thought Lydia was walking on the streets of gold in the kingdom of God rather than the dusty roads of Galilee.

Alexandra wished the outlaws had abducted her instead of her lively sister. Lydia must be terribly frightened. But then Lydia would have been forced to cut James's face. Alexandra swayed on her feet as the image of the deadly sharp knife slicing into her brother's cheek played through her mind. Stealing money hadn't been enough for the robbers. They had played a cruel game, enjoying the wretched fear it wrought.

James gave a loud cry. Father's slave, Goda, was attempting to cleanse her brother's wound.

Alexandra moved closer to James. "Take your hands away. The bleeding has slowed," she soothed. "Let Goda have a look at it."

"It stings like a burn," James complained, sniffling, but he lowered his hands. White flesh glistened beneath a wash of pink blood. The knife had cut deep into the meaty part of the cheek, flaying it open like the belly of a fish.

Another wave of nausea arose. Alexandra swallowed. "It will need to be stitched," she said as calmly as she could.

Father shoved his way between them. He inspected the diagonal cut crossing James's right cheek, then poked at it with his finger.

"Ouch," James squawked, falling back.

"Hold still," Father ordered. James clenched his teeth and submitted to the exam. Father made a sound of disgust. "It will take a dozen stitches to close the cut. You are going to have a scar the length of my finger."

James's lower lip wobbled.

Father wrinkled his nose. "This means the ruin of all my plans."

"Plans?" James said.

Father ignored the question. "You won't be able to serve as a priest."

"But all my friends are to be priests. And...I...I..." James began to wail and covered his face.

"Perhaps the Lord has other plans for you," Alexandra said rubbing her brother's back as the full implications of the attack washed over her. The Lord's priests must be without blemish. Poor James. He could talk of nothing but becoming a priest. Now he would never stand at the Lord's altar.

An annoyed look crossed Father's face. "Stop your blubbering."

Alexandra grabbed her father's sleeve. "Allow Goda to tend to *your* wounds. I will take care of James."

Father pointed a finger in her face. "Don't tell me what to do."

She lowered her eyes. "Forgive me." Better he storm at her than James. Though not much older than her brother and sister, she watched over them as if they were her children, a practice she had followed since their mother had died twelve years ago.

Father turned his back on them.

Alexandra put her arms around James. His shoulders shook from the force of his weeping. Her heart ached for him and for Lydia. The horror of the past hour had changed their destinies. All that remained to be seen was the depth and breadth of the damage.

CHAPTER 2

Jerusalem frothed like the sea in a storm. More than one hundred thousand Jews from the four corners of the world, all wearing pure white garments, poured into the walled courtyard surrounding the Temple, eager to celebrate the holiest day of the year. *Yom Kippur.*

Nathan guided his six-year-old brother, Timothy, to the shade of the south gate. Rumor had it the Onias Family would be making their first public appearance since they were attacked.

Nathan had led Simeon and his children to the safety of a small inn four weeks ago. He'd spent all his time since then searching the hills and caves surrounding his Galilean home, but he hadn't found any sign of Lydia or her captors.

He'd gone straight to the Onias's grand home upon arriving in Jerusalem two days ago to report what he knew and had been turned away. Nathan shook his head. Nothing about the matter sat right. He planned to get an explanation from the Pharisee.

The crowd surrounding them buzzed more loudly, then quieted and parted.

"Here they come," Timothy squealed excitedly, pointing at Simeon Onias riding high on a sedan chair carried by four rugged slaves.

Nathan patted his brother's head. "Hush, Monkey."

The thin middle-aged woman standing in front of Nathan elbowed her husband. "I told you. The Onias boy's scar is bright as day. He won't be able to be a priest now."

Nathan flinched. James's scar hadn't healed right. It pulsed, ugly and purple, on the boy's ashen face.

The husband of the loud-mouthed woman stroked his grizzled beard. "Everyone says the older sister cut the boy. Do you think it's true?"

Alexandra was half-hidden behind the sedan chair. Head held high, her bearing was regal.

The loud woman craned her neck for a better view. "She does have a cold-blooded look about her."

"Hold your tongues," Nathan growled through clenched teeth. He admired Alexandra's poise and prayed the gossips were wrong. Shedding another person's blood had a way of eating at your soul. If the story proved true. His fists balled.

Onias's bald slave walked behind the chair holding his master. Nathan pushed through the press of people, grabbed the slave's arm, and drew him aside.

The eunuch's wrinkled brow arched. "What can I do for you?"

"Tell me why your master won't see me."

The slave held out his hand. He wanted money for the information.

Impatient and annoyed, Nathan clapped his hand to the pocket of his tunic. The leather pouch he carried barely made a bulge, holding enough money to pay the

Temple tax and to buy a few essentials. "Go." Nathan waved the sly man on.

"I take goods as well."

Nathan made a sound of disgust. "You are as odious as your master."

The bald man's smirk slipped.

"Go," Nathan said again. "I'll talk to Simeon myself."

"Master Onias wants you to stop the search for his daughter. He will take care of the matter in his own way." Message delivered for free, the slave slithered off.

Nathan found Timothy, then followed the Onias family across the stone-paved courtyard and watched Alexandra enter the arched entryway to the Women's Court. A wide swath opened around her. No aunts or cousins stepped forward to greet her. Thanks to false reports saying the rebels had defiled her and her sister, Alexandra was being treated like a leper. She was adrift. Alone. Friendless.

Simeon and James moved on, careless of her plight. *Curse them.*

Incensed, Nathan entered the Men's Court and guided Timothy to the back, to the lattice screen dividing the men's and women's sections. He caught Mary's attention and signaled his sister to join them.

She hurried over. Brown eyes alight, twelve-year-old Mary spoke in a rush. "Nathan, I swear, one peek of High Priest Hyrcanus and I would have—"

Nathan tapped his finger to the end of her nose. "Hush, little lamb," he said, "I have a kindness to ask of you." He pointed. "Alexandra Onias is in need of a friend. Sweet lamb that you are, I am sure she would welcome your company."

Mary blinked and swallowed. "But the Onias family

belong to the righteous. And we farm and own goats and sheep."

He squeezed his sister's shoulder. "Here you are, in your well-washed white gown, and she is in hers. Today, you are all righteous daughters of Israel." He gave her a gentle nudge. "Go on, now."

He understood Mary's doubt. Olive farmers and Pharisees lived in different worlds.

Pharisees strived for spotless purity.

Farming entailed tasks leading to defilement.

Blessed with a kind heart and a warm nature, Mary soon engaged Alexandra in conversation. His sister turned and smiled at him, drawing Alexandra's attention.

Sad, lovely eyes shone on him. There was no sign of reproach on her face in spite of his failure to keep his promise. With such a father, she was undoubtedly used to disappointment. Nathan rapped his knuckles against the stone latticework. He wouldn't fail her too. He'd find Lydia, with or without Simeon Onias's permission. But not on his own. Upper Galilee was pocked with countless caves. He'd need help to search through all of them.

A gruff whisper filled his ear. "The Onias girl would make a fine wife for you, olive farmer."

Nathan turned and grinned at Herod of Idumea. "I heard you and your father were back from Egypt."

Black-eyed and dark-skinned, Herod's large, white teeth gleamed as he smiled back and clapped Nathan on the shoulder. "You missed a good battle, friend." Then he nodded toward Alexandra. "A high-ranking priest's daughter is not likely to come more cheaply."

"I heard she was supposed to marry a wealthy priest,

but the man ended the engagement." Nathan exhaled heavily. To ensure the purity of the priestly line, priests were not allowed to marry women who had been taken as captives. Alexandra had only been held for a brief time, and her father had been present the whole time, but it was enough to disqualify her.

Nathan couldn't stop staring at her. Priest's daughters didn't come more beautiful than Alexandra Onias. It had been a long time since he craved wealth. Her refined loveliness made him wish he was richest man in the land.

Herod crossed his arms over his wide chest. "If her father wishes to gain even half the money he might have gotten for her, he'll have to marry her off to a wealthy man outside the priestly families, a man with ambition looking to make an alliance with a family of means and influence."

Nathan stubbed his sandal into the stone-paved ground. "Do you know who might make an offer?"

"She's a pretty thing," Herod remarked. "I ought to marry her myself."

Nathan's head snapped up. "What?"

Herod laughed and waggled his brows. "So, you are taken with her?"

Not about to admit to it, Nathan offered a sour grin back. "I am horrified for the girl's sake, not mine."

The priestly procession moved toward them, putting an end to the conversation. A hush fell over the crowd and faces filled with reverent awe.

High Priest John Hyrcanus padded by on bare feet, flanked by the Captain of the Temple and the Director of the daily sacrifices. Next came a priest holding up the sacred breastplate engraved with the names of the twelve tribes and decorated with twelve different precious gems, sparkling brightly.

The rest of the priests followed, hundreds and hundreds of them, taking their places between the Levite singers and musicians lining the Temple stairs. Though Nathan had witnessed the grand spectacle annually, from boyhood on, it never lost its luster. But today it brought no joy.

He prayed for peace of mind as High Priest Hyrcanus donned the sacred vestments, and as the bull and goats were sacrificed, and as the blood was sprinkled on the altar, but his conscience continued to accuse. Soon the moment everyone had been waiting for arrived. Like the trumpets of a thousand angels, loud song reverberated through the courtyard. "YAHWEH!" The *Shem ha-Meforash*—the excellent name of God—spoken out loud only once a year. It was what made *Yom Kippur* the highest of the holy days.

Nathan fell on his knees and pressed his face against the cold paving stones. "Praise be the glorious name of his kingdom forever and ever," he yelled, joining his voice with the people of God, longing to feel at one with his brethren.

Herod shouted louder than anyone. Did Herod feel the same crushing guilt Nathan did? Ten years ago, allied with the Romans and Mark Antony, they had fought their way into Jerusalem and retaken the city. Jews had killed Jews.

And now Nathan had committed himself to hunting down his friends and neighbors. He would go out of his way to keep from lifting a sword against them. But what if it couldn't be avoided? What if he had to spill blood?

The congregation stood. Nathan felt a divide opening between him and the people of God, and his insides
knotted.

High Priest Hyrcanus took burning coals from the
altar, put them in the golden censer, took up two hand-
fuls of incense, and went behind the veil woven with
blue, purple, and scarlet thread. Smoke rose and curled
heavenward.

Nathan inhaled the balsam and cinnamon, the smell
of God's forgiveness and mercy. It offered no comfort.

John Hyrcanus reappeared, and the Levite musicians
and singers burst into song. Hyrcanus took off the gem-
encrusted breastplate and hurried away from the Holy
of Holies.

Herod laughed and shook his woolly head. "Some
high priest he makes. Look at him. He is scared half to
death."

"You are one to criticize," Nathan chided. "You put
him in office."

"With your help."

"Yes, but I feel only shame for it now." Collecting
a number of curious stares from the departing crowd,
Nathan lowered his voice, "We shed blood to make Hyrcanus High Priest."

Herod patted Nathan on the shoulder. "Don't be so
hard on yourself, olive farmer. There was plenty of
blame to go around."

"I'm glad to see you're in a generous mood. I have a
favor to ask."

Herod pretended to fall backward. "You...accept my
help?" He put his hand to his heart. "I never thought to
see the day."

The corners of Nathan's mouth twitched. "Stop, you

overgrown barbarian." He glanced toward the Women's Court. "I want you to help me track down the men who attacked the Onias family."

Who knew? If Nathan rescued Lydia, he might get the opportunity to speak to Alexandra again. A fellow could always hope.

Alexandra made her way to the arched opening leading out of the Women's Court. The pleasing girl who had befriended her chatted away at her side. People continued to point and stare. Alexandra ignored them. What was a little embarrassment? Compared to what her sister must be suffering it was nothing. She focused on the young girl's pink-cheeked face. "Bless you for being so kind."

The girl's smile widened. "Will you be joining the maiden's dance in the vineyard?" This was the night all the unmarried girls got to dance under the stars, hoping to catch the eye of the young men who came to watch. Many marriages would be arranged before the evening ended.

Alexandra shook her head and bit her lip. She was supposed to dance tonight and make her engagement to Philip Peter official. But not now. Her intended husband had run out of his sandals in his haste to distance himself from her disgrace.

Alexandra sighed. "What's your name, dear?"

The girl's eyes shimmered. "Mary. I'm Mary and, oh, you *have* to come. It will be such fun." She skipped a step or two, then twirled in a small circle and clutched her hands to her chest. "I have been waiting all my life to join the dancing. Father says no, but," she nodded towards the Men's Court "Nathan has promised to speak to Father."

Alexandra's gaze shifted. Nathan of Rumah's dark brown eyes met hers. The sun emerged from behind a cloud and shone bright on waves of his black, glossy curls. The east wind rose. The dry desert air blew warm on her face and ruffled through his chin-length hair.

A strange sensation curled through her.

Mary shook her arm. "Here come my mother and aunts and cousins."

Alexandra forced her eyes away from the farmer. A small group of women moved toward them, smiling and waving. Wives and daughters of farmers or laborers, they had sun-browned faces and red-chapped hands.

A tall, straight-backed woman stepped forward. "Come along, Mary, the feast is waiting to be prepared." She looked too young to be Nathan's mother. She must be his stepmother.

Mary waved back. "I'm coming. I just need to say goodbye." The girl fluttered in place like a butterfly about to take flight. "Convince your father to bring you to the maiden's dance, and you and I can dance together."

"I will do my best, but please don't be disappointed if I'm not there," Alexandra cautioned. For the first time since the attack, she smiled. "But, I hope you get to dance. And, I hope it is even more wonderful than your dreams."

Mary touched Alexandra's sleeve. The light in her eyes dimmed. "I pray you get your sister back soon."

A painful lump lodged in Alexandra's throat. "Tell your brother I said thank you for all his kindnesses."

"Nathan feels guilty about what happened."

Alexandra blinked. That made no sense.

"Mary," the girl's mother called.

"Oh, I'm sorry. I've got to go. Goodbye," Mary said, and then she raced off.

Alexandra watched the sweet girl and the other women join a large group of men. Nathan was among them, with a young boy swinging on his arm. Nathan felt guilty? But why?

"Nathan of Rumah is an intriguing man, is he not?"

Alexandra jumped. "James, I...I..." She turned toward her brother. "Oh, look at you." The sun had burned the scar running across his face. "I begged you to put ointment on before going out." She reached up. James jerked away, fear shining in his eyes.

The horrid image returned—James's blood dripping from the shining blade. Her stomach clenched and she pulled her hand back.

Her father arrived on his sedan chair. "Festival joy, Matthias," he said to a passing friend. Turning back to them, he wagged his finger at James. "You will thank me someday for making you come to the Temple." He nodded his head at the slaves carrying his chair. "Even though it's meant letting these oxen haul me about like sack of wheat, it was worth it. Since the first time my father carried me on his shoulders to the Temple, until this day, I have never missed one of the required feasts."

James's face puckered. He turned his back on the familiar boast.

Alexandria swallowed the bitter taste in her mouth and offered the customary response, "May it be so, Father, until you lie in the grave with your fathers."

Her father's shoulders sagged low. "Take me home,"

he commanded the slaves.

Though she ought to follow, she stayed behind. "Father is a proud man."

James blew out a harsh breath. "Then why isn't he doing more to find Lydia? I begged Father to send me out with hired men to look for her. He laughed in my face." Her brother wrinkled his nose at her look of amazement. "Do you think Nathan of Rumah would abandon his sister to bandits?"

She glanced between James and Nathan. They were both dressed in white, the similarity stopped there. A scholar, her brother was thin and pale, whereas the olive farmer, Nathan, was rugged and bronzed. Avoiding her brother's question, she said, "Father paid the ransom."

"Yes, and we have nothing to show for it. Father wants to continue to negotiate with the bandits. He told Nathan of Rumah to stop looking for Lydia."

She rubbed her hands over her arms. What horrible things was Lydia suffering? She must be frightened half to death. "I don't understand why Father won't talk to Nathan."

James frowned. "I don't know and I don't care. I'm going to go talk to the olive farmer myself." He stalked off after Nathan.

Alexandra's heart sped up. Hundreds of festival goers brushed past her. She should already be walking behind her father, but her feet refused to move. She watched James go. There was no telling what trouble her rash brother might get into if left on his own. She stared in the direction her father had gone. She wasn't convinced he would do what was best for Lydia.

Alexandra took a deep breath and hurried to catch

up with James. "Wait for me," she called.

Her brother's eyes widened. "You are full of surprises of late, Sister."

She winced. "Father will be furious when he realizes we didn't follow him home."

James gave her a long look. "He'll be twice as angry with you."

A chill went through her. She walked faster. "All I care about is getting Lydia back. Nothing else matters."

CHAPTER 3

Leaving his family behind, Nathan threaded his way through the press of people returning to their campsites. Temporary tent cities ringed Jerusalem, filled with Jews who flocked to the holy city to observe Yom Kippur in obedience to the commands of God. Nathan's family had pitched their tent in the same spot in the Kidron Valley for generations. He knew every rock along the steep, twisting path between Jerusalem and the Mount of Olives.

He hurried and caught up with Hezekiah. "*Shalom*, my friend. Did you speak to Judas? Is he going to return Lydia to her family?" Nathan liked Hezekiah and had been immensely relieved when he learned the competent, well-respected leader of the rebellion hadn't had anything to do with the attack on the Onias family.

"*Shalom*, Nathan," Hezekiah said. A barrel of a man, he sobered. "My cousin doesn't think he's done anything wrong."

Nathan could only shake his head. Judas also claimed he was the Messiah, the one anointed of the Lord to usher in the promised kingdom. The man did have a way about him. Learned and engaging, Judas drew men in with his zealous speeches and his fiery hatred of Rome. Impatient to inflict harsher punishment on Roman sympathizers, Judas and his followers had broken away from the main body of rebels a month ago. Something Nathan would have known, if he allowed anyone to talk to him on the subject.

"Your cousin crossed the line," Nathan said.

Hezekiah's large chest heaved. "You're right."

"You saw the boy's scar?"

The rebel leader's face grew grim and he nodded.

Nathan looked his friend in the eye. "You know as well as I do that Judas needs to be stopped. Lead me to him or tell me where he's hiding. I promise to take him to the proper authorities."

Hezekiah's frown deepened. "I can't. Our leaders are unfit judges. They are adulterous, lovers of money who've gotten in bed with Rome."

Nathan exhaled heavily. The favorite rhetoric of the zealots was hard to argue against. "I agree. The Sanhedrin is ripe with corruption. And Simeon Onias is probably the worst judge of the whole lot, but it doesn't excuse what your cousin did."

Hezekiah kicked a small rock out of his path. "I gave Judas a good scolding."

"He needs to give the girl back to her family."

The rebel leader winced. "Judas gave me a message for Simeon Onias, concerning his daughter." He rubbed his forehead. "You're not going to like what he has to say."

Nathan looked back up at the city and squinted against the rays of the dying sun, and spotted Alexandra and James Onias coming toward him. His gut contracted. "It looks as though you are about to have the opportunity to speak to Simeon's son and daughter."

"Now? No, no, no." Hezekiah waved as though warding off a charging animal. "Sarah will hang me by my toes if I'm late for dinner." The gregarious man laughed and smoothed his neat beard. "Bring Simeon's children to my tent later tonight. I will give them Judas's message and we can work on finding a mutually satisfying solution for everyone."

"I will present your offer to them and if they find it acceptable I will bring them to you." Nathan missed the barrel-chested man's company. "It's been too long since we talked."

Hezekiah patted Nathan's shoulder. "Tell your father we missed him and hope to see him in the Men's Court."

Nathan smiled. "The trip from Galilee to Jerusalem exhausts him. I told him he should stay home. But you know my father. He loves coming to the Temple to worship with the Lord's people."

"Give him our wishes for a happy festival and seasons of joy to the family."

Nathan returned the blessing, "Time of gladness to you and your family."

Hezekiah waved goodbye and continued on his way. Nathan reversed direction. A moment later he came upon his brother and sister. Timothy cradled an arm full of rocks against his once-spotless tunic. Mary's face was creased with disapproval.

Timothy gave him a toothy smile. "Where are you going?"

Nathan tousled the boy's fine hair. "I am going to invite a pair of friendless souls to eat at our fire." He didn't know if James and Alexandra Onias would, or could, accept. They might observe the same strict dietary regime as their Pharisee father, but an invitation would be given.

Always up for an adventure, Timothy brightened. "Can I come too?"

"Mother won't thank you for inviting more guests," Mary said.

A fretful sort, his stepmother was easily frazzled, but she was also unfailingly hospitable.

"The two of you best hurry along and help your mother, then."

"Nathannnnn," they whined in unison.

He laughed. "The sooner dinner is over, the sooner you can join your friends."

Timothy dumped his load of rocks on the side of the road and took off at a run. Mary held fast. She twisted her hands together. "All my friends will be dancing in the vineyard. You promised to ask Father."

"Father is worried. He doesn't want you to marry too young."

His sister's cheeks turned rosy-red. "I don't want to make eyes at the young men. I just want to dance among the trees and the lights." She sighed and hugged herself. "It's so beautiful and dream-like, and, and per-fect."

Nathan hated the idea of his young sister growing up. "I'm sure Father will agree to it."

Mary smiled wide and clapped. "I'm doubly glad, because I told Alexandra Onias I would dance beside her if she came to the maiden's dance, and here she comes, now. Oh, I hope Alexandra and her brother are the ones you're inviting to eat with us. She says she won't be dancing. But you can help me to convince her otherwise."

Nathan raised a brow. "The Onias girls have never joined the dancing before."

"How would you know, Nathan?" his sister teased.

"Because..." he said through gritted teeth "...your mother takes it upon herself every year to point out any maiden making her first appearance in the vineyards." It was a signal the girl was of marriageable age. Rhoda enjoyed the support of the entire family in her campaign to see him married. He pointed a warning finger. "No matchmaking tonight. Alexandra and her brother might take such teasing seriously and be offended."

A smile lingered on Mary's lips. "It's usually bothersome to eat with religious guests. But Alexandra isn't prudish or standoffish. And she has lovely gray eyes, don't you think?"

Nathan watched Alexandra draw closer. "I hadn't noticed." He winced at the lie.

Mary surprised him with a hug. "Thank you, Nathan. Tonight is going to be wonderful. I just know it."

He patted her back. "I won't allow it to be anything but perfect, dear lamb."

Mary wrinkled her nose at the endearment.

He turned her about and gave her a gentle push. "Go help your mother."

She danced off humming.

Nathan took a deep breath and headed up the steep incline toward Alexandra and James Onias.

Alexandra's heart was about to beat out of her chest. How many times had she'd stared out her bedroom window, watching people come and go from the Kidron

Valley, wishing she could walk the winding road leading to the Mount of Olives. Now here she was, doing it.

It was dreamlike. Up above, Jerusalem was washed in gold, a shining beacon of safety. Down below, night crept after men, women, and children, threatening to overtake them before they reached the safety of their tents.

She spotted Nathan of Rumah coming toward them and edged closer to James. "Do you see him?"

James nodded.

Alexandra frowned. "How did he know we were following him?"

James waved. "He was a soldier. They notice everything."

Many men had visited her father after the attack, regaling him with tales of Nathan's days fighting in the Jewish army. It was easy to imagine. Tall and powerfully built, Nathan of Rumah moved with ease and grace. But he'd left soldiering and returned home to the family farm. How had he become a soldier? Why had he given it up?

Nathan drew nearer. She licked her lips. "James, how did an olive farmer from Galilee in the north end up friends with Herod from Idumea in the south?"

Her brother grinned. "You've been spying on Father? I didn't know you were so sly."

Her face heated. "I'm not, but I couldn't stay in my room. I had to find out what I could about Lydia."

"Father says Herod is a dog. Shall I mention it to Nathan?"

"James..."

Her brother laughed. "*Shalom*, good man," James called out.

The hard angles of Nathan's face dissolved into a breath-robbing smile. Alexandra's insides contracted. She shouldn't be staring. It wasn't proper. But she couldn't make herself look away.

Nathan made brief eye contact with her before coming to a stop in front of her brother. "How are you? I tried to visit you."

She hadn't imagined it. His voice was as gentle and comforting as a soft, summer rain. And, though he'd addressed James, she knew the questions were for her. She inclined her head slightly in answer.

James swiped his hand at the people flowing past them. "Aside from being a sideshow in today's circus, we are fine." He stuck his finger in Nathan's face. "Why haven't you found Lydia yet?"

Alexandra's toes curled. Her brother's poisonous attitude was embarrassing and worrisome.

The color drained from Nathan's face. "Come, walk with me, and we will talk."

She put her head down and moved forward.

"I'm sorry I wasn't able to keep my promise," Nathan said. He paused and cleared his throat.

She found the courage to look up. Her breath caught. Nathan was staring at her over James's head. She opened her mouth to say his apology wasn't necessary, but her tongue wouldn't work. Her father never allowed her or Lydia to speak to men. She and her intended husband, Philip Peter, had never shared a word.

But she'd already talked to Nathan, the day of the attack. Yes, and her father had called her a whore.

A hot updraft of wind caught and lifted Nathan's dark curls as he spoke. "Finding Lydia is going to be difficult."

A mountain-sized hole opened up inside Alexandra. She dipped her chin and rubbed at her forehead. *My dear, dear Lydia. What are they doing to you? What are you suffering?*

"We will get her back. I promise," Nathan said.

"I know." Her voice shook. She swallowed and looked up at Nathan. "I believe you. I do."

Some of the tension went out of Nathan. "Herod of Idumea has agreed to help me hunt down Judas."

She swayed on her feet. Herod and his Idumean soldiers were going to join the search for Lydia. What would Father say?

"Alexandra?" Her brother tapped her arm. "When was the last time you ate? Goda told Father you aren't eating enough to keep a mouse alive."

Today was a day of fasting, so she hadn't eaten. What about yesterday? It was hard to think. She sighed. "I can't remember."

Nathan moved to her side. "Come and break the fast with my family. After dinner I will introduce you to someone who might be able to help Lydia's cause."

She straightened. She hadn't dared hope for such a promising lead.

"I always wanted to visit the festival campsites," James said and walked on. "Come along, Alexandra," he called back.

She looked back toward the city. They'd be away that much longer.

"I can take you home, if you'd like," Nathan offered.

A boisterous group of boys ran past them. One of them almost collided with her brother. James shook his fist at them. Why did he have to be so prickly? "James wants to go," she said.

"But he didn't ask what you wanted."

"Me?" She frowned. "It is for the man to tell the woman what to do."

Nathan raised a brow. "James is not fit to order a donkey about, never mind another person."

She bit her lip to keep from laughing. "I will stay for my brother, and for Lydia." Her smile died. "Can you tell me more about the men who took Lydia?"

"Let's catch up with your brother. He will want to hear what I have to say."

The road grew more rutted. They rounded a sharp curve and found James digging a rock out of his sandal. Scowling, he joined them.

Alexandra resisted the urge to fuss over him. "Nathan has agreed to share what he knows with us."

"Judas the Zealot and the twenty, or so, men following him were part of a larger group of rebels dedicated to forcing the Romans out of the land," Nathan said. "I know them well. They are my friends and neighbors."

James narrowed his eyes at Nathan. "Why aren't you one of them?"

Nathan pulled on his collar. "I went with them a few times at the start, hoping to talk them out of it. They wouldn't listen. Five years later they're more convinced than ever of their cause."

A heaviness filled Alexandra. Nathan seemed too good, too perfect to have associated with criminals. But he wasn't all loveliness. He'd been a soldier in the Jewish army and probably killed many men. She rubbed her arms.

James's purple scar pulsed. "So you have been looking the other way while your friends attack innocent people?"

Alexandra winced at the bald assessment.

Nathan hung his head. "I've closed my eyes and ears to it and tried to stay clear of trouble. I promised my family I was done with war and fighting." He laughed without humor. "Hearing my excuses out loud makes me realize how pitiful they sound."

She admired his honesty and took comfort in the knowledge he honored his promises, because it meant he'd invest equal diligence in keeping the vow he'd made to her. "What have the authorities done to stop the bandits?" she asked.

The corners of Nathan's mouth turned down. "Practically nothing. The rebels live in plain sight and enjoy the support of most people. The current governor of Galilee has sent out men a time or two, but I don't think he wants to find Hezekiah and Judas, for fear of riling everyone up."

"Who is Hezekiah?" James pointed at his scar. "And what does he have to do with this?"

"Hezekiah is the man I'm going to take you to see, Nathan said. "He and Judas are cousins. Judas's ideas have always been more radical than Hezekiah's. They parted ways a few weeks before you were attacked. Judas and his men have gone into hiding in a remote part of Galilee."

Her brother's brows rose. "Hezekiah is in Jerusalem. Why doesn't someone arrest him?"

"Hezekiah has many supporters," Nathan said.

A chill went through Alexandra. "You and Hezekiah are on speaking terms?"

Nathan frowned. "I told you, the rebels are my friends and neighbors."

A bitter taste filled Alexandra's mouth. She hadn't

considered the fact that the festival campground would be full of people loyal to the men who had attacked her family. *Lord, please grant me strength and grace.*

CHAPTER 4

They left the road and entered an orchard. Alexandra's pulse quickened.

Loud talk and laughter soon filled the air. Nathan led them on a zigzagging path through a maze of trees and tents, the smell of roasted lamb swirling about them.

They came to an ancient, gnarled olive tree sheltering two black tents. A tall woman, probably Mary's mother, worked over a cook fire at the edge of the leafy canopy.

Alexandra and James followed Nathan to the larger tent. The flaps were rolled up, and a small man sat on a large, cushy pillow in the middle of the shelter. His face lit. "Son, did all go well?"

Nathan crouched down next to the frail man. "It did. I'm sorry you had to miss it. You look a bit stronger now."

The aged man waved his hand. "It was nothing. A mere inconvenience."

Nathan laughed. "You could be on your deathbed and you'd say the same thing."

Merriment danced in the older man's rheumy eyes.

"I feel much better, and I'm glad of it, seeing you have invited more mouths to eat my food and to drink my wine."

Nathan held out a hand, inviting her and her brother to come closer. "James and Alexandra Onias, it pleases me to introduce you to my father, Joseph of Rumah."

Alexandra bowed her head, already liking the kindly, old man. It was a shame his health was so poor.

Joseph smiled and patted a nearby pillow. "Come, tell me how the sacrifices went. I could hear the shouts from here."

James stood fast. A scowl marred his face. "After traveling so far, I am surprised you stayed away from the Temple."

Alexandra hunched her shoulders at her brother's rudeness.

The elderly man's smile never faltered. "There is a week yet to go. I hope to attend a service at the Temple at least once before returning to Galilee."

James shared a knowing look with her. "Our father was beaten half to death, yet he insisted on attending the required festival."

A twinkle entered the old man's eyes "Ah, but your father is a religious man. He carries a heavy burden. I'm but a poor farmer."

"Father. Father." The clatter of slapping feet put an end to the uncomfortable conversation. Mary and the apple-cheeked boy Alexandra had seen with Nathan earlier today raced up to Joseph.

Mary spoke in a rush, "Timothy called me a silly sheep and told me to stop baaing over the maiden's dance." She dropped to her knees and took hold of her father's hand. "I want to dance with the other maidens.

Can I?" She looked over to Nathan for support.

Alexandra held her breath, hoping the girl would get her wish.

Nathan smiled and winked. "All of Mary's friends will join the dancing."

Joseph patted Mary's hand. "As much as I dislike it, I suppose I have to accept you are growing up. You have my blessing. You may go."

Mary threw her arms about her father's neck. "Thank you. Thank you."

She stood and gave Nathan a hug, and then she wrapped her arms around Alexandra.

Surprised, Alexandra laughed.

Mary moved on to Timothy. The boy made a cross-eyed face. Everybody chuckled.

The feel of Mary's warm arms wrapped around her lingered with Alexandra, making her wonder what it would be like to have a life filled with loving hugs.

Joseph pointed a finger at Mary. "Promise me you will ignore the young men who line up to watch the dance and choose a wife. Give me the pleasure of your company for a few more years, Daughter."

Alexandra sighed, marveling at the high regard Joseph had for Mary. Her own father thought unwed daughters a heavy burden. Alexandra and Lydia's abrupt fall from grace at least had the virtue of proving him correct.

"I promise," Mary said. She turned her happy face up to Alexandra. "Are you going to join the maiden's dance?"

Though she hated to disappoint the dear girl, it couldn't be helped. Her father would rage at her if she joined the dance in the vineyard. Alexandra opened her mouth to say no.

But James answered for her. "My sister would be happy to join you."

Alexandra's stomach knotted. Had an evil spirit got hold of her brother's tongue?

Mary clapped and hopped in a small circle.

Alexandra smoothed her tunic. Her fingers shook. She looked up. Nathan was staring at her. She swallowed. Unnerved, she wanted to run back to the safety of her bed chamber. But she couldn't. She'd come here to find out all she could about Lydia. More remained to be done. Alexandra clasped her trembling hands and tried to smile.

Joseph of Rumah's wife stopped by the tent entrance. "The food is ready."

"Rhoda, come and meet our guests," Joseph said.

The tall woman wiped her hands on her apron. "Move to the table and we can talk there."

Noise and confusion reigned from tent to table, but the family quickly sorted themselves out. Colorful mats ranged around the large, flat stone that served as a makeshift dining area. It looked nowhere near as comfortable as the cushioned couches and raised platforms the Onias family ate from, but the hospitality around the stone table more than made up for any deficiency. And something smelled delicious. Alexandra's stomach growled.

She stopped short. In all the excitement it hadn't occurred to her they would be eating at an unclean table. A strict Pharisee, her father practiced a form of ritual pureness deemed rigorous even by stringent Pharisaical standards. Moses' Law listed objects or persons considered unclean, and another whole set of directives aimed at making one clean after coming in contact with the unclean. Unlike common Jews, who either did not have the time, or the means, or the inclination to avoid the unclean, Pharisees aimed for perpetual purity. The Pharisaical strictures regarding the proper handling and preparation of food were particularly onerous. They were so exacting, in fact, some women marrying Pharisees had provisions written into the marriage contract requiring the husband to maintain two kitchens, one for himself and one for his family.

Alexandra whispered a discreet warning to her brother. "Father would not want us to partake of their food."

"Our dear father," James said, achieving a sarcastic note despite mumbling, "need not ever know."

Appetite gone, she struggled to get her food down. Gradually, though, thanks to the soothing influence of the Rumah family's amiably chatter, she began to relax and enjoy the meal.

She was fascinated by the active part Mary and Rhoda took in the discussions. Alexandra and Lydia were never invited to speak or give their opinion on any matter. When their father had company, she and her sister had to stay in their room.

"Alexandra," Joseph said, directing attention to her. "I hope you did not spill tears over Philip Peter. I think it disgraceful of the family to make a new engagement for their son so soon after breaking the agreement they had with your father."

A flavorful chunk of meat lodged burr-like in her throat. Embarrassed, she turned to James and silently begged him to speak for her.

His eyes were as impatient as his words. "Answer the

man."

Though surrounded by friendly and encouraging faces, she couldn't make her mouth work. The dreadful silence stretched on and on.

James exhaled an exasperated breath.

Rhoda clapped to gain their attention. "Eat, eat, or you will have no time to deliver the olive oil."

Dinner was soon over and the family dissolved into a frenzy of hectic activity. Under Nathan's deft supervision, the unruly clamor ended with the campsite set right and Joseph settled in bed for the night. Mary and Timothy burst with merry excitement.

Alexandra's trepidation grew and grew at the prospect of meeting the cousin of the man holding Lydia. Then there was the maiden's dance to worry over.

Too quickly it was time to go. Rhoda stayed behind with Joseph. The children and Nathan leading the way, Alexandra left the Rumah campsite behind and walked deeper into the olive orchard.

Alexandra walked in the Kingdom of Heaven. Or so it seemed. The glow from a thousand campfires lit their way. Laughing children darted to and fro. Savory smells abounded. Ripples of cool air washed over her face. Silhouetted against the black sky, the naked branches of the olive trees stretched upward. *The trees of the field shall clap their hands.* The fanciful words of the psalm played over and over through her mind.

Buoyed along like a bubble on the still air, the dreamlike quality of the night burst when she came face-to-face with the leader of the Galilean bandits. Hezekiah left behind the large group of men sitting around his fire and came over and embraced Nathan in a big bear hug.

Hezekiah didn't look as menacing as Alexandra had expected. His smile was jovial.

Nathan clapped the man on the back. Turning to her and James, he introduced them.

The older man sobered. "Please accept my sincere apology for your unfortunate trouble."

"Unfortunate?" James said indignant.

"Judas mistook your father for a Roman sympathizer."

Alexandra felt as though the ground moved below her feet. The trial they had endured, and still suffered from, was the result of a simple mistake?

Through the buzzing in her ears, she heard Nathan ask, "Why is Judas still holding the girl?"

Hezekiah smoothed his neat beard. "Judas claims the girl wants to stay."

James bristled. "We paid the criminal a generous ransom to get Lydia back."

Hezekiah held out empty hands. "Judas characterized it as a wedding present."

Mortified, Alexandra stepped forward. "You speak lies. Lydia is all goodness. She would never consent to marrying a thief and murderer."

Hezekiah narrowed his eyes at her and the other men in the camp grumbled loudly over her interference. James huffed and spluttered.

Nathan of Rumah remained an isle of calm. His brown eyes locked with her gray ones. "I think it best if you leave. Will you trust me to take care of this matter for you?"

Alexandra nodded.

Nathan sent her off in Mary's care.

The sweet girl's nonstop chatter barely registering, Alexandra let herself be led blindly along. After winding this way and that, Mary eventually pulled her to a stop. Festive music sounded and someone took hold of her free hand. Propelled on her way once more, what initially seemed a blur of lights slowly resolved, revealing hundreds of winking lamps strung among grapevines and the twinkling of thousands of stars overhead.

Dozens of girls wearing glowing white gowns weaved in and out of leafy lanes, sweet laughter trailing behind them. Instantly enchanted, Alexandra felt her burdens ease.

The line of girls contracted. She and Mary were pressed close together. Breathless and full of joy, the young girl confided, "I will remember this night for the rest of my life! Bless you, bless you, bless you, Alexandra Onias, for coming with me tonight."

Pace quickening as the string of maidens uncoiled, Mary squealed and said, "here we go again."

Alexandra joined in the fun, skipping in time with the maidens and the music. The carefree bliss seduced. Drawn into the spirit of the maidens' dance, she laughed and leaped and twirled. For the first time in her life she felt wholly alive.

Mary tugged on her hand. "Nathan has come."

The onlookers a mere blur, Alexandra focused on finding his handsome face. She caught a glimpse of large, doe eyes. *Lydia? But her sister couldn't possibly be here.* Alexandra twisted around for another look.

Mary crashed into her and Alexandra fell face-first into the dirt. She craned her head back to see whose feet she had landed on and found Philip Peter, the man she had hoped to marry, glaring down at her. She scrambled to her feet.

Philip Peter jumped back. "Away with you, woman!" Face thunderous, he held his hands up, warding her off. "The Lord as my witness," he yelled, beseeching the astonished onlookers, "I washed my hands of this woman. Yet she shamelessly throws herself at me."

Frantic to escape, Alexandra fell back on her heels. Feet hopelessly tangled in the hem of her gown, she toppled over backwards and came to rest in a pair of outstretched arms.

CHAPTER 5

Alexandra Onias's delicate back pressed warm against Nathan's chest. Tempted to pull her closer, he set her back on her feet.

Alexandra's white dress was covered in dirt and her head covering hung down her back, exposing her long, thick hair to view. She cried out in dismay and clapped her hands to her head.

Nathan went to work helping her right the heavy drapery. Loose tendrils of hair floated about his face. Hints of lily of the valley teased at his nose. Transfixed by the riot of brown curls, he allowed his gaze to slide lower, following the trail of shimmering locks down to the small of her back. The ringlets twirled frustratingly out of sight beneath the edge of the elaborately embroidered scarf. Resisting the urge to pull a curl free, he helped her draw the band of white cloth back into place.

She raised her face to his. Like a lamb caught in the wolf's mouth, pure terror radiated from her gray eyes. "Lydia is here. I saw Lydia."

He scanned the crowd. Seeing no sign of the bandit named Judas, he turned to the idiot making the unholy ruckus. Phillip Peter was ruthlessly savaging Alexandra to protect his spotless image. The fool needed his neck wrung. Alexandra Onias's good name had already suffered enough harm.

Nathan pointed a warning finger in Phillip's purple-tinged face. "Leave the girl alone."

Absolute quiet descended over the vineyard.

Satisfied, Nathan turned his attention to the stunned onlookers. "This was nothing more than a simple accident. Alexandra Onias came to the vineyard tonight at my sister's request. This is Mary's first maiden dance. She has dreamed of this evening all her life. It would be cruel to allow a small misunderstanding to ruin her happiness and the other girls' joy."

Facing the white-clad maidens, he said, "Come, girls, return to your dancing." He called out to the musicians, "Play. Play." A few awkward notes sounded, and then the familiar rhythm once more filled the air. The girls stood rooted in place. "Dance, dance." He waved his arms in a shooing motion at the wide-eyed maidens, coaxing and cajoling until they formed a line and linked hands.

The girls glanced nervously between him and Alexandra. If she balked, all was lost. Nathan stopped before her. Her soft gray eyes met his. He whispered low and urgent, "Dance, Alexandra. Laugh and dance as though nothing is amiss, or you will be ruined forever."

She took a tentative step.

He smiled and nodded encouragingly.

Alexandra nudged Mary with her elbow, who in turn prodded the side of the girl standing next to her. More jostling ensued, but finally, like an ungainly camel caravan getting underway, the maidens' procession lurched into motion.

Nathan walked alongside, teasingly hectoring them. After one trip about the vineyard path, most of the girls were laughing and skipping. Another turn around the leafy trail and Alexandra Onias managed a weak smile.

Assured all was well, Nathan took a spot among the circle of onlookers and shared a smile with Mary and Alexandra each time they whirled by.

Minus the cold veil of upper-class refinement, Alexandra appeared the incarnation of the pretty, young maidens who had haunted his dreams from his youth onward. Worry and unhappiness eased, she moved with easy grace. Her eyes sparkled bright, putting the brilliance of the rising moon to shame.

Too soon the dance came to an end. Loud shouts of congratulations drowned out the last fading notes of music. "Blessed marriage, Joseph and Judith! Happiness and joy, Phillip Peter and Martha!"

The middle-aged priest standing next to Nathan slapped his back. "Long life and happiness to you and your bride on this fine night."

Taken aback, Nathan opened his mouth to straighten out the misunderstanding. More calls of felicitation rained down on him.

"Blessed marriage, Nathan and Alexandra!"

"Peace and prosperity, Nathan and Alexandra!"

He clamped his mouth shut again.

"What has happened here?" James Onias stood at Nathan's side.

Nathan had stared at Alexandra far too long, making people believe he wished to marry her. And she had stared back at him, the traditional signal for accepting a proposal.

His heart sank. He wouldn't be able to talk himself out of this, not with a family member as a witness. "Tell your father to expect me tomorrow to negotiate the terms of the marriage contract."

After asking a friend to escort Alexandra and James Onias home, and answering his family's noisy questions, Nathan escaped the campsite and headed for a quiet refuge. The gnarled trunk of a squat olive tree at his back, he ran his fingernail over an oblong olive leaf. Its clean, light scent filled the air.

The memory of Alexandra's warm back pressed against him returned. She was all loveliness and beauty. And he'd be taking her to live in a one-room house made from mud and fieldstone.

He crushed the leaf, tossed it aside, and lifted his face toward heaven. "Is the jest on me or her? Because I'm not sure whether to laugh or cry."

Moonshine winked at him through the leafy canopy. He pounded the ground with a balled up fist and shouted at the dark. "I didn't want to marry."

The outer darkness spoke back. "So, go hang yourself."

Nathan jumped to his feet and reached for his sword. His hand came up full of air because, *foolish him,* he no longer carried a weapon.

A point of steel dug into his back.

"Are you armed?" a familiar voice asked.

"Be careful with that thing, Bear," Nathan said.

The hairy man laughed.

Two dozen men appeared and fanned out in a circle. Nathan's neighbors. One face stood out in particular.

"Silas? Who's watching over your sheep?"

The thin man's hooded eyes burned brighter. "I gave the flock to my brother."

Dread flickered inside of Nathan. The shepherd had turned dark and moody after the death of his wife. He was a man with nothing to lose and they made the most dangerous of opponents.

Judas the Zealot stepped out of the shadows.

Nathan shot a dirty look at him. "Hezekiah told me you were up in the mountains."

Judas laughed. "I will be soon enough."

"What do you want with me?" Nathan growled.

An unkempt beard dominated Judas's plain face. "I wanted to offer you another chance to join us."

"Why? Was terrorizing young women and studious men too taxing for you?" The sword in Nathan's back twisted deeper.

Judas waved Bear away. "This is your opportunity to redeem yourself, Nathan. Help us drive the Romans out of the land."

"I've said no, more than once."

Judas signaled for someone to step forward. "I thought your upcoming marriage might change your mind."

A young woman appeared. Judas touched his hand to her elbow. "Tell your future brother-in-law where your loyalties lie."

Nathan wasn't sure what he found more amazing —the speed with which the news of his accidental marriage proposal had traveled through the pilgrim's camp, or coming face-to-face with Lydia Onias. Alexandra had said she'd seen her sister.

Lydia moved closer to Judas. Her voice was a mere

whisper, "No King but the Lord."

The earnest recital of the rebel anthem chilled Nathan to the bone. He addressed her with due gentleness, "Lydia Onias? Your family is worried about you."

The young woman flinched.

Judas interceded. "Lydia is my wife."

Nathan's fist balled. He wanted to beat Judas into the ground for what he'd done to the young woman. "I would hear it from the girl."

Judas handed Lydia off to Silas and turned back to Nathan. "Tell Simeon Onias to go back to his careful study of the Torah and leave Lydia to me. Tell him it is a wiser and healthier path."

"Are you mad?" Nathan held his hand out toward the captive woman. "Lydia."

Judas shoved Nathan backward. "Keep out of this, lest my men and I pay an unwelcome visit to your farm."

"You viper!" Nathan lunged for Judas.

A dozen men launched themselves at Nathan, knocking him down.

"Let him up," Judas yelled.

Nathan climbed to his feet. He searched for Lydia, but didn't see her. "Lydia Onias, step forward."

The rebel leader stepped closer until he was nose to nose with Nathan. His breath smelled of roast lamb. "Go home and live in peace. Forget about Lydia. Forget about me. And I will let you and yours live in peace."

Then the rebel leader slowly backed away and vanished into the dark with his men.

Nathan scrubbed his face. He started to follow after Judas, but stopped. "Job's bones!" He punched the air. "I need a sword."

◆ ◆ ◆

"The bridegroom is at the door." The slave's announcement bounced off the stone walls and high ceiling of the dining alcove, rattling Alexandra to her core. Hands shaking, she set a tunic and the blue and white fringe used to decorate it beside her on the reclining couch.

Nathan of Rumah had come.

"Good tidings, daughter." Her father addressed her without looking up from the scroll he and James were studying. "Nathan of Rumah possesses at least one worthy trait. He is a man of his word. It will save me the odious task of taking him to court to make him marry you."

James spun the toy top he'd been fiddling with. "Heaven knows the poor farmer does not possess much more than his good word."

Alexandra squirmed in her seat. She hated the thought Nathan was being forced to marry her.

"What of the dowry?" James asked, scooping up the spinning red top.

"Yes..." Father gave a quiet laugh. "I expect the farmer's humble offering to at least amuse."

"Why not ask a service of him like the patriarchs in the days of old?" James cast a mocking look at her. "Surely, our Alexandra is worth more than a few trifling amphora of olive oil. Task the bridegroom with slaying Judas and finding Lydia. It should be relatively easy with Lydia walking about Jerusalem in plain sight."

Alexandra looked down at her lap. Father and James had laughed in her face at her insistence she had seen Lydia at the maiden's dance. The rest of the night had been taken up explaining to Father why an olive farmer would appear today to make a marriage proposal, a task that proved difficult, because everything had happened so quickly. Worry for her sister had the merit of saving Alexandra from dwelling too long on her own predicament. But the time of reckoning had arrived.

She trembled. *Lord, be merciful.*

Father gave a great sigh. "Daughters are a sore trial. Come, girl..." Distracted by something of interest in the text, he paused to ponder it. An agonizing amount of time passed before he finished his thought. "You have kept your prospective husband waiting long enough. Go greet the man you played the whore with." The characterization of the preceding evening's events, though predictable, hurt. "Since you are on such familiar terms with the man, you may wash his feet."

"Me?" Positive she'd misheard, she looked up. "But Goda usually—"

"Daughter." Fixing a withering look on her, he said, "You best find ways to serve your husband. The angels know you won't be much use to anybody on a Galilean olive farm."

She flinched. The reproof stung, for it hit directly on her fears and doubts. She stood.

James snickered. "Poor, Alexandra. You will stand out like a lily in a turnip patch among the other farmers' wives."

She sighed.

"I'm sorry. I shouldn't have said that," James said.

Father's face twisted. "Alexandra deserves what she gets. Has not the sage said, 'the marriage of the daughter of a learned man and an ignoramus will not be a successful one'?"

Alexandra hurried out, lest her father pound her over the head with further wise sayings. Arriving at the front door much too quickly, she slowed and approached the small alcove off the main door as if venturing toward the pits of hell. Her heart sped up at the sound of sandals pacing over tile. She stopped. Father and James were right. A marriage between her and the olive farmer would be a disaster.

She must convince Nathan of Rumah a proposal wasn't necessary.

She took a deep breath.

Nathan poked his head around the corner. The large brown eyes trained on her were as inscrutable as they were long-lashed and beautiful. Was he angry with her for getting him into this horrible mess? Or, like her, terribly embarrassed?

Summoning up her courage, she edged her way past the large stranger filling the doorway. She had spent all morning telling herself Nathan of Rumah was not so different from Father, James, and Phillip Peter. The nearness of his powerfully built body incinerated the lie to ashy nothingness.

Goda appeared with a carafe of water. The bald slave handed her the container and disappeared before she thought to stop him.

She rushed to fill the washbasin. Water splashed everywhere.

"Let me." Nathan took the carafe from her trembling hands. His fingers brushed over hers. Her breath caught. The roomy alcove suddenly felt small and cramped. "My feet are clean," Nathan said.

"Father insists everyone wash their feet before entering his home."

Nathan shrugged, sat on the bench, and reached for the tie of his sandal.

She knelt and brushed his hand aside and tugged at the bow fastened about a muscled calf. Fingers moving as though they belonged to someone else, she unwound the tie and slipped the sandal off his foot.

"You can speak to me. I don't bite." Nathan's deep voice reverberated through her.

The sandal clattered to the floor.

She bit her lip. A three-legged donkey had more claim to grace than she. What a fuss. And over such a simple task. She and her sister had sat in this very spot many, many times washing the dust from each other's feet.

She dared a look. "Forgive me."

He offered her a small smile.

His full lips and soft mouth mesmerized. Heaven above, she was staring.

She reached for the other sandal. Shaking, she fumbled the leather tie into a stubborn knot. Her face heated. She sat back. Her eye was drawn to an old wound, a wide gouge running through the meaty part of his lower leg. She winced. It had to have been excruciatingly painful. She traced her fingers over the long, puckered scar. It must have occurred while he was fighting with the Jewish army.

She drew in a sharp breath. An ex-soldier was here to negotiate a marriage contract for her. A soldier. Panic rose like vomit. They'd never suit. She'd been raised to be the quiet, dutiful wife of a religious man. Nathan needed a wife as bold and lively as he. She'd be too dull and bland for him.

Nathan's hand covered hers. "This is not necessary.

I made a point of visiting the ritual bath closest to your home. If my feet are clean enough for the Temple grounds, they are clean enough for your father's house."

"You don't have to marry me," she said. "I release you from any obligation you feel you owe me."

Goda reappeared. "May I be of assistance?"

"Leave us," Nathan ordered, his scowl ferocious.

The slave turned and fled.

Nathan released her hand and patted the bench, inviting her to sit next to him. "Slaves are useful creatures, are they not?"

Puzzled by the turn of the conversation, she frowned.

Nathan bent forward and laced up his sandal. "The slave was sent to catch us spending time alone together, so he can testify against me in court if I refuse to marry you."

A sinking sensation took hold. "Father said something about taking you to court."

Nathan exhaled heavily. "I'd almost convinced myself your father would refuse my marriage proposal. But it appears he wants us to marry. Do you know what he hopes to gain by it?"

She squeezed her eyes closed. *What are you up to, Father?* "I think it might be related to our trip to Galilee." She made herself look Nathan in the eye. "I never should have gone to your camp. You don't need to pay for my mistake. Go, and I will tell Father I sent you away. But...but..." Her lip trembled. "Could you...could you continue to search for Lydia?"

Nathan's brown eyes softened. "I keep my promises. And I told your father to expect me today, so we could negotiate the terms of our marriage contract." He stood. "Take me to your father."

She sighed and rose to her feet. *Lord, this is no way to start a marriage. Have mercy. Move in my father or Nathan. Help them to see what a mistake this would be.*

Nathan followed Alexandra, steeling himself for the coming interview with her father. The tidy alcove occupied a small corner of an open-air court featuring a rectangular reflection pool. His doubt doubled when he saw the rich surroundings. The stone walls and paved floor of the courtyard were decorated with colorful tile mosaics. Elaborate stone archways stood opposite each other, leading to the wings of the grand home. A tangle of dried melon vines trailed up the twin stone staircases climbing the walls to the upper rooms. What was he doing in a rich man's home?

The thought of taking Alexandra Onias to the humble dwelling he had grown up in made him sick. His sturdy house wouldn't fill one corner of this two-story behemoth. Her bed chamber was probably bigger than his whole house.

"Which room is yours?" he asked. Lattice-screened windows looked out over the courtyard. A matching set of windows lined the exterior walls. The interior shutters stood open to catch the autumn breeze.

"There." Alexandra stopped and pointed to a spot over the front entryway. "Lydia and I share it." She faltered. "I saw Lydia last night. And I froze. And next I knew, people were congratulating me on my coming marriage." A rosy flush crossed her cheeks. "My father and brother do not believe I saw Lydia."

"Why not?"

"Because they believe women are liars and mischief-makers." She choked on a sob. "I swear I saw Lydia."

"I spoke with your sister."

"Thank the Lord." Relief flooded her voice. "My prayers are answered."

He reached his hand to his neck and rubbed the tightening muscles. "Surely you have not been asking the Lord to give you an olive farmer for a husband."

She twisted her hands in the folds of her tunic. "Thank you for being so kind. You are a good man."

His conscience roared to life. "There are things you ought to know about me."

"Good, you agree with me...we shouldn't marry."

"That's not what I said."

The bald slave came around the corner. A few moments later, Nathan stood off to one side of the dining alcove listening to James and Alexandra try to reason with their father. They knelt before the old man, who was seated regally on a long couch surrounded by a surfeit of plush pillows. The grand opulence of the palace-like home lost much of its luster in the presence of the master of the house.

"Lydia is dead to me." Simeon Onias's perpetual scowl had worn deep grooves in his sober face. "I will hear no more of the matter."

James frown was equally grim. "Judas is making us look foolish."

"Us?" The disdainful smile Simeon offered his son curdled Nathan's stomach.

James's scarred face turned ashen.

"Please, Father," Alexandra pleaded.

"Silence!" Simeon pointed a finger at his daughter. "You and your sister are a pair of wanton harlots, deserving of your mercenary husbands."

Nathan flinched. *Mercenary?*

Alexandra glanced back at him. Her mortification on his behalf cooled his ire.

"Father," Alexandra tried again. "Lydia has done nothing wrong. Don't abandon her to the bandits."

Simeon turned purple with rage. "Hold your tongue, woman."

Nathan stepped forward and glared down at the hateful man. "Perhaps we should move on to the betrothal."

Simeon Onias's less-than-pleasurable company made Nathan wonder if Lydia wasn't better off where she was. Mad and wrong-headed as Judas was, he was also engaging and charismatic.

Simeon directed his anger toward Nathan. "Do you plan to double your dishonor by refusing to marry my daughter?"

"You see that I am here." He was happy to marry Alexandra, if only to take away her from her wretched father.

Simeon narrowed his eyes at him. "Why isn't your father with you? He should be here to negotiate the marriage contract on your behalf."

"My father's health is failing." Mindful of the courtesy due an elder, Nathan moderated his tone. "He sends his regrets. Have no fear, he gave me careful instructions for the *mohar.*"

"Yes, yes, I accept whatever gifts your family can offer for my daughter," Simeon said.

Nathan and his father had struggled long and hard to come up with an appropriate gift for the esteemed family. The price the groom's family paid to the bride's family for the privilege of marrying their daughter was a simple matter among the poor. He wished they hadn't bothered.

Nathan held onto his temper. "Why are you willing to part with your daughter for so little? Surely there are men with more wealth than I have who would be willing to overlook recent unfortunate events in order to marry a priest's daughter?"

Simeon's lips curled in a nasty smile. "I'm glad to see you're not a total ignoramus."

Nathan spoke through clenched teeth. "Sorry to disappoint you."

The obnoxious man crooked his finger.

Nathan knelt on a pillow so they were at eye level.

Simeon propped his chin on his hands. "Why you, a lowly nobody, you are asking yourself. As the scriptures say, they that plow iniquity and sow wickedness, reap the same. My daughters have shamed me. They deserve unworthy husbands."

Nathan's fists itched to knock the smirk off the pious man's face. "While it's gratifying to know my iniquity has been of benefit to someone, I hope you won't take offense when I make your daughter the happiest woman in Judea."

He glanced back at Alexandra. Flustered, she looked away. He hoped he wasn't giving her false hope. He stood a better chance of being named the next emperor of Rome than he did of fulfilling the outlandish boast.

"You?" Simeon laughed. "You have chosen a shoe too big for your foot, olive farmer."

James snickered, a foreshadowing of the merciless banter Nathan was likely to endure for marrying above his class.

"I wasn't looking for a shoe," Nathan reminded them.

Simeon picked up a sheet of parchment and waved it in Nathan's face. "You will soon be rich, but I fear you will always have a poor man's mind."

"Rich?" Nathan echoed, wary. It was customary for the bride's parents to offer the groom a gift on her behalf. His expectations had been modest. How much money were they talking about?

"Read the dowry contract to him," Simeon said, passing the parchment to his son.

Nathan snatched the document away from James. "I can read." He deciphered the pertinent parts. The dowry was generous. Very generous.

Holy angels in heaven—marriage to Alexandra Onias was going to make him ungodly rich.

CHAPTER 6

Alexandra held her breath and watched Nathan read the marriage contract. His guarded face gave nothing away. The generousness of the dowry was worrisome. Nathan wasn't in a position to demand a single shekel, never mind a fortune. The money would come with strings attached. Nathan must suspect as much. Perhaps he'd turn it down.

She shifted in place. *Say no, Nathan. Please say no.*

Father laughed and leaned forward. "So, the Romans taught you more than just how to kill, did they? Delightful. I hadn't counted on having a thinking man for a son-in-law."

Nathan tossed the parchment at her father. "I accept your terms."

Alexandra's breath left her lungs in a big whoosh. Of course he said yes. No man in his right mind would walk away from a small fortune. She'd been a fool to think otherwise. Her heart sped up. God save her, she was going to be a farm wife. She might as well grow feathers and call herself a duck.

Nathan turned to her. Her mouth was hanging open like a sacrificial ox who'd had its neck slit open. His brow furrowed and a pained look entered his eyes. She didn't mean to hurt or insult him. She clapped her hand over her mouth. Again, probably not the most encouraging of signals.

Her neck and face felt red-hot. She put her hand to her throat. She could do better. "I am sure the marriage will prove pleasing."

Nathan faced Father. "I do have one stipulation. I want to wait until spring to marry."

Sweet relief filled Alexandra. Six months. She'd have six months to prepare for the marriage.

Father tossed the contract aside. "Why wait? Do you need time to get over another girl?"

Alexandra froze. The possibility hadn't occurred to her. A handsome, well-formed man like Nathan must have many admirers. He ought to be married already. What if he'd been waiting for someone special? She couldn't look at him. She didn't want to see it in his eyes if it was true.

His warm voice filled her ear. "My heart is free."

She swallowed. "I'm glad of it," she whispered.

Nathan sat back on his heels and speared her father with a dirty look. "We need to wait to shut the mouths of the gossips. We can't have anyone saying our first child is illegitimate."

She gasped and touched Nathan's arm. "I'm not...they didn't...you don't believe..."

Nathan's warm, steady hands enfolded hers. "I know nothing happened. Even if it had, it wouldn't stop me from marrying you."

Flabbergasted, she couldn't make her mouth work. Nathan of Rumah was full of strange ideas. And, he was holding her hand. He acted as though nothing was amiss. If men and women held hands in the privacy of their homes it was news to her.

"He has country manners," James complained.

Father wrinkled his nose. "Army life corrupted him."

Nathan squeezed her fingers and released them.

She clasped his hand and gave him a steady look. "I don't mind."

His smile reached his eyes. He turned to her father. "If you can spare your daughter, I will take Alexandra out for a walk."

Bubbles of laughter rose inside her at the idea of Father missing her company.

Father shook his head, as she knew he would. "I won't have my daughter traipsing all over Jerusalem like some common maiden."

Nathan stood and pulled her to her feet. "I want to introduce your daughter to her new life, and we need to spend time getting to know each other." His hand tightened around hers. "I refuse to enter the marriage bed as strangers."

Her face heated. Head-swirling thoughts intruded.

"Talk now," Father sputtered. "No one is stopping you."

"We are going out for a walk."

"I gave you my answer."

Nathan grabbed up the marriage contract and waved it in father's face. "Do you want me to sign this or not."

"You won't walk away. Not with so much money at stake."

Nathan just smiled. Alexandra wanted to throw her arms around him. She didn't quite understand why he was marrying her, but clearly it wasn't for her father's money.

Father opened his mouth and closed it again. He looked Nathan up and down. "You've got audacity to spare, I see." Father rang the small bell he always kept at his side.

Goda appeared with inkpot and stylus.

Nathan took the brass pen, dipped it, and held it over the paper. He turned to her. "Are you satisfied with the terms of the contract?"

"Olive farmer," Father's voice was condescending. "You are the head of the household. You decide what's best for her."

Nathan arched his brow at her. "Alexandra?"

Her mouth went dry. A drop of ink plopped onto the parchment. His question was genuine. He wanted to know her thoughts and concerns. She had no idea what was in the contract. "Is it fair to you?"

The corner of his mouth lifted with a wry smile. "It's more than fair."

"Then it pleases me as well."

Father made an exasperated noise. "Do you want to ask Goda what he thinks?"

Nathan winked at her. Putting stylus to paper, he signed with a flourish, writing his name in large, looping letters.

She smiled to herself. Nathan of Rumah might be a penniless farmer, but he wasn't about to grovel at the feet of other men, no matter how rich or important they might be. He was a man a woman would be proud to call husband.

Father snatched up the contract. "Go for your walk, and take James along. Alexandra needs an escort for decency's sake."

"Come along, James," Nathan said agreeably, taking

hold of her hand again.

"One more thing, olive farmer..." Father blew on the parchment to dry the wet ink. "Try not to be the total barbarian. Keep your hands off of her in public, at least."

Nathan dropped her hand and the color drained from his face. He walked away without a backward glance. Alexandra hurried after him, pushed along by her father's cruel laugh.

Nathan paced about the open-air courtyard, waiting for Alexandra to retrieve her cloak for their walk. His fists curled and uncurled. He wanted to go back into the dining alcove and smash Simeon Onias in the face, except it would prove the hateful man correct when he'd called Nathan a barbarian. Not that the prudish Pharisee's opinion meant anything to Nathan. No, it was Alexandra he was worried about. Did she see him as a barbarian?

He heard her door open. He walked over to the staircase leading to the upper rooms. Alexandra paused on the top step. A tremulous smile crossed her lips. His muscles went slack.

She'd exchanged the heavy veil covering her face for a bluebird-colored headscarf. The bright blue accentuated her gray eyes and thick, dark hair, making them all the more striking. But what had the blood draining from his head, was the sight of her full, red lips.

"Why did you change your veil?" he asked, his voice thick.

Her eyes widened.

He clasped his hands behind his back and pretended

an interest in the melon vines climbing the garden wall.

The tap of her feet skipping over stone had the air backing up in his lungs. She stopped on the last stair. "I thought it would please you. The wives and daughters of farmers don't wear heavy veils."

Her anxious voice had him looking back at her. "Long veils are too cumbersome for the work they do. But, I don't expect you to dress like Mary and Rhoda."

"I want to."

The faint scent of lily of the valley curled around him. He swallowed. A woman didn't put on perfume and pleasing clothes if she was repulsed by a man. "Veil, or no veil, you please me."

She blushed, and looked engagingly flustered. "Where are we going on our walk?"

Tempted to kiss her, he took a step back. "Where would you like to go?"

"Anywhere but the Temple."

He laughed. "That is a decisive answer."

She turned brighter red. "I didn't mean to be disrespectful. Father believes it best for women to stay at home. So the Temple is the only place I ever go."

"Amen," James called out. A ball of impatience, he stood at the door with his hand on the latch. "The one time Father did take Alexandra and Lydia somewhere we were attacked by bandits."

"Why was your father in Galilee, anyway?" Nathan asked, the question nagging at him anew. "Pharisees are a rare sight there. And I've never seen one in Upper Galilee."

Brother and sister shared an uncomfortable look.

James fidgeted some more. "Father was asked to

examine pieces of stone found by a shepherd, who claimed he had found a fragment of Moses' tablets of commandments. Next we knew we were racing off to Galilee." He traced his finger under the stitched scar crossing his face. "But, the bandits found us before we found the shepherd."

Nathan raised a brow. "Similar stories go around from time to time. But, strangely, none of the shepherds I know have said anything about it."

Alexandra frowned. "I fear Father might not have been telling us the truth."

James yanked the door open. "He won't let me ask a single question about the cursed trip." All gangly arms and legs, he tramped outside.

Nathan led Alexandra out onto the marble-columned porch. Her face lit up. "Goda is building the *sukkah*." She clapped her hands in delight. "*Sukkot* is my favorite feast."

Her enthusiasm over the temporary shelters being erected for the coming harvest celebration was endearing. Most of the Onias's neighbors were outside their large homes, constructing similar looking *sukkahs*.

Alexandra sighed. "I've always wanted to help build the *sukkah*."

"Goda looks like he could use some help," Nathan said, and headed down the stone stairs. Alexandra remained rooted in place. He turned back. "What's the matter?"

"Father wouldn't want me to help."

"I bet he wouldn't," Nathan mumbled, going back for her. He almost took her hand, but caught himself in time. He couldn't wait to take her home to the privacy of the farm.

Loud clapping sounded next door. An elderly priest had his hands raised toward heaven, celebrating the placing of the last branch atop his *sukkah*. The old man, his sons, and his grandsons would sleep in the small hut each night of the festival week, as a reminder of the time when the Hebrew people lived in tents in the wilderness, without permanent home or country.

Alexandra came down the steps. "Have you and your family built your booth yet?"

He bit down on a laugh. "We don't have to. We already sleep in tents."

"Oh, I guess you do. Will you continue to live in tents now...now that you..." Her cheeks turned a pretty shade of pink and she lowered her eyes.

"Now that you have made me rich," he finished.

She glanced up.

He winked. "There is nothing to be embarrassed about. Neither of us planned for it to happen. But, as for buying or building a home in Jerusalem for the required pilgrimages to the Temple, I don't know."

Nathan rocked back on his heels. His eyes swept over the marble and stone homes lining both sides of the road. This district was a new one. Most of Jerusalem was far older and more modest. Hezekiah, Judas and the other rebels loved to complain about the Roman or Greek influences spoiling the purity of the Holy City, and these homes represented everything they hated. He tried to imagine himself living in one.

He shook his head. "Ten years ago, I'd have loved the idea. Now our tent, and being a part of the generations of pilgrims who gather every year in the Kidron Valley, suits me very well." But he couldn't ask Alexandra to live in a tent, even if it was only for a few weeks each year. He rubbed the back of his neck.

"Are you coming?" James said, waiting for them on the edge of the street.

Nathan gave Alexandra an apologetic smile. "Could we discuss this later, after I've had time to digest the change in my, ah, circumstances?" He made a face. "Being rich is more complicated than I expected." He waved to James. "Come and help me and your sister finish the *sukkah*."

"Father told Goda to build it," James said, but he trudged back to the half-finished hut and picked up a palm frond.

Alexandra rushed down the stairs and joined her brother. Nathan followed. She took a spindly myrtle branch from Goda and laced it among the leafy olive and palm branches.

James pushed the slave aside and threw a frond onto the flat roof.

"Be careful to leave the branches loose, so the stars can shine through," Nathan instructed.

The neighbors all stopped and stared, but Alexandra and James were too engrossed to notice. A lemony smell enveloped them as Alexandra passed the final branch to her brother. "Here, you do it."

James stood on his tiptoe, looking for the perfect spot. He held his tunic against his body and stretched his arm out to thread the myrtle branch into place. Then he wiped his hands clean while Alexandra clapped. A muted cheer went up along the street, and James raised his arms and smiled, a rare and pleasant sight.

Three black-clad Pharisees approached, wearing unhappy faces. "Alexandra Onias, why aren't you wearing a proper veil?" The tallest one demanded.

Alexandra froze.

Nathan straightened. "Direct your questions to me, sirs. I am her betrothed husband."

Wearing piety like armor, the men held fast. "You must be the olive farmer from Galilee," another of them said. "You haven't had the advantage of sitting under proper teaching we enjoy in Jerusalem, so I will do you the favor of offering a warning. If you allow your wife go about with an uncovered face, she will use her wiles to entice men into adultery. Women are weak, unfaithful creatures. They can't help themselves."

Nathan managed to hold onto his patience. "While I appreciate your concern, I have consulted the scriptures and my conscience on this matter and I must respectfully disagree with you." The Pharisees' mouths flopped open. Nathan turned to Alexandra and James. "Come along," he said, walking away from an argument he had no hope of winning.

"I want to go to the bazaars," James demanded.

Nathan nodded. "Very well. I want to take a look at the weapon smith's swords."

Alexandra's step hitched. "Swords?"

CHAPTER 7

During feast weeks festival-goers descended on Jerusalem's bazaars as thick as locusts, buying up spices, medicines, metal goods, and the countless other items a trip to a major city provided.

Nathan paid no attention to the crowds. He couldn't stop watching Alexandra and her wide-eyed amazement at every little thing in the bazaar. They stopped before a display of alabaster perfume bottles. She reached toward a miniature white vial, but pulled her hand back at the last instant.

Nathan picked up the small bottle and pressed it into her hand. "No one will mind. The merchants want you to take a closer look."

She smiled and ran her thumb over the chalk-like stone.

"Is this your favorite market?" he guessed.

"I don't have a favorite."

Nathan nodded. "My sister loves them all, too."

"No, um..." Alexandra blushed. "I, ah, never visit them, so..."

He arched his brows. "Never? You truly have never been permitted to visit the bazaars?"

She winced. "Father says a woman's place is at home."

Nathan's mouth snapped closed. He knew Pharisees lived lives of seclusion, but he had never imagined the extent of their isolation.

James snatched the alabaster jar away from his sister and plunked it back down on the mat. "Women are weak creatures. I'm surprised Alexandra hasn't collapsed from the unfamiliar excitement."

Nathan burst into laughter. From what he'd seen, Alexandra Onias wasn't the fainting type.

Alexandra bit her lip, as though trying not to smile. "I appreciate your concern, James. But, I'm not tired."

James shot a sour scowl at her. "Who said you were?" He stomped off.

Alexandra sighed.

Nathan sobered. "Forgive me. I didn't mean to laugh. I would go mad if I was cooped up as you have been. How do you bear it?"

She rubbed her arms. "It's been terribly quiet without Lydia to keep me company."

He exhaled a heavy breath. "We will get your sister back."

Her eyes met his. "When?"

"Soon." Someone bumped into him. "Let's catch up with James."

They found the boy at the weapon smith's stall.

Rows of blades glistened under the midday sun. Nathan picked up a sword with a broad, flat blade. Weighted and balanced perfectly, it felt made for his hand. He slashed it through the air.

James looked over Nathan's shoulder. "Are you going to buy it?"

Nathan laid the weapon down and traced his finger

over its smooth length. "No. It's too costly."

"Ask Father for the money," James said picking up a jewel-handled dagger. "Or borrow the coins. You will soon be rich as Croesus. You'll be able to buy anything you want then."

Nathan rubbed his neck. He didn't trust Simeon Onias and wouldn't be indebted to the man. But he didn't feel it would be wise to admit it. "The money is not mine, not yet. But, I know someone who will lend me a sword."

A blade swished past his nose.

He leaned back and threw a protective arm in front of Alexandra. "Put it down before you hurt somebody," he ordered, adding under his breath, *like yourself, young idiot.*

James reluctantly obeyed.

Nathan hefted the jeweled dagger. Holding it up to the sun, he inspected the blade. "When you are fighting close enough to feel your enemy's breath on your face, the swifter man will fare best. Carry a light knife." He pointed the blade at James. "The tip could save your life."

The boy cringed backward.

Alexandra gave a small cry. Her eyes were locked on the dagger held to her brother's scarred face.

Who was the careless idiot now?

"Forgive me." Nathan threw the weapon onto the table. "Would you mind if we leave the market now? I need to make another stop."

Alexandra and James blinked and nodded.

Nathan led them out of the bazaar and through a set of arched gates. Leaving the old city behind, they followed the Second Wall. The sound of steady chinking filled the air even before the worksite came into view. Improvements to the city wall were underway, some ten years after Nathan and his fellow soldiers had broken it down taking Jerusalem away from an opposing band of Jews.

His stomach knotted. He was a bloody man, one more comfortable handling a sword than a pruning hook, and he had no business marrying, especially not a highborn woman who had led an extremely sheltered life.

He glanced over at Alexandra. Composed once more, a rosy color suffused her cheeks as she watched as the stonemasons wrestled an oversize block into place, raising a gray cloud of dust.

Nathan scanned the construction site, searching for Herod, but couldn't see his friend anywhere. "Stay here, while I go speak to the master builder," he said.

James walked on. "I want to take a closer look at what they're doing," he called over his shoulder.

Nathan's teeth ground together. "Is your brother always this obstinate?"

The clatter of hooves over stone drowned out Alexandra's answer. A large white horse charged toward them. Alexandra gasped and backed up against him.

Recognizing the ruggedly built rider, Nathan's frown gave way to a smile.

Herod pulled the powerful animal to a rearing halt, slid off the horse, and tossed the reins to a surprised stoneworker. Winded and laughing, Herod exclaimed, "Olive farmer! I have a message for you. But first, I have to have a word with my master builder."

"Please excuse Herod," Nathan told Alexandra.

She released her breath. "Does he always crash about

headlong like this?"

Herod was speaking animatedly with the supervisor, gesturing wildly with his hands, explaining what he wanted done.

Nathan laughed. "I'm afraid so. Next to fighting, nothing fires Herod up more than building things." Nathan pointed to James, who was standing beside Herod, listening intently to what was being said. "Watch and see if Herod doesn't talk your brother into helping him."

Alexandra looked skeptical. "My brother hates getting dirty."

"Herod is a hard man to say no to. And I ought to know. He convinced me to help him dig many, many holes and to lift thousands of rocks."

"Why? What were you building?"

Nathan gestured broadly toward Herod. "We were young and believed we were destined to be mighty soldiers. So, we copied Roman tactics, like building temporary shelters each time we bedded down for the night. Only Herod always wanted to construct elaborate defenses and, more often than not, he convinced me to help."

The master builder and Herod had finished their business. Herod said something to James, and led the boy over to the surveyors' station.

"See?" Nathan shook his head and laughed.

The surveyors moved off, giving Herod and James access to the *groma*, a long wooden pole with a cross arm attached to the top. They took turns looking down the cross arm, the older man giving the younger man a lesson in surveying.

Alexandra's brows furrowed. "What are they

doing?"

"Checking to see if the wall is level."

"Father would love it if James showed half this interest in his studies."

Nathan's lips curved upward. "Herod can be very engaging when he wants to be. The first time I saw him, he was racing a huge, white stallion across a valley floor. He was stretched out over the horse's neck, urging his mount forward. He outraced and outshone every other horseman there."

The fateful day was stamped like a seal on Nathan's memory.

Herod pulling his horse to a stop a hair's breadth from Nathan. Although he was only twelve years old at the time, Nathan stood his ground, impressing both himself and Herod.

Herod jumped off the magnificent horse and offered the reins to Nathan. "Give it a try?"

A large group of boys gathered around them.

Ignoring the snickers behind him, Nathan looked up, up, and up into the stallion's wild eyes. He reached a hand to the horse's flaring nose. Warm puffs of air hit his face. A soft muzzle filled his palm. "Pray, yes," he replied.

Herod petted the horse and spoke softly to it. "We have a brave one here, Ajax. Pray, do not try, straight off, to break his neck."

"Indeed, Ajax," Nathan's voice broke and squeaked. "allow me one turn around the valley before sending me to my grave." He turned to Herod. "My name is Nathan of Rumah in case you, ah, need to bear my remains home."

Herod threw his head back and laughed. When he got his wind back he said, "I am Herod of Idumea."

Nathan didn't see any hint of guile or mockery hidden in

the other boy's steady black eyes. Lord be praised because Nathan had his heart set on riding the magnificent horse.

Herod pressed his face affectionately against the stallion's long white neck. "Ajax is fussy about who rides him. I had better give you a few instructions before you climb aboard the evil devil." Herod reached over and punched Nathan's arm companionably. "Though I expect you will do a fine. You have the look of a born horseman about you."

Nathan shrugged. "And that was that. From then on, when I came to Jerusalem with my family for the feasts, I spent all my time around Herod's fire. We soon became fast friends."

Eyes the size of dinner plates, Alexandra asked, "What made you leave the army?"

"My family had need of me," Nathan lied. "My mother died and my father's health failed, I returned home to run the farm." *Coward, coward, coward.* The truth was that he had learned to hate being a soldier. When he received word of his mother's death, he hadn't been able to get home fast enough.

An ox-drawn cart filled with stones rattled past, putting an end to the uncomfortable conversation.

"Olive farmer!" Herod came roaring back toward them. He cupped Nathan's face and kissed him on both cheeks. "Happy marriage to you, young fox."

Nathan clapped Herod on the back. "At the speed the news is traveling, it ought to have reached Egypt by now."

"You saved me a trip," Herod said in his usual big and booming voice. "I planned to pay you a visit later, to invite you to the banquet High Priest Hyrcanus is hosting tomorrow night in honor of my father."

Nathan groaned. "You know my answer. I promised

my family I'd stay clear of your father and his behind-the-door intrigues."

Herod stumbled backward in exaggerated fashion. "My father involved in secret plots? Your lack of faith wounds me."

Nathan grinned. "If you were on stage, the audience would be pelting you with rotten fruit."

"Jerusalem needs a theater to liven things up." Herod wriggled his brows. "Or, even better, a Roman-style bathhouse. It's mind-numbingly boring around here."

"A bathhouse in Jerusalem?" Nathan rolled his eyes. "Are you insane?"

Herod's smile widened. "Come to the banquet. It's the least you can do, since you are going to drag me into the wilds of Galilee in hunt of your highway bandits. Come, and you can petition my father for help. He always liked you. I bet he'll offer you men and money."

Nathan glanced over at Alexandra. She was gazing at him expectantly. He expelled a resigned breath. "What time do you want me there?"

"The food and drink starts flowing at sundown."

Nathan looked down and scuffed his sandal against the ground. "You wouldn't happen to have a sword I could borrow?"

Herod burst out laughing.

Nathan straightened and frowned.

Wheezing, Herod pointed his thumb over his shoulder. "Only a few thousand hidden close buy. I'll dig one up for you before tomorrow." He turned his lightening-bright smile on Alexandra. "Are you sure you can handle this brute? To this day, my father's army talks about Nathan and how he single-handedly cut down a squad of men. They call him—"

"Don't say it," Nathan roared. "Not another word."

Alexandra went unnaturally still.

CHAPTER 8

Stone grated against stone, drowning out Herod's laugh.

Alexandra focused on the stoneworkers pushing another carved block into place. They wiped the dust from their hands, stood back and examined the city wall. James joined the workers and struck up a conversation.

She finally let herself look at Nathan. He wore a pained expression. Her heart ached for him. Though rattled by the image of Nathan as a bloody warrior, she wasn't going to give Herod the satisfaction of gloating over it. Herod was the brute, not Nathan. She turned and scowled at the overgrown bully. "I'm sure Nathan was a skilled soldier."

Herod ignored her and clapped Nathan on the back. "Good luck in your marriage." Then he strode off.

Nathan rubbed at his neck. "This was a bad idea. I'll take you home."

"No it wasn't." She moved closer to him, touched her elbow to his, to show him she wasn't frightened or repulsed by him. Full of questions, she said, "I hope we are able to go out for another walk before you go back to

Galilee."

James joined them and waved a finger in her face. "For shame, woman, you are barely espoused and already nagging." He turned his frown on Nathan. "Go on without me. I'm going to stay and watch the work on the wall." Not giving them a chance to reply, James walked away.

Nathan offered her a tentative smile. "If anyone is a clamorous woman, it's your brother."

She breathed easier, seeing the tension leave him. "My brother would be outraged if he heard you comparing him to a woman."

Nathan led her back to the road. "Your brother and father need a lesson in kindness. My mother would have set the goats on Father and me if we had dared treat her so."

"Truly?" she asked, astonished and amused.

Eyes alight with fond memories she could only envy, he said, "No, but she threatened it often enough."

Alexandra smiled. She hadn't had enough smiles in her life, an injustice Nathan of Rumah appeared determined to correct. *Praise heaven.* "Do you even own goats?" she asked.

"Yes, and sheep and chickens." He shrugged. "It is a farm, with all the usual smell and dirt."

Oh. She hadn't considered the unpleasant aspects of farm life. She quickly compared it the quiet bed chamber waiting her return. "I believe it will suit me."

Nathan offered her a doubtful look.

She opened her mouth and closed it. No amount of assurance on her part would convince him she was hardy and able, rather than fragile and needing protection. She would make the best farmer's wife who ever lived, she told herself. Fresh doubts arose. She pushed them away.

They walked in silence past houses and shops. People filled the street, rushing about preparing for the festival. They came to a repaired section of city wall. Nathan stopped and nodded. "Here's where we came over. Herod was on one side of me and his father on the other side. I was frightened half to death." A haunted look filled his eyes

A chill went through her. "In the final battle?" she asked. Jerusalem had changed hands three times in five years during the last war.

"Yes." Nathan exhaled heavily. "It's been ten years. Can you believe that?"

She tried picturing him, marching with the Roman soldiers. "You must have been just a boy."

His smile was grim. "I was seventeen. Herod was sixteen. We were big for our age and full of ourselves."

A young girl herself then, she'd been sick with fright and done what she could to comfort her terrified brother and sister. Nausea rolled through her, recalling the horrid screams and bloodthirsty shouts.

"You killed my nephew." The accusation came from behind them.

Nathan flinched.

An elderly bent-backed man stood in the doorway of a nearby house, staring hatefully at Nathan.

Alexandra moved closer to Nathan.

The man's wrinkled face reddened. "I saw you do it." He pointed at the very spot in the wall they were discussing. Spittle flew from his mouth. "You cut John down like he was a dog."

"Your nephew should have stayed inside," Nathan

said, the tension vibrating off him.

"Let's go," Alexandra whispered.

The old man tossed a hateful look at Nathan. "My nephew was an ardent supporter of Hasmond. He couldn't stay home."

People began to gather around.

"I'm sorry," Nathan said. He took her elbow and steered her past the onlookers.

"Murderer!" the old man yelled after them.

Nathan hunched his shoulders and lengthened his stride. Alexandra walked faster. They rounded a corner.

"Does this happen often?" she asked.

"Now and then. Most of the men who fought for Hasmond have either left the country or are in hiding." Misery marred his face.

Her brow furrowed. "I think the reason you don't own a sword is because you had your fill of violence and killing. And now my family's troubles will put a sword back into your hands."

Nathan tapped his chest. "I am to blame. Not you."

Her stomach knotted. Nathan had wounds deeper than the ones scarring his body. It wasn't fair to ask him to pick up the sword again. The image of Lydia's frightened face arose for the thousandth time. If only there was another way. But there wasn't. She loved Lydia too much to release Nathan from his promise.

The courts of the Temple pulsed with life and music. It was the first night of *Sukkot*, when all Israel slept in ramshackle booths to remind the people when they were a nation without land or permanent homes, and when all the men danced with joy before the Lord.

Alexandra sat with thousands of other women in the temporary gallery erected especially for the Water Drawing Festival. The Men's Court held a smaller set of benches set aside for white-bearded men too feeble to join in the dancing.

The courtyard was bright as day thanks to four golden lamps holding more than a hundred oil-soaked logs. They were set high on pedestals accessible only by ladders, and priests climbed up and down from the fiery lamps, throwing armload after armload of clothes onto the red-hot embers, disposing of last year's priestly garments.

Alexandra kept a firm grip on the wooden bench. The abrupt change of direction in her life was dizzying. Betrothed this morning, tonight she'd entered the Women's Court alone and found herself the center of untoward curiosity. Nathan's stepmother and sister, as well as numerous aunts and cousins, had rushed forward and taken her into their fold. By marrying Nathan, she wasn't just getting a husband, she was also gaining a loving, boisterous family. And Nathan got Father and James. A poor trade indeed.

Mary leaned close and pointed. "There's Nathan. Do you see him, next to Herod?

Alexandra's pulse beat faster.

Mary wrinkled her nose. "Herod ought to take a seat among the graybeards. He has absolutely no talent for dancing. Our Nathan, though..." Love and pride filled her voice. "He was born to dance for the Lord."

Handsome at rest, Nathan looked utterly breathtaking as he jumped, spun and clapped in time to the lively music. He picked up a torch and tossed it high. Herod caught it without missing a beat. Another torch flew upward and another. Herod plucked them out of the air as nimbly as the first. A loud cheer went up. More flaming brands filled the sky. Herod juggled seven, then eight torches. His fellow soldiers roared their approval. And why not? Confident, bold, and able, Herod was a natural leader. Nathan had the same qualities. It was easy to see why they'd become friends.

"Oh," Mary cried, "Father is going to join the dancing."

Alexandra winced watching Joseph of Rumah's halting progress. Nathan spotted his father and ran to help. Greeting his father with a hug, Nathan led the old man by the arm into the middle of a circle formed by friends, probably their neighbors. Helped along by the men's hoots and howls of approval, Joseph of Rumah soon spun round and round. Though no whirling dervish, the old man acquitted himself quite well. At least until he lost his balance. Nathan caught his father, kissed him on both cheeks, and set him on his feet. Joseph of Rumah patted his son's face.

Alexandra smiled through her sadness. She wished her father and James loved each other half as much as Nathan and Joseph did.

The night passed too quickly. A blast from a trumpet signaled it was time to take up the *lulab* and the dancing came to an end. All the men moved to the piles of boughs placed about the Men's Court and picked up tied bundles of myrtle, willow, palm, and citron branches. They raised the boughs high and waved them back and forth.

Alexandra reached under the wooden bench and wrapped her fingers around a leafy bough. The women stood as one. Like a peacock spreading its feathers, they lifted the long fronds of *lulab* high overhead and moved them side to side. The smell of lemon saturated the air.

All eyes turned east. The orange ball of the rising sun filled the sky and cast a warm yellow glow over the Levites lining the Temple steps, singing the words of a psalm. *"Someday the Holy One, blessed be He, will give a dance for the righteous and He will save us. This is the Lord, we have waited for Him and He will sit among them in the Garden of Eden, and each one will point His finger at him, saying 'Lo, this is our God, we have waited for Him'."*

Though it was probably blasphemous, Alexandra's eyes went to her betrothed. A man sent from the Lord. Nathan would rescue Lydia. She doubted there was any man in Judea or Galilee better suited to the task. She believed it with all her heart. The marriage though...She hadn't made peace with it. Yes, Nathan was handsome and kind, but they came from different worlds. They'd never suit. She sighed. There'd be time enough to worry about it after Lydia was safe. Spring was a long way off. Anything could happen between then and now.

The singing ended and the crowd shuffled to the exits. Nathan waited for them outside the Women's Court, standing with her father and James amid a crush of people.

Nathan spotted her and smiled. James yawned and waved. "Nathan wanted you to spend the day at his campsite," her brother announced when Alexandra, Mary, and Rhoda stepped out of the Women's Court. "Father said no."

Her father's face became more pinched. "The impatient fool can come to you, if he is that anxious to see you."

Alexandra's face heated. She gave Nathan an apologetic look.

He smiled and winked. "Will you be free to see me this afternoon?"

Warmth rushed through her. She bit her lip and nodded.

Someone in the jostling crowd bumped into her father. He grunted and fell forward.

"Watch where you're going," James said.

Alexandra caught her father as he fell. They toppled to the ground. Father's weight pinned her in place.

Nathan landed on his knees beside her and dragged her free. Father writhed like a worm beside her. A knife was sticking out his back. A red circle bloomed on his costly white cloak.

A large roaring filled her ears. James screeched and screeched like he had the day of the attacks. Her vision blurred. A large, steady hand squeezed her arm. "Your father will be fine. I promise." Nathan's voice soothed. "It's a small knife. The wound is superficial. A few stitches and your father will be his usual unpleasant self."

She choked on a laugh and dabbed at her damp eyes.

Mary knelt beside her, concern writ on her young face. "May I help?"

Alexandra pushed a loose strand of hair back under her scarf. "I'm fine, dear. Go talk to James." Rolled up like a ball on the ground, her brother continued to wail. Rhoda was patting his back. Alexandra's heart ached for him. "Tell James Father is only injured."

Alexandra turned back in time to see Nathan pull the wicked knife free. Bile rose in her throat. She swallowed. Someone gave Nathan a robe. He pressed the white garment to the wound and looked up at her.

"What? why?" she asked.

Nathan eyes clouded. "Someone wanted to send a message to your father."

She blinked. "I don't understand."

"Your father angered the wrong person or people. The knife is a warning."

"Help me up," Father demanded.

Nathan removed the bloodstained robe. The bleeding had slowed to a trickle. "What's the name of your physician?" Nathan asked.

"Mathew the Younger," Alexandra said.

Nathan turned the man who had handed him the robe. "Pinhas, go find Matthew. Tell him to meet us at Simeon Onias's home." The man took off at a run.

Nathan helped her father sit up.

"Can I do something?" Alexandra asked.

Nathan's steady eyes met hers. "Prepare for the wedding. We will marry at the end of the week."

Her face heated. She raised her hand to her throat. "But you said we would wait until spring."

Her betrothed winced. "It can't be helped. Your father has been attacked twice. I won't wait for a third." His lips firmed. "I can't trust him to keep you safe."

Holy angels in heaven, he was in earnest. A few days hence, they'd be man and wife.

CHAPTER 9

The high priest's palace was perched on a hill in the Upper City, presiding over the homes of Jerusalem's wealthiest families. John Hyrcanus's home was actually a compound comprised of private residences, offices, rituals baths, gardens, servant's quarters, guard barracks, and a prison. Nathan nodded to the palace guards and walked under a tall gateway.

He slowed and let out a low whistle. Their high priest lived well.

A servant approached, walking with a noticeable limp. The man's red hair was fading to white. "The banquet honoring Antipater is being held in the reception hall. Shall I show you the way?"

Nathan laughed. "Indeed. It's my first visit to the palace, but you could probably tell by the way my mouth is hanging open."

The servant held out his hand, inviting Nathan to follow him across the stone-paved courtyard. "How did you manage an invitation?"

"I'm a friend of Herod's. I'm here to ask a favor from his father." He was almost certain Antipater would give him men to help in the search for Lydia Onias. Nathan also planned to share his neighbors' grievances with Antipater, in hopes of quelling the worst of the unrest in Galilee.

The servant snorted. "You've come at a good time. Antipater is spreading coins as generously as a farmer sowing seed."

"Antipater always was fond of using bribes to make friends," Nathan said looking forward to seeing the gregarious man again.

"He's a clever one." The slave shook his head. "The money he is giving out isn't even his. It comes from the Temple treasury."

Nathan ground his teeth. "Does High Priest Hyrcanus know about it?"

The servant snickered. "Probably not. Hyrcanus follows Antipater as blindly as a lamb trailing a shepherd."

The servant led him under a domed archway leading to a spacious inner courtyard. Raised beds of roses cascaded toward a marble-carved fountain. The sweet smell of the pink, orange, and red blooms mixed with the fruity fragrance of the citron trees lining the walls of the garden. White turtledoves cooed contentedly among green boughs dotted with yellow fruit.

"Queen Salome loved roses," the servant explained.

"Were you here during her reign?" Nathan asked. He'd been a boy when Salome died.

The slave's reddish head bobbed up and down. "Those were good years." His voice was wistful. "The last twenty years have been a trial. Her worthless son and nephew aren't fit to carry the queen's chamber pot."

The two men being the current high priest, John Hyrcanus, and his nephew, Hasmond.

"They've certainly made a mess of things," Nathan agreed.

Several wars had been fought to determine which man would sit as high priest. Hasmond had ousted his uncle and ruled in his place for a short while. Nathan had fought in the last battle ten years ago, when Hyrcanus regained the coveted office of high priest. He still wasn't sure of the right or wrong of it. "Do you think Hasmond made a better leader than Hyrcanus?"

The servant swiped his hand through the air. "Hasmond is a whiny liar. I'll stick with Hyrcanus. I know a lot of folks hate having Antipater run things from behind the scenes, but I think the country could do worse."

Leaving the rose garden behind, the slave led Nathan up a wide marble staircase and down a hallway lined with Corinthian columns. Dozens of embroidered tapestries decorated with religious symbols hung from the walls.

They entered a cavernous banquet hall. The walls and ceiling were painted in muted shades of brown with gold leaf accents and flourishes. An army of servants carried trays piled high with food smelling of roasted meat and rich spices.

The lavish excess of the surroundings left a bad taste in Nathan's mouth. The Temple tax he and all other Israelites paid every year had paid for all this. He might not have begrudged the high priest his luxurious palace and wealth, but Nathan was friends with several priests who struggled to get by. Meanwhile, Hyrcanus and a handful of other families grew richer and richer. It was wrong. It was one of reasons his friends and neighbors had taken up arms.

The red-haired servant lifted a bony arm and pointed. "Do you see Antipater? He's standing beside Hyrcanus, with a delegation of high and mighty foreigners."

Engaged in a lively discussion with the visitors, Antipater looked hale and hardy as ever. Hyrcanus stood off to the side. Bored and indolent, he showed no interest in the conversation.

The servant's rheumy eyes met Nathan's. "Do you know what Hyrcanus said when his nephew ousted him from power?"

This ought to be good.

"*I never wanted to be High Priest.*" The old man shook his head. "Then Antipater comes along and convinces the fickle man otherwise."

Herod came roaring toward Nathan. The servant bowed and took his leave.

"Olive farmer." Herod wrapped Nathan up in a bear hug. "I'll take you to my father. He'll thank you for saving him from the Egyptian ambassador. The fellow is first-rate bore."

Antipater smiled as they approached. He kissed Nathan on both cheeks. "How are you? How's the family?"

Nathan returned the greeting and stepped back. "My father's health remains frail," he said, lest Antipater or Herod think they had a chance of talking him into rejoining the army.

Antipater turned toward High Priest Hyrcanus. "This is the Galilean farmer I was telling you about."

"*Shalom,*" Hyrcanus said without looking at Nathan. "My feet ache." The priest shuffled in place. "I need to sit down or my ankles will swell like melons."

Antipater offered Nathan an apologetic look. "The members of the Sanhedrin are up in arms over the attack on one of their own in Jerusalem."

Nathan made a sour face. "It's about time." The Great Court had mostly ignored the assaults on Roman sympathizers in Galilee.

Antipater nodded toward the seats reserved for the Sanhedrin. "Curiously enough, I've heard from all judges, except one. Simeon Onias." Antipater's brows rose. "The fractious man is always bleating complaints. Do you have any guess as to why he's keeping quiet or why he was stabbed?"

Nathan exhaled heavily. "No. I don't." His soon to be father-in-law refused to discuss the attack.

High Priest Hyrcanus blinked to life. "Rome is to blame for the trouble in Galilee. I only wanted the Romans to remove my nephew from power. How was I to know they would stay?" The priest lowered his voice. "Can't we ask them to leave?"

"No," Herod said, rolling his eyes. "We've told you a thousand times why not. If Rome leaves, Parthia will swoop in behind them. The Parthians will rape and rob the country and leave it in ruin. Rome taxes may be burdensome, but they build roads and aqueducts. It's in their interest to see us prosper." Herod turned to Nathan. "Am I lying?"

"I've been telling my rebellious neighbors the same thing," Nathan said. "They don't want to hear it."

Antipater leaned in closer. "Once Julius Caesar consolidates his power back home, he plans to march on Parthia, and make Rome the undisputed ruler of the world."

The high priest sighed, again. "You're right. Of

course, you're right." He gave Antipater a sheepish look. "May I go eat now?"

Antipater pursed his lips and nodded curtly.

Hyrcanus hobbled away.

Nathan shook his head. It was hard to respect the man.

"Good riddance," Herod growled.

Antipater lifted his hand and signaled to someone. A blond-haired, blue-eyed giant rose from a nearby table.

Nathan's eyes widened.

"My new bodyguard, Kadar," Antipater explained.

Nathan rocked on his heels. "He would have made Goliath look small."

Herod grunted. "He throws a hard punch."

"Tested the man already, have you?" Nathan asked.

Herod grinned. "Believe me, I won't be doing it again anytime soon. I just wish I'd seen him first and made him my man."

It took a lot to earn Herod's respect. The comment told Nathan all he needed to know about Kadar.

The giant joined them.

Antipater put a hand on Nathan's shoulder. "Herod and I have to go accept official thanks from the Egyptian ambassador for saving Cleopatra's pretty neck. Tell Kadar what you need to hunt down the outlaws and he will see that you get it."

Antipater and Herod took their leave.

A black-robed Pharisee sitting at the next table lobbed an insult at father and son. "Idumean dogs." His fellow Pharisees murmured their approval.

Kadar raised a brow. "Idumean? What is this?" The giant's accent was as heavy as it was guttural, marking him as a recent migrant to the civilized world.

Nathan had never come across an honest-to-good-ness barbarian. Indecently pleased, he smiled and called up his rusty but serviceable Greek. "Idumea was a small tribal nation east of Jerusalem. One hundred and twenty years ago the Hasmoeans..." Nathan pointed at High Priest's table. "...converted the Idumeans to Judaism with the tips of their swords. Many people consider Antipater and Herod to be Jews in name only."

The giant laughed. "I'd say the Idumeans are the ones with the right to gripe. You Jews forced them to be circumcised, and now you hate them for it? And you call me a barbarian."

Nathan winced.

Kadar scanned the room. "Antipater told me the Pharisees hate him because they fear he wants to be king, but you Jews don't have a king."

"We don't. And many people like it that way. The rebels I'm trying to hunt down have a motto. No king but the Lord. The power Antipater holds over our high priest makes people nervous."

Kadar straightened and reached for his sword. "I don't like the looks of this."

Nathan looked across the room to the head table. A Roman courier stood at Antipater's side. Herod and his three brothers all wore troubled faces. The news rippled its way back to them. Julius Caesar had summoned Antipater to Syria to face charges of treason.

Kadar frowned at Nathan. "Don't count on any help from Antipater now. He suddenly has more than enough problems of his own."

Nathan studied Herod, worried for him. Antipater could be put to death if convicted. Nathan shuddered.

Herod would go stark, raving mad if it happened.

CHAPTER 10

The sound of singing drifted through the open window, announcing the approach of the bridegroom. Alexandra pressed her hot cheek against the cold stones of the lattice window and peered down the road, waiting for her betrothed to appear.

She was getting married. Not in the spring as planned, but this very hour. Though nervous, the idea did not displease her.

And here he came. Nathan of Rumah.

Dressed in a simple white tunic, his black, curly hair was lit by the rays of the setting sun. Surrounded by his friends, he sang the wedding songs with the same enthusiasm they did. As the wedding party came even with the house, Nathan peered up at her window. A smile spread across his face. He'd spotted her watching him. Her pulse sped up dizzyingly.

"Alexandra, come away from the window," her aunt commanded.

The bedroom door banged open and her cousins charged in. Beyond excited at the prospect of walking in the wedding procession, the young girls spoke over one another, encouraging her to hurry.

"He's here."

"Come quick."

"Alexandra, why are you still holding your veil? Put it on. Put it on."

Alexandra took her time. The day of her marriage might not wait, but the hour certainly could.

Aunt Anna held out the wedding veil. "I am shocked your father agreed to this hasty marriage. The gossips are already chattering over it."

Alexandra dipped down to allow her aunt to slip the long, transparent covering over her head. "I am just grateful Father is alive and able to agree or disagree with anything."

"Praise the Lord, the evil devil who attacked your father used a woman's knife," Aunt Anna said and stood back to examine her work.

Praise the Lord, indeed. Her father had only suffered a flesh wound. He was already halfway healed.

A shiver snaked through Alexandra as she recalled the sight of the bloody knife. She was developing a deep loathing for the hateful weapon, and she wondered if she'd ever be able to pick up a simple cooking knife and not see blood.

Tears beaded in her aunt's eyes. "You are the image of my sister. A maiden's wedding day should be full of joy. Your father ought to have put the young man off."

Alexandra lifted the veil and kissed her aunt's cheek. "Nathan is worried for my safety." And for good reason. Her father had been unusually quiet on the subject, convincing her that he was, indeed, involved in some unpleasant scheme.

Lowering the veil, Alexandra skimmed her fingers over the fine stitchwork decorating the border of the sheer cloth. Lydia had worked many, many hours on it. Alexandra's throat closed. She wished her sister was here. The loss of Lydia was a low, constant ache.

Her aunt stepped back and her young cousins charged forward. Corralling Alexandra, they pushed her through the doorway. She watched her step for fear their enthusiasm would send her tumbling down the stairway.

"Ho, children," a firm male voice commanded.

The girls went instantly quiet. Alexandra drew her foot back and scanned the large, open-air courtyard below. A roomful of wedding guests holding garlands of myrtle smiled up at her. One face stood out from the others.

Nathan.

Two weeks ago, he had come to Jerusalem to observe *Yom Kippur* and *Sukkot*. Two weeks ago he didn't know her. Today he would marry a wife bringing him a pack of trouble. Poor man. What must he feel? Bewildered? Trapped? Displeased?

He stepped forward. "Take care with the bride." A lovely smile spread across his face. "She is a priceless treasure." Holding out his hand, he beckoned her to him.

Unfamiliar joy took hold. *Gracious God, praise You for Your loving kindness toward me.* Not only did Nathan not resent her, he actually seemed pleased to marry her.

Behind her, Aunt Anna laughed derisively. "The boy will stop his sweet-tongued ways once he has your father's money in his pocket. Just you wait and see."

Alexandra didn't believe it. Nathan was a good and honorable man.

His smile began to fade. She hurried down the stairs,

lest he believe her unhappy or reluctant to marry. Stopping a hairsbreadth away, she placed her hand against his open palm.

All she could manage was a whisper. "Take me to your tent."

His smile faded and his eyes grew intent. He swallowed. The long muscles in his neck flexed. His straight jaw and rugged cheekbones called out to be touched. She settled for pressing her palm closer to his.

His mouth brushed her ear. "You look utterly beautiful."

The whispered words purled at the nape of her neck and down her spine. She took a deep breath.

Myrtle garlands were placed around their necks. The floral smell soothed. Together she and Nathan moved toward the door. He held her hand tight, resisting his friends' efforts to pull him free and place him at the head of the marriage procession.

They stepped outside. A loud buzzing greeted them. All of Jerusalem had come out to watch the poor olive farmer take home his rich bride. How had she forgotten the gawkers? She'd stood at her window all day, watching the crowds gather and build like storm clouds around her home.

Her brief pause elicited a raised brow from Nathan.

And what of it, his amused smile asked. Was she having second thoughts?

She lifted her chin and pressed closer to him.

They left her home behind. Alexandra's cousins led the wedding procession through the streets and lanes of Jerusalem. Dressed in laced-trimmed white gowns, they skipped in time to the musicians' festive songs. Torch-bearers lit the way, and merriment and joy abounded as they trod the winding road to the Mount of Olives, then wove their way through the orchard.

Nathan's father, Joseph, stood waiting for them at the door of his tent. Moonlight shimmered on the spindly branches of the ancient olive tree guarding the camp. The walls of the tent were rolled up out of the way, and two simple, wooden chairs sat facing each other. Joseph invited the bridal party under the canopy. The guests gathered around.

This wasn't the wedding of Alexandra's imagination. Hers was to have been a grand affair, celebrated with fanfare at the door of a prestigious synagogue, followed by a sumptuous banquet. But the simple beauty of the orchard suited her tastes and temperament better than any grand celebration would have.

"Daughter." Joseph stepped forward and kissed Alexandra on the forehead. "Welcome home." She smiled, loving the frail man already.

Joseph nodded for her to begin.

Nathan released her hand and took his place on the groom's chair. She circled him once. Six more times to go around the bridegroom and her part would be over. She studied his broad shoulders and wide chest. A warrior through and through, vitality pulsed off him. Her toes curled and her stomach flipped. She prayed he'd find her as pleasing as she found him.

Legs shaky and weak, she finally was able to slide down onto the bride's chair. Aunt Anna and Nathan's stepmother, Rhoda, stood behind her. Unable to meet Nathan's eyes, Alexandra studied her feet. The silence dragged on and on. She lifted her chin.

Nathan was watching her. "It's not too late to stop," he whispered. Concern and conviction shadowed his brown eyes. He looked as vulnerable as he had when that stranger called him a murderer.

She folded her hands together and sat up straighter. "I'm nervous." She nodded toward the wedding guests. "I'm not used to being the center of attention." Which was also true.

Nathan's brow smoothed. "Keep your eyes on me, and we will get through this together."

She smiled. Though a warrior, he also was incredibly kind.

Joseph passed a silver-flecked stone goblet to Nathan. He lifted the cup and drank, his beautiful brown eyes remaining intent on her. He held the cup out. She laid her hands on top of his, directed the cup to her mouth, and drank deeply. Pleasant warmth washed through her, and it wasn't solely due to the wine.

The rest of the ceremony went by in a blur.

They moved outside.

A bonfire blazed bright, shooting sparks up into the starry sky. Merry music filled the air. Children raced after one another. Platters of food appeared. Nathan led her to a reed mat, where they sat. Rhoda gave them a plate holding luscious, red grapes and creamy, white goat cheese.

Father and James sat off to the side looking miserable. Used to sitting or reclining on couches, they shifted back and forth on the thin mats. Lydia would have loved it. Always dreaming about her own wedding, she would have found the evening enchanting.

Alexandra's smile faltered. If Judas the Zealot had indeed taken Lydia as a wife, her sister would never have her dream wedding. Not now.

Mary raced up. Breathless and rosy-cheeked, she

knelt down beside Alexandra. "Come and dance. Rhoda and most of the other women who live in Rumah have agreed to dance in your honor."

Alexandra eyed the women gathering by the fire. The mothers, sisters, and cousins of the men who had attacked her family. The men of Rumah stood off to the side. One of them might be responsible for stabbing her father.

Mary pointed. "Judith sends her apologies for the hurt her son caused you and your family." A small, frail woman waved a red-chapped hand. "Judith promises to do her best to persuade Judas to release your sister."

The air backed up in Alexandra's lungs. Everybody was staring, waiting to see what she would do.

A hand touched her elbow. Nathan's warm breath filled her ear. "No one will blame you if you refuse." He had invited these people, his friends and neighbors. He obviously wanted to live in peace with them. But he wasn't going to force her to do the same.

Her disgust with them fizzled. What would hating them accomplish? It wouldn't get her sister back. How long could she hold onto her bitterness? If the Lord willed it, she would live among these people from now until her death.

Alexandra took a deep breath and stood.

Nathan fingers skimmed over her wrist. "Thank you."

Her eyes met his. She forced a smile to her lips.

"Be sure to watch your step, now. The last time you danced..." Nathan's eyes sparkled with mischief.

Yes, she'd tripped and fallen into his arms.

Her smile turned real.

Mary led Alexandra over to the women. Greetings

and blessings rained down on her. She nodded and was friendly in return. The sour taste in her mouth would be worth it if even one of them decided to champion for Lydia's release.

The musicians struck up a new song. Mary clapped and waved for Alexandra to follow her. After a couple of turns around the bonfire, she began to relax. Then Herod of Idumea walked into camp. Alexandra stumbled. Nathan jumped up and greeted his old friend. Herod pulled Nathan off to the side.

A two-fold increase in the tempo of the music sent Alexandra and the others dancers whirling around the fire. Though she should be watching her feet, she kept peeking up at Nathan and Herod. Nathan frowned and seemed to be arguing against whatever Herod was saying. She grew dizzier and dizzier. She lost sight of them briefly, then spotted Herod leaving the way he'd come. From his satisfied smile, she'd say he'd been the winner of the short argument.

Where was Nathan? She looked one way and then the other.

The music slowed and stopped.

She wobbled in place.

Nathan took her elbow, saving her from another fall. His warm breath curled around her ear. "Are you ready to retire?"

He was asking permission to take her to the marriage bed.

God save her, she wasn't half-ready.

Alexandra's heart pounded loudly in her ears, but not loudly enough to drown out the noise of the wedding guests celebrating the imminent consummation of her marriage. She sat on her knees in the middle of the plush bedroll filling the small tent. An oil lamp burned dimly overhead. Nathan stood at the door studying her. His cinnamon-colored eyes flamed with intensity. She didn't want to be embarrassed, but was anyway.

He took a step toward her.

Her spine stiffened.

Pausing, he looked away from her and made a pretense of examining the tent, a tent he was undoubtedly thoroughly familiar with.

Bless him. He wasn't going to force or rush her.

Nathan found a pillow and sat on the hard-packed ground at the foot of the bed. His gaze settled on her again. "I am as uneasy as you are."

Not true. He looked calm as a reflection pool on a windless day. She couldn't fault his motives though. The lie was meant to soothe and encourage her.

She asked the question nagging at her. "What about your wish to wait until spring to marry? What if I conceive immediately? People might suspect our child is illegitimate."

"I considered putting off our joining." He gave half a smile. "Not for long, mind you. And seeing you now, so lovely, with your hair down and barely dressed, I am doubly glad I decided against it. I am mulish when it comes to keeping oaths. I would be suffering quite badly now if I had decided to put off our wedding night." His lips twitched with a smile. "If it worries you, you are welcome to persuade me otherwise."

Had the plentiful wine gone to his head? It was his decision to make, not hers. She meekly demurred. "You know best."

His smile broadened. "Moses' wife probably said so for the first thirty-nine years they wandered around the desert."

More loud cheers erupted outside the tent. They shared embarrassed looks. The noise faded. Nathan turned serious. "The real reason I insisted we wait until spring to marry was to give you time to get used to the idea." His eyes softened. "But the Lord had other plans. And here we are."

A cold draft swirled around her. She shivered. The gauzy tunic she wore felt cobweb-thin.

Nathan came and kneeled before her. "Come, let me warm you."

She rose to her knees. The nearness of him provided heat enough for ten tents. His large, strong hands moved over her with unsettling gentleness. Whispered words floated about her. "Don't be afraid."

She laid her hands on his chest and pressed her body to his. He smelled of myrtle and rich spices. She thrilled to the feel of his heart beating strong and fast against her palms.

"Lex?" The sound of the intimate name on Nathan's husky breath burned through her. Their noses brushed. His mouth lingered above hers. She longed for his kisses, but his lips skimmed her face.

"Nathan," she whispered the name against his cheek.

Still, he held back.

She turned her lips into his face and tasted of his smooth, salty skin. Nathan's chest expanded beneath her hands with his indrawn breath.

Her mouth grazed his. Hints of nuts and honey lingered on his lips. She licked her tongue along the velvet ridge of his upper lip, igniting a holy fire between them.

And now his hands were everywhere, fingers kneading and stroking.

Suddenly kissing Nathan felt as vital to her as her next breath. Stretching higher on her knees, she wrapped her arms around his neck and touched her lips to his. The soft melding flashed into urgent, ardent seeking. Pushed by ravenous needs she never guessed lived inside her, she nipped at Nathan's lips. He made a feral noise deep in his throat. And still it wasn't enough. She opened her mouth and cried out her pleasure at his tongue stroking over hers.

Nathan gave a guttural groan and set her away from him. "Slow..." He panted for breaths between words. "...got to...slow...down."

Had she offended him? Been too bold and brazen? Why hadn't she remained still and taken what he had to give instead of...of... she couldn't even say the words to herself.

Why? Because she was impatient to taste, touch, feel, and experience every last thing. She shuddered at her lack of restraint and what Nathan must think. Disgusted with herself, she turned her head away.

Nathan gave his first order as her husband. "Look at me."

She swallowed and squeezed her eyelids more tightly closed.

"Wife." His voice was kind but firm.

She forced her eyes open. Her husband was staring at her as though he'd encountered a strange creature.

Weeks of emotional upheaval since the roadside attack finally caught up with her. She burst into tears.

Nathan lifted her onto his lap and cradled her in his arms. "Did I hurt you? I promised myself I would

take care with you. And then I was grabbing you and..."
Shame writ large in his eyes, he turned his head away.

The truth dawned. He wasn't disgusted with her, but with himself.

Glad for the excuse to touch him, and wanting to console him as he'd comforted her, she took his face in her hand and made him look at her. "It felt wonderful."

He smiled weakly. "I...you..." shy now, he said, "You, ah, caught me off guard with your eagerness."

She spoke in a rush, "Did I offend you? I couldn't help it." Then it was her turn to be shy. "You are so beautiful...I...I...got carried away."

"Beautiful?" The dull light in the tent made it hard to tell, but she thought he was blushing.

She covered her mouth. "This is why I keep my thoughts to myself."

He arched a brow. "What other intriguing ideas are swirling around your interesting mind?"

Kiss me again, topped the list. But, she just shook her head.

He persisted. "No? I bet you are full of surprises."

She sealed her lips more firmly.

His chest rumbled with a laugh. "I like surprises."

Taking him at his word, she circled his neck with her arms and kissed him until they were both breathless. She pulled back.

Strong desire marked his features. "I could grow very fond of the unexpected."

And yes, beautiful was precisely the right word for him.

She slid off his lap, lay back on the plush bedroll, and held her arms out to him.

The sound of the ongoing wedding feast penetrated the low buzzing in Alexandra's ears. She wouldn't have believed it possible to forget the boisterous crowd just outside the tent, but she had. Wonderfully sore, she cherished the ache. Alexandra crossed her arms over her belly. Nathan's seed lay deep within her. She was a full woman now, and, if God granted, she would soon be with child.

Nathan stirred. Now here was pure blessing. He wasn't the husband she'd dreamed of having. *It is not a complaint*, she hastily explained, lest the heavenly hosts take offense. Generous to a fault, Nathan had been careful with her, bridling his own pulsing need. It was a beginning full of promise, a promise she planned to fully explore.

Nathan propped himself up on an elbow. If not for his careful study of her, she might have undertaken a more thorough study of his equally naked body.

He traced his finger along her temple and down her jaw. "You have lovely skin. So soft and fair. I promise to hire a lady's servant for you as soon as we arrive home."

She pulled a blanket over her body and sat up. "No. Please don't. I don't want to be treated any differently than Rhoda or Mary."

He held his hands out. "Show me your hands." She touched her fingers to his. He turned her hands palm up. "I won't..." his voice was rough with emotion "...watch your lovely, supple skin grow raw and red from work a servant can easily do."

She searched for an answer that would satisfy both of them. Although more than a little nervous about how she would fare with farm life, the last thing she wanted was to be treated like visiting royalty. "Please wait a few months, see how matters go. If I turn out to be a hopeless cause or troublesome…"

She would not fail. She'd spent her whole life sitting in her room with nothing important to do. Here was an opportunity to help and be of use, and she wasn't about to let it slip through her fingers. *Please, please, please, don't make me beg.* She would, though, because it was that important.

"I will give you three months." Nathan held up a staying finger. "A favor merits a favor."

His tone warned her she wasn't going to like what he had to say.

"Herod wants me to go to Syria with him."

She winced. Nathan was supposed to resume the search for Lydia. "Will you go?"

"Herod says he will join the hunt for your sister, if I agree to help him."

"Help him how?"

"Herod doesn't scare easily. But Caesar's summons has him very worried. He wants to be distracted and he thinks my company will help." Nathan shrugged. "Herod *is* bullying me into going, but he's my friend and…"

"And, you want to help him," she finished for him. "I know my sister's troubles are not as important to you as Herod, but Lydia is good and loving and…" Alexandra's lip wobbled. Tears filled her eyes. She pulled the thin blanket up under her chin.

Nathan sat up and lifted her onto his lap. His warm breath filled her ear. "Don't cry. I haven't forgotten about your sister. But I need help. Antipater will keep all his men close until the matter with Caesar is settled. If I'm in Syria and all goes well, I'll stand a good chance of getting men for the search immediately. Especially if Herod speaks to his father on our behalf."

She dried her eyes on the corner of the blanket. Getting Lydia back was turning out to be more complicated than she'd imagined. "How soon do you have to go?"

Nathan skimmed his fingers along the loose ends of hair falling over her arm. "Too soon for me."

A shiver went through her. "How long will you be away?"

"Ahhh...about that." For the first time since they'd met he looked unsure of himself. "I'd like you to come with me. If you find the idea too loathsome, I won't force you to go."

She blinked in surprise. "I'll go."

Nathan's brows rose. "Are you sure? We will be spending most of our time with the Idumeans, Antipater and Herod, and mingling with pagans. You might see some shocking things."

"I'll risk it to be with you." Blushing at the bold confession, she ducked her head.

Nathan's knuckles caressed her jaw. He tilted her chin up. "I'm glad you said yes. I hated the idea of getting home and straightway leaving you behind. I prepared all kinds of arguments to convince you." Nathan's voice turned husky. "And I can be quite persuasive when I want something as much as I want you."

The weight of Nathan's confession made her insides contract. "What made you think I wouldn't want to go?"

"Your father is a Pharisee."

"And?" she asked.

Nathan shrugged. "And Pharisees do not go out

among sinners."

She pulled away from him. He was as nervous about taking her to Galilee as she was about going there. Though they were both Israelites, she and Nathan lived in different worlds. This was his roundabout way of asking if she was as fastidious about observing the Law as her father.

She offered him a reassuring smile. "Pharisees do not go to live in Galilee. And, in case you haven't noticed, I am not dressed in the Pharisee's flowing robes or looking for the nearest ritual bath to cleanse myself."

He hooked his finger on the blanket trapped under her arms. "At the moment you are very un-Pharisee-like."

A flash of heat went through her. She swallowed. He was trying to make light of it, but she knew he had strong doubts about the marriage. "If I had married Phillip Peter I would have tried hard to adhere to Pharisaical standards. But, I am your wife, and so I must learn to live and move among your people."

His brown eyes grew serious. "Whether you like it or not?"

She brushed her lips over his and pulled back. "But I will love it. Because you will teach me to love it." She let go of the blanket.

Nathan's breath hitched.

She drew his callused hands to her waist. "Take me to my new home and teach me to love everything about it."

CHAPTER 11

T he sky hung like a dingy gray blanket over the Mount of Olives. Fat drops of dew clung to the trees, tents, rocks, and grass. Smoking campfires snapped and hissed. People moved slowly about their campsites, worn and tired from two weeks of festivities.

Nathan led Alexandra up the winding road to Jerusalem. He was taking her to say her final goodbyes to her family, and to collect the promised dowry. He also planned to, once again, raise the topic of Lydia.

He brushed his hand down Alexandra's arm. "There's still time to buy a donkey for you to ride."

She smiled politely. "No, thank you, Nathan. I will walk like everyone else."

He exhaled heavily. Afraid the week-long, journey north would be too hard on her, he tried a different approach. "No one will think less of you for it. My father will be riding. He'd enjoy your company."

She shook her head. Without warning, she veered off the dirt road and knelt down beside a patch of flowers. Picking a purple bloom, she held it to her nose, closed her eyes, and inhaled. Her lips curved upward. Pleasure shone on her face, the same way it did when they made love.

His loins tightened. The first two nights in the marriage bed ought to have satiated his hunger for her, but like a few drops of golden honey, it whetted his appetite for more. He'd gone to her on their wedding night hoping she wouldn't be frightened or disgusted by him. Her passion and eagerness when he had her in his arms was a delight he hoped to enjoy again and again.

She plucked a handful of flowers and rejoined him. A short while later they entered the city and passed a group of Greek-speaking Jews who stood outside an inn, preparing to go home. Judging from their refined clothes and manners, they most likely came from as far away as Rome.

"Every year it seems as though more and more pilgrims come to Jerusalem," Alexandra observed. "I wonder why?"

"Blame Julius Caesar," he said.

Her brows rose. "Caesar?"

He laughed. "Caesar was responsible for clearing the Great Sea of pirates, making it safe for Jews from all over the world to come to Jerusalem for the feasts."

She pondered it for a moment. "Do you think you'll get to meet Caesar while he's in Syria?"

"I hope so. He is an up-and-coming-man in Rome. His name's on everybody's lips, and I want to see what all the fuss is about."

She smiled but tried to hide it.

Intrigued, he smiled too. "What?"

She waved a dismissive hand. "Never mind."

"You can't raise my curiosity and not tell me."

A red blush rose on her cheeks. "I was thinking about

what I want to see in Syria."

He brushed his arm against hers. "And?"

"I can't wait to see the pagan statues," she said in a rush. "To see what all the fuss over idol worship is about."

He clapped a hand to his forehead. "I forgot about the statues. Half of the figures are naked and some..." Unseemly images flashed through his mind. He slapped his forehead again. "I can't take you to Syria."

Alexandra ducked her head and smiled. They both knew he wouldn't leave her behind.

They walked in silence the rest of the way to Simeon Onias's home. The bald slave met them at the door and led them down a high-ceilinged, marbled-floor hallway before showing them into an opulent sitting room.

Nathan groaned inwardly at the rich surroundings. What was he doing taking a gently raised woman to live on a remote olive farm, in a two-room mud and rock house? If the walk to Galilee didn't do Alexandra in, the primitive life awaiting her surely would.

He approached the low, cushioned, reclining couches where his new father-in-law and brother-in-law sat studying a Torah scroll. They remained seated, sparing him the necessity of greeting them with a kiss to the cheek.

Nathan bowed his head. "Father, Brother." He addressed Simeon, "How are you fairing? Is your wound continuing to heal well?"

The corners of Simeon Onias's mouth sagged lower. "Stop with the pleasantries. We both know you don't like me."

Nathan smiled. "I don't, but your directness is refreshing. Let me be open in return. What do you want me to do with Lydia, once I find her?"

Simeon's brows arched. "You are awfully sure of yourself, young pup."

Nathan struggled to remain respectful. "Do you want me to return Lydia to you?"

"Fine, fine. I may have use for her yet." The cantankerous man plucked a tattered cloth pouch off his couch and tossed it.

Nathan caught the bag. Coins jangled together. "What's this?"

"A dowry payment."

"A payment? I thought—"

"You thought wrong," Simeon snapped. "The contract didn't state when or how the dowry was to be paid, leaving it to my discretion. Consider this your first lesson in being a rich man. What's not said in a contract is as important as what is said."

Nathan's fists balled. Though he'd been a bit apprehensive about handling the small fortune, he'd sooner kiss a pig than admit it now. He narrowed his eyes at Simeon. "We will get along fine without your money."

The pious man smiled. "I'm sure you will. Now take my daughter and go."

Nathan glanced at Alexandra. His bold boast was true for him and his family—he didn't want Simeon Onias's money. But what about his highborn wife? Would she beg him to go groveling to her father for money once she realized just how poor he was?

Calm and lovely as a rose garden at sunset, his wife took a step forward. "James. Father. I will think of you every day."

Her brother started to rise.

Simeon waved the boy back and scowled up at Alexandra. "You're keeping James away from his studies. Bid us farewell and go."

She bowed her head.

Nathan took hold of her limp hand and squeezed her fingers. He wished there was more he could do to comfort her. Tempted to throw the bag of coins fisted in his other hand at her hateful father, he refrained. The gesture was a luxury his family couldn't afford.

Simeon gave him a smug smile. "Expect to hear from me."

The statement had an ominous ring. Not bothering with parting words, Nathan turned his back on his father-in-law, tucked Alexandra's hand into the crook of his elbow, and led her out of the cold house.

Nathan walked beside Alexandra, leading a donkey which refused to be rushed. His family had been making the trek between Galilee and Jerusalem with the same families for generations, folks from the villages and farms surrounding his olive farm, about a hundred people in all. They watched out for each other as best they could.

Days of traveling in the rain had left everyone sniffling and coughing. Everyone except Alexandra. And here he had been worried about her. He might have enjoyed a good laugh at his own expense if not for the weary slope of Alexandra's delicate shoulders. Not only wasn't she sick, she had spent the whole time acting as nursemaid to them all, unselfishly attending to men, women, and children related to the men who had attacked her family.

He'd married a generous, forgiving woman. The extent of her goodness would soon be tested. "We're almost to the farm," he said.

Alexandra shaded her eyes and peered into the distance. "Can you see it yet?"

He ran his hand down her back. "No. The hills are in the way. Two more to go and we'll be there."

Pinhas stood off to the side of the rocky trail, waiting for them to catch up. "*Shalom Shabbat*," he said falling in beside them.

Nathan offered his friend a weak smile. "What do you think? Will there be enough time to set the tents before sunset?"

The band of weary travelers had been pushing hard all day to reach his home before the start of *Shabbat*. They would stay with his family all tomorrow, observing the day of rest as the Law of Moses demanded.

The rugged stonecutter nodded. "Barely. We ought to go ahead of the others and begin the work."

Nathan glanced over at Alexandra. He'd wanted to be with her when she got her first look at the farm. But Pinhas was the right.

Alexandra lifted her arm and pointed. "I see smoke."

Smoke? Nathan's head snapped around. A curl of white showed against the gray horizon.

Nathan pushed the rope tied to the donkey into Alexandra's hands. Her brow was furrowed with concern. "I have to go," he apologized. "The smoke is close to the farm. I'll send Timothy back to help you."

Not waiting for a reply, Nathan raced off. He dug his sandals into the ground, kicking up rocks and dirt.

Pinhas followed.

Lungs close to bursting, Nathan crested the hill overlooking the farm. White smoke rose from the hole in the roof. He scanned the yard, looking for the person or people bold enough to enter his home and kindle a cook fire. He saw a lone horse grazing in front of the house.

Nathan braced his hands on his thighs and gasped for breath. He'd predicted something like this would happen. Living next to the olive orchard was practical. It was also isolated and unprotected, which is why the majority of the people choose to live in walled cities and villages. Nathan repeated his concern every time they left the house unattended to go to Jerusalem for the required feasts. And every time his father would say, "Trust in the Lord" or "The Lord will provide." Nathan took no satisfaction in being proven correct.

Pinhas came to a halt beside him. Panting, he asked, "Is the house safe?"

Nathan straightened. "You were thinking the same thing I was. Good. I'd hate to think I am growing to be an old, worried woman."

Pinhas nodded. "Let's go greet your visitor."

A man stood at the threshold, watching them.

They approached the house with caution. Then Nathan recognized the woolly head. Herod had never visited before. "What are you doing here?" Nathan called out.

Herod grinned and waved a greeting.

Assured bad news wasn't in the offing, Nathan walked past Herod and took a quick look around the house. Everything appeared in order. "Come with me," he told Herod. "We'll talk while I draw water for the animals." Nathan patted Pinhas's shoulder. "The last of the old wine is in those large jars out back. You'll need help carrying them."

They headed toward the well. As other travelers started to arrive, Nathan fired off instructions for them as well.

Herod reached the well first and grabbed the worn, two-handled pitcher sitting on the rim of the ancient, rock-walled well. Lowering the jug into the water, he said, "You are an efficient leader."

"I'm not rejoining the army," Nathan declared for the thousandth time.

Herod dumped water into the clay trough. "Your talents are wasted out here."

"And you are the most stubborn man I know."

Herod dropped the pitcher back into the deep pit. "Can you honestly say you don't miss fighting?"

A line of children carrying water containers of all shapes and sizes formed at the well. Nathan took the rope from Herod and dragged up the full vessel and emptied it into a waiting pot. "Why are you here?"

The children stared wide-eyed at Herod, unsure whether to be afraid or not.

Herod bared his teeth at the youngsters and growled. His leery audience tumbled over each other in their haste to get away from the formidable man.

Laughter softening his eyes, Herod turned back to Nathan. "My men still talk about your exploits. I saw a glimpse of the Angel of Death when you came charging over that hill."

Nathan ground his teeth and whacked the pitcher against Herod's chest. "Stop."

Angel of death. Nathan had earned the name from Antipater on the heels of a particularly horrific battle. A name Nathan hated, as Herod knew.

Unfazed, the big man threw the water pot over the

side of the well again. "Is that any way to treat your bodyguard?"

"Bodyguard?"

Herod hauled on the rope. "My father wants to make sure you arrive safely in Syria."

"He could not want it too badly, since he sent you." Nathan stepped aside, narrowly escaping the gusher of water whizzing past his ear. "Alexandra will be making the trip with us," he said.

His friend frowned and handed the empty pitcher back. "Are you sure that's wise? What if Judas or Hezekiah make trouble for you?"

"Of all the foolish..." Nathan rolled his eyes. "They'd never do real harm to me." Annoyed at the skeptical grin that earned, he pointed a warning finger. "Your father is the one who had better start paying attention to the rebels."

Herod's smile vanished. "He's got bigger problems. The treason charge has Father worried."

Antipater had backed Pompey against Julius Caesar in the latest go-around of civil wars plaguing Rome. Many Israelites hoped Caesar was going to strip Antipater of power, or, better yet, execute him.

Nathan wasn't convinced it would happen. "Yes, but Antipater's soldiers fought alongside Caesar's army in Egypt. That has to count for something."

"You would think so." Herod shook his head with disgust. "But Hasmond has come out of hiding. Again. He's in Syria already, speaking lies against my father. The damnable snake."

"Watch your mouth around the children," Nathan growled. But the majority of his displeasure was for John Hyrcanus and his nephew, Hasmond, and their never-ending bickering over which worthless member of the Maccabeus family would sit as high priest.

Herod rolled his thick shoulders. "There is a bright side to the trip to Syria. The governor has some amusements planned."

Nathan narrowed his eyes at Herod. "I'm not going to find myself in a line with the jesters, dwarves, and lions, am I?"

Herod threw his head back and laughed. "No, but I'd pay to see it. The governor is going to hold some tournaments. Wrestling, swordsmanship, horse races, and the like. I'm in the mood for some bruising competition. Plan on going up against me. I want to see how soft you've become."

Nathan snorted. "If anyone's soft, it's you."

Herod clapped him on the back. "You must be brave as ever." He nodded toward Alexandra, who was just entering the yard. "Or you wouldn't consider bringing Simeon Onias's daughter to live in a two-room hovel."

Nathan took a deep breath and went to meet Alexandra.

Alexandra stood aside as the travelers swarmed over the farmyard and got to work setting up camp. She eyed the stone and mud house at the center of the activity. Despite Nathan's repeated warnings about the size of the house, she was still taken aback by how small it was. The rolling hills surrounding the home had a quiet beauty she liked. She couldn't wait to explore the depths of the ancient olive orchard. But the house.

"You didn't faint. That's something."

She turned at the sound of Nathan's voice. He walked

toward her as though headed to his doom.

She put on a smile. "You have the whole valley to yourself. How lovely." The last farm they'd passed was several miles behind them.

He raised a brow. "The next time I see your father I will have to ask him if the scriptures say anything about a tactful wife being a blessing to her husband. If not, they should."

Her smile became real. Since they were at the center of a whirlwind of activity, and she was anxious to fit in and be helpful, she spread her hands. "What can I do?"

The tension went out of Nathan's shoulders. "I have to go set up tents." He backed up a few steps. "But, I'm sure Rhoda could use help preparing the *Shabbat* meal. I'll be along shortly to give you the grand tour of the house." He winked and spun away.

The sinking sun at her back, Alexander hurried to the home's open door and peeked inside. Nobody was around. A round, tan mat was laid out on a hard-packed dirt floor. Smaller, matching woven mats circled it. Loaves of bread jutted out of a large basket sitting in the middle of the table.

She stepped inside. Tools of all shapes and sizes filled one corner. She crossed the room. Rhoda came rushing out the back room and crashed into her, dislodging the pitcher the older woman was carrying. Water splashed everywhere.

Alexandra gasped. "I'm so sorry. Where are the rags? I'll dry the floor. Or I can go for more water."

The careworn woman continued to frown. "You can help me by sitting down over there, out of the way." She pointed to the opposite corner. Then she rushed outside.

Alexandra winced and wiped her hand over her wet tunic. She was so anxious to please Rhoda, but Nathan's stepmother remained standoffish. This small accident wouldn't help.

Mary and Timothy burst through the door and skidded to a stop in front of Alexandra.

"Did you hear the news?" Timothy asked breathlessly, pushing his hair out of his face.

Alexandra bit her lip to keep from smiling. "Did Bartholomew's donkey bite someone again?"

Brother and sister shook their heads.

Mary clapped. "There's not enough time to put up all the tents, so Pinhas and his family are going to sleep with us. You will love it. Pinhas and Nathan tell funny stories about when they were boys. They make us laugh and laugh."

The house already felt cramped. More people would soon crowd inside. The walls of the small home seemed to press closer. Alexandra swallowed and filled her lungs with air, while there was some still to spare.

A short while later eleven people sat around the mat table. Herod had been invited to spend the night, too.

Rhoda leaned forward and lit a simple clay lamp. The smell of warm olive oil filled the air.

Joseph spoke the words of the Psalms. *"Seek the Lord, and his strength, seek his face evermore."*

A chorus of approval went up. Olives, dates, bread, and wine were passed around the table. Everyone fell to talking.

Alexandra started to relax. Nathan touched her arm and leaned closer. "How are you?"

Her legs were starting to go numb from sitting on them. "I'm fine," she said.

He offered her a dubious look.

Pinhas called for everyone's attention. He reached behind his back, grabbed up a woven bag, handed it to Alexandra, and offered her a sheepish smile. "A wedding gift."

Whatever it held was heavy. Alexandra peeked inside and pulled out a pair of stone-hewn cups and plates.

The others watched her expectantly.

"I carved them myself." Pinhas shrugged. "I'm sure they're not as fine as the ones your father uses."

Alexandra ran her hand over the polished rim of the cup. She'd lived surrounded in luxury, but without the happiness and love abounding here. If anyone had been deprived, it was her. She offered Pinhas a smile. "They are beautiful. Thank you."

Her blessing given, the rest of the family felt free to exclaim over them.

Mary asked to see the dishes.

Herod stood and walked across the room. "Your roof's leaking."

Nathan and Pinhas jumped to their feet. Nathan grabbed up a lamp and inspected the wall and poked it with his finger. "We must have had some heavy rain while we were away. A fair amount of mud has washed away."

Everyone looked up at the ceiling.

Nathan lowered the lamp. "The roof needs rolling. I was going to wait until after *Shabbat*, but I don't think it will keep." He turned and headed toward the door. "I'll be right back." Another moment and creaking came from overhead.

"Awww," Timothy said disappointed. "Nathan's feet

didn't come through the roof. Alexandra won't get the chance to hear Nathan say bad words. My brother is funny when he's angry," the boy informed her helpfully.

Alexandra tipped her head back. "This occurs regularly? Err...what is the matter...if you don't mind my asking?"

"It's a mere inconvenience," Joseph assured her.

"It would be easier to list what's not wrong with the house," Pinhas said, earning laughter from the others. "A tile roof would solve the problem, but it costs too much to bring tile to Galilee, so the roofs in these parts are made of timbers, packed with clay. Heavy rain wreaks havoc with them. Nathan is using a stone roller to repack the clay."

"Did the rain weaken the wall?" Joseph asked.

Pinhas squinted up at the corner. "I'm not sure. It's too dark to tell. A thorough inspection will have to wait until daylight."

"Daughter?"

It took Alexandra a moment to realize Joseph was addressing her and another moment to make herself look away from the ceiling. "Yes?"

A small, unassuming man, Joseph of Rumah would be easy to overlook, that was until he smiled. Like the sun rising over Temple, his joyful face brightened the room. "The Lord has brought you here to bless us."

It was her turn to say something. She couldn't very well dismiss the praise, as it was directed at Lord God. She agreed with the most modest reply she could think of. "Amen."

"Amen," Nathan added, coming into the room and closing the door.

Though it obviously caused him pain, her father-in-law sat up straighter and offered Alexandra more wine. "After trying my patience all these years with a fieldstone and mud house..." a wry smile crossed his lips "...the good Lord has given us means to improve our circumstances. Nathan, Rhoda and I think it's time to build a new house. We want to hire Pinhas to make a sturdy limestone-block house. What do you say, Daughter?"

"Ahhh..." Alexandra stammered. Job's bones, he wasn't teasing. Her father-in-law wanted to know what she thought. Or was he asking her permission? And what would her father say to that? A giddy laugh bubbled up.

The earnest faces staring at her sobered her. She didn't want these good people to feel beholden to her because of the dowry. There was no question about it, they needed a new house, especially with mud-smeared walls threatening to slide down onto the hard-packed, dirt floor.

She managed a small nod.

Cheers went up.

Joseph pointed his face toward heaven. "Bless the Lord."

Nathan sat down. His mat was nearer to Alexandra's than before, thanks, no doubt, to Mary pushing it closer. He spoke in her ear. "My father's great faith puts me to shame."

"Amen," she whispered back.

Nathan threw his head back and laughed and laughed. She clapped her hand over her mouth.

"What did she say?" everyone asked.

Alexandra knitted her hands together. She couldn't remember ever celebrating a more enjoyable *Shabbat*.

"I said, 'Bless the Lord, for he has given me a wonderful new home and family.'"

A short while later, Nathan stretched his arms and yawned. "I don't know about everybody else, but I'm exhausted."

The suggestion had everyone moving to get ready for bed. Everyone except Alexandra, who stood in the middle of the room looking confused and tense.

Nathan touched his hand to her elbow. "Can you stand one more night of sleeping out in the open?"

A look of relief crossed her pretty face. "Yes."

Pinhas stopped beside them and handed the *Shabbat* lamp to Nathan. "I hate to chase you out of your own house."

Nathan patted his friend's arm. "You're not."

When a cool mass of air moved through the house, Nathan looked up in time to see the door closing behind Herod. "Where is he going?"

Pinhas shuffled in place. "He told me to tell you he'll be back in a couple days. He's going to Sepphoris to retrieve a wedding present for you."

Nathan frowned at the door.

Pinhas read his mind. "It's a long way to travel on *Shabbat*."

The Law said, six days you shall work, and on the seventh day you shall rest that your ox and your ass may rest, and the son of your handmaid, and the stranger may be refreshed. The problem was the Laws of Moses were interpreted as many different ways as there were men calling themselves Israelites. Nathan tried to be lenient in his judgment of others. But Herod always had pushed things to the limit.

Nathan exhaled heavily. "Are you going to gainsay the pigheaded man? Because I'm not."

Pinhas' brows shot up. "No. Not even if Goliath and his five oversized brothers were backing me up."

Nathan laughed and slapped Pinhas on the back. "I'll see you in the morning."

Alexandra returned with the blankets. Nathan led her to the door and opened it.

A week had passed since they'd lain together as man and wife. He couldn't help wondering if she would come to him as eagerly as the first few times.

They went outside. "Where are we going?" she asked, examining the stars shining overhead.

He pointed to the ladder leaning against the side of the house. "Up there."

She stopped abruptly. He bumped into her.

"On the roof? Truly?" She couldn't have sounded more delighted. "When it is especially hot, James and father sleep on the roof. Lydia and I are always envious."

He kissed the top of her head. "You seem an easy woman to please."

Alexandra's soft laugh warmed his belly. "The subject of nagging wives came up quite often among my father and his friends. I vowed my husband would have no reason to speak thus about me."

Nathan rubbed her arm. "Telling me what you like or don't like is not nagging. You have left behind an easy life for a hard one. Sleeping with a roof over your head, albeit a leaky one, is not too much to ask." He directed her to the ladder. "Climb slowly, and make sure your tunic doesn't get caught underfoot."

He stepped up onto the rung behind her.

Halfway up, she paused and looked down at him. "It was not always an easy life." Though barely discernible, her words were filled with aching sadness. "You don't need to worry over me so. I am not as fragile as you think."

Nathan put his hand on her calf and gave it a reassuring squeeze. "It has been given to me to worry over you."

She slipped away from him. "And it has been given to me to obey you."

Reaching the roof a few steps behind her, he set the lamp and bedrolls aside and wrapped his arms around his wife. "Why do I feel like I am losing this argument?"

Her soft breath filled his ear. "Why are you are letting me win?"

"Because winning at all costs is not always the wisest course." Being a soldier had not all been for naught. He'd learned a helpful thing or two.

He felt her shiver. Though reluctant to release her, he set about righting the bed mats and covers atop a mound of straw.

Alexandra bent to help. "The straw looks fresh."

"I managed to find time to carry some up here." He placed the burning lamp next to the ladder. "Whether inside or out, we are going to be sleeping on a clay floor. At least we have some privacy up here."

"Bless heaven," Alexandra replied.

He smiled. "I didn't think I'd ever be attracted to a religious woman, but you are proving me wrong." He held out his hand. "Come lay with me."

They stretched out on the hay and turned to each other.

"What fault do you find with religious women?" she

whispered.

"They are usually very strict about observing the Law." He stroked his hand over the curve of her hip. If he didn't have a yard full of guests he would be tempted to strip her bare.

She pressed closer to him. Her soft fingers slid over his face. Her mouth found his. Warm lips trailed down his neck. She ignited a fire deep within him.

He promised himself he would treat her with respect. *Be gentle with her*, he reminded himself, straining to remain still.

Her slim leg slid over his thigh. Her breasts brushed against his chest.

He sucked in a breath. "I come undone with you in my arms."

She went still. The dim moonlight glowed in her eyes. "Is that bad?'

"No." He traced his finger up the curve of her spine and brushed her lips with his. "Making love with you makes me a holier man, especially during *Shabbat*," he said, his voice hoarse with need.

She smiled against his mouth. "*Shabbat*?"

He kissed her nose. "*Shabbat* is a day for enjoying what the Lord has supplied and for meditating on his commands."

Her warm breath spilled down his neck. "And, which of the commands are you meditating on presently?" Her tongue circled over-sensitized skin.

"Umm...let me think...it is not good for man to be alone...that's one." Another moment and he would have trouble remembering his name, never mind the commands. "I seem to recall something along the lines of 'be fruitful and multiply.'"

She laughed low. Her teeth nipped at his chin.

He groaned. She sat up and twisted her way out of her tunic.

Pale moonlight glowed on her unbound hair and ivory skin. Her beauty made him want to weep. What had he done to deserve so precious a gift?

He reached for her.

She pushed him back and stretched out on top of him. "*Shabbat* is a day for enjoying and not doing." The warmth of her breath brushed over his chest, raising his flesh. "Let me pleasure you."

He moaned. "Lex. Have mercy...If you go on like this I might not be able to hold back. I am an untamed brute. Please...I will hate myself if I hurt you."

She held his face. "You are not a brute."

Her faith in him was heartening.

She pressed her mouth to his and blew a teasing ticklish blast of air. She smiled at his spluttering surprise. "I am not a girl who must be protected."

He sobered. "I am a man. And men are..." Did he really want to explain the workings of a man's body to his new bride? "Just go carefully," he warned.

She shackled his hands and pushed them over his head. Her warm, wet mouth brushed over his lips. "I promise to go slowly, if it is what you wish."

He closed his eyes and groaned a silent prayer. *Good angels above, save me!*

Hours later a voice woke Nathan out of a sound sleep. "Nathan! Nathan!"

The urgent tone set Nathan on instant alert. He untangled himself from Alexandra. "Get dressed," he directed her and crawled over to the edge of the roof.

Peter ben Eli stood at the door, torch in one hand and knocking with the other. "Nathan!"

Peter owned an olive farm a day's walk south of here. The matter must be urgent for him to come so far during *Shabbat*.

"What's wrong?" Nathan asked.

Peter's head jerked up. He moved to the base of the ladder. "I know where Judas the Zealot is."

Alexandra scrambled up beside Nathan. "Lydia? This man knows where Lydia is?"

Uneasy over his lovely wife's close proximity to the edge of the roof, Nathan took hold of her upper arm. She was trembling. He put his arm around her and pulled her close. "Many thanks, Peter. I am in your debt." This was exactly the lead he'd been hoping and praying for.

CHAPTER 12

Nathan and Pinhas ducked under the craggy mouth of a cave, not bothering to avoid the dripping water. "Do you see anything?" Nathan said.

Pinhas knelt. "A large party spent time here. But the coals in the cook fire are several days old. If it was Judas, he's likely miles away by now."

Disappointed, Nathan shook his head.

They moved back outside. The midday sun parted the somber gray clouds.

"At least the walk home should be drier," Nathan said, struggling to find a bright side. Their clothes were drenched and their hair was plastered to their heads thanks to traveling a day and a half through driving rain.

Pinhas grunted and gave Nathan a leery look. "What will you do with Judas when you find him?"

The memory of Alexandra's stark terror in the wake of the ambush replayed through Nathan's mind. His blood heated. "The attack wasn't your usual raid." His fingers curled around the hilt of the sword strapped to his waist. "Judas didn't just ambush the Onias family.

He took great pleasure in torturing them."

Pinhas eyes locked onto Nathan's sword. "You plan to kill him?"

"No," Nathan said, releasing the hilt like it was a red-hot poker. He bent and picked up one of the small stones littering the ground and heaved it. "Much as I'd like to, I plan to hand the fiend over to the Sanhedrin. The courts can decide his fate." He turned to Pinhas. "I hear Hezekiah has another raid planned."

His friend's face hardened. "Don't ask for details. I don't want to have to lie to you."

"Hezekiah's rebellion will end badly," Nathan warned. "I feel it in my bones. Promise me you will stay out of it."

"Hezekiah is a good man," Pinhas countered. "A man worth supporting."

Nathan scrubbed his face. "I don't doubt Hezekiah's sincerity. I know he believes he's doing the Lord's will. I've also thought long and hard about the verses of scripture he uses to justify the raids, but I can't see it the way he does."

Nathan and Pinhas had spent hours discussing the scriptures and wondering together how best to understand them. Hezekiah and his followers had definite ideas regarding the meaning of the holy writings, the teachers of Israel had theirs, and the Sadducees, Pharisees, and Essenes had theirs. Who had the right of it? Nathan knew what he believed, but he would keep searching the scriptures and continue to pray for insight.

"I hate the division it causes," Nathan finally said. "I hate that Jews are fighting Jews." His voice dropped to a whisper. "I hate that you and I don't see eye to eye over the rebels, old friend."

Pinhas picked up a jagged rock and examined it. "I don't care one way or the other about hunting down Roman sympathizers. But my fellow priests are another matter. Did you know Justus and Saul are so desperate for money they are ready to place their daughters as bondmaids?"

Nathan winced. "I plan on expanding my olive groves. I will hire them to work with me."

"That's good of you, Nathan. And I'm thankful for the extra money I will earn building your house. But you can't singlehandedly employ every destitute priest in Galilee. Even if you could, you shouldn't have to. The Law makes provision for us. But High Priest Hyrcanus and his bloodsucking relations are taking what should rightfully be given to us common priests."

Pinhas performed his priestly duties at the Temple two times a year, receiving only a small share of the pelts from the animals sacrificed. The rest of the time he worked as a stonecutter. Poor priests without a trade, such as Justus and Saul, struggled to get by. A state of affairs stinking to heaven, given the river of coins and goods flowing into the Temple treasury. All God's priests ought to be well provided for. But the bulk of the wealth was funneled off to members of High Priest Hyrcanus's inner circle. Hezekiah and his rebels wanted this, and many other wrongs, set right.

Nathan remembered Alexandra's blood-spattered veil and James Onias's ugly, purple scar. He crossed his arms to keep his hand from clasping his sword again. "I hate the corruption, but the raids aren't the answer." He looked his friend in the eye. "I plan to do everything in my power to stop Hezekiah, as well as Judas."

The rock in Pinhas' hand slipped to the ground. "It's why you've taken up with Herod again, isn't it?"

Nathan's gut knotted. Pinhas had taken it hard when Nathan joined the army back when they were boys. The gentle-hearted man never understood Nathan's love for the military and had been deeply hurt when Nathan had set aside their friendship to become fast friends with Herod. But Pinhas didn't hold it against Nathan. When Nathan had quit soldiering and returned to the farm, shaken to his very core, Pinhas had welcomed Nathan home with open arms, never uttering a word of censure.

Nathan wanted to look away, but didn't. "I need Herod's help. But it stops there. The last thing I want is for this to cause trouble between—" his voice cracked.

Pinhas squeezed Nathan's shoulder. "Promise me you will talk to Hezekiah before you do anything."

Nathan cleared his throat. "I was going to ask you to arrange a meeting."

"I'm glad to hear it." Pinhas clapped his back. "By the way, I like Alexandra immensely. She is good for you."

"She's going to be very disappointed when I return without her sister."

"I'll speak to Hezekiah about the girl."

"I welcome the help." Nathan cinched his sword belt tighter about his waist. "Let's go home."

Two days later Nathan and Pinhas crested the small knoll behind his home. Nathan's heart stopped. One wall of the house had collapsed. Mary and Timothy and a third person pawed at the wreckage. "No," Nathan yelled and raced down the hill.

Dizzy with fear, he dropped down on his knees beside Mary. The right half of Rhoda's body was pinned under the muddy wreckage. Herod was there, and he and Timothy shoveled the mud away with their hands. There was no sign of Lex or his father.

His sister threw her arms around him. "Nath...Nathan..." Beyond hysterical, the poor thing could barely get her words out. "Mother...Mother is hurt."

Rhoda was spluttering complaints. Nathan took it as a good sign. He gripped Mary's arms and shook her gently to get her attention. "Where are Alexandra and Father?"

"Inside." Tears poured down the girl's muddy face. "Alexandra was inside the house with Father."

Nathan groaned. His father's bed was tucked up against the wall closest to where the partition had given way. Dread and despair constricting his chest, Nathan ran to the house and grabbed for the door. It swung away from him.

Alexandra stood before him, supporting his father with her arm.

"Thank God." Nathan wrapped his arms around the pair and hugged them for dear life. "Thank God...I..."

His father gripped his arm. "We heard the cries. Who's hurt?"

"They're freeing Rhoda. She doesn't appear too badly hurt," Nathan assured his father. He led the pair to a safe spot, then turned his attention to helping Pinhas, Herod, and Timothy free Rhoda. Together they quickly removed the rest of the dirt. Rhoda winced and cried out when they tried to lift her.

"Let me examine her," Herod ordered. Pinhas and Timothy moved aside.

Herod's hands moved methodically over Rhoda's limbs, checking for broken bones. He nodded at the wreckage. "I've heard that heavy rain is brutal on these rock and mud houses. Has this happened before?"

"Not in my lifetime," Nathan said. Breathing easier, he surveyed the yard. Two horses grazed nearby. "Who does the second horse belong to?"

Herod grinned. "It's yours."

"Mine?"

"It's a wedding gift."

"It's a warhorse," Nathan growled.

"It will get you to Syria."

"I can't leave my family. Not now."

Herod finished his inspection. "Your arm's broken," he told Rhoda. "But I think between Nathan and I we can set it."

"You know how to set bones?" Alexandra stood behind them, holding a stone cup.

Nathan took the cup of water and patted the ground, inviting her to join them.

"Physicians are few and far between when an army is on the move or on the battlefield," Nathan explained. "Herod and I have mended a few broken limbs in our day. We'll splint it and pray the bone heals well."

"Stop talking and get on with it," Rhoda said.

Nathan patted her good arm. "It shouldn't take long."

"I'll go find what we need," Herod said, standing and heading toward what remained of the house.

Alexandra shifted closer to his stepmother and carefully propped her up. Gently caressing the side of Rhoda's face, Alexandra crooned to her, "Be strong for just a little bit longer. We'll soon have you tucked into a soft bed."

Nathan held the cup of water to Rhoda's lips. She sipped at it. He allowed himself to examine to Alexandra. "How are you?"

She offered him a tired smile. "I am glad you are home."

Indecently pleased with the reply, he winked at her.

A pink blush spread across her glistening cheeks. The perspiration pearling on her face was the lone sign that something out of the ordinary had happened. He admired and appreciated her calm in the face of trouble.

Nathan gave Rhoda another sip of water, then returned his attention to Lex. "I am proud of you. Thank you for taking care of my father, for making sure he got out of the house."

Flustered, Alexandra lowered her eyes. "It was nothing."

He scanned the barren hillsides surrounding his home "Out here we have only each other to depend on. You did well."

Alexandra lifted her chin and gave him an uncertain look. If they were alone he would tease a smile out of her. She wasn't used to compliments—a sad shame he planned to correct.

Rhoda knocked the cup aside. "If I drink any more I'll spring a leak." She cringed and rubbed her arm. "Help me sit up."

Nathan smiled down at Rhoda. "Give us a few moments to ready the tents." He stood and turned to Pinhas. "We'll have to get started on the new house right away. In the meantime, we can set up the festival tents and live in them."

Timothy gave a whoop of approval and raced over to hug Nathan about the waist.

"I'm glad one of us is happy with the plan." He rumpled the boy's hair. "I'll patch the old house back together again, and we can put it to use as an animal pen."

Alexandra's gray eyes lit up.

At a guess he would say she was amused at the idea she'd been living in a home barely fit for livestock. Bless her for her healthy sense of humor.

Amber twilight settled around the quiet farmstead. Alexandra peered down into the dark well. Tugging hard on the rope, she promised her aching arms this was the last jug of water she would lug today. Rhoda was resting comfortably, the animals were watered, the clothes washed, dinner prepared and eaten.

She couldn't remember a day half so satisfying. Or exhausting.

"Here, let me help." Nathan hauled the pail up the rest of the way and set it on the ground. Turning to her, he took her fisted hands and tugged her fingers down, revealing the raw, red welts she had hoped to hide from him.

He frowned and drew her into his arms. "My heart broke when I saw the wall down. I thought I'd lost you...I..."

This was not the lecture she'd expected. She pressed her face to his solid chest. His heart beat fast against her ear. She'd never felt more safe and wanted, sheltered in his embrace.

His mouth moved against her hair. "I'm glad you weren't hurt." He set her at arm's length and smiled. "Come. My father wants a word with us."

Unnerved by the summons, she tidied her hair.

Nathan took her hand, hefted the pail, and headed toward the tents. The small tent was to be all theirs. Praise heaven.

They stepped inside the big tent. Oil lamps cast up a soft glow. Pinhas and Herod lounged by the entrance. Rhoda was resting on a bed along the back wall. Joseph, Mary, and Timothy sat around the large, circular mat serving as a table. Nathan and Alexandra joined them.

Nathan poured wine into a cup and pressed it into her hand.

Joseph offered them a tired smile. "Herod says Rhoda's arm will need most of the winter to heal. I want to hire a bondmaiden to help with the work."

The children gave their noisy approval.

"What do you say, Daughter?" Joseph asked.

Though she'd done fairly well today, Alexandra knew she wasn't ready to replace her mother-in-law. The stoic woman usually worked from morning to night serving the family's many needs. She turned to Nathan.

His smile was sympathetic. He knew she didn't want a slave to do her work. "It's for you to decide," he said.

She swallowed and looked around the table. Expectant faces glowed at her. A prickly heat crept up her neck. For her whole life she'd wanted this, wanted what she thought or felt to matter to someone. She never guessed it would prove so unsettling. She rubbed her sweaty palms on her tunic. "I think it might take two bondmaidens to replace Rhoda." She laughed with the others, then returned her focus to her kindly father-in-law. "I will be grateful for the help."

She ducked her head. Nathan's leg tapped hers and his fingers pressed lightly into her elbow. "Breathe," he whispered.

She inhaled deeply and let her breath go. And felt much better for it.

"Son, I want you and Alexandra to make the trip to Syria," Joseph said.

Her head snapped up.

Nathan wore an incredulous look. "But the house."

Her father-in-law waved the problem aside. "Men can be hired to assist Pinhas. Herod has need of you."

Alexandra looked over at Herod, hoping he'd release Nathan from his promise.

The career soldier set down his cup of wine. "I'd like you to be there."

Nathan grimaced. "You can find other men to amuse you."

"Antipater and Herod are not asking you to go to war with them," Joseph said. "They are asking for a show of support. Their friends are few and far between just now."

Herod nodded. "Once I know my father is safe, I'll give you men to help build your house and to hunt down the bandits holding your sister-in-law.

Nathan's shoulders fell. He touched his hand to hers. "What do you think?"

Herod trained his black eyes on her.

It was all she could do to keep from squirming. Crossing Herod would be a mistake, especially since he held Lydia's fate in his hands. And Nathan was convinced he needed Herod's help to locate and retrieve her sister. Alexandra forced herself to stop twisting the folds of her tunic. "We promised we'd go."

Nathan laughed without humor. "I can't argue with that."

Herod's satisfied smile made her toes curl.

"I'll need to time to contract a bondmaiden and hire workmen," Nathan said.

Herod picked up his cup, drained his wine, and held it out for a refill. "I'll give you tomorrow to see to your affairs."

Alexandra stared up at the large gray-and-white-dappled warhorse named Royal. Another wave of dizziness struck. Holy angels! She was going to have to climb way, way up there and ride atop the spirited creature's back. Royal galloped as fast as lightning. She'd watched with her heart in her throat yesterday while Nathan and Herod tore across the hills on their horses.

The whole family was out in the yard to say goodbye, even Rhoda, who was up for the first time since the accident, her injured arm hanging in a sling. Herod was already mounted on his white stallion, more than ready to begin the journey to Syria. Nathan was stowing food in the leather packs that hung from the felt-covered wooden saddle.

He came around to her side of the horse. "Are you ready?"

She reached out and patted Royal's soft, velvety nose and looked into the horse's big black eyes. "You're a good boy, Royal. Yes, you are."

She liked the horse, she just didn't like the idea of riding on him. Romans rode horses. Israelites walked or used donkeys.

Nathan climbed into the saddle and helped her up.

Royal pranced in place.

"Job's bones," she cried out, wrapping her arms

around Nathan's waist and burying her face in his back.

The family chuckled and called out encouragements. Nathan patted her hand. "I promise to go slowly."

"You can stay behind," Herod said, circling his horse closer to Royal and aiming his comments at Alexandra. "I'd bet good money the trip will prove too taxing for you." He wagged his brows. "We haven't left the yard and you are already being a pest."

Alexandra's spine stiffened. A pest? Too taxing? She'd walk through a pit of snakes or jump into a pool of crocodiles just to prove him wrong.

A growl reverberated through Nathan. "Don't bully my wife."

Herod shrugged. "I meant well."

"Of course," Alexandra muttered through gritted teeth.

Royal tossed his head and neighed loudly. She yelped and grabbed Nathan.

Herod rumbled with laughter and shook his head. "I'll wait for you over the next hill." He flicked the reins and the white stallion surged ahead.

Alexandra sighed loudly. It felt as though she was competing with Herod for Nathan's loyalty. Could she win such a battle? A gray cloak of doubt wrapped itself around her. She prayed it was a test she'd never have to face.

Joseph, Rhoda, Mary, and Timothy came closer and laid their hands on Nathan and her, wishing God's speed on them.

The bondmaid, Sapphira, approached and patted the horse's nose. She turned her freckled face up to Nathan. "Have a safe trip, my lord."

"You don't need to call me lord," Nathan said. "You are part of our family."

Sapphira smiled shyly. "I'm happy you chose me, Nathan."

Alexandra blinked. Something in the girl's tone didn't settle right. Sapphira's eyes met hers. The slave maiden blushed and dipped her head.

Nathan nudged Royal forward and the family waved and called out more farewells.

Alexandra looked back at the pretty bondmaid. Sapphira was staring at Nathan. The girl was smitten with him. Well, who could blame her? Alexandra tightened her hold on Nathan and tried not to dislike the young girl.

Joining Herod, they rode over hill after hill. The hours rolled by. The terrain became rockier and steeper the further north they went. Impatient with the slow pace, Herod volunteered to ride ahead to find a place to camp for the night.

She laid her face against Nathan's warm back and noticed again the steady bump of his sword against her leg. The hilt bounced against his hip with each step the horse took.

"How does it feel to wear a sword after all this time?" she asked.

He laughed softly. "Good and bad. I like knowing I am equipped to defend you. But I feel less like my father's son. It's hard to put it into words. When I take a sword into my hand, I feel at one with it—like I was born to swing a length of steel. Yet my father is a peaceful farmer. Where did this talent for violence come from?"

"Talent for violence?" She wrinkled her nose. "I have a hard time imagining it."

"I assure you that, come time for a battle, you wouldn't be able to tell me from a barbarian. I might as well have been born a Celt, I become that much the brute." He squeezed her hand. "There's a reason I never talk to my family and friends about my days fighting with the Jewish army."

"Something terrible happened, didn't it?" A shiver went through her. She wanted to help ease his pain, but dreaded what she might learn.

His muscles went rigid under her hand. "I shed a lot of blood."

"And?" she coaxed.

He rubbed the back of his neck and rolled his shoulders. "It doesn't matter now." He urged the horse into a gallop.

Alexandra swallowed back a yelp and held tight to her husband. It did matter. And they would have this conversation again.

CHAPTER 13

Alexandra lay beside Nathan on a straw mattress, staring up at a ceiling painted with cherubs lounging about on fluffy clouds. They'd been in Antioch four days now. As formal members of Antipater's large delegation, she and Nathan had been assigned a small but comfortable room in the Governor of Syria's palace-fortress. The room had the sole amenity she cared about—privacy. A luxury they'd taken advantage of to indulge in some mid-morning lovemaking.

She sat up, pulling a cover with her. "I'm surprised Herod hasn't come looking for you yet."

"Give him time." Nathan stretched and yawned. "The day's still young."

"Herod is very fond of your company. It's no wonder, fighting side by side the way you two did."

A long pause ensued. She held her breath. Please let him trust her enough to share the inner sadness and anguish he carried close to his heart. He'd done so much for her. She wanted to repay the kindness.

Nathan twisted a lock of her hair around his finger. "Herod is very fond of beating me into the ground, as you've probably noticed. I've gone up against him twice with a sword in the last two days and lost both times." He kissed her and pulled away. "You don't have to keep coming to the arena to watch. You've seen all there is to see."

She wriggled her nose at the suggestion.

There was a knock at the door. "Wait a moment," Nathan called out. They scrambled up and quickly got dressed.

She finished securing her bluebird-colored head cover just as Nathan pulled the door open.

Herod of Idumea stood in the doorway wearing a licentious grin. "I'm on my way to the jewel of a temple everyone is talking about. Come with me. I'd like the company."

Nathan laughed. "I knew you'd have to see it." He looked back at her. "I won't be long," he apologized.

"Take me with you." Alexandra rushed her words. "Please."

Nathan gave her a sympathetic look.

Herod studied her with some amusement. "What makes you want to visit Jupiter's temple? Thinking of converting to paganism, are you?"

She managed a polite smile. "Me? Never. Are you?" She resisted the urge to take a step back. Using wit on Herod might be as wise as poking a venomous snake with a stick.

Nathan was trying not to smile. Herod laughed outright. "You sound spirited enough to survive a tour of Antioch's back alleys."

Interpreting his answer as a yes, she grabbed her cloak off the hook by the door and followed Nathan and Herod on a zigzagging path through the palace's maze of narrow stone corridors. Her stomach churned and her heart beat fast, but it wasn't because of the coming adventure. She hoped to find a few moments to speak privately with Herod about Nathan's fighting days. A daunting thought, indeed.

They emerged from the dark innards of the palace into bright daylight.

Herod led them to the edge of a long, steep stairway, where they could see the city stretched out in all directions. Her breath caught. So many people. All of them busy with their own lives. The road running behind the governor's residence teemed with activity, most of it involving people and animals trying to navigate around each other. Workmen crawled over the face of a half-finished tower. Closer at hand, a team of oxen strained to haul a pillar upright. Antioch was bursting with evidence of prosperity.

"You can see the roof of the temple from here." Herod pointed.

The abundance of gold-leaf trim was practically blinding.

"The builders must have melted a river of gold," Nathan said admiringly. Scanning the city, he emitted a soft whistle. "I can't believe how much Antioch has changed since the last time I was here."

Herod nodded. "The Romans arrived twenty years ago and they've just kept building and building."

Alexandra moved closer to Nathan. "When were you here last? Was it with the army?"

Nathan blanched.

Her stomach dropped. She wished she hadn't said anything.

Herod turned a quizzical eye on her. Remembering

her father's rants about the evils of pushy women, it required all her determination not to look down.

Herod squeezed Nathan's shoulder. "It was close to ten years ago. Those were heady days, weren't they? My father's army joining forces with Mark Antony's army here in Syria, and then marching on Jerusalem."

Alexandra had been a young, frightened girl at the time, quaking at the sounds of battle outside her home. It was hard to believe Nathan had been one the soldiers she had so feared.

Nathan scrubbed his hand over his face. "What's Antony up to these days?"

Herod grinned wide. "Wherever he is, you know he's drinking and whoring himself into an early grave."

Nathan glanced over at her.

Equal parts fascinated and embarrassed, she felt her face flame.

"Stay close to me," Herod said, chuckling and moving on.

They descended the steps and waded into a river of people. Herod veered down a tunnel-like lane lined with multi-level tenement buildings. The ground floors were given over to shops decorated with colorful pictures of the goods sold within. They crossed a major intersection and passed a bakery that filled the neighborhood with the fragrance of freshly baked bread. Alexandra's mouth watered and her stomach growled.

Then the street narrowed and the shops became dingier. The stick figures drawn on one wall caught Alexandra's eye. She stopped. But no, the images were indeed what she had thought. The paintings showed men and women engaged in various sexual acts, complete with a list of prices.

A hand touched her arm. She jumped. Nathan scowled at his friend. "Come along, while I go wring our guide's clever neck."

Herod held his hands up. Incorrigible grin in place, he feigned innocence. "What?"

The door to the disreputable establishment banged open and three whores tumbled outside. Gathering around Herod, they fawned over him. Alexandra stared, aghast and amazed. Despite appearing too old and fat to do most of what was so boldly illustrated on the wall, the giggling trio assured their potential customer that, given enough *sestertii*, they were willing to have a go at most anything.

Nathan's hand touched the small of Alexandra's back, encouraging her to move on. She looked back, half-expecting to see Herod take the women up on their offer.

Herod was walking backward away from the women, laughing so hard he could barely breathe. "Sorry, ladies," he gasped. "I'm busy just now, but I will keep you in mind for another day."

A thousand questions bouncing around her mind, Alexandra leaned closer to Nathan. "Do people actually —"

He cut her off with a terse, "We'll talk later."

They certainly would. She sighed. "Antioch has proved very interesting so far."

Nathan smiled. "Interesting? *You* are interesting."

"And very curious, I think."

"You think you're curious?"

Alexandra laughed, relieved he was amused. She knew he'd been afraid she'd hate Syria or find it offensive. She'd wondered about it too. "How could I know?"

she answered. "Aside from the disastrous trip to Galilee with my family and outings to the Temple, my whole life was lived inside the four walls of my father's house."

Nathan frowned. "What about your relations...aunts and uncles? Surely you went to visit them."

"Not after my mother died."

Nathan came to a stop. "You told me you'd had a hard life. I just never imagined—"

Herod, who'd outpaced them and reached the end of the street, turned and yelled, "What's taking you so long? The temple's just around this corner."

Nathan waved Herod on and focused his kind eyes on her again. "I know the strictest of the strict Pharisees are zealous in guarding the purity of their wives and daughters. But your father's measure seems extreme, even for Pharisees."

She swallowed. "I wish that was the case."

Nathan's brow lifted questioningly.

"If Father kept us locked away because his conscience toward God demanded it, I could excuse it. But the truth is my father scarcely thought of us at all."

Nathan put his arms around her and rubbed her back. She tucked her head under his chin, listening to his heart beat against her ear. What an absolutely lovely feeling. She touched her hands to his waist. "And now here I am, visiting pagan Syria with my husband the olive farmer. And I am too fascinated by it all to be the least offended."

Nathan kissed her forehead. "We'd best be on our way before Herod comes and drags us to the temple."

She sighed. "He doesn't have a lot of patience, does he?"

"Hardly any, and someday it's going to get him into trouble."

The lane emptied out onto a busy boulevard. They found Herod standing at the bottom of the tall rows of stone steps leading up to a white-walled temple. Slender marble columns loomed overhead. Creamy white statuettes, atop pedestals festooned with ornate rosettes, stood watch over a plaza full of worshippers coming and going from the temple.

Standing this close to a pagan temple made Alexandra's skin crawl. Moses' Law was deadly clear. The Lord God hated idolatry.

Nathan offered her a reassuring smile. "We won't stay long."

Herod slung one arm over Nathan's shoulder. "Look at the exacting detail displayed in the grapevine. Have you ever seen more beautiful work? If I were building a palace or a temple, I would insist on making it as fine as this."

Nathan grinned. "Are you still holding on to those other absurd notions of yours?"

So she wasn't the only one who thought the idea incredible.

Herod shook his head in mock dismay. "Absurd notions?" He turned his boyish smile on her. "You have to agree, Judea is a backward nation. A first-class amphitheater and bathing facility would bring Jerusalem into the present age."

"Jerusalem?" The idea was beyond foreign. It must violate one of the commands of God, though she couldn't think which one. "Would the Sanhedrin allow it?" she asked.

"The Sanhedrin?" Herod's rude hand gesture made it

clear what he thought of the rulers of Israel. "Those asses have no imagination. Jerusalem could be the jewel of the east. Why can't anyone besides me see that?"

She and Nathan shared astonished looks.

It was hard to know what to make of Herod. Though an obnoxious braggart, he also had another side, an imaginative, idealistic side that evidenced itself when he spoke of his vision for his country and its people. He dreamed of a Jerusalem called the jewel of the east.

Nathan and Herod fell into a discussion involving porticos and lintels. Alexandra wandered over to a statue of a smiling woman dressed in a flowing garment. An invisible wind molded the gown to the lush curves of her body. Alexandra touched a fold in the dress. The cold immovable stone beneath her fingers felt at odds with the movement and life bursting from the statue.

Nathan and Herod joined her. Alexandra pulled her hand back. "Who is she?"

Herod stood with his hands on his hips studying the statue, a glint of appreciation in his eyes. "She is Fortuna, the Roman goddess of fate and prosperity."

Alexandra shaded her eyes and examined the line of statues bordering the plaza. The mosaics, paintings, and statues depicting man and beast found around every corner in Syria still came as a surprise.

Nathan's arm brushed against her arm. "Jerusalem is probably the only place in the world devoid of images."

The dictates of Moses' Law prohibited graven images. A fact she had taken for granted. "Then we Israelites are the strange ones and not the gentiles?" The idea made her proud and sad, all at the same time.

A loud fanfare sounded.

"He's here," Herod said.

Trumpet-blowing heralds filled the main thoroughfare. Next came a hundred red-caped Roman soldiers seated on spirited warhorses. This was followed by the main attraction, a tall, white stallion carrying a man outfitted in a gold cuirass and a red-crested helmet. Julius Caesar. Military aides dressed in bronze breastplates rode on either side of him, followed by more red-clad soldiers.

Transfixed by the spectacle, Alexandra tried imagining Nathan and Herod marching with the Roman army. An easy task, given that they were every bit as much warriors as the men riding by. She had a harder time dismissing the question of whether or not men serving the Lord, God of Israel should be marching with Romans. Her father would answer with a definite no. Thankfully, Nathan was done with that life. Herod was welcome to answer to his own conscience on the matter.

They watched until the soldiers disappeared from view.

Nathan rocked back on his heels. "I'll give Julius Caesar one thing, he puts on a good show."

"Public executions always draw a crowd," Herod said, grim-faced.

Nathan moved closer to his distraught friend. "Have faith. Your father has no peer when it comes to escaping danger."

Herod shook off his malaise and led them down an alley crowded with people and shops. An old man came around a corner carrying a thick, crusty round of rye bread. Alexandra rubbed her growling stomach and gazed after the man until he walked out of sight. Turning around, she bumped into a wide chest. A hasty apology on her lips, she looked up to find Nathan smiling down at her. He raised one brow. "Hungry?"

"Famished to distraction, apparently."

Brown eyes twinkling, Nathan turned and disappeared into a shop with a large loaf of bread painted on the wall above the doorway.

"You couldn't have found a better man to champion your cause." Herod's mouth was indecently close to her ear. "Nathan was a first-rate soldier."

She ducked her shoulders and turned around. Grateful Herod was the one to start the conversation, she came straight to the point. "What happened to Nathan when he fought with you and the Romans?"

Herod shrugged. "I wish I knew."

"Why don't I believe you?"

"Because you are too clever for your own good, that's why." Herod's smile dimmed. "Nathan saved my life more than once. He is the kind of man anyone would want at their side in a fight. He will pursue your attackers unto his last breath. He would die to protect you."

She put a hand to her heart. "I wouldn't want him to."

Unholy glee lit black eyes. "That's where you and I differ. I want Nathan by my side in battle, ready to throw his life away for me, for my father, for my brothers. And I finally have hope of luring him back. Thanks to you."

Unease prickled through her. "Me? What do you mean?"

"I've been trying for ten years to lure Nathan off the farm. He isn't married to you two months yet and here he is in Syria." Herod clapped his hands together mockingly. "Well done, Alexandra, well done."

She blinked. "You want Nathan to rejoin the Jewish army? He won't do it."

"He will if he wants my help apprehending Judas the Zealot." Herod's lips curled back from his large, white teeth. "I predict Nathan will be riding as one of my men before you've been married six months. He will say yes for *your* sake."

Her mind spun dizzyingly. She didn't doubt Nathan's selflessness. He'd be forced to return to a life he'd sworn off, one still haunting him. She reeled back. Someone caught her by the arm.

"Alexandra?" Nathan held a small loaf of bread out toward her. Concern furrowed his brows. "Are you unwell?"

She took the loaf and smiled weakly. She hated worrying him. "I just need to eat." Turning a cold eye on Herod, she said, "I was just telling your friend not to underestimate me. I'm stronger than I look, especially if I feel threatened." And a threat was just what Herod's little talk was all about. She took a large bite of bread. The tasteless, glutinous mass swelled in her mouth. She chewed with dogged determination, praying she wouldn't disgrace herself by vomiting or crying.

Nathan would *not* be rejoining the army. Not if she had any say in the matter.

The next evening the cavernous fortress-palace overflowed with guests. Musicians plucked at stringed instruments and blew into reed horns. But Nathan couldn't hear a note over the din filling the great hall. The chance to lay eyes on Julius Caesar had brought every man of any consequence from hundreds of miles around to the banquet. Nathan had hated leaving Alexandra behind, but queens were the only women deemed worthy of the coveted invitation.

Antipater had been given a seat of honor on a raised dais. He was seated among richly dressed dignitaries who reclined on cushioned couches, eating and drinking off silver dinnerware. Nathan, Kadar, Herod, and Antipater's three older sons sat at the back of the hall on wooden benches lining plank tables.

A palace slave set a platter of roast pigeon in front of Nathan. Already full, he pushed the dish in Kadar's direction. Antipater's oversized bodyguard grabbed a golden-brown bird by the leg and dropped it on his plate. He pointed a finger toward the head table. "Is Hasmond the one with the long, pinched face?"

Nathan grimaced and nodded. "I hoped I'd never have to see his rat face again."

The blond-haired giant's rumbling laugh attracted some stares. "Put some whiskers on him and he *would* pass for a nervous rodent." Kadar turned his piercing blue eyes on Nathan. "I heard you were a soldier in Antipater's army when they chased the rat out of Jerusalem with the help of a Roman army."

Nathan plucked a red grape from a bowl of fruit. "Herod and I marched beside one of Julius Caesar's nephews, Mark Antony. Have you heard of him?"

Kadar nodded and took a bite out of the crisp pigeon. "A hard-drinking, hard-fighting soldier." The giant swallowed and licked his lips. "You must have gotten quite an education."

Nathan popped the grape into his mouth. Those days were best forgotten. He jerked his thumb toward

Herod, who was guzzling down wine as fast as his cup was filled. "Antony and Herod got along famously."

Kadar grinned. "I bet they did."

Nathan shrugged. "The coming trial has everyone on edge. And I've got the bruises to prove it." He rubbed his upper arm where Herod had hit him with the flat side of his sword earlier.

Kadar's white teeth flashed. "You've held your own in the arena and racing your horse. I'll give you that, olive farmer."

Disgusted by how satisfying he found the compliment, Nathan hid it behind a shrug. "Blame Herod. He runs his mouth until he gets me spitting mad."

Kadar laughed. "Herod can't pour enough venom on Hasmond. Do you think the rat can convince Caesar to execute Antipater?"

Nathan looked across the room to the man who had been like a second father. He exhaled heavily. "I wasn't surprised when Antipater chose Pompey. Pompey headed the first Roman army to enter Jerusalem. The two men defeated Hasmond's forces and set John Hyrcanus up as high priest."

"I heard Antipater agonized over the decision."

Nathan grabbed up his clay cup. "I'm sure Hasmond was ecstatic when he learned of Pompey's defeat and death. The rat couldn't get to Caesar fast enough to accuse Antipater." Nathan drained the last of his wine. "Antipater's success in Egypt ought to help his cause."

Herod swung toward Nathan and joined the conversation. "Egypt? My father won the war for Caesar and Cleopatra." Herod lifted his mug over his head. "More wine here!"

Nathan plugged his ears. "Yell louder. They might

not have heard you in Rome."

Herod gave him a companionable shake. "You should have been with us. You'd have loved it. First we sneaked through the desert and took the northern gateway of Pelusium. The big battle was even better. Outnumbered two to one and hit from both sides by the enemy, we fought our way out, held the flanks, and earned Caesar's praise."

A slave came around with wine. Nathan covered his cup.

Herod knocked Nathan's hand aside and held the fat goblet up so the slave could fill it. Herod passed the cup back to Nathan and raised his own. Herod looked up and down the table. "Drink a toast with me. To Rome and Caesar."

Nathan groaned and raised his cup.

"To Rome and Caesar," the men around him shouted, but he made it into a soft prayer. "Save us from Rome and Caesar."

Sextus, nephew of Julius Caesar, came strolling up. "Mind if I join you?" Herod and Sextus had struck up a friendship over the past few days.

Herod grinned. "Come to join the fun?"

Sextus stabbed his thumb back toward the head table. "They've been talking taxes for the last hour." He turned his friendly smile on Nathan. "Nice race today. Your horse has real heart. I thought you were going to come back and win."

"He is a good horse," Nathan said genially, liking the friendly man.

Herod's barking laugh turned heads. "Nathan's horse almost beat the horse you bet on, didn't it?"

Sextus waggled his brows. "I nearly soiled my tunic

at the close finish."

Herod clapped Nathan on the back. "Tomorrow you better bet on the olive farmer, here. He's due for a win."

The corners of Sextus's mouth turned down. "Actually, I stopped by to tell you your father's hearing will take place tomorrow."

The table went silent.

A slave brought another tray of food. Herod knocked the platter aside, sending nuts and olives sailing overhead.

Nathan steeled himself for a long night.

Light streamed through the open window, promising a beautiful day ahead. Nathan hated the thought of getting out of bed.

"You're worried about the hearing?" Alexandra asked sleepily.

He rolled over and pulled his lovely wife into his arms. Her slender back warmed his chest. "It's that obvious?"

"You usually sleep like the dead."

They'd been married long enough now for them to know intimate things about each other. The thought gave him pause. "It's been a long time since I've felt this close to another person," he said, running his fingers over the sprinkle of freckles midway down her upper arm. Outside of Lex's mother or a nurse, he was likely the only person who'd ever see or touch the lovely light brown flecks. He brushed a kiss over the soft juncture between her neck and shoulder. "This is going to sound strange, but combat is similar to marriage."

Lex laughed. "How so?"

"I mean it in a good way. It forms intimate bonds between the participants. I didn't realize how much I'd missed it. The intimacy."

Lex rolled onto her back and studied him, her eyes wary. "Would you ever consider rejoining the army?"

His muscles tensed. "Why do you ask? Are you having an easier time picturing me as a soldier?"

She swallowed and nodded.

He relished the swordplay and the company of soldiers more than he liked to admit, and had wanted her to come to Syria for this very reason, wanted her to know the kind of man she'd married. So why did her unease prick? His breath left him in a rush. "The truth is, if Antipater's army only went to battle against foreign foes like Parthia I might sorely regret quitting the army. But I fear our country is facing more internal warfare. Jews killing Jews. I won't go down that path again."

Lex's brow furrowed. "Are matters so dire?"

Lonely despair struck, the kind he'd experienced as a young man moments before scaling the walls of Jerusalem. "If Antipater is found guilty and crucified, Herod and his brothers will go to war. The Lord alone knows how many people will die then."

"Do you think they'd go so far?"

"I know they will." He brushed a knuckle along Lex's jaw, needing the contact. The idea of disappointing or failing her was intolerable. "I don't want to frighten you, but you need to be prepared to leave at a moment's notice in case things go badly."

He looked heavenward. *I will kill whoever I must to protect the wife you gifted to me, Lord. I pray it doesn't come to that. Please don't let it come to that.*

The fortress-like palace housing the governor of Syria served many functions. Today it was a Roman court of law. Seated in the front, Nathan had a perfect view of a servant unfolding Caesar's *curule*. The chair's curved golden legs formed a wide X, upon which a plush cushion was placed. The armless, backless design of the seat was meant to encourage the official using it to finish his business in a timely manner. And a quick end to this matter was just what was called for.

Nathan had never seen Herod so on edge. His friend was ready to jump out of his skin.

Caesar and a small cadre of tribunes entered the hall from a side door and climbed the steps to the top of an octagonal dais. Serious and decisive, Caesar plowed his way through case after case. Nathan could see why the whole world was abuzz over Julius Caesar. Of average height and build, it wasn't his physical appearance that impressed. What separated him from his fellows was the way he conducted himself. He had a bold demeanor, revealing a man comfortable with welding power on and off the battlefield.

Finally the head tribune delivered the summons the assembled Jews had been waiting for. "The court calls on Antigonus Hasmond."

Antipater's accuser stepped forward. Herod growled menacingly. Nathan sat forward, ready to restrain his friend.

"State the charges you bring against Antipater of Idumea," the tribune ordered.

Caesar's eyes stayed on a paper he was studying.

Hasmond shuffled from foot to foot, looking unsure how to proceed. "I will wait until Caesar is ready to give the matter his full attention."

Caesar looked up. Eyes twin black pinpoints, he stared Hasmond down.

Hasmond pulled at the neckline of his tunic. "Ah-hh...I...ah...have letters from some of Jerusalem's most prominent men accusing the Idumean usurper of using oppressive and intimidating tactics against the people."

Idumean usurper? Nathan shook his head. The insult was a new one to him. The derogatory term referred to Antipater, of course.

Caesar waved Hasmond forward. A tribune collected the letters. The sovereign head of the world's most powerful nation took the time to examine several of the documents. "I get the gist. Go on."

Confidence returning, Hasmond spoke louder, "Antipater has attempted to have me killed."

The audience murmured. Herod leaned forward. "If he tells any more lies about my father. I'll do more than threaten him."

"Easy, friend," Nathan whispered, laying a hand on his arm.

Hasmond ticked his points off on his fingers. "Antipater paid Pompey to poison my father and to have my brother executed. Antipater took up arms alongside Pompey to defeat you."

What could Antipater possibly say to the last charge, which was indisputably true and the most damning? The tension in the court climbed. People shifted in their seats.

Hasmond held a third finger. "Antipater stole the throne of high priest from me and gave it to my uncle." The rat-faced schemer's whiny voice grated.

Caesar must have thought so too, for he put his hand

up, ending Hasmond's testimony.

The head tribune's deep voice echoed through the hall, "Antipater of Idumea, come forward and answer the charges against you."

Wide-shouldered and solidly built, Antipater marched to the dais like a man without a care in the world. Nathan couldn't help but smile.

Antipater laid out his case with military precision designed to impress a fellow soldier, ending with a charge of his own "I, too, have sworn testimony from leading citizens of Jerusalem." Antipater handed the documents to a tribune. "May I approach the dais?"

Caesar nodded his approval. Antipater stepped closer and proceeded to roll up his sleeves. Nathan had known the wily old man long enough to know he was up to something. Antipater held both arms out. "Here is my true defense. I shed blood for you.

Caesar set the papers down and examined Antipater's arms.

Antipater turned and showed his arms to a rapt audience. Red-rimmed scars marred the old man's tawny skin. "I shed blood for Rome and for Caesar."

Nathan remembered all the reasons he loved and admired Antipater.

Caesar stared back blank-faced. He waved a hand, indicating he had heard enough, then put his head together with his advisors to discuss the case.

Everyone held their breath. Nathan kept an eye on Herod. Fists balled and lips pursed tight, he couldn't have looked grimmer.

The meeting on the dais broke up. Caesar set one bundle of papers aside in favor of another. He passed a single sheet to the head tribune. The man cleared his throat. "Antipater of Idumea is hereby acquitted of all charges."

Wild cheers and loud groans filled the room and Caesar smiled for the first time all day.

The head tribune called for quiet. He proceeded to read from a prepared statement, one extolling Antipater's every virtue. Hasmond twitched each time his foe was praised.

The head tribune traded the statement for a more official-looking document. His voice rang out again, "By decree of the Roman Senate, Antipater of Idumea is granted Roman citizenship."

The incredible news set the audience buzzing. The hum grew louder when Antipater was named governor of Judea and John Hyrcanus was confirmed as high priest.

Herod clapped Nathan on the back. "This is it, olive farmer. We are on our way."

Stunned, Nathan wondered where it would all lead.

Herod saw only the good. The family's fortunes had gone from fair to a future with unlimited possibilities. A highly coveted honor, Roman citizenship brought rank and riches with it.

Nathan saw potential for plenty of trouble. Roman citizenship would serve to sink the family's reputation to a new low among their fellow Israelites, who regarded all things foreign as suspect. Rebels like Hezekiah and Judas would use the news to stir up more unrest in Galilee. The Pharisees, who could rile up the people faster than anyone, would spew volcanic-worthy fury upon learning Rome meant to interfere in religious matters, especially on an issue as vital as who would sit as high priest.

The head tribune went on, "In honor of the Jewish army who fought valiantly in Egypt, Julius Caesar grants special status to the province of Judea."

All the Jews present cheered.

Nathan's worries dissolved. Favored nation status meant taxes would be greatly reduced. And no taxes would be levied for the sabbatical years when the Law decreed the fields must lay fallow. On the almost-too-good-to-be-true-list, all tribute collected would go to John Hyrcanus and not Rome. Jewish youths would not be forced to serve in the army. And the Jewish people would not have to feed and quarter Roman troops.

Soundly defeated, Hasmond slunk away.

Last on the official agenda came a list of political appointments. The most notable one named Julius Caesar's nephew Sextus Caesar as the next governor of Syria.

Court was dismissed. Herod and Nathan found Sextus and offered him their congratulations.

Pleasantries exchanged, Sextus said, "Herod, my assistance is yours for the asking."

Herod bowed respectfully. "I will pass your offer on to my father."

Sextus turned his sharp gaze on Nathan. "The same goes for you, olive farmer."

Nathan smiled. "You know what I want."

Sextus grinned. "Use of my private bath." They all laughed. Nathan had been pestering Herod for a few hours' use of the governor's personal bath. Nathan wanted Lex to experience the luxury of a real Roman bath.

"I'll see what I can do," Sextus promised.

A call for order claimed their attention. Antipater

stood atop the dais. "Caesar has been gracious enough to accept my proposal for dividing Judea into four districts, each of which will be administered by one of my four sons. My youngest son, Herod, is hereby named governor of Galilee. My son, Phasael—"

"Damnation," Herod said through gritted teeth.

Nathan leaned closer to his friend. "I thought you'd be overjoyed." He'd listened to Herod talk for hours about the great things he would do once he got the chance to hold an important office.

"My skills should be put to use in Jerusalem and not the God-forsaken backcountry. Galilee doesn't own one respectable fortress. It will take months to bring the fortifications up to half standards."

Nathan winced. The new governor of Galilee was likely to be busy and distracted for the foreseeable future, leaving him on his own in his quest to apprehend Judas the Zealot.

CHAPTER 14

The colorful pennants ringing the circular amphitheater snapped and waved overhead. Succulent smells of roasting meats and nuts competed with the smell of freshly spilled blood, the latter courtesy of the one-hundred plus animals slaughtered for sport at the start of the day's entertainment.

Foreign as all this was to Alexandra, nothing compared to the sight of Nathan clothed in a short-sleeved, mid-thigh length roman-style tunic. His muscled arms and thick legs rivaled those of the marble statuary of the pagan gods dotting the city.

Swords clashed again in the arena below. The air backed up in Alexandra's throat watching Herod beat Nathan down with his sword. The crowd roared their approval. She gripped the edge of her seat. Nathan assured her the fighting was all in fun, but it looked deadly serious to her.

Herod's very young and very foolish wife, Doris, leaned closer to Alexandra. "You don't look well."

"Someone is going to get hurt," Alexandra said through gritted teeth.

Doris waved her hand at the suggestion. The thin gold coins dangling from her bracelet jingled, mimicking her tinkling voice. "It's just rough play."

Alexandra bit her tongue. Herod was a bully. That's what he was. He was also without rival: outfighting, outracing, and outmatching every opponent he'd faced this week, including Nathan. They'd fought four times, with Herod pushing Nathan harder than he pushed anyone else. Nathan made light of the dark bruises lining his arms and legs, but the sight made her see red.

Herod smashed his sword down with extra force, and Nathan's sword clattered to the ground. A quick flick of the wrist and Herod's weapon slashed across Nathan's thigh, leaving a light trail of blood.

Alexandra sprang to her feet. A surprised look crossed Nathan's face. The bloodthirsty crowd jumped up and cheered wildly. The strike was no accident. Nathan was bleeding because Herod wanted it so. Everybody present knew it and yelled the louder for it.

Swaying where she stood, she pressed her fists to her mouth. The injury was superficial; even so, her head spun at the sight of the blood. Nathan had warned her of the arena's brutality, warned her she'd be sickened by what she saw, warned her she'd be better off staying to her room. Excruciating as it was to watch, she couldn't stay away.

Herod allowed Nathan to reclaim his sword. The ecstatic crowd cheered anew.

Alexandra wanted the fight done with. Now.

Doris slipped a bolstering arm under her elbow. "You, poor thing," she cooed. "Herod's surprised you've held up so well."

"Me?" The tiresome girl couldn't be serious. "I am no

concern of Herod's."

"Oh, I wouldn't call it concern, exactly." Doris pressed as close as her ample bosom allowed and confided, "You've disappointed my husband."

Engulfed by a cloying, cloud of perfume, Alexandra was tempted to plug her nose. "What are you talking about?"

"My husband is goading your husband, hoping to enrage him."

Swords held at the ready, Herod and Nathan circled one another wearily. Alexandra shot a dirty look at Doris. "Why would he do that?"

"Nathan had quite a reputation as a soldier. They called him the angel of death. Herod thinks you..." Doris poked Alexandra's arm for emphasis "...a sheltered, squeamish, priest's daughter who will go scurrying home to your father once you get a glimpse of..." she giggled and pitched her voice low "...the angel of death."

Herod said something and laughed. The color drained out of Nathan's face. Alexandra's heart began racing again.

Nathan feinted left, shifted his weight forward, and went on the attack. Red-faced with rage, he beat his sword against the other blade, forcing Herod to use his sword as a shield. Metal screeched over metal. Herod tripped and fell. Nathan pressed the point of his sword into Herod's neck.

The crowd cheered wildly. Alexandra stood on her toes, straining to see them. Herod offered up his weapon.

A long, agonizing moment passed.

Alexandra gnawed her knuckles. Everything in her

wanted to yell, *Stop it! Stop it! Stop it!*

Nathan eased his sword back. "Your bath? Or your life?"

A few nervous laughs went up from the spectators.

A slow smile crossed Herod's face. "I'll take my life. But, don't think I wasn't tempted to choose the bath. What with all the marble and gold."

Alexandra sagged with relief. *Praise heaven.* Nathan wanted use of the governor's private bath. He'd promised her he'd find a way to secure them some time alone there. She laughed. The fighting was just play, after all.

Nathan held a hand out. Herod grabbed hold and let Nathan help him to his feet. The spectators went wild. Alexandra cheered and applauded too, clapping until her hands hurt.

On his way out the arena, Nathan stopped and scanned the stands for her. Spotting her, he bowed theatrically.

Angels above! How could one feel vitally alive and scared unto death, all at the same time? She loved it. She hated it. It was much the same with her beautiful, warrior husband. He excited her and frightened her, this man known as the angel of death. She wasn't afraid for her safety. Rather, she was afraid a man as vital and virile as he would tire of someone as silent and shy as she.

Doris divined her thought. "Herod used to look at me the same way, too. You wait. Your man will take a slave to bed. They all do sooner or later."

Alexandra ignored the unhappy woman's comments, hoping it would discourage her, but Doris went blithely on. As usual.

"Herod purchased his latest plaything from Sextus

Caesar." Doris sighed. "Does Nathan own a slave girl?"

Alexandra put her hand to her cheek as though she'd been slapped across the face. "Yes, a bondmaid."

"Oh, they are even worse," Doris assured her. "Girls sold as bond slaves always marry their masters. The girl's father will insist. It probably says so in the contract."

Alexandra didn't know what the contract said because, *foolish her*, she'd assured Nathan the matter was his to settle. An image flashed through her mind of Nathan holding Sapphira in his strong arms. Alexandra's stomach rolled. Nathan would never betray her so. Would he?

Floating in the water behind Nathan, Alexandra moved a soft sponge in slow circles over his broad shoulders.

"Ah..." Nathan's voice echoed softly off the marbled walls of their private sanctuary. "There's almost nothing I enjoy more than a good Roman bath."

"My father's pool can't compare," she agreed.

Flickering light cast by oil sconces skipped over the water, illuminating the mottled bruises on her husband's arm. Beaten and battered as he was, he hadn't once complained. She hugged him around the waist and pressed a soft kiss to his shoulder.

Nathan pulled her around to face him. His callused hands moved down her sides. "There's a good reason the baths are different. We Israelites are concerned with ritual purity, so our pools tend to be utilitarian, whereas the Romans are concerned with pleasure and relaxation. They are so fond of them they've built opulent pools from here to Rome."

She wrapped her legs around his hips. "It sounds as though you've visited plenty of Roman baths."

Nathan nudged her toward deeper water. "I traveled far and wide with Antipater's army. We never missed a chance to see chariot racing or visit the theaters and baths wherever we were." His hands flexed against her waist. "Are you disgusted with me for indulging in worldly pleasures?"

She gave him a reassuring kiss. "No. I can't find it in my heart to hate pagans because they did not have the good sense to be born among the Lord's chosen people."

He smiled. "We think alike on the subject." He kissed her on the nose. "Tell me what is bothering you."

She gritted her teeth, and asked the question eating at her. "When you visited those places did you ever bed with slave girls?"

The soft lapping of water filled the widening silence.

Sorrow darkened his brown eyes. "I did." Displaying more vulnerability now than he had when facing the fiercest of opponents in the arena, he whispered the last of his words. "I don't want to lie to you. Do you despise me?"

"It hurts." The words burned in her throat. "What I hate is the idea that another woman has known you intimately as..." She pressed her lips to his mouth and dipped her tongue inside, then pulled back. "I wanted it to be special. Just between you and me."

He touched his forehead to hers. "I know. And I'm sorry and...I don't know what else to say."

"Many men take slaves to bed." She squeezed her eyes shut. "Even after they are married."

Nathan jerked back. "I won't."

She made herself look at him. "Yes...but Abraham, Jacob, and David did. Herod and some of the others have."

"I swear to you on Moses' Law," Nathan spoke each word slowly and vehemently. "I will not take another woman to my bed. You are worried about Sapphira?"

She nodded. Of course, she didn't think of the bond slave as Sapphira. She thought of her as the poor, needy priest's daughter who couldn't wait to bear a child with the newly rich olive farmer. Rot her.

Nathan pulled away. His eyes couldn't have looked sadder. "The girl's family needs the money. As soon as Sapphira is of age I will find a husband for her. Or I can send her away now."

Alexandra wasn't hateful enough to want to force the family to go begging, but she was selfish enough to resent the thought of sheltering a girl who might grow to rival her for Nathan's affections. Life had been far simpler when she'd been given no choice in matters. She felt naked and exposed, and it didn't have to do with the pool water barely covering her breasts. "Sapphira can stay," she said, then added, "I'm usually quite reasonable."

Nathan's fingers traced lightly over the sensitive bones at the base of her neck. His voice was a soft murmur. "I am a man who will only ever want one woman." He looked up into her eyes. "You are that woman."

Tears of relief flooded her eyes. "Make love to me," she demanded.

The water barely stirred about them as Nathan's warm lips moved over her skin.

CHAPTER 15

F raying mats circled a sputtering blaze. The fidgety innkeeper lurked in the doorway of the small, dismal establishment, ready to rush out and sell more stale food and sour drink to the large traveling party. The accommodations were the best to be had, and the sad part was, Nathan had stayed in far worse inns, in far smaller towns.

Herod and his men passed pitchers of wine with the same abandon they swapped war stories, crude language, and crass innuendos.

Nathan cringed for Alexandra's sake. Traveling with soldiers for company was a mistake. Not that he'd been given much choice. Deciding at the last hour to make a cursory inspection of Galilee, Herod packed his wife, Doris, off to Idumea with his father and informed Nathan that the new governor of Galilee and his men would escort Nathan and Alexandra to Rumah.

Nathan should have stood his ground and traveled home with a paid guard rather than subject Lex to this uncouth band. He didn't remember acting and talking this foully when he was a soldier, but Herod's knowing smile told him differently.

He leaned close to Alexandra and offered an apology. "They've started early tonight. We'd best go inside." Herod held out a staying hand. "Don't go yet." He turned to his men. "Knock off the nonsense," he barked. Sitting up straighter, he leaned forward. "I've been thinking about the governorship." A born administrator, Herod always had a plan at the ready.

"And?" Nathan prompted.

Herod's black eyes gleamed intently. "I don't know a damnable thing about Galilee. I want to hire you to advise me on local matters."

Stifling a groan, Nathan gave Herod a direct look. "I will help you as often as I can." Nathan pressed his hand discreetly to Lex's leg. "But my family is my first priority." Lex shifted closer to him.

Herod clucked his tongue in disgust. "Anyone can manage your farm."

"I don't want anyone else managing it."

"As governor of Galilee I could order you to do it."

No one was going to ride roughshod over Nathan. He stared Herod down. "I don't have time to traipse back and forth between the farm and your post."

Herod threw his hands up. "If you won't do it for me, then do it for your friends and neighbors, to save them from suffering from my mistakes."

Nathan blew out a frustrated breath. An argument with merit—how could he say no? "Look..." Nathan strived to sound reasonable. "...if I believe you are about to make an idiotic blunder, I'll tell you friend to friend."

Herod opened his mouth. A loud fart ripped the air. A burst of belly-busting laughter followed.

Nathan frowned at Herod's men.

Herod gave them a dirty look. The grinning idiots pointed out the guilty man, a strapping young soldier looking shamelessly proud of the impolite deed.

Nathan took hold of Alexandra's hand and helped her to her feet. "Goodnight, gentlemen," he said, glad for the excuse to escape Herod's badgering.

Nathan directed Lex to the small lane fronting the inn. "Do you mind taking a walk? I don't know about you, but I'm not in any hurry to bed down in the grubby cubbyhole the innkeeper calls a bedroom."

Alexandra looped her arm through his. "The first two inns we tried didn't look any better."

Late arriving in town, they'd had to settle for the last available rooms. The Lion's Den Inn. A flea-bitten pile of rocks was what it was.

They passed by a newly built shop. "I hardly recognize Cadasa. The town was a simple watering hole before the Romans arrived. A small village has sprung up since the last time I was here."

Lex remained quiet.

He never should have brought his sheltered bride on this trip. "I am sorry to expose you to the men's crude behavior. Soldiers are little better than brute beasts." She'd watched him duel like a soldier in the arena, race his horse around a track watched over by foreign idols, and socialize with Romans in sumptuous banqueting halls, all without comment.

Lex came to a stop and turned her face up to his. The moonlight illuminated her soft beauty. "You are nothing like Herod and his men."

The coward in him wanted to give her leave to believe the best about him. He cleared his throat and fought past the bitter taste in his mouth. "In here," He guided her hands to his chest and pressed her palms to his heart. "I am like them or worse."

Tears welled in her gray eyes. "Herod thought I'd run back to my father when I learned you are called the angel of death."

He flinched, hearing the ugly name fall from her lips.

She began to tremble. "Were you...were you hoping I would beg for a divorce after seeing you fight in the arena?"

"No. For the love of...no." He hugged her hard. "But you have to be disgusted, now that you know what kind of man you married."

She wrapped her arms around him and pressed against him. "I married a good man, and nothing I saw or heard in Syria changed my mind."

Relief washed through him.

Then a high-pitched scream tore through the dark. Panicked shouts and confused noise followed.

Nathan drew his dagger. He'd gone over enough walls in the middle of the night to recognize the sounds of victims taken unaware and of attackers screaming like the demons of hell.

"Someone is laying siege to the village. Come," he said. He took Lex's hand and ran for the inn. Pushing her inside, he dashed into their small room, grabbed up his sword, and headed back to the door. He touched Lex's arm. "Don't stir from here until I get back." The innkeeper and his wife wore terrified looks. "Bar the door behind me," he commanded, and raced into the dark.

Frightened villagers peeked out their doors. A dog barked a warning at him. He rounded a corner and found Herod standing in the doorway of a tiny inn holding a blood-soaked body. A woman wailed in the background. "We came too late to help," Herod said, his face pinched. "Bandits robbed the guests, then stabbed the innkeeper." He passed the limp body over to two of his men.

Screams and shouts came from down the lane.

Nathan and Herod took off at a run. Herod's soldiers poured out of the inn and raced to catch up.

They came to another inn, this one lit by lamps. The sight of a bloody man lying on the ground and a host of bewildered souls roaming the yard struck soul-robbing fear into Nathan. "Lex!" he howled, reversing course and charging back toward the Lion's Den Inn.

This was Hezekiah and Judas's handiwork. He was sure of it. They were at it again. Striking out at so-called Roman sympathizers. Tonight they'd turned their wrath on Cadasa's innkeepers. And the innkeeper hiding Lex might well open his door to fellow Galileans turned bandits, not realizing he'd become a target. Nathan would kill Judas with his bare hands if the cretin dared to lay one finger on her.

He couldn't move fast enough. His feet felt like they were mired in deep clay. Breath ragged, he rounded the last corner. Up ahead, he saw a man pushing someone over the low wall running behind the Lion's Den Inn.

What if the rebels carried Lex off like they had Lydia? His stomach lurched. *Please, God, no!* Nathan raced to the mud wall and threw one leg over it.

"Nathan. Nathan," a frightened voice called out.

He hugged the wall to keep from going over. "Lex?" Dropping to the ground, he scrambled over the dirt, heading toward the sound of her beautiful, wonderful voice. He met her coming around the corner of the inn. "Lex!" He pulled her into his arms and hugged her tight.

He was too relieved to be angry with her for ignoring his order to stay inside.

She pressed up against him.

A winded Herod stopped beside them.

"What happened? What was all the screaming about?" Lex asked.

"Those damnable bandits are what happened," Herod growled. He took a few steps toward the wall and scanned the dark. "I'll send men after them, although I'm not holding out much hope that they'll catch anyone." His voice turned quiet and deadly. "These raids are unacceptable. My first priority will be to put an end to them."

The throbbing pressure in Nathan's head increased. Hezekiah didn't know it, but he'd riled the wrong man.

Herod patted Nathan on the shoulder as he walked past. "Let's go clean up this mess."

An hour later, with all the villagers accounted for, the injured stitched up, and soldiers posted as lookouts, Nathan and Herod returned to the inn. Herod sent the frazzled innkeeper, his wife, and the other guests off to their beds and called a meeting.

More than ready to be alone with Lex, Nathan took her hand and headed for their tiny room.

"Not so fast, olive farmer," Herod called out, flinging a straw mat.

Nathan caught the mat. "It's been a long day."

"Stop looking so grim," Herod ordered, then his grin faded. "Stay. We need to have a talk about your friends."

"Do you mind?" Nathan asked Lex. She shook her head and let go of his hand. He watched until she slipped behind the door of their small bedroom, then joined the men.

Oil lamps burned next to baskets filled with bread. Cups brimming with wine stood at the ready. The smell of human sweat and mildewed hay kept the place from feeling cozy. He eyed the men sitting around a blanket spread out on the floor in the middle of inn's main room. Malchus and Obodas had been riding with Herod forever. The rest of the Herod's Idumean soldiers were strangers to Nathan.

Herod lifted his squat goblet. "To your wife. She handled tonight's chaos admirably. She is a stronger, braver woman than I first supposed." Herod wasn't a flatterer, meaning the compliment was high praise, indeed.

Nathan smiled. "I am continually surprised by Alexandra. She is a rare gem."

The men hooted and howled. Herod cocked an eyebrow. "If she's as clever as she is courageous, you, my man, are in trouble."

Let them laugh. Nathan could handle that kind of trouble every day. He came to the point. "What are you planning to do about *my* rebel friends?"

"Rebels?" Herod grabbed a loaf of bread and tore off a chunk. "They are common thieves and thugs." Herod waved the remains of the barley loaf in Nathan's direction.

Nathan shook his head. "If it was only so simple. Hezekiah and Judas have been wreaking havoc all over Galilee and getting away with it. And do you know why? Because ninety-nine out of a hundred Galileans either support them or are willing to overlook their lawless deeds."

Obodas spoke up, "And here I thought the scoundrels were just good at hiding."

"They are." Nathan drank deeply from his cup. "Plus, the hills in upper Galilee are riddled with caves ideal for their purposes. You are going to need help from the locals to find Hezekiah and Judas."

Herod stuffed a piece of bread into his mouth. "You still haven't told us why the people support them."

Nathan cringed. He'd hoped to avoid admitting the truth. "The people believe Hezekiah is the next Mattathias Maccabeus."

Herod threw his head back and laughed. "No, no, no. You are jesting?"

Nathan shifted uncomfortably. The others shared puzzled looks.

Herod dried his eyes on his sleeve. "These dullards don't know who Mattathias Maccabeus is. Tell them while I try to catch my...br...br..." Herod fell to laughing again.

Nathan rolled his eyes. *Give me patience,* he prayed. Sizing up the half-godless Idumean soldiers, he amended the request. *Make that baskets and baskets of patience.*

"Listen up, dolts," Nathan said. Chunks of bread sailed toward him. He deftly ducked out of the way and continued. "Around three hundred years ago the Greek conqueror, Alexander the Great, had barely finished conquering this part of the world and subjugating it to Greek rule when he suddenly fell ill and died. But thanks to the generals who proceeded him his influence survives to this day."

Herod slowed down laughing and offered a comment. "It's why we and every nation west of here speak Greek as a second language." Herod was no dolt. He had paid attention to his tutors, especially the ones giving

lessons about conquering generals and military cam-
paigns. Herod's favorite teachings from scriptures had
to do with the battles fought by great men of war such
as Joshua and David.

"Thank you, Rabbi Marglus," Nathan said, calling
Herod by the name of the humorless teacher they both
had dreaded to see darken the door as boys.

The men whooped at the banter.

Looking properly revolted, Herod said, "Get back to
Alexander."

Nathan bit back a smile. "After Alexander died, the
empire he'd built was divided between his generals.
Judea, and other small nations bordering the middle
ground, changed hands on a regular basis between
the opposing realms. This went on for several generations until Judea came under the rule an insane des-
pot named Antiochus Epiphanes, who got it into his
head to destroy Hebrew traditions and religion. Enter
Mattathias Maccabeus, a priest and the great, great,
great grandfather of High Priest, John Hyrcanus. A family better known as the Hasmoeans."

The light of understanding finally dawned in the
men's eyes. They nodded.

Nathan sliced his finger across his neck. "Maccabeus and his sons ousted Antiochus Epiphanes and the
Greeks out of Judea for good and became beloved figures because of it. Hezekiah and Judas believe they've
been anointed to drive the Romans out of the land."

Herod started laughing all over again.

Nathan frowned. "What about this amuses you?"

"The Hasmoeans are...are..." Herod paused for breath
"...the Hasmoeans are responsible for convincing my
Idumean ancestors to give up idol worship and to con-

vert to Judaism. It wasn't much of a choice, since it was either circumcision or death by the sword." Black eyes twinkling with mischief, Herod continued. "If the Hasmoeans had left well enough alone, my father and brothers and I would be at home minding our own business instead of supporting Roman rule."

Nathan choked. "You and your father sitting at home, peaceful as lambs. Tell me another fable."

Herod pressed his hand to his chest. "Your lack of faith wounds me."

Nathan rolled his eyes. "Give me your plan for dealing with the rebels—and how you're going to do it without offending all of Galilee—and I'll be impressed."

Herod sobered and leaned forward. "Very well, here's what I'm thinking."

Alexandra lay awake, straining to hear the muffled conversation going on beyond the curtain. The loud snores coming from the cubbyholes to either side of her tiny room blocked most of what was said. She caught a few words—rebels, caves, Judas.

The image of the zealot's mocking face loomed before her.

She squeezed her eyes shut. A low roar filled her ears. She released a steadying breath. Uncurling her fists from the blanket, she pulled the sturdy cover up under her chin and brought her husband's face to mind.

What a fine man Nathan was. Beautiful brown eyes and thick curly hair. Bold, brave, intelligent, and possessing a clever wit, Nathan had burst like a brilliant star into her drab existence. She'd been prepared to be an obedient and virtuous wife. And had prayed for a loyal and upright spouse in return. Instead, she was coming to love her husband. How extraordinary. How wonderful.

But Nathan was not all light and beauty. He kept warning her he had a dark side. She still hadn't truly believed the reports painting him as the angel of death. Until tonight. In the wake of the bandit attack, a wild ferocity had darkened his face, making her afraid for him.

It seemed like hours before Nathan pushed aside the curtain and came to bed. Alexandra lifted the covers and he lay down, bringing the cold with him. The steady drone of Herod and his men talking and laughing drifted into the dark sanctuary.

"You're so warm," Nathan whispered.

She turned to him. "How did it go?"

"Herod asked me to ride as one of his men again," he said, drawing her close.

She pressed her body to his. "I think that is for the best." Nathan the olive farmer was a reasonable and prudent man. The angel of death had looked capable of committing dark deeds aplenty, the type of man bold and reckless enough to think nothing of single-handedly taking on a band of criminals.

Nathan stroked her back. "My commitment to Herod wouldn't end there."

"Why not?"

"If I want to have a part in apprehending Judas, then I will have to become one of his official advisors. Herod can track down the rebels without me, but he might be heavy-handed about it."

"What did you tell him?"

He kissed her forehead. "I told him I needed to talk to you about it first."

Flustered, she stammered, "That is thoughtful of you, Nathan. But...but..."

His warm breath filled her ear. "I'm in earnest. We need to discuss what's best for us."

For us. What a lovely thought.

Anxious to be of real help, she searched her mind for the wise, sensible thing to say. Painfully aware Nathan was waiting for her response, she blew out an exasperated breath. "I begin to sympathize with my brother's propensity to spout nonsense."

Nathan's soft laugh tickled her ear. "Just tell me what you are thinking."

She shivered and traced her fingers over his chest. "I think Herod is an oversized bully." She felt Nathan's lips curve upward against her ear. She pressed a kiss to Nathan's neck. "Herod won't be content to have you as an advisor. He will do or say anything to force you to rejoin his father's army."

Nathan's calloused fingers stroked her arm. "It's not too late to break with Herod. I can hire men to help hunt down Judas."

It sounded promising. "Could you find men as skilled as Herod's soldiers?"

"No. But I'll manage."

"I want Lydia back, but..." She cupped Nathan's face and drew him down until their noses touched. "I would see her lost to the bandits forever rather than risk having you killed."

Nathan kissed her nose. "You saw for yourself, I'm an able soldier."

Her throat closed. "I wish I was worrying for no

cause. But, I have seen what Judas is capable of." She squeezed her eyes shut, but the terrible image came, a bloom of red welling and spilling down James's deathly-white cheek. The walls of the tomb-like room closed around her.

Nathan rubbed her arms. "Tell me what happened," he whispered.

She scratched lightly at his chest with a fingernail. "I'd rather forget that day. Can't we go back to talking about Herod's demand?"

Nathan shifted so his body sheltered hers. "I'm sorry to cause you pain, but I want to know everything."

The attack was permanently imprinted upon her mind. Her mouth turned dry as dust. "Judas and his men came rushing at us from all sides. They reeked of strong drink. After the initial confusion died down, Judas placed dice in my brother's hand and forced him to throw them. The lots landed in the dirt." A tremble went through her. "It fell on me to maim James. Lydia was condemned to go with the bandits." She had pleaded with the bandits, begged them to show mercy.

"Tell me the rest," Nathan coaxed gently.

She exhaled a ragged breath. "Judas placed a long, ugly knife in my hand. Three men grabbed my brother's head and arms and held him in place. Poor James began to cry hysterically. Lydia and I were weeping. Father was screeching curses at the bandits. Judas was yelling into my ear, 'Cut him. Cut him.' My hand shook violently. I nearly dropped the knife. I touched the blade to James's face, but I couldn't do it. I couldn't." A sob bubbled up. "Judas slapped me hard across the face."

Nathan growled low in his throat. "I'm sorry I came too late to save you from the evil you suffered." His body settled more firmly against hers. "Forgive me for pushing, but I want to hear it all."

She squeezed her eyes shut. "Judas' hand closed over mine and he guided the knife to slash across my brother's face. James screamed pitifully and blood spurted over his clothes and onto my sleeve." She gagged on the confession. Nathan's cool fingers slid over her face and tucked her hair behind her ears.

She swallowed, but couldn't get rid of the bitter taste filling her mouth. "Then they released us and shoved James and me to the ground. Lydia joined us, and we wept and hugged. Father continued to screech. The bandits turned their attention on Father and beat him senseless." Black despair welled up. "Then they tore Lydia away from us and fled."

Nathan groaned. "My God. I had no idea Judas had descended so low."

Alexandra turned her face aside. "It would have been better if I'd been the one kidnapped. I'm stronger than Lydia. My feelings aren't as sensitive as hers."

Nathan stroked her hair. "Your strength amazes me. Not many people could move past such an experience as well as you have."

"My brother accuses me of being cold and uncaring."

"James is an idiot."

She smiled, but tears stung her eyes. "I'm hateful, that's what I am...these days I am happy Lydia was kidnapped instead of me...otherwise, I wouldn't be married to you...and isn't that the most selfish thing you've ever heard?"

"Lex?" The white outline of his tunic framed Nathan's wide shoulders. His face remained hidden from her.

She released a shuddering breath. "Yes?"

"You don't need to feel guilty about what happened," he said soothingly. "Our marriage was meant to be. Though it grieves me you had to suffer violence, I doubt our paths would have crossed without help from Judas."

She wiped at her eyes, hating that she'd cried. "Help? That is a strange word for evil."

"Forgive me. It's my poor attempt to sum up the scriptures. Do you know the passage I mean? 'You thought evil against me, but the Lord meant it unto the good'." Nathan pressed a soft kiss to her forehead. "What Judas did was atrocious. But it brought you into my life, and I count that a very good thing." Nathan's voice hitched and deepened. "There's more I want to say, but I won't have you hear it here, in this armpit of a place, with the dark between us and with Herod and his men practically snoring at our feet."

The confession made her indecently happy. She ran her hands up and down his strong arms.

His lips grazed her face. "Surely, as the Lord has given you to me, Lex, he has also given it to me to put an end to Judas' evil ways. You know that, don't you?"

Her hands stilled and her stomach went back to feeling sick. "I do, but I hate it, nonetheless." She had another secret to share, one making her glad for the dark. "It is why I thank the Lord you are the soldier they call the angel of death."

Nathan tensed and started to pull away. She held tighter to him.

"Let me up." There was a dangerous edge to the command.

"Listen to me...*please!*" He stopped struggling. She

pressed her palms to his chest. "I am glad you fight like the angel of death, because I am less frightened knowing you are a fierce, experienced warrior. You will rescue Lydia. And you will bring her home to us. I know you will."

"Job's bones, Lex," he said without heat. "You make me sound noble."

"That's because you are noble. Marrying me was the good and decent thing to do. Going after Lydia is beyond kind."

A shudder went through him. "You should be disgusted with me."

"But I'm not."

"What about Herod?"

Alexandra sighed. "I think we should accept Herod's self-serving offer. And, though it amounts to throwing our lot in with vipers...I think it the safest way. We can worry later about extracting you from the snake pit."

"We?" Nathan asked. "As in you and me, together?"

She laughed, pulled him down, and gave him a smacking kiss. "Fool. We are talking about saving your neck and not my reticence over spouting every notion that pops into my head."

"Very well." The doubt tingeing Nathan's agreement sobered her. "We will throw our lot in with Herod and hope we don't live to regret it."

CHAPTER 16

They'd been home from Syria for six weeks, and the hunt for the rebels was finally underway. Nathan was both relieved and apprehensive. He, Lex, Joseph, and Rhoda had spent countless hours discussing the best way to proceed. Their plan called for Nathan to help Herod see the wisdom in letting all of the rebels go except Judas.

Meanwhile, Joseph would try to contact Hezekiah, who had gone into hiding with his men, and convince him to put his sword away in favor of taking the rebel grievances to the Sanhedrin.

Everybody ought to be satisfied. The rebels could return home to their families. Herod could boast to his Roman overlords he had restored peace to the land. And Nathan could fulfill his promise to reunite Lydia with her family and see that Judas the Zealot was punished.

Leading Royal by the reins, Nathan walked beside Lex on the hard-packed path he'd trod more times than he could count. The family was accompanying him as far as the village of Rumah. They'd brought along some olive oil to trade for goods they were running short of. From there Nathan would go on to meet Herod and begin the search for Judas.

He turned and walked backward, checking to make sure his father and stepmother hadn't fallen too far behind. The donkeys carrying Joseph and Rhoda continued to shuffle along at the same abysmally slow pace. Nathan smiled, watching his father gesture enthusiastically as he talked. The frail man looked healthier than he had in ages. And, miracle of miracles, Rhoda was in a rare, relaxed mood, laughing at whatever it was his father was saying.

Nathan heard Mary and Timothy yelling excitedly. He turned around and saw his brother and sister racing toward the gates of the walled village in the distance. They ran past the slave maiden, Sapphira, who was trying without success to hurry along the donkey she'd been assigned to lead.

Royal nickered and tossed his head. Nathan tightened his hold on the reins and pulled the gelding's head down to his shoulder. The horse sniffed at his neck. "Good boy," he said, rubbing the long, velvety nose.

"The poor dear," Lex said, staring up ahead.

Nathan wasn't sure if she was referring to Sapphira, who was anxious to get the village and spend time visiting with her family, or to the donkey plodding along under the load of two oversized jars filled with olive oil.

He touched his fingers to the back of Lex's arm. "Do you mind if I go relieve Sapphira of her burden?" He was extra careful in his dealings with the slave maiden, not wanting to give Lex any cause for concern over the girl.

Lex's brow furrowed briefly. "Ride Royal and I will catch up with you."

He climbed atop the saddle, made a clicking noise, and the horse bounded forward. The blast of warm wind to his face was a mere tease. He pulled the horse to a stop next to Sapphira and held out his hand for the lead. "I will take the donkey the rest of the way."

Passing him the rope, Sapphira glanced up shyly. "Bless you, Nathan. It's very kind of you." A red blush showed beneath her pretty freckles.

He still thought of Mary and Sapphira as girls, but they were closer to being young women than children, and he'd do well to treat them thus. He broke eye contact and made his voice cold and distant. "Go. Enjoy the company of your family while you can."

Sapphira ducked her head, spun around, and took off toward Rumah. The donkey brayed a forlorn complaint. "Hang on little fellow, we are almost there," Nathan said.

He looked back at Lex. She'd stepped off the road and was picking flowers. Straightening up, she lifted a bouquet of early blooming crocuses to her nose. Stray strands of hair danced around her face. She noticed him watching her.

He waved. "Take your time."

But she was already hurrying toward him, the spray of flowers bobbing from side to side as she pushed her hair back under her kerchief. She arrived at his side breathless and flushed. Hugging the horse around the neck, she rested her face against Royal's black mane and smiled up at him. A yellow petal clung to her cheek. "I can lead the donkey the rest of the way."

The cover of cool reserve she'd worn when they first met had deceived. This was the real Lex. He brushed the back of his hand over her soft skin. "I'm going to miss you."

Her eyes warmed. "I am glad I please you."

"I was not just speaking of the nights," he explained, even as his loins tightened. "I meant you, Lex...Alexandra Onias."

Her eyes widened in surprise. He hated that she underestimated her worth. That was her father's doing, and an injustice he planned to redress.

He heard Timothy calling his name, and turned to see the boy racing toward them as fast as his small legs would carry him.

Lex stepped back from the horse. Timothy arrived huffing and puffing. "Nathan, hurry. You have to come."

"What's wrong?" Nathan asked.

The boy danced in place. "It's Mary. She's spitting mad."

"Here." Nathan tossed the lead rope to Lex. "Be firm with the beast and she shouldn't cause you too much trouble." He bent forward and reached for Timothy.

His brother grabbed hold of Nathan's arm. "Hurry, you know how Mary can be."

He hoisted the boy up. "Our sweet lamb has turned into a lioness, has she? But she just got to the village. What could have happened in so short a time?"

"I don't know." Timothy circled his arms about Nathan's waist. "But I've never seen her so furious." And the little imp ought to know, as he frequently went out of his way to rile his sister.

Nathan turned the horse in a circle and saw his father and Rhoda trying to spur their donkeys on. He stopped beside Lex. Concern filled her eyes. "Mary will be fine. As for the person foolish enough to annoy our sweet lamb..." He offered Lex a chagrined smile and nodded in his parents' direction. "Please wait for them and let them know there's no need to hurry."

Nudging his knees against the horse's sides, they set off at a lope down the road. "Hold on tight," he warned Timothy. A slight flick of the reins, and Royal was flying towards Rumah.

Nathan slowed the horse to a trot as they passed under the arched clay gate.

Mary was standing at the threshold of a tidy stone house, pounding her fist against a wooden door. A good portion of the Rumah's residents stood outside their homes, watching the spectacle. What had gotten into the girl? The house she was assaulting belonged to Bartholomew ben Judah, the grandfather of Mary's best friend, Tabitha. A town elder and the wealthiest resident of the village, Bartholomew had a habit of pushing his jowly face into everyone else's business.

Nathan looked back at Timothy. "What did you do to irritate Bartholomew?"

"Me?" The boy's brows shot up. "I got here and went straight inside the baker's shop. Old Zeb told me I wasn't welcome in his shop anymore, and he led me outside by my ear." Timothy pinched Nathan's ear in demonstration.

Nathan frowned and pushed the sticky fingers aside. "So why is your sister yelling at Bartholomew instead of pounding on old Zeb's door?"

Timothy shrugged. "Mary was already arguing with Tabitha's grandfather when I saw her." He scrunched his nose up and snarled in imitation. "And I ran as fast as I could to you."

Nathan squeezed the boy's knee. "Let's go see if we can calm Mary." He jumped off the horse and helped

Timothy down.

The door to Bartholomew's house swung open and Bartholomew stuck his plump face outside. "Get away from my door!" he yelled in Mary's face.

Did his sister have the sense to back down? No. She went nose-to-nose with the respected elder.

Bartholomew backpedaled. Mary followed. Nathan reached her in two strides and grabbed hold of her skirt. She swung around with her fists up and stopped short. "Nathan." She turned and pointed an accusing finger. "Bartholomew called you a traitor, and he said I can no longer be friends with Tabitha." Exhaling a loud breath, she crossed her arms, obviously expecting Nathan to take over where she had left off.

Though he appreciated her outrage on his behalf, she wasn't considering the cost. Bartholomew had the power to ruin Mary's reputation. One word from the hard-hearted man and most of Rumah would avoid her like a leper.

Nathan gave his sister a firm look. She gritted her teeth and marched away. "Fine! I will go and visit Judith. I like *her* grandfather." She stomped to the next house. Judith's father and mother saw Mary coming and herded their brood back inside their home and shut their door in her face. Mary spun around, burst into tears, and ran to Nathan.

He gathered her in his arms. She buried her face in his tunic and wept inconsolably. He rubbed her back. "All will be well, sweet lamb."

Bartholomew frowned. "Take her and go home. You are not welcome in Rumah." The man's beefy jowls sagged lower. "None of you are welcome here."

A loud buzzing filled Nathan's ears. "You are expelling us from the village?"

Bartholomew eyes screwed up in disdain. "You chose to turn your back on your friends by siding with Herod and Rome. We choose to shut our doors to traitors."

Nathan's hand went to the hilt of his sword. Bartholomew's face drained of color.

A hand covered his. "Son, what's the trouble?" The sound of his father's steadying voice stopped Nathan cold.

He let go of the sword handle as if holding of a red-hot coal. *Job's bones! What did he mean to do? Run the tiresome man through over an insult?* This whole business with the rebels had him on edge.

Nathan looked around and saw the rest of his family had reached town. He sent Mary to her mother. Rhoda wrapped her arms around the distraught girl and scowled at the gawkers.

Timothy, who had more of Father's calm nature than his siblings, had taken charge of the donkeys. Fear and confusion clouded his young eyes. Lex stood with her arm wrapped tight about her middle. Nathan could tell from her anguished frown she was blaming herself for the trouble. Plenty of others were at fault: Judas the Zealot and Hezekiah for spilling blood; Nathan and his father for not standing sooner against the rebels; Bartholomew for stirring up the villagers of Rumah against his family. Lex was wholly innocent.

Nathan managed to answer his father evenly, "Bartholomew says we are no longer welcome here."

"Surely Elder Bartholomew does not speak for you all?" Joseph asked, gazing around at his neighbors.

Nathan walked to the middle of the narrow dirt road and stared down the fifty-plus families who called

Rumah home. They stood beside the doors of their solid stone houses, eyeing him warily.

He could not believe what was happening. Bartholomew was trying to run his family off like a pack of stray dogs? Nathan took his name from Rumah. As a boy he had run up and down this street with his friends, who were now men of influence here. The women of the village had helped raise him, scolding or praising him as needed. He'd learned the scriptures at the feet of the town elders. He attended synagogue, almost daily, with all the men staring at him.

Surely they had an ally or two. "Who among you will stand up for your good friend Joseph?" Nathan asked. No one stirred.

Nathan's dead mother wasn't from Rumah, and his father was an only child, but several of his father's cousins lived in the village. Nathan addressed the eldest directly. "Potiphar?" The stooped-backed man stroked fretfully at his long beard and stared off into the distance, letting his silence speak for him.

Nathan turned in a circle, seeking a sympathetic face. Still getting no response, he tried reasoning with them. "Judas the Zealot is crazed. Someone has to stop him." To the last person, their faces remained closed to him.

Where was Pinhas? Surely, Pinhas would stand up for him? Nathan twisted back around toward his friend's modest house. Pinhas and his family was nowhere to be seen. The stonemason hadn't been out to the farm in over a week, either. Nathan had assumed Pinhas was busy with other matters.

Realization cracked like thunder. His lifelong friend had deserted him.

◆ ◆ ◆

Nathan rode beside Herod, guiding Royal through the large herd of sheep swirling around two shepherd boys. Three weeks spent roaming Galilee, questioning every farmer, shepherd, or traveler they'd come across, and Herod and his band of thirty men were no closer to locating the rebels than when they'd begun.

Nathan dismounted and walked toward the nervous shepherds. The taller and skinnier of the two looked familiar.

Herod stayed in his saddle and spoke to the boys, "I am looking for information." He shook the cloth bag dangling from his fingers. Coins jingled. "Have you seen or heard anything of a large group of bandits said to be wandering in the area?"

The eyes of the tall, thin boy darted between Herod and the small sack. The younger one screwed his face up in distaste. His sharp, overlarge teeth protruded over his lower lip, making him looking like an angry badger. "We've seen none but those we count as friends."

"Peter!" the older boy scolded, elbowing his companion.

"Saul!" The angry badger turned his snarl on the skinny boy. "John Rumah is my friend as much as he is yours."

Herod laughed. The harsh bark scattered the sheep. The boys backed up a step and gripped tighter to their gnarled, wooden, shepherd's crooks.

Peter's unwitting remark represented the first promising lead of the expedition. Nathan stepped between Herod and the skittish boys. "John Rumah is my neighbor." He pointed his finger at the skinny youth. "I believe you are Mark the Younger's brother?"

"I know you." The boy's face twisted with hate. "You are the filthy Roman-lover hunting down Hezekiah."

Nathan winced. He ought to be used to the names people were calling him, but it cut deep each time it happened.

Herod jumped off his horse. "Shut your foul mouth," he roared, charging at the boys.

The terrified shepherds looked all arms and legs as they scrambled out of the angry man's way. Herod stepped on the thin boy's sandaled foot, tumbling him over backward. Saul gave a loud cry and landed hard on his backside, losing hold of his shepherd's crook. Herod snatched it up and pointed it at the boy. "You need a lesson in respect, dung mouth."

Hate and defiance simmered behind the tears filling the boy's eyes. Nathan was just feeling sorry for young Saul when he sucked in his cheeks and spat, spraying wet goo over Herod's hairy shins.

Herod hefted the wooden staff over his head. "Why you, little..."

Nathan jumped in front of Herod. "Whoa, whoa." He locked his hand around his friend's broad wrist. "You won't earn information this way."

"You're defending the little fiend?" Herod tried to yank his arm free.

Nathan tightened his grip. "When did you take up the practice of menacing helpless children?" Nathan made his voice reasonable. "The inhabitants of Galilee are spoiling for a fight. If you take a stick to a shepherd boy, it will only add fuel to their hatred." The arm under his hand went slack. *Thank the holy angels.* Nathan released his hold and stepped back.

Herod tossed the wooden staff at the boy. "Watch your tongue. Or you just might provoke someone to cut the vile instrument out of your mouth."

The young shepherd hugged the crooked stick to his breast and stuck his lower lip out defiantly. Nathan admired the boy's brave front, foolhardy as it was.

"Find out what they know," Herod ordered, stalking off.

The shepherds glared hatefully at Nathan. He told them the same thing he'd been telling anyone who would hear him out, "If you see Hezekiah give him a message from me. Tell him if he turns Judas over to Herod and gives up his raiding, he and his men can return home with no fear of being arrested." The boys' lips stayed sealed shut. He sighed to himself. These two were more likely to kiss a pig than talk to him.

"Question them," Nathan told the second-in-command before heading off to where Herod stood under the shade of a wild olive tree. Nathan pulled on the collar of his winter tunic, wishing he'd brought a summer-weight one. Reaching the tree, he plucked off a cluster of cream-colored flowers and rubbed the waxy petals between his fingers. The unusually warm spring had the trees blooming early. Too early. If a killing frost struck now he could lose his entire olive crop.

Herod leaned back against the tree. "The little brats wouldn't talk to you, either?"

Nathan crushed the sprig of flowers against his palm. "It seems my reputation is no better than yours."

"You weren't expecting this, were you?"

"No." Nathan opened his hand, spilling the ruined buds onto the ground. "And I am more the fool for it. I was so busy warning you to take the peoples' zealousness for Hezekiah's cause seriously, I forgot to heed my own advice."

Herod grinned. "You should see your face."

"Go ahead and laugh. But you don't have to live in Galilee for the rest of your life."

Herod squeezed Nathan's shoulder. "If it gets too bad for you here...know you will always find a warm welcome in my household."

The scorn Nathan saw in the eyes of his fellow Galileans chafed more than an ill-fitting sandal, and Pinhas' betrayal continued to eat at him like a festering sore. Yet here was Herod rallying around him. "You are a good friend, and I appreciate the generous offer." Nathan stopped to clear his throat. "But don't expect me to come knocking at your door anytime soon. I won't be run out of my own country without a fight."

Herod regarded him thoughtfully. "It sounds like an ugly war."

An uneasy queasiness filled Nathan. "The sooner we find Hezekiah and Judas the better."

Fresh off the trail from the hunt for the rebels, Nathan couldn't resist attending synagogue before heading home. Stopping to purify himself, he opened the door leading to the small stone bath attached to the house of prayer which served the whole community. Few families were prosperous enough to have their own baths, and Nathan would be counted among them when his house was finished. He wondered again at the abrupt changes to his life. *Where is this all leading, Lord?* The prayer was never far from his mind.

The ritual pool was crude compared to a Roman

bath. Comprised of side-by-side steps, the bather walked down one set of stairs ritually unclean and walked up the other set of stairs ritually pure. He removed his sandals and washed his feet. As modesty reigned supreme among Israelites, he went into the water fully clothed. The water didn't quite reach his neck. He dipped down until it lapped against his chin. If it wasn't considered sacrilegious by some, he'd be tempted to linger. He moved on.

Putting on a clean tunic, he exited the small enclosure and walked around to the front of the stone building. Unadorned and plain, Rumah's synagogue had nothing to commend it. But Nathan loved it nonetheless. It was a second home to him.

He reached for the door latch. The warmth of the rising sun hitting his back felt good. He stepped inside. Greeted by voices lifted in reverent song, he paused to let his eyes adjust to the dim interior. The singing trailed off.

He checked his father's seat. Empty. Unease crept up Nathan's spine. Joseph loved synagogue and came as often as his health allowed. He scanned the benches lining three out of the four the walls, searching for friendly or open faces. A good portion of the town's men and boys were present, and they all wore the same scowl. Proof his father hadn't been able to convince any of them to throw their support behind Nathan.

Synagogue was supposed to be a place of sanctuary. Putting the tenet to the test, he took a deep breath and headed for his seat. A low grumble went up. He ignored it and sat down. Pinhas always sat to Nathan's right, but his friend was nowhere to be seen. Nathan wasn't sure whether to be glad or relieved. John ben Simon was in his usual spot to the other side of Nathan. He nodded good morning to the stonemason. "*Shalom*, John." John's answer was to get up and move to the opposite side of the room. Nathan flinched.

It was time for the reading of the scriptures. No one moved. All eyes were trained on him. The silence stretched on and on. If none of them would begin the reading, he would. He got up and marched to the wall reserved for the Holy Ark and stomped up the small set of stairs leading to the wooden cupboard holding the Torah scrolls.

"Stop! No!" a chorus of voices called out.

Nathan heard someone coming up behind him. He spun around and came face to face with Bartholomew, the man responsible for making him an outcast in the village. Bartholomew pointed a thick finger at Nathan. "Leave. Go. You are no longer welcome here, Nathan ben Joseph."

Nathan's hands balled.

Rage marred Bartholomew's puffy face. It mirrored the black fury surging through Nathan's blood. He choked. What was he doing? Did he mean to start a fistfight in the house of prayer? He rolled his shoulders and flexed his fingers. "Elder Bartholomew, surely we can put our differences aside for synagogue."

Bartholomew rested his arms on his round stomach. "You assume wrong."

Nathan couldn't believe it was coming down to this. "My father will die of grief if you bar him from synagogue."

"You are a rich man now." Bartholomew smiled smugly. "Build your own house of prayer. Pay a scribe to make you a copy of the Holy Books."

Nathan blinked repeatedly. Build himself a house of prayer? It was the way of things in Jerusalem. The holy city boasted dozens and dozens of synagogues, many built thanks to differences that couldn't be solved. Most Galilean towns were too poor to have even one house of prayer. If he was going to build a synagogue—as likely as deciding to erect a statue of Zeus in his orchard—Rumah would be the dead last place he'd put it. He found his voice again, "You are in earnest?"

Bartholomew's thick lips firmed.

Nathan gritted his teeth together, lest he say something he'd regret, made his way to the door, stepped outside, and exhaled exaggeratedly. What an unholy mess. Eager to talk to his father and to hold Lex in his arms, he headed for his horse. Racing around the corner of the building, he came face to face with Pinhas and Hezekiah.

Pinhas and *Hezekiah* together?

CHAPTER 17

Nathan could hardly believe his eyes. Pinhas and Hezekiah had their arms slung over each other's shoulders, laughing over something. They halted

Nathan reeled on his feet. "*Shalom*, Pinhas. Hezekiah."

The rebel leader appeared unperturbed, an impressive feat, as he surely hadn't expected to find Nathan in Rumah, attending synagogue. That's because Nathan was supposed to be away for another week. Only Herod had called the hunt off early.

Pinhas stared at Nathan opened-mouthed. Nathan gave his friend a hard look. "Don't tell me you've joined them?"

The stonemason stood taller. "*The Lord has said, I will deliver you out of the hand of the wicked, and I will redeem you out of the hand of the oppressor.*" Pinhas quoted from the prophet, Jeremiah.

"Don't do this," Nathan implored his friend.

Pinhas wavered. "I...I—"

"Turn back while you can, *traitor*," Hezekiah said.

Nathan gritted his teeth against the insult and kept

his focus on Pinhas. "Would you leave Martha husbandless and baby Simon fatherless?"

Hezekiah laid his hand on Pinhas' arm. "Remember what the Lord says, '*I will preserve the fatherless. And let the widows trust in me*'."

Pinhas exchanged a troubled look between them. What was Nathan supposed to say to that? There was much about Hezekiah he admired. He was a devout man of faith who feared the Lord. It was easy to see why others listened and followed him.

Hezekiah's present suffering would only increase his fame. Normally fastidious about his appearance, the rebel leader's unkempt beard, stained clothing, and tired eyes spoke of a man fighting to stay one step ahead of his enemies. He smelled of sweat and dirt. Nathan imagined three weeks on horseback had left him looking equally weary and rumpled. How had they come to this? His anger drained away. "Hear me out," he said. "Turn Judas over to the Sanhedrin and you will all be free to return home to your families."

Hezekiah frowned. "I pray the Lord forgives you." He walked on.

Pinhas lowered his eyes and followed Hezekiah.

The sunny day became black as night to Nathan.

Alexandra woke up alone in her bed. The tent was cold without Nathan there to warm it. Time had crawled by as she waited for him to return from hunting the bandits. *Please help him to find Lydia. Please keep him safe.*

The sound of the goats bawling to be fed and milked —a job she was in no hurry to get to— almost made her miss her brother, James. He woke up as grumpy as the goats, but his irascibility had the merit of sometimes making her smile.

She laid her palm on her flat stomach. Married for four months, she had hoped to be with child by now. *Spare me from a barren womb, Lord.* A woman could be forgiven many other failings. Besides, it was too soon to worry. "But I am worried," she confessed to the heavens.

The goats' cries grew louder. Alexandra sighed, threw back the covers and crawled out of bed. Shivering against the cold, she donned her warmest tunic and stepped outside the tent. She studied the idle outlines of the half-finished stone house. Pinhas refused to complete the work, resisting her father-in-law's friendly overtures. Joseph's attempts to make peace with his neighbors had proved equally fruitless. He gave up the task, saying a colony of lepers would find a warmer welcome in Rumah than the family would right now.

She tipped her head back and sought solace in the beauty of the crisp, blue sky. *Lord, why? Nathan and his family are such good people.*

She rubbed her arms and made her way across the yard. The goats heard her coming and their bleating grew more insistent. She stopped outside the mud house turned stable. Not particularly convinced she'd meet with any more success at milking the goats today than she had yesterday, or the day before that, or the day before that. She squared her shoulders, opened the door and stepped inside.

"Baaah, to you, fool beasts." She plugged her nose. "Phew...and you are extra smelly today."

She grabbed a rake and mucked the soiled straw into

one corner. Ignoring the goats butting up against her, she put down fresh bedding, filled the water trough, poured sour-smelling grain into the manger, and the easy work was done.

She eyed the goats with disfavor, sighed, and placed a stool next to Blossom. "Good old girl," she said running her hand over the goat's white, bristly fur. She set a bowl under the animal. A few massaging strokes of her fingers and the swish, swish of liquid hitting pottery mixed with the munch, munch of the goats chewing their food.

Finished with docile Blossom, Alexandra turned her scowl on her arch nemesis, a feisty she-goat bearing a distinctive patch of white on its nose. Everyone called the goat Star. Everyone except her. She pointed a warning finger at the creature. "You be good today, Jezebel."

Moving ever so slowly, Alexandra pushed the stool and milk dish into position. Prepared with a new strategy today, she reached into her pocket and eased out a chunk of honeycomb. "Here, Jezebel. This ought to distract you, Spawn of Satan." Slipping the bribe into the goat's mouth, she cautiously took her seat and moved her hand closer and closer to the nearest udder.

Like a dog digging at fleas, the goat lifted her hind leg and batted at her. A sharp hoof dinged her fingers. "*Ow.* Look what you've done." She sucked at a stinging cut.

So much for today's plan.

Drawing a calming breath, she laid a hand on the goat's side. Using her shoulder to block the goat's hind leg, the way Nathan had taught her, she reached under the goat. Jezebel turned and kicked. The powerful hooves hit Alexandra in the chest, knocking her backward off the stool. She landed hard on her back at the same time she saw Jezebel's feet land in the pottered bowl, spilling Blossom's milk into the hay. "*Drat!*"

"Are you all right?"

Startled she sat halfway up. "*Ouch.*" Covering the small knot of pain in her chest, she flopped back into the hay. "You're home."

"Lie still," Nathan said, crossing the room.

She rolled her eyes. "How much of my inept display did you witness?" Most likely he'd seen enough to confirm the fact she was a helpless ninny when it came to animals.

Nathan knelt down beside her. "And here I thought you'd be happy to see me." Though he teased, concern clouded his eyes. "I hate to think about the bruises you're going to have."

She smiled half-heartedly. "I'll be fine. I'm more embarrassed than hurt." She touched the back of her hand to his face. "I am happy to see you, but just not under these...ah, circumstances." And wasn't that much more dignified than saying she'd been outsmarted by a four-legged, cud-chewing she-devil.

Nathan kissed her forehead. "It's not your fault." He pointed a finger at guilty animal. "One more trick out of you, Jezebel, and you are going to find yourself the guest of honor at a family feast."

Alexandra grimaced. "Jezebel? You heard that, huh? I thought I was being so clever, giving her the honeycomb."

Nathan made a face. "The foolish beast is too stubborn for her own good." He looked back at Alexandra and frowned. No doubt thinking Jezebel and his wife were quite a pair.

She held out her hands. "Could you help me up? I'm

finding it hard to carry on a dignified conversation with goats wandering around my head."

Nathan smiled. He scooped her off the ground as though she weighed nothing, righted the stool, set her down, and proceeded to brush the hay from her clothes. A goat bumped Alexandra in the back. Nathan shooed it away.

She twined her fingers together. "I have a confession to make."

The hand rubbing over her back slowed. "It sounds serious."

"I think you should know..." she blew at the stray wisps of hair tickling her nose "...I hate goats." The silky strands settled back onto her face.

"Is that so?" Nathan tucked the renegade curls behind her ear. "You could take charge of the turtle-doves."

"Start small and work my way up to goats? Is that it?"

Nathan smiled. "Yes. Or we could hire more help."

She knew this was coming. She sighed and dug her fingernail at the miniscule pieces of chaff sticking to her tunic. "Yes...I suppose you should."

"You are good at stitchwork." Nathan's hand covered hers. "Mary loves her new apron."

She made herself look up and smile. While she appreciated his attempt to console her, she wouldn't have him feeling sorry for her. "I will not give up trying new tasks. Some needlework is fine. But too much of it makes me cross-eyed." And didn't she sound peevish and immature? She couldn't help it. There had to be something more useful she could contribute to the family and to the running of the farm, she just hadn't found her role here. But she would.

Finished brushing her clothes, Nathan walked over to the door, stuck his head around the corner, and yelled for Mary and Sapphira.

Alexandra covered her face. "Did you have to do that? I'd rather the others didn't hear I let the goats get the best of me. *Again.*"

"The girls can finish the milking." Nathan walked back to her side. "If you are feeling up to a walk, there's something I want to show you."

Mary came bounding through the door. "Nathan, you're home!" Not waiting for an explanation, she rushed over and kissed Nathan on the cheek.

Nathan hugged the young girl. "*Shalom,* to you, sweet lamb," he said, giving his sister an indulgent smile.

Mary turned to her. "*Shalom,* Alexandra."

Alexandra tried to stand. "*Ow.*" A stab of pain made her sit back down. She pressed her hands to her chest. "Dumb goats," she muttered.

Nathan's warm hand massaged her neck. "Perhaps you should go lie down."

Mary squatted down beside her. "What's the matter, poor dear?"

Alexandra waved off the attention. "It's nothing."

Sapphira came through the barn door, followed by Rhoda.

"Nathan." Rhoda nodded briskly. "Did the girls do something wrong?"

"*Shalom* to you, Rhoda," Nathan said. "It's nice to see you, too." Rhoda made an impatient face. Nathan laughed and went on. "The girls, I am sure, have been nothing but angelic."

Mary and Sapphira giggled.

Nathan smiled and winked at them. "It is the goats

who are in a pesky mood. They are extra frisky this morning. I think it best to have Mary and Sapphira finish the milking."

Alexandra fidgeted under Rhoda's appraising gaze. Her aggravation with her daughter-in-law showed clear in her weary eyes. The older woman wiped her flour-covered hands on a rag. "Very well," she said. "Sapphira can manage alone. I need Mary's help in the house."

Rhoda shooed Mary out the door ahead of her. Alexandra sighed. Nathan squeezed her shoulder. "Don't let Rhoda's bad mood bother you. She is easily put out of sorts."

A truth Alexandra understood too well, as annoying her mother-in-law was the sole task she excelled at. The worst of it was that Rhoda's disgust had merit. Like now for instance. There was much work to be done—the goats' accusing baas were growing more impatient the longer they waited to be relieved of the milk swelling their udders; a double portion of grain needed to be ground today in preparation for *Shabbat*; the olive trees needed pruning—yet the family had been called away from their chores to cluck over her.

Alexandra forced a bright smile onto her face. "I think it's time we get out of Sapphira's way." She addressed the young maid directly, "I'm sorry you have to clean up my mess. I promise to make it up to you."

The servant's cheeks blushed prettily. "I'm glad to be of service, good woman." She dipped her face respectfully and was turning her attention to the goats when Nathan stopped her.

"Sapphira."

The girl glanced back at him and blushed brighter.

"Yes?"

"Leave the soiled hay for me to clean up," he told her.

"Thank you, Nathan."

Every jealous bone in Alexandra's body took exception to the simple exchange. Clearing her throat louder than necessary, she said, "Nathan, you had something you wanted to show me?"

Nathan sat down on his haunches, so they were at eye level. "The walk will be too much for you. It will wait."

She touched her sore chest. He might be right. Opening her mouth to agree, she bit back the words upon spying Sapphira's pleased smile. The annoyingly competent slave-maid was kneeling beside Jezebel, and, of course, the horrid goat stood perfectly motionless for the girl. The rhythmic hiss, hiss of milk splashing into the pottered bowl set Alexandra's teeth on edge.

Alexandra suspected that if she were with child she wouldn't feel half so threatened by the strong, capable slave maiden. The problem was that Sapphira possessed all the qualities a farmer could hope to find in a wife. With her generous hips and budding breasts, the girl looked the picture of fertility. Sapphira would, no doubt, conceive a child on her wedding night and bear her happy husband many, many sons. Drat the girl.

And now to top it all off, she could hear herself sounding hateful and mean. Nathan had not given her any cause to worry where Sapphira was concerned, instead going out of his way to reassure Alexandra.

That might all change if she remained childless.

Nathan led Lex out of the barn and into the orchard. White blossoms blanketed the olive trees like freshly fallen snow. Sheltered under the ivory canopy, his sore heart took solace in the fragrant smells, the chirping birdsong, and the gentle stroke of the breeze brushing his skin. The peacefulness of the place made him want to stay there forever.

"Paradise couldn't be more beautiful," Lex said in hushed awe.

"Paradise indeed," he agreed. "I was hoping I'd be home before budding season passed. This is my favorite time of the year. I wanted to share it with you. I am almost tempted to pull up our tent and pitch it here."

"Oh, yes. It sounds wonderful."

He smiled. His refined, highborn wife was at war with the goats and she was excited at the prospect of sleeping in an olive orchard. God couldn't be overly angry with him, to give him Lex.

She glanced up at him. "How did the hunt go?"

"It was totally fruitless, until this morning...when I ran into Hezekiah as I was leaving Rumah." Lex's gray eyes widened. He shared what had happened.

"What do we do now?"

"We?" He wriggled his brows at her. Lex laughed. At least, one aspect of his life was headed in the right direction. Lex was blooming to life before his eyes. "We will need to find new buyers for our olives because no one in Rumah, or Galilee for that matter, will purchase a drop of oil from our orchard. We'll have to sell it to the Greeks."

He drew her to a stop beside a row of saplings growing in the heart of the olive grove. A gentle breeze arose. Iridescent petals floated past them. Lex reached her delicate fingers to the flowers. "The people here seem extra-leery of gentiles. But you and your father think very differently. Is it because of your time in the army?"

"No, it is because of my mother."

"Your mother?" Lex gave him her full attention.

"She was not from here. She was from Gamala."

"Your mother was from Decapolis? So she was used to living beside pagans." A mix of Jews and pagans lived in a group of cities located on the other side of the Sea of Galilee and the River Jordan in a region called Decapolis. Curiosity danced in Lex's eyes. "But how did she end up in Rumah?"

It had been a long time since Nathan had talked with anyone about his mother, who hadn't let his father get away with anything. His father never minded, saying he had won the most important arguments when she agreed to marry him. He smiled thinking about his father as a young man. "Like me, my father got it in his mind to leave the olive farm. He worked as a fisherman on the Sea of Galilee. He met my mother in the fish market, wooed her with moonlit boat rides, convinced her to marry him, and to come and live here as a farmer's wife."

Lex studied him. "You look like her, don't you?"

"According to my father I am the very image of my mother."

She touched his face. "She must have been very beautiful."

Nathan inhaled deeply. He'd been trying hard to keep his hands to himself because he didn't trust himself to stop touching Lex once he started. Control stripped away, he skimmed his fingers up the length of Lex's long, elegant neck. She closed her eyes and tipped her head back, exposing the soft flesh edging her jaw. He touched his tongue to her warm skin and stroked her slim waist.

He heard his name being called and groaned. Lex whimpered. He tried to step away, but Lex wrapped her arms around him. Desperation heated her whisper. "I can't wait until night. Take me somewhere private. I want to join with you."

Blood pounding in his ears, he gasped, "I missed you, Lex. I missed everything about you." With great remorse, he gently set her away. And just in time too.

Timothy came bounding through the trees. "Nathan," he called excitedly. Nathan held out an arm and Timothy scrambled his way up Nathan's side and hugged him hard around the neck. "Guess what?"

"What, monkey?" Nathan tousled the boy's fine hair.

"We have company." Timothy turned his grin on Alexandra. "Your father and brother have come to see you."

Lex's face drained of color.

CHAPTER 18

Nathan stepped out of the orchard and looked across the grassy valley to the low knoll beyond. The whole family stood outside the tents, fussing over Simeon and James Onias. Timothy was already halfway down the hill, racing toward the others. "Any guess as to why your father is here?" he asked Lex, only she was no longer beside him. "Lex?" He turned around. At first glance he didn't see her. She stood half-hidden behind the gnarled trunk of an ancient olive tree chewing nervously at her lip and staring hard at her father and brother. "Lex," he called a little louder.

She flinched, then hurried to catch up. Stopping beside him, her eyes remained fixed on the yard. "I wish the house was built," she said.

Finishing the house was at the top of the long list of projects needing his attention. Entertaining visitors meant more delay. That was merely irritating. Simeon Onias bearing witness to his daughter's present living conditions cut deeply. "He should have warned us he was coming," Nathan said, more sharply than he meant to.

Lex wrung her hands, her eyes haunted. "I can't imagine what possessed my father to travel through Galilee alone. Again. James must have been frightened half to death."

Nathan put his arm around her shoulder and rubbed his hand up and down her arm. "Whatever the trouble is, we will manage it together."

Lex sighed and offered him a weak smile. "It's strange...my father coming here, don't you think?"

Nathan scratched his chin and peered across the field at his father-in-law. "This makes it twice now your father has ventured into Galilee. I doubt he's here to hunt for religious relics." That was the excuse Simeon Onias had used last time. "Let's go find out what he's up to now."

Setting out across the field, Nathan saw Simeon and James weren't alone. The bald slave stood off to the side, tending a handful of donkeys. One of the animals was loaded down with mesh sacks and straw baskets. A young woman was traveling with them as well. It was probably too much to hope Simeon had somehow managed to secure Lydia's release.

Lex slowed. "Elizabeth. What is she doing here?" Her breath hitched. "Elizabeth and James must have married."

"You don't sound pleased."

"Her father and my father are cousins. They wanted James and Elizabeth to marry, but Father and Cousin Nehonya have been feuding. Besides, I didn't think Elizabeth was of age yet."

Nathan studied the new bride more closely. Of average height and weight, there was nothing remarkable about her, except she looked young. Very young. "How old is she?" he asked.

"Twelve, or thirteen, at the most."

Nathan winced on the girl's behalf.

They crossed the yard and joined the others.

Nathan forced a smile. "*Shalom* to you, Father Simeon. James. We could hardly believe our eyes."

Simeon Onias's frown deepened. "Nathan of Rumah, I would have a private word with you."

No greeting. No acknowledgement of his daughter. No pleasantries. *Rot the old prune.* Nathan gave his father-in-law a hard look. "What brings you here?"

"What brought me here?" Simeon mocked, sarcasm dripping from each word. "I received word you have joined forces with Herod. Something my dear children knew but failed to mention." The unhappy man narrowed his eyes at Alexandra and James. Lex blushed. James turned and walked back to the donkeys.

"Blame me," Nathan said. "Asking for Herod's help was my decision. I thought it the quickest, surest way to find your daughter." Simeon's complaint didn't come as a surprise. Pharisees whole-heartedly resented Antipater for interfering in Temple matters. Antipater's recent successes must be making them even more nervous.

"You are to end all contact with Herod," Simeon ordered. "Leave the thinking to me, farmer, from now on."

Give me patience, Nathan prayed, biting his tongue for the sake of the others. Glancing around, he saw that Lex and Elizabeth were exchanging uncomfortable frowns. Mary and Sapphira sidled closer and closer to Rhoda. Fidgety as always, his step-mother wiped and re-wiped her hands in her apron. Timothy played happily in the sand at his mother's feet, oblivious to the tension.

Then Nathan looked toward his father. Joseph tipped his head in the direction of the largest tent. Food and drink might—or might not—serve as a palliative to Simeon's bad mood. Nonetheless Joseph, who was unfailingly polite and hospitable, would do his best to placate their unfriendly guests.

Nathan held out a hand toward the tent. "Come and sit. We can discuss the matter over the morning meal."

At the mention of food Timothy whooped loudly, dumped the sand from his hands and threw himself at Nathan.

Simeon reared back as though coming face to face with a striking snake. Thankfully, Lex intercepted Timothy before he could climb monkey-like up Nathan's side.

"Why? I never. I..." Simeon Onias spluttered.

Lex whispered a few words in Timothy's ear and the boy grinned and went and hid behind Rhoda. Nathan smiled his thanks at Lex.

She in turn smiled brightly at her father. "Welcome to my new home." At Simeon's glowering frown, she moved quickly on to her father's cousin. "Elizabeth, you are married? This is so unexpected." The new bride blushed.

Nathan must have met the girl at his and Lex's wedding, but he couldn't recall her specifically.

Simeon Onias pushed Elizabeth aside to scowl ferociously at his daughter. "I see your manners have already been corrupted. Go find a proper head covering, you Jezebel."

Lex's face and neck turned bright red.

Nathan could hardly believe his ears. He stepped between Lex and her father and put his finger in the man's face. "Alexandra is my wife and answers to no man but me."

Simeon smirked and something about the smug smile raised the hairs on the back of Nathan's neck.

Joseph clapped for their attention. "My home is a house of peace. Come, let us eat."

A cloud of awkwardness overshadowing them, they headed inside the tent. Basins of water and clean towels were set out for the travelers. Simeon, James, and Elizabeth washed the journey's dust from their hands and feet. Timothy helped Nathan tie back the tent flaps to allow the sun in. Mary and Lex set extra straw mats around the large woven oval that served as the table. Rhoda and Sapphira raced to and fro, arms loaded with stone-carved bowls filled with dates, bread, and olive oil.

Nathan turned to check on their guests and cringed as Sapphira collided with the Pharisee.

Knocked back a step, the man's face twisted with disgust. "Fool, slave! Watch your step!"

Sapphira burst into tears.

"Hold on." Nathan moved to intercede, but Lex was quicker.

She stepped between her father and Sapphira. "It was my fault," Lex spoke hurriedly. "I should have been paying better attention."

Simeon turned his wrath on his daughter. "None of your excuses, Alexandra! You were taught how to run a proper household. You need to keep a tight rein on your slaves or they will take advantage."

"Yes, Father," Lex murmured.

Simeon fussed with the thick folds of his richly embroidered garments. "Don't stand there gaping at me.

Come and help straighten my robe."

Lex patted Sapphira's arm comfortingly, and then knelt before her father, making a production of plucking and pulling at nonexistent wrinkles.

If Nathan ground his teeth together any harder they would shatter. Lex had said her life wasn't always easy. Hard is what it had been. Too damnably hard. How many times had she had her ears and heart blistered because she'd stepped in the way of her father's wrath on behalf of her brother and sister, like she was doing now for Sapphira? How often had she sacrificed her pride and feelings on the altar of Simeon Onias's self-righteous tirades? Was it any wonder she was skittish about speaking her mind?

Not about to allow the puffed-up peacock to lord it over Lex even one more moment, Nathan walked over and knelt down beside her. Her eyes widened in surprise. He winked back mischievously, gently pushed her hands aside, and tugged hard on the hem of Simeon's expensive robe.

Simeon batted at his tunic. "Enough! I wanted my clothes righted. Not torn from my back." Sticking his nose in the air, he walked away.

"Sit down, already," Rhoda admonished, claiming the attention.

Lex blew out a tremulous breath. Nathan stood and offered her his hand. "You are brave as a lioness defending her cubs," he whispered, helping her to her feet.

"I'm sorry your family has to suffer my father's impatience," she said, barely able to meet his eyes.

Her discomfort killed Nathan. He made a promise, "The Lord as my witness, you will never suffer another cruel word from your father. Not while I breathe."

Lex's small smile of gratitude pierced his heart all over again.

Joseph waved everyone to the table. "Come and eat." Simeon sat to the right of Joseph in the place of honor. Nathan took the seat opposite his father-in-law. James chose a spot as far away from his father as possible. James's young wife looked about uncertainly. Joseph offered Elizabeth a kind smile. "Sit next to your husband, child."

Frowning, she circled around the table and kneeled down beside Simeon Onias.

Nathan's jaw dropped. Elizabeth and Simeon Onias were man and wife?

Honest as ever, Timothy blurted out what everyone else was thinking, "Alexandra's father is really old. He should have married someone his own age."

Elizabeth stared at her lap, her cheeks blotchy and red.

Nathan's appetite deserted him. It wasn't just because of Elizabeth's tender age. Marrying daughters off shortly after they started their monthly flow, when there could be little doubt about virginity, was a common enough practice. But giving a young girl to a nasty old, dried-up stick of a man like Simeon struck Nathan as the height of cruelty. It was the equivalent of forcing Mary to wed an uncle, and a hard-hearted, ill-tempered uncle at that.

"Merciful angels!" Simeon scowled in disgust. "You'd think I murdered someone, the way you all are frowning at me."

"Father," Lex's voice shook.

"No more of your impertinence, Alexandra." The fussy man rearranged his legs. "I get enough of that from

Elizabeth. My wife talks enough for ten foolish women, but she is learning to keep silent."

Nathan squeezed Lex's elbow. What he wanted to do was plant his fist in Simeon Onias's hateful mouth.

Lex chewed her lip a moment. "But...but...I thought you and Cousin Nehonya weren't speaking."

"Stop." Simeon held a hand up. "What has gotten into you, Alexandra? You are acting as headstrong as your fool brother."

"That's unfair of you, Father," James interrupted. "After all, Alexandra married the man you selected for her." Lex's brother aimed his bitter brown eyes at Nathan. "Father wanted useful sons-in-laws. Are you prepared to be useful?"

Nathan's suspicion that Simeon was up to something deepened. "If my conscience allows it," he said.

"James," Simeon warned.

The boy traced his fingers over his empty plate. "Father's angry with me. He promised cousin Nehonya I would marry Elizabeth. But I refused."

A collective gasp went up at the unthinkable rebellion. Fathers reigned supreme as the head of the household, and children, be they ten years old or thirty and ten, were duty-bound to obey their fathers.

Simeon scowled some more at his son. "My cousin insisted on a marriage between his family and mine as a condition for our reconciliation." Simeon shrugged. "So I married the girl."

"Reconciliation?" Lex looked between her father and brother. "I am happy to hear it. It is good news."

"Hold on, Sister," James drawled. "Before you get all misty-eyed over the fact we are one big, happy family again, you need to hear why father and cousin Nehonya have set their differences aside. They're scheming to make Father the next high priest."

"High priest?" Lex sat up straighter. "Is it true?" she asked Elizabeth. The child bride looked to Simeon for direction. The old prune's cheeks were puffed to the point of bursting.

"Is James teasing?" Mary asked.

"Truly?" Sapphira clapped delightedly. "My father will rejoice to have a righteous man sit as high priest."

Timothy hopped up from his mat and came and leaned on Nathan's shoulder. "Why do we need a new high priest? Did John Hyrcanus die?"

Rhoda shook her finger at Timothy. "John Hyrcanus is alive and well. Now, go back to your seat. Though heaven knows the man ought to be dead, eating all the rich food he does."

Nathan peeled Timothy's hands off his neck "Mind you mother, monkey," he said, and exchanged an incredulous look with his father. Was Simeon Onias addled? The Hasmonean family had reigned as high priests for the past one hundred and twenty years. It would take nothing less than war to unseat them.

"Cease your caterwauling!" Simeon Onias put his hands over his ears. The tent went silent. Simeon lowered his arms and leveled a withering look at James. "You have said more than enough."

"Does the boy speak true?" Nathan asked, hoping he'd misunderstood. "Surely, you're not entertaining the wild notion of becoming high priest?"

"Wild notion?" The pious man's mouth puckered. "My family owns the rightful claim to the office of high priest. My forefathers come from the line of Zadok, who was appointed high priest by King David. The

Hasmoeans and John Hyrcanus are common priests. My cousin and I mean to set matters right."

The argument had more than a little merit. The Pharisees had been at odds with the Sadducees for years over this very point. If not for his strong misgivings about his father-in-law, Nathan might have found the idea more to his liking. "Sapphira's father will not be the only one glad to hear it," he admitted with reluctance. "People are tired of the Hasmoeans' corrupt practices. If you can straddle the line between the Sadducee and Pharisee's camps..." a task Nathan feared his wily father-in-law would be more than able to perform "...you will find many in Galilee who will support you."

Simeon frowned at James. "Did any of what your sister's husband said penetrate your thick hide? People are tired of the Hasmoeans. What do you have to say to that?"

James rested his elbows on his knees and propped his chin in his hands. "I am tired of you, Father. What do you have to say to that?"

"Father. James." Lex pleaded.

"James," her brother mimicked. "You won't be so judgmental when you hear what Father wants from your husband."

Lex's eyes flashed and her spine stiffened. "My husband is a capable and quick-minded man, able to hold his own with the best and brightest of men." Nathan watched with admiration. Lex had never appeared more beautiful or more strong.

"Soldiers are useful creatures," Simeon agreed. Kneading the gray hair edging his long, wiry beard between his fingers, he studied Nathan for an uncomfortably long time. "You had quite the reputation as a soldier. It's said some called you the angel of death."

Nathan's blood went cold. "Hold your tongue, old man."

Simeon laughed. "Yes, I can see it's true. You do possess a dangerous side."

Nathan emitted a low growl. "You go too far." A steady hand landed on his arm.

"Nathan." Lex's soft plea cooled his anger.

"Tell us what you want," Joseph said.

Simeon cleared his throat. "I want your son to gather an army for me and lead them into battle against the Hasmoeans."

Temper reviving, Nathan barked, "Are you mad?"

"My cousin and I have purchased arms enough for one thousand men." Simeon raised his brows at Nathan. "Is that sane enough for you?"

"Wait, wait, wait." The tent went dark around Nathan. There were so many things wrong with what his father-in-law proposed he wasn't sure where to start. He took a deep breath. "Antipater has an army three times that size, filled with experienced soldiers. And don't forget the three Roman legions sitting in Syria, waiting to pounce at the first sign of rebellion. You can't—"

Simeon's fork clattered onto his plate. "Leave Antipater and Rome to me. You worry about raising an army."

Nathan pointed his finger at his father-in-law. "Stop your jabbering and listen. You thought wrong. I'm not a soldier. Find someone else to lead your army. I agreed to search for your daughter and nothing else. You will have no hope of getting Lydia back if you go to war against Antipater."

Simeon waved his hand. "I've received report she is with child. Judas the Zealot is welcome to keep the shameless wanton. She is of no use to me in that condition."

"With child?" Lex cried.

Nathan squeezed Lex's shoulder and shot a dirty look at Simeon. Did the man have one feeling bone in his body? Disparaging his blameless daughter so, and announcing her pregnancy as though reporting yesterday's gossip? And who was giving Simeon those reports? And why didn't Nathan know anything about it? He was sure of one thing. He wanted nothing to do with his father-in-law's intrigues and trickery. The sooner he set the old fool straight, the better.

"I promised to get Lydia back, and I will." Nathan worked to keep his voice calm. "And even if I wanted to lead your army, I couldn't. I promised my father I would not take up a sword again. That aside, I'm begging you to reconsider. Going to war against Antipater is a mistake."

"No. You are the one who needs to think again." Simeon pointed a bony finger at him. "Refuse to cooperate and you won't see another shekel of Alexandra's dowry. Hear me, Farmer. Say no to me, and I will beggar you and your family."

"Keep your money," Nathan bellowed. He surged to his feet, loosened the straps of his sandals, took them off, and slapped the heels against his palm. "Hear me, you old snake. I will walk naked through the streets of Jerusalem before I accept a crumb from you." He threw the sandals at his father-in-law's chest, repaying insult with insult. Simeon nearly toppled over backward, setting off a chorus of surprised cries.

Disgusted with himself for allowing his hateful father-in-law to get under his skin, Nathan did an about-face and marched out of the tent.

CHAPTER 19

Alexandra watched the only happiness she'd ever known disappear with Nathan as he stormed out of the tent. She would gladly sacrifice ten lifetimes' worth of joy to save Nathan and his family from her father's schemes. His promise to beggar Nathan's family was not an empty threat.

Her father truly believed he should be high priest. Over the years, he had frequently discussed intrigue and strategy with influential men regarding how best to take his rightful place. He'd met secretly, a time or two, with Antipater, but had come away sorely disappointed.

Leave it to her father to take the drastic action of raising his own army. Rigid and single-minded in his purity practices, he would seek the office of high priest with equal passion. If she believed for one moment that her father was acting for the sake of the Lord and the Holy Scriptures, he might have gained her sympathy. But she knew all too well that he was motivated by his overblown pride.

Alexandra rose to her feet to go after Nathan.

"Daughter." The sound of her father's voice chilled

like a blast of frost from the mouth of God. She sat back on her heels and forced herself to look at her father.

His gray eyes sat like lumps of wet charcoal in his face. "I am disappointed in your husband. I had great hopes for him."

Her face heated. "Nathan is a good, honest man."

Joseph, Rhoda, Mary, Timothy, and Sapphira joined her in defending Nathan.

"Hold your tongues and listen," Father ordered. The full weight of his contempt landed back on her. "The olive farmer didn't hear me out. I have another offer to make. It concerns his marriage to you."

She lifted her hand to her constricted throat. *Please, please, Lord,* she begged *don't let him say what I'm afraid he is going to say.*

Her father's mouth turned down. "I'd rather have my own man heading my army. But I have other options. My brother is ready to leave Egypt and throw his money and influence my way."

Alexandra groaned. Uncle Jacob made the pilgrimage to Jerusalem every few years. Every bit as pompous as her father, Jacob had a huge potbelly. She blurted out her disbelief, "You want Nathan to divorce me, so you can give me in marriage to Uncle Jacob? I thought you despised the idea of uncles and nieces marrying?"

James laughed harshly. "How is that for throwing away one's beliefs? Aren't you proud to call such a man Father?"

Alexandra winced. The barb was as sharp as it was apt. Everyone in Judea knew Simeon Onias had left the Sadducees to join the Pharisees and thereafter railed loudly against the Sadducees' corrupt ways. He was among the chief critics of the Sadducees' practice of intermarriage between uncles and nieces, a cold-blooded tactic for keeping wealth and power in the hands of the few. It made the marriage he was proposing that much more hypocritical.

Lightheaded, Alexandra clutched her stomach. "Nathan won't divorce me."

Her father plucked at his beard. "He will if he knows what's good for him." He narrowed his eyes at her. "You aren't with child, are you?" He read the despondency in her eyes. "No? Good. Good," he said with satisfaction. "Jacob wants to try to get sons on you. Sarah just delivered daughter number eight. I imagine my brother probably wants to jump off a cliff about now."

Lex licked her parched lips. "Jacob is going to divorce Sarah?"

Her father made a sound of disgust. "No. My brother claims he is fond of the old carp. You will be Jacob's second wife."

Her father turned and addressed Joseph. "If you and your son want to be rid of me, all Nathan has to do is divorce Alexandra. I will give you a generous settlement and leave your family to live in peace."

"Nathan doesn't want to divorce Alexandra," Mary protested, her voice rife with confusion.

Lex wished the problem was so simple. Oh, she knew Nathan would kick hard against divorcing her. But, in the end, what choice would he have? He couldn't let his family come to ruin. She wouldn't let it happen. Hugging herself, she rocked in place, already mourning the loss of her beautiful, kind husband.

The meal over and the tent put to rights, Alexandra

went searching for Nathan. She found him at the far end of the orchard, climbing an old, twisted olive tree. The ancient tree boasted a knobby trunk half as wide as it was tall, capped with a mushroom-shaped canopy of bright, white flowers.

Nathan leaned out over a craggy limb and hacked at a flower-lined bough with a short hooked blade. The spindly branch tumbled to the ground. "I'm sorry for deserting you," he said by way of greeting her. "I let my temper get the best of me."

She picked up a cast-off sprig loaded with blossoms. "Should you be trimming the trees in your present...ah, mood? Look at all the flowers."

Nathan reached over his head, snapped off a white bud, and twirled it between his fingers. "One olive is born for every twenty flowers that bloom. It goes against sense, but by cutting away branches and making openings for the sun, I'll get more olives. The old women hereabouts tell the tale of the olive tree that talked to its farmer and told him, 'keep my brother away from me and take his share from me.' My father has a saying, too. 'One branch allowed access to full sunlight will produce more fruit than two that touch.'" Tossing the flower away, he scanned the branches over his head. "The best time for pruning is right after the harvest. But I was too busy to get to it this year."

Nathan sliced another limb free. The bough twirled in small circles as it fell and came to rest at her feet. She toyed at it with her sandal. "It's because my family's woes distracted you from your work. And now my father is threatening you. And I don't see any way out of this mess."

Nathan jumped to the ground and stood before her.

"I plan to plant more trees. But it will take eight or ten years for new trees to bear fruit. We will have to live frugally until then." Shadow and light played over the sharp planes of his concerned face.

Her throat tightened. "You can't believe I would mind?"

"I mind. You having to live poor wasn't in the contract I made with your father."

She hid her face in her hands. "Father says he will give you a generous settlement if you divorce me."

"He what? Why?" Nathan fingers circled her wrists and he gently pulled her hands into his. "Never mind, I've seen how his mind works. He uses his children like game pieces. He wants to marry you off to someone else, doesn't he?"

"My uncle." A shudder went through her. "It might be for the best."

"Not for *me*. And certainly not for *you*."

"What about your family. What about Timothy and Mary?"

His hands squeezed hers. "They'll fare just fine. Rhoda will be unhappy about losing Sapphira. We'll have to send the slave maiden home if we can't work out some other agreement with her father." He smiled and winked. "I don't expect you will miss Sapphira overmuch, will you?"

Alexandra's face warmed.

Nathan turned grave. "It will mean more work for you."

"I don't mind." She moved closer to him. "I despise what my father is doing to you."

"Don't worry about me. I know how to be poor." His eyes softened. "Trying to learn to live without you...now, that would ruin me." He wrapped his arms around her and buried his mouth in her hair. "I love you, Lex. Tell me you are happy to throw in your lot with a poor farmer."

He actually believed she would choose riches over him? She ran her hands over his arms and back, memorizing the lines and angles of his well-formed body. Then she tried to imagine herself returning to the stifling confines of her life in Jerusalem. "Nathan, I will live in a tent for the rest of my life, and count myself blessed above all women if you are there with me." She swallowed back tears. "I love you. And I adore your family. And I love this farm...well maybe not the goats and Jezebel, but everything else."

She felt Nathan's lips curve with a smile. "We could serve goat tonight for dinner and wish Jezebel and your father both to Hades."

"Jezebel deserves better," she protested half-heartedly. Her voice fell to a whisper. "I wouldn't regret the loss of the money one bit, except it had the virtue of making up for all the trouble I've caused you."

Nathan leaned back and looked her in the eyes. "Your father's money means nothing to me." He traced his finger along her jaw and then over her heart. "You, and you alone, are my prize."

Her husband valued *her*. The thought amazed and warmed her. But, she couldn't fully enjoy it. "Father won't be happy with us."

Nathan turned grim. "Simeon Onias can't return home soon enough to please me."

That night Lex and Nathan moved into the large

tent, leaving the small tent to James, Elizabeth, and Father.

Her head pillowed on her arm, Lex lay facing Nathan. Beyond his shoulder, dim shadows cast by oil lamps wavered ghost-like across the tent's weathered walls. Rhoda and Joseph lay on their backs, side by side, holding hands and talking over the day's events. Timothy, Mary, and Sapphira were stretched out on their stomachs, facing one another, playing at a guessing game.

Lex imagined the mood in the small tent was dismal.

Her family and Nathan's couldn't be more different. "Your father's stoicism would put the patience of Job to shame," she said, marveling at her father-in-law's serene demeanor in the face of her father's ferocious, foul mood.

Nathan's warm laugh ruffled her hair. "I made my father angry enough once that he actually swore."

"No."

"It shocked me contrite. For a day or two, anyway." Nathan's smile dimmed. "A few hours in your father's company has given me new respect for you. It's amazing he has any friends, or that he ever speaks to women, given his attitude."

"Father is highly respected among his peers." She grinned at the sour face Nathan made. "You and your father are the strange ones. I've never seen men treat women with as much esteem as you two. Mary is blessed to have you as her brother."

"Don't praise me for doing what is right. Besides, I had a good example. My father never speaks disparagingly to women. Or of them, for that matter." He lifted his hand and tucked a stray strand of hair behind her ear. "I've listened to the elders read the story of

Eve tempting Adam to eat the forbidden fruit dozens of times. And, I've considered, at length, the teaching that all women are evil seductresses, ready to commit adultery or fornication, but I couldn't find it in the scriptures. My father and I have debated the matter at synagogue with the elders, but our view gets little consideration."

Lex could only blink. He kissed her on the nose. "I know. It's very presumptuous of olive farmers to argue with the teachers of Israel over the Law of Moses." He shrugged. "Weren't Abraham and King David shepherds? I don't believe the Lord holds my lowly status against me."

She found her tongue. "My father would turn purple if you said such things in his hearing."

Nathan snickered. "Your father is highly learned. I'm sure he'd talk circles around me."

She covered his mouth with her fingers. "You mistake me. I would enjoy hearing you argue scripture with my father."

He blew a puff of air through his lips, tickling her palm, then tugged her hand down. "Lord forbid. I learned not to waste my breath on men like him."

She snuggled closer to Nathan. "I'm glad you are here to warm me. The nights have been long and cold without you."

"Lex?" She could hear the need in his voice. "Remember what I said about wanting to pitch the tent in the orchard?"

Desire spiraled through her. "We don't need a tent. Tents are for the old."

"Amen," Rhoda said loudly.

Nathan laughed. "I think we're being invited to

leave."

"God bless you, children," Joseph called after them as they scooped up their blankets and tumbled out of the tent.

Hands clasped, they raced across the field, laughing and whooping like a pair of demented hyenas. They barely made it past the first row of trees when Nathan dragged her to a stop. She looped her arms around his neck and practically inhaled him whole, kissing his lips, chin, and neck. Nathan's hands and mouth were everywhere. Limbs hopelessly entwined, they toppled over.

Nathan rolled on top of her, pinned her to the ground, and kissed her breathless.

She pushed at his chest. "Wait...wait," she was laughing so hard her sides ached. "Let's go deeper into the orchard, before...before..."

He shifted his weight to his elbow and peered down at her. "You are too tempting to resist, my lovely wife. I see you and I want you." The light of the rising moon highlighted the bold lines of his face. His warm breaths purled against her ear. The ends of his dark, curly hair brushed over her cheeks.

A shiver went through her. "Come, my husband. Come have your fill of me."

The moon stood high above the tops of the trees by the time Alexandra and Nathan spread their blankets out in the heart of the orchard. Nathan drew the covers over them and wrapped his body around hers. Warm for the first time in weeks, she fell into a deep sleep.

Hours later she woke up shivering.

Nathan awoke with a start. "No!" he cried, jumping to his feet. He slipped and almost fell.

Alexandra sat up. The white puffs of her breath clung to her mouth like the bands of a death shroud. A thick layer of icy white frost coated the ground, rocks, and trees. Olive blossoms twinkled like costly diamonds against the frigid blue sky. Eerie silence had replaced the birdsong.

The icy cold sliced to the quick as she realized what she was looking at.

A killer frost.

CHAPTER 20

Nathan reached up and snapped off a frozen bud from the gnarled tree. He held the delicate blossom out on his open palm and watched the ice melt away. The edges of the white flower were curled and browned. His eyes told him what his heart already knew—this year's olive crop was a total loss. He threw the dead flower back at the tree. "Lord, why?" he groaned. "Why this year?"

Lex hugged him from behind. "Nathan, you're frightening me."

He turned into his wife's embrace, wrapped his arms around her, and laid his face on her head. "Forgive me. I'm frustrated. We'll have to rethink where we go from here." He pulled back and looked at Lex. "I won't change my mind about your father's offer."

"Of course not. But...but, I feel guilty you and your family will have to suffer. When you could solve all your problems by divorcing—"

He kissed her, pressing and pressing until she surrendered and kissed him back. Satisfied he had her attention, he released her. "No more talk of divorce. Are we agreed?"

Eyes gray and large as a pair of plump doves, she nod-ded.

"Good," he said. "As long as we're together, every-thing else will work itself out." He took hold of her hand. "Let's go break the bad news to the others."

Later that day Nathan steered Royal to the right, ceding the center of the narrow dirt road to the noisy donkey caravan kicking up a trail of dust on its weekly trek between the Galilean capital of Sepphoris and the small towns and villages lining the Sea of Galilee. His father had sent him out, ostensibly to assess the reach of the killing frost—the damage appeared limited to a swath of valleys north and south of his farm—but Na-than's real purpose was to have a word with Herod about Simeon Onias's damnable plan to form an army.

Nathan waved a greeting to the last of the traders and licked his lips, savoring the sour, salty remains of the pickled fish he'd purchased during a quick foray into Magdala to ask after Herod's whereabouts. The newly minted governor split his time between a small out-post on the Sea of Galilee and a run-down fortress to the west, in Sepphoris. Herod was currently in Sepphoris. The nominal capital of Galilee, it was the only sizable city in the region, numbering around eight thousand people.

A few miles short of his destination, Nathan rode past the watchful eyes of the inhabitants of Nazareth. He pulled Royal to a stop at the sight of a tall, blond-headed man ducking out the door of a low-slung house. "Kadar," Nathan called out to Antipater's oversized bodyguard. "You are the last person in the world I'd expect to find in Nazareth."

The giant man walked toward Nathan, mischief shining in his pale blue eyes. "All hail the mighty olive farmer."

Nathan made a face.

Kadar's rumbling laugh scared off the group of curious children trailing after the giant soldier. The big man gave a bronze coin to a boy bravely holding the reins to his midnight-black stallion, Satan. Kadar led the horse over to Nathan. "Herod sent me down here to hire some of the local craftsmen to make furniture and pottery and baskets and any other items the town can supply to keep a working fortress going."

Kadar nodded at a group of women drawing water from a well. "It's a good bet Nazareth has never seen the type of money Herod is spending."

Nathan shifted in his saddle. "It's because the few hundred people calling Nazareth home have never come across the force that is Herod on a mission." Given a decrepit fortress, Antipater's youngest son would work and work on the garrison until it outshone his brothers' strongholds.

Kadar frowned. "What's happened, olive farmer? You look like you swallowed a thorn bush."

Nathan checked the position of the sun. "I have an important matter to discuss with Herod." It was late afternoon. Home was a half-day trip away. "My plan is to be off by first light tomorrow."

Agile for a big man, Kadar swung gracefully up onto the back of his stallion. "Herod won't like that you can't stay. With both of us here, he'll want to arrange some horse races and sword fights."

Nathan exhaled heavily. "So, what's brought you into

Galilee?"

"Antipater sent me up here to warn Herod to expect trouble."

More bad news was the last thing Nathan needed to hear. "What's happened now?"

Kadar nudged his horse into a slow walk. "You're gonna love this. The city of Athens voted to give Antipater a golden crown and to erect a bronze statue in his honor."

Nathan winced and prodded Royal ahead. "Why would Athens do such a thing?"

Kadar shrugged. "Antipater said it's because Julius Caesar named him governor of Judea and bestowed most favored nation status on the Hebrew nation, and now Athens and others are trying to curry favor with Caesar by claiming Antipater as their friend, too."

Nathan shook his head in disgust. "I suppose they want to place the cursed statue in a prominent place, such as the Acropolis or Mars Hill?"

Kadar laughed. "No. Nothing so grand. It will stand in a marketplace next to a Temple to the goddess, Hera."

"Grand?" Nathan asked, miffed. That was the problem with converts to Judaism. The Idumeans didn't appreciate the zeal true Jews had for the Commandments of God—*thou shalt not make unto thee any graven image.* Nathan clutched Royal's reins tighter. "Antipater agreed to this blasphemy?"

"Oh, it's worse than that. You know how Antipater's careful to deflect all honors away from himself and onto High Priest Hyrcanus?"

Nathan groaned. "And Hyrcanus didn't have the backbone to say no to Athens."

Kadar merely raised his brows.

A statue? Of John Hyrcanus? Nathan gnashed his teeth. "Job's bones!" The loud complaint garnered curious stares from the handful of men milling flour at Nazareth's communal grindstone. He lowered his voice. "All Judea will be pulling their hair out over Hyrcanus's idolatry."

Kadar's smile was apologetic. "I imagine your rebel friends will kick up hard over this."

"They no longer count themselves my friends," Nathan reported glumly. "But you're right. Hezekiah never misses an opportunity to denounce the corrupt practices of Hyrcanus and his greedy associates. What measures has Herod taken?"

"He's sent out extra men to scout for trouble."

"Herod will want to hear the news I bring, then," Nathan said.

Nazareth behind them, they urged their horses into a gallop. Pushing their mounts hard, they raced across the rolling hills until Sepphoris came into view. Situated atop a steep rise, the fortress city stood like a watchful sentinel over the valley floor. Established by the Hasmoneans after they had liberated Israel from Greek rule, it was the strongest, wealthiest city in the region, boasting two-storied homes, several thriving bazaars, and hefty city walls.

A short while later they slowed their sweating steeds to a walk and passed through the crumbling gates. They steered the horses to the back of an old fortress, suffering from a collection of haphazard additions. The ring of metal hitting on metal called out to them. Rounding the corner to the stable complex, they encountered a crude version of a Roman *gyrus*, a circular wooden corral used to train cavalry riders and horses.

Herod stood at the arena's chest-high wall, oversee-ing a mock battle. He signaled the flaggers stationed around the ring to wave the fight to an end. Good-na-tured banter replaced swordplay.

Nathan smiled as agreeable memories of his rough-and-ready life in Antipater's military camps flooded back. Had he and Herod been that young and cocky? Yes. And probably more so. If providence pushed Na-than back to soldiering, he'd choose to serve under Herod and not Simeon Onias.

Herod growled some instructions to the soldiers, sobering them. The men remounted their horses. The flags dropped and they came out fighting.

Nathan slid off Royal, tossed the reins to a waiting slave, and followed Kadar across the yard to the *gyrus*.

"I've seen eunuchs fight with more spirit!" Kadar's voice boomed above the sound of whinnying horses and the shrill clash of steel.

Herod swung around. "It's about time you showed up, you barbarian bas—" He spotted Nathan. His frown deepened. "Olive farmer. It's nice of you to finally get around to telling me Hezekiah showed up at your syna-gogue. My scouts reported it to me this time yester-day."

"I had problems of my own," Nathan said evenly. He clapped his friend's shoulder. "What's put you in a foul mood?"

"Phasael sent Herod a friendly greeting," Kadar ex-plained. The age-old rivalry between Antipater's sons was exceeded only by their intense loyalty to one an-other.

Herod pulled a crumpled scroll from his pocket and shoved it at Nathan. "My brother is living the life of splendor at the governor's gilded palace in Jerusalem, entertaining High Priest Hyrcanus and Roman officials, while I'm chasing after desert rats and living in a fort that's falling down around my ears."

Nathan pulled the string holding the scroll closed. "Phasael is the eldest. It's only natural your father made him governor of Judea."

Herod snatched the letter back. "Thanks, you cold-hearted dog." He stuffed the thin roll back into his pocket. "I tell you one thing. I won't sit up here meek as a mouse and allow my brothers to grab all the glory. I'll make sure my father remembers I'm out here."

The determination in Herod's voice worried Nathan. He cleared his throat. "I have—"

Herod held up a hand. "Hold on." He climbed over the *gyrus'* high wooden wall, jumped into the fray of horses and men, and yanked a soldier off his saddle. The beefy man landed on his backside in the dirt, putting an abrupt end to the mock battle.

Nathan and Kadar rested their elbows on the wall, ready to enjoy the show.

"Keep your shield up, you cretin halfwit!" Herod yelled. He tore the leather oval away from the stunned man and thumped him over the head with it. "Did you listen to a thing I said? You knock aside the blows from your enemy's sword and wait for him to expose his neck. Let him make the first mistake."

Nathan smiled. "Herod's as tough a commander as his father."

"Maybe better," Kadar remarked. He gave Nathan a sideways look. "His brothers know it, too. And work extra hard to humble him."

"They're wasting their time," Nathan said. "A dozen

bull elephants couldn't contain Herod's ambitions."

Herod tossed the shield back at the soldier and swiped his hands at the rest of his men. "Go. Get out of here."

Nathan winced. "I wish he had some of his father's patience."

Herod jumped back over the wall and dropped to his feet beside them. "I'm ready to resume the hunt for the bandits," he announced.

Nathan drummed his fingers against the leather scabbard at his side. "You'll want to hear what I have to tell you first."

Herod invited Nathan to follow him. "Talk to me while we walk. I have a mountain of business to attend to before tomorrow. We ride out at first light."

Nathan lengthened his stride and caught up with Herod. "I can't go with you."

Herod came to an abrupt stop. "Why, in the name of the Creator, not?" His unhappiness didn't last past Nathan's explanation of his plight.

The next morning the governor of Galilee rode out of the fort with a hundred men at his back, indecently pleased at the prospect of helping Nathan recover from the loss of his olive crop. Nathan was tasked with keeping an eye on Simeon Onias. And Herod resumed the hunt for the rebels.

Nathan didn't leave Sepphoris at dawn as planned. News of the killer frost and of his arrival at the fortress had spread like wildfire from gossiping slave to gossiping slave. A friend of his father who was in failing health had asked Nathan to visit with him.

A few hours later Nathan stood at the entrance of the fortress stable, impatiently waiting for a slave to saddle his horse. Hearing his name, he turned around. Kadar strode toward him.

Red-faced and winded, the giant man greeted Nathan with a frown. "A messenger just arrived. A scout spotted Judas the Zealot on the move, with his men."

The stable slave led Royal over and passed the reins to Nathan. Nathan patted the horse's neck. "Thank the Lord. It's about time something went right. If I ride hard, I can catch up with Herod and give him the report."

"You don't understand. The scout reported seeing Judas and his band leave Rumah and head up the trail toward your farm."

Judas wouldn't dare attack his family, Nathan told himself, even as the image of Judas' angry face loomed before him. He leaned heavily against Royal. "Lex...Father..." he groaned as the twin blasts of heat and rage consumed him.

CHAPTER 21

T he goats' urgent bawling pricked at Alexandra's ears. Heels scuffing over the dirt floor, she pushed the circling animals out of the way. "Shoo goat, shoo." The ripe smell of musty hay and animal dung stung at her eyes and nose.

Much as she disliked her present company, it was heavenly compared to being penned-up inside the tent with her unhappy father. Nathan would be home soon. Everything would be better with Nathan here.

She retrieved a long-handled fork from the corner and dug into the soiled straw vigorously enough that dust and chaff swirled upward. She jabbed and tossed with force, taking her frustration out on the hay. Beads of moisture trickled down her back. Once she was finished piling the dirty straw in the corner, she wiped her damp forehead and modestly flapped the folds of her tunic to cool off a bit.

Suddenly bright light flooded the barn. She jumped and spun around. A man stood in the open doorway, the fiery rays of the sun shooting out from behind his head and arms. Her mouth went dry as the man stepped inside and closed the door.

She backed up and almost tripped over a goat. "Who's there?"

"It's me, fool woman," her father growled.

Her relief was brief. She had volunteered to milk the goats, believing the dirty barn was the safest place to hide from her fastidious father. "May I help you with something?" she asked.

Her father inspected the place with a curled up nose. "Your husband brought you to live in a place fit for goats?"

Her back stiffened. "This was a cozy home. But then it rained buckets and the wall caved in and..."

Her father targeted her with his hard eyes.

Flustered, her voice grew smaller. "Nathan's building us a stone house."

Studying her with the same intensity he used when musing over a difficult passage from the Torah, he said, "You don't actually believe you are strong and robust enough to help your husband eke a living out of the dirt, do you?"

No she didn't, and it frightened her half to death.

Her father closed the distance between them and circled his fingers around her slender wrist. "You take after the women in your mother's family. They are all pale, weak creatures, accustomed to having slaves waiting on them hand and foot." He shook her unresisting arm and dropped it. "Now that indentured slave, Sapphira, she comes from hardy stock. She is a big, strong girl. Not thin and weak like you. She is the kind of wife Nathan needs."

Lex examined her fingers and palm. Unlike the slave maiden's red and roughened skin, her hands were pink and soft. Was it any wonder Rhoda favored Sapphira?

The country-bred girl could work circles around Lex. And, Lord forbid, if Rhoda grew ill or died—Alexandra would be lost without the older woman's help and guidance. "Nathan wants me as his wife," she said as much to herself as her father.

He gave her a pitying look. "He says so now."

Mary came skipping into the barn. "Mother sent me out to help. She is afraid the goats won't behave for you and that you'll get kicked again."

Her father turned and walked out the door, chuckling as he went.

Lex clenched her teeth and managed a small smile for Mary.

Unfortunately, she and her sweet sister-in-law finished the outside chores too quickly to suit her and she had to return to the tent. Father watched her every move all through the morning chores and breakfast. Feeling as though she had two left hands, she knelt beside the reed-mat table and pulled it toward her. *Don't let him upset you. Ignore him,* her mind repeated over and over. She rolled the mat up tight and hugged it to her chest. Hurrying to stand, she toppled over. "Clumsy oaf," she grumbled, tugging on the long veil caught under one knee. She'd donned the cumbersome headdress to please her father—a clear waste of her time.

Sapphira rushed over and grabbed the mat from Alexandra. "Be careful, or you'll tear it to pieces and Rhoda will have to mend it. The poor woman has enough work to do as it is."

Alexandra stole a glance at her father.

A thin smile crossed his lips.

She gathered her dirt-stained veil to her waist and stood. Chin held high, she walked straight-backed across the tent and threw the flap back. A few steps outside the door, she tossed the veil aside and ran toward the orchard. Her breath hitching, she raced behind the trees and fell to her knees and buried her face in her hands.

"Lord, I'm trying," she sobbed. "But I'm tired and afraid. And there's so much to learn and so much work to do." *The cooking and mending and tending the garden and washing the clothes and on and on and on.* "If I had more time. If I was strong like Sapphira."

A branch broke with a loud snap, startling her. She stared straight ahead.

Her father-in-law appeared from behind a squat tree, carrying a limb lined with withered flowers. "Alexandra?" Concern etched his face. He came and sat down in the grass beside her.

She hated being caught sniveling like an unhappy child. She scrubbed her sleeve over her wet eyes. "Did Rhoda send you to find me? I'm sorry. I needed a few moments alone." Could she sound anymore selfish or weak? Tears welled up. She sprang to her feet.

"Please stay." Her father-in-law patted the ground.

A sparrow darted past her. She followed its flight and watched it join a flock of birds roosting in the treetops. "You must think me the weakest, most unworthy woman to ever grace your noble orchard."

"Rhoda and I are worried about you. Sit and talk with me."

She plopped back down and hung her head on her drawn-up knees. "I don't mean to be a bother. I know I don't belong here. I tried to tell Nathan, but he wouldn't listen to me. He'll heed you, Father," she choked on the endearment. This kind, wonderful man wasn't going to be her father-in-law much longer. Regret stuck in her throat like a fist. "You have to convince Nathan to divorce me."

"Divorce? Unworthy woman?" Joseph's voice was kindness itself. "What's this nonsense? Rhoda and I think of you as a beloved daughter."

"You are the kindest person I've ever known." She looked up at him and sighed. "But, I think Rhoda would be relieved to see me go."

"If my fretful wife wants be rid of anybody, it is your father. Or, as Rhoda calls him, Beelzebub." Joseph's smile faded. "Rhoda gets out of humor when she's worried. Don't hold it against her."

"No. Never."

Fondness shone in his eyes. "Rhoda can't help but fuss and worry. It's what she does for those she loves."

Although grateful to learn she did have Joseph and Rhoda's good opinion, Lex still had her doubts. "I adore and care about you and Rhoda and Mary and Timothy with all my heart, but..."

"But, nothing," Joseph said. "You make my son happy. That's all that matters. Everything else is an inconvenience. "

Her brows rose. "My father? The killing frost?"

Joseph's serene smile didn't falter. He held the small tree branch up, twirled it between his fingers, tossed it over his shoulder, and wiped his hands clean. "Mere nuisances. I have my family. It's more than Job had."

The story was a favorite of Alexandra's. Job lost his wealth, and all ten of his children, and suffered boils from head to foot, and yet he did not curse God.

"*Naked I came out of my mother's womb and naked shall I return*," Joseph quoted. "*The Lord gave, and Lord has taken away, blessed be the name of the Lord."*

Here was a man with the same spirit as Job. Come what may, Joseph of Rumah trusted in the Lord. "Is faith as simple as that?" she asked.

Joseph smiled. "It is for me."

She shook her head in wonder. Her thoughts went to her father. Simeon Onias wasn't at peace with himself or God. He would wreck everything and anyone to right what he perceived to be the wrongs done him. What a horrible way to live. She looked solemnly back at Joseph. "I will try to live by the same rule. To view trouble as a mere inconvenience."

The sparrows roosting overhead squawked loudly and lifted as one. She looked up. A dozen or more men emerged from the trees and swarmed toward her and Joseph. Her blood turned cold. Judas the Zealot led the men, brandishing the sharp-edged knife Alexandra remembered all too well.

CHAPTER 22

Alexandra wrapped an arm around Joseph.

Judas loomed over them as he signaled his men to spread out to either side of him. Breathing hard, he turned his bright eyes on her. "Where's your husband? And your father?"

Heart beating out of her chest, she forced air past her clogged throat. "Nathan is away." *Thank the Lord. Please let him be far, far way.*

Judas' scowl deepened. "Away where?"

Summoning up her courage, she narrowed her eyes at the outlaw. "Return Lydia to us, and Nathan will stop hunting for you."

"Lydia is my wife." Judas came closer and pointed a long, dirty finger at her. "Lydia belongs to me."

He smelled of dank smoke and sweat. Her sister shared a bed with this glassy-eyed man. Lex swallowed the bile rising in her throat. *My poor, poor Lydia. What you must be suffering.* "Let Lydia go. I beg—"

Judas lunged toward her.

She cringed backward, just as Joseph leaned over to shield her. "No! Leave her be!"

Judas shoved Joseph aside, grabbed a hank of Lex's

hair, and yanked her to her feet. The knife flashed in her face. The knife that had sliced through James. The knife she had held. Her knees buckled.

Joseph stood and raised his hands. "Don't hurt her. We'll do whatever you say."

Judas hot breath and bushy beard raked her neck. "Do not speak Lydia's name again. Do you understand?"

Lex choked out an answer. "I...I understand."

Her father-in-law stepped closer. "Let my dear daughter go, I beg you, and tell me what's troubling you."

Judas pulled her against his bony body. "Why has Nathan turned against me? The Lord's anointed."

Alexandra's skin crawled. She struggled against the arm holding her in place.

Joseph stepped closer. "Don't fight him, Alexandra. The Lord will see us through this." His soothing voice calmed her.

She stilled.

Joseph offered her a reassuring smile, then looked up at Judas. "Please. Come sit at my table and discuss the matter over food and drink."

Alexandra held her breath. The arm pressing at her shoulders went slack.

Judas laughed and pushed her aside. He slid his knife beneath his belt and put his arm around Joseph. "You always were more reasonable than your son." They walked in the direction of the tent. "So, where's Nathan? You expect him soon?" Judas couldn't have sounded friendlier.

Lex clasped her shaking hands to her waist and followed. She hoped her dear father-in-law knew what he was doing. She wished Nathan were here. And was grateful to heaven he wasn't.

They left the orchard and crossed the field. Timothy saw them coming and waved. Water sloshed over the sides of the jar clutched in his arms. His smile fell. He dropped the jug and raced inside the big tent.

A moment later Rhoda, Mary, and Sapphira followed Timothy outside. James and Elizabeth came out of the small tent to investigate what all the excitement was about.

The red slash crossing James's face blazed like a beacon triggering sharp images that flashed through Alexandra's mind. Blood welling and spilling over James's pale cheek. The knife slick with blood. Red droplets splattering her white tunic. *Don't fight Judas*, her father-in-law had said. Her hands fisted. She hated to disobey Joseph. But if things turned ugly, she was prepared do whatever she must to keep Judas from hurting her family.

The outlaw leader stopped beside the well and ordered Alexandra to fill the men's water pouches. The raiders gathered around her and loaded her arms with water skins. Judas commanded the men to spread out and search the grounds.

Rhoda gathered Timothy and Mary under her arms. "Husband, what do they want with us?"

The raider acting as the second-in-command called out from the other side of the yard. "There's no sign of Nathan or Onias."

Alexandra released a relieved breath. For all she knew Nathan might have come home while she was in the orchard. He was safe. For now.

"Where's Father?" she asked James, lowering the water jug down into the well.

Her brother fidgeted in place as the raiders fanned out around them in a large circle. "Father went into Rumah to attend synagogue. And good riddance, too. We don't need his screeching."

Judas grinned nastily. "I remember you did your share of crying last time we met." His fellow raiders laughed.

James gritted his teeth. "Go away. Leave before you regret coming here."

Alexandra's heart went out to her brother and his attempt at bravery.

Judas slashed his knife through the air and bluffed a move toward James. Her brother jumped behind Cousin Elizabeth. The raiders split their sides laughing.

"You seem extra feisty today," Judas commented, rummaging through the leather pouch hanging from his belt. He dug out a set of bone-carved dice.

Alexandra's breath hitched. The rope slipped out of her hands. The water jug crashed back into the well.

Judas tossed the dice and caught them. Tossed them up and caught them. James's eyes were glued on the dice. Lex knew she should do something, but what?

Joseph clapped his hands. "Why don't we move inside the tent? Rhoda will set out some bread and our best olive oil."

A guttural cry went up and James raced past Alexandra. She wanted to go after him, but her feet wouldn't work. *No, no, no! What are you doing James?*

Howling, her brother lowered his head and rammed the rebel leader in the stomach. Caught off guard, Judas stumbled backward. The dice flew through the air.

James jammed his shoulder into Judas' midsection. "Run, Lex! Run!"

The rebel leader lifted his knife high over his head. Alexandra lunged for the deadly weapon. Joseph was closer. Her father-in-law grabbed Judas' upraised arm. The rebel leader thrust his elbow back, knocking the frail man off his feet. Joseph landed on his back. His head crashed against the well with a loud crack.

Everyone froze in place.

❖ ❖ ❖

The stables whirled in a blur around Nathan at the news that Judas the Zealot was on the march and heading to his farm. He gripped Royal's reins, ready to ride the horse into the ground to get home.

"Hold up," a booming voice called. "I'll ride with you."

"I can't wait." Nathan threw his leg over Royal's back. Judas was a dead man if he touched any of them. Nathan would rip the mad devil apart with his own hands.

A hand fisted in his tunic and yanked him off the horse.

"Rot you!" Nathan yelled. He twisted around and threw a punch.

Kadar deflected his fist. "Listen to sense," the big man said.

"What sense?" Nathan threw up his hands. "Judas the Zealot is going to do God knows what to my family. And you want to stand around discussing it?"

The blond giant raised a brow. "I didn't think Jews said the name God out loud. It's always 'the Lord this' and 'the Lord that.' And you," Kadar pointed a finger at him "I've never heard you take the Lord's name in vain."

"You're purposely trying to slow me down, aren't you?" Nathan didn't have time for a lecture from the

Torah, especially one coming from a barbarian. "Go hang yourself!" he said, turning back to Royal.

Kadar gripped Royal's bridle. "Run in there like you're Sampson brandishing the jawbone of an ass and you'll get them and yourself killed."

Nathan hunched his shoulders against the level-headed argument. Damnation! Kadar was right. Nathan directed his frustration at the stable boy. "Stop staring and go saddle the man's horse." The boy scurried away.

Kadar let go of Royal and called a man out of the shadows.

Nathan recognized the diminutive soldier as Herod's fastest horseman and most reliable messenger. Kadar pressed a silver coin into the messenger's hand. "Find Herod and tell him what you told me. Do it in record time and there's a bag of coins in it for you."

The man nodded and disappeared back into the shadows.

Nathan crossed his arm over his chest. "I'm not waiting for Herod to show up in Rumah."

A flicker of surprise crossed Kadar's face. "We'll need every available man to track Judas down."

Nathan's stomach lurched. "Judas is going to be long gone from the farm before I get there, isn't he?" He ran his hand over his face. "Of course he is." The next terrible thought presented itself. "What if Judas takes Lex or Mary captive like he took Lydia? It could be months before we get another lead." He smashed his fist into the thick wooden beam framing the barn's double doors. Royal whinnied and pranced in a circle.

Kadar put a hand on his shoulder. "If that happens, Herod will turn Galilee upside down to get them back."

"You're right. But at what price?" Nathan flexed

his throbbing fingers. "Forgive me. I'm not thinking straight."

A slave led Kadar's big black stallion over to where they stood. "Rumah's a good half-day ride north of here from what I remember?" Kadar asked, as he climbed aboard Satan.

Nathan gave a curt nod and swung up onto Royal's back. He'd never felt more helpless or impatient. *Lord, give me strength and a clear mind for my family's sake.* He snapped the reins. The horse jumped ahead. "Try to keep up," he called back.

CHAPTER 23

J oseph lay motionless, his head cocked to one side. Alexandra fell on her knees beside him. Rhoda raced over and dropped down next to Joseph, lifted her husband's hand and squeezed his fingers. "Joseph," she coaxed. "Please, Joseph. Talk to me." There was no response.

Lex pressed her ear to her father-in-law's chest and listened but only heard the loud thumping of her own heart. But then, *praise heaven,* she felt the steady rise and fall of his breast against her cheek. "He's breathing," she assured Rhoda.

"Thank the good Lord," Rhoda's voice wobbled. "We'll need a blanket to move him inside."

It was eerily quiet. Lex sat up and looked around. Judas had his arms out, holding everyone back. He and his raiders appeared almost as anxious over the old man's welfare as Joseph's loved ones.

James was pinned down in the dirt by a large, sandaled foot planted in the middle of his back. Misery was written all over his face. "I didn't mean for Joseph to get hurt."

Lex brushed aside the stray hairs hanging in her face.

"It's not your fault." Though frustrated and irritated with her brother, he didn't deserve the blame. Her eyes returned to Judas. "You've made your point." She was amazed by her own calm. "Leave now, and I'll try to convince Nathan not to kill you."

Judas lowered his arms. "We'll go." He smiled and her scalp and skin prickled from fear of what was coming next. "But we're taking the girls." He snapped his fingers and the raiders nearest Mary, Sapphira, and Elizabeth grabbed hold of them. The frightened girls wailed and looked to Lex and Rhoda for salvation.

Alexandra leaped to her feet. "No! You can't." She moved towards the girls. A somber, long-faced raider blocked her way. The imposing man pressed the flat of his blade to her stomach.

Ignoring her, Judas walked over to Joseph's prone body. He laid his hand on Rhoda's shoulder. "This was an accident. Tell Nathan I didn't mean to hurt Joseph."

Rhoda glared up at the raider. "My Joseph won't hold it against you. As for Nathan, he's not quite as forgiving as his father." She pointed a long, knobby finger at the rebel leader. "Judas Maccabee, be warned, if you take my Mary, Nathan will hunt you down like a dog.

Judas' face hardened. "He can try. But he will fail. I'm the Lord's Anointed. The Lord is my refuge."

The other raiders shuffled in place. Judas motioned his men to move out. The girls' cries became higher pitched.

Alexandra pushed against the blade holding her back. There had to be a way to stop Judas. He was obsessed with Lydia.

What if—? It might work.

"Wait!" she yelled. "Leave the girls and take me. You

like Lydia. You will like me, too."

Judas stopped and narrowed his eyes at her.

She swallowed. "I promise you will like me as much as you do Lydia." Lust flickered through Judas' dark eyes.

Bile rose in her throat. She forced herself to smile. "I promise to please you." What else could she use to tempt him? Money, perhaps? It worked with most people. "Leave the girls and take me and James. My father would pay a great deal of money to get his only son back."

"Lex!" James squawked. "I told you I was sorry. I didn't mean to hurt the old man. Why are you punishing me like this?" He squirmed under the foot holding him in place, causing his tunic to ride up and expose his skinny white legs.

The raiders laughed and laughed.

Judas hooted hardest of all. Gasping for breath, the rebel leader wiped his eyes dry. "This is too entertaining to pass up. Though it may prove troublesome, I'm going to take you two and the girls."

"What?" Lex asked, outraged. Hands clasped onto both her arms.

"You heard me," Judas said.

He gave a shrill whistle and he and his men moved out, herding the women ahead of them. James's tormentor slung the kicking and screaming boy over his shoulder. Cousin Elizabeth was taking matters well, but poor Mary and Sapphira were sobbing their eyes out and reaching their arms out to Rhoda. Timothy stood beside Rhoda comforting his mother. The distraught woman rocked on her knees. Her doleful keening was the piercing cry used to mourn the loss of a loved one. Alexandra wasn't sure if her mother-in-law was grieving for the girls or for Joseph, who remained as motionless as a statue.

Two raiders stayed behind to fill the water skins. It was all too easy to imagine the men running their swords through Rhoda, Joseph, and Timothy on their way out of the yard. Alexandra squeezed her eyes closed. *Keep them safe, Lord. Please, please keep us all safe.*

Cresting the hill leading out of the valley, Alexandra turned her head around for one last look at the farm. Though it had been her home for only a few short months, it was dear to her. Undeterred by the sight of the half-built house and barren orchard, she thought it the most beautiful place on Earth. Would she ever set eyes on it again? Would she get to run through the fields again with Nathan? Or make love with Nathan under the trees?

She stubbed her toe on a rock. Her ragged cry had nothing to do with her foot.

They walked all that day and halfway through the night. Mary, Sapphira, Elizabeth, James, and Alexandra each stumbled and fell at some point. The raiders pushed them remorselessly on. A pucker bush poked into Alexandra's ankle. She ignored it, wondering, once again, how much longer it would be before she could get off her aching feet. A short while later a scout returned. An excited buzz went up among the raiders. A dim glow appeared up ahead. The pace quickened. Head-high scrub gave way to a clearing and flaring light.

Squinting against the sudden brightness, Alexandra saw a dozen or so men standing outside a cave entrance, hefting torches. A woman came out of the rock den. She hesitated, then moved forward.

Lydia. It was Lydia.

Her sister ran past Alexandra and into Judas the Zealot's open arms.

◆ ◆ ◆

Nathan leaned over Royal's neck and willed the horse to run faster. They'd stopped just once, at Kadar's insistence, to water the horses. Nathan didn't bother prodding his exhausted steed. The blond giant would just cut him off, as he had every time Nathan pushed too hard. The same questions raced through his mind. Did trouble await them? Was the family safe and well? Could Lex survive another encounter with Judas?

The hillocks guarding the farm came into view. *Praise the Lord God.* Halfway up a knoll Nathan gave the halt signal. They pulled the horses to a stop and dismounted.

Kadar flexed his neck and rolled his massive shoulders. "I wondered if you planned to ride in there like a horseman from hell."

"I'd love to." Nathan stared up the hill. He could have had Lex in his arms by now. Pushing the tempting notion aside, he turned back to Kadar. "Even though it's a good bet Judas and his men are long gone, it'd be foolish to charge in blind. We'll leave the horses here and approach on foot. If you sense the least danger, spill blood first and ask questions later."

Kadar's white teeth flashed with a wolfish grin. "Herod said you have a good head for battle."

"Battle?" Nathan snorted. "Judas isn't a soldier. It will be more like a brawl."

Kadar shrugged. "It's all the same to me." He slapped Nathan on the back. "You take the point and I'll watch the rear."

They hobbled the horses and headed out at a jog. Nathan moved quickly and silently, the palms of his hands sweaty from gripping and re-gripping his sword. He swept his eyes back and forth, alert for signs of trouble. His body hummed, ready to burst into action. Combat tactics played through his mind. Strike first. Strike hard. Antipater shouting, *'Keep your mind on the enemy and keep your sword up, and you might just get to keep your ugly head on your shoulders.'*

And Nathan remembered why he loved soldiering—he was good at it. He made an adequate farmer, but he was ten times a better soldier. And today, with his family's lives at stake, he was thankful this was so.

Cresting the hill, Nathan and Kadar dropped to their bellies and crawled forward until the farm came into view. They hid behind a clump of weeds and studied the yard. Simeon Onias was seated outside the small tent reading from a scroll, while his servant, Goda, brought him food and drink. Timothy came out of the main tent and hurried toward the well. Nathan exhaled. Nothing looked amiss.

Kadar rose to his knees. "I don't see any sign of the rebels. Let's move in."

They ran in a low crouch to the safety of the barn and stopped and listened and waited. It was too quiet. Where was everybody? Rhoda and the girls ought to be busy preparing dinner. They watched and waited some more. Bursting with impatience, Nathan tapped his fingers against his thigh. Finally Kadar gave the all clear sign and they stepped out into the open. Timothy spotted them and raced forward. Nathan got ready to catch the boisterous boy in his arms, but his brother crumpled into a sobbing ball at his feet.

Nathan and Kadar exchanged grim looks. Nathan crouched down beside Timothy and patted the boy's heaving shoulders. "What's wrong? Tell me what happened." Unable to get a coherent word out of the inconsolable boy, he scooped his brother up and walked toward Simeon Onias.

His father-in-law pursed his lips. "You're too late," he complained. "Judas and his band of thieves came and stole James away while you were out gallivanting. And now I'll have to pay a king's ransom to get the infernal boy back." The prim man passed his empty dinner plate to the slave standing at his side. "More bread and olives, Goda."

Nathan shook his head in disgust and glanced at the main tent. "Where are the others?" he asked, uneasy no one had come outside to greet them.

"Judas took the girls," Simeon said nonchalantly. "He is welcome to keep them, as far as I'm concerned."

Nathan hugged Timothy closer. "Girls? Who...who did Judas take?"

The slave returned with a full plate of food. Simeon inspected the dish and plucked up a plump olive and waved it at Nathan. "The fool fiend took them all. My wife, your wife, your sister, that incompetent slave maiden."

Nathan looked heavenward. "No! No! No!"

Timothy cried harder.

A hand shook Nathan's arm. "Give me the boy."

Nathan collected himself and passed his brother over to Kadar. Timothy wrapped his arm around the big man's neck. Anger wouldn't get Lex and Mary back.

The giant sheathed his sword. His blue eyes iced

over. "Find out what that puffed-up peacock knows before I wring his neck."

Simeon opened his mouth to complain. Nathan bent down so he was at nose level with his father-in-law. "How long ago did Judas leave?"

"I was at Synagogue when they came. They were gone by the time I returned." The spiteful man's mouth curved with a smile. "I do have one piece of information you might find interesting." Simeon raised his stone goblet and waved it. "Goda, fetch me more wine. And, bring a cup for my son-in-law. He'll need it after he hears his wife offered to play the harlot with Judas." Nathan growled. Simeon smiled primly. "Alexandra begged Judas to take her. She promised to please him."

Nathan knocked the cup out of his father-in-law's hand. "Stop with your lies you horrible old man."

Indignant, the Pharisee sniffed. "If you don't believe me, go ask your stepmother."

"I've heard enough." Nathan stood. "I'm going to go talk to my father. He'll tell me what I need to know."

Simeon plucked a piece of lint from his expensive robe. "Your father won't be any use to you. He's dead."

The world went dark. Nathan braced his hands on his knees. "What did you say?"

"Your father is dead," Simeon repeated matter-of-factly.

Nathan drew back his arm and punched the hateful man in the face. A loud crunch was followed by blood spurting in all directions. Simeon howled and fell over backward, clutching his nose.

Nathan stared at the big tent. *My father is dead...my father is dead.*

Kadar squeezed his shoulder. "Do you want me to

go find Rhoda and offer to help?" Help prepare Joseph's body for burial—that's what Kadar meant.

Nathan's stomach knotted. "No. It's my place to bury my..." his voice wavered. He cleared his throat. "I'll go to Rhoda. She will be expecting me."

Kadar patted Timothy's back. "I'll take care of what needs doing out here."

Nathan turned toward the main tent. He took one faltering step. Then another. And reached the tent entrance far too soon. Teetering on the edge of a bottomless pit, a place bereft of his good, kind father, he took a deep breath and eased the flap back.

Joseph was laid out in the middle of the floor. Rhoda knelt next to her husband, lovingly washing the pale, lifeless body. She sang softly as she worked. The tender affection underpinning her rough, uneven voice added poignancy to the hymn of love.

As the apple tree among the trees of the wood, so is my beloved among the sons, I sat down under his shadow with great delight, and his fruit was sweet to my taste.

Others saw a careworn woman in Rhoda. Not Joseph. The sentimental song would have pleased his father to no end.

Nathan squeezed his eyes closed. *Lord, I'm not as strong as my father. I don't want any wife but Lex. Have mercy. Keep her safe.*

"Nathan." Rhoda straightened. "Thank heaven you're home."

He kneeled down beside his stepmother and dragged the wet cloth from her hand. "Let me help."

Rhoda held her hand out for the rag. "Leave this to me and go after my Mary and your Lex."

"How long ago did the devils leave?"

Rhoda sighed. "Shortly after the morning meal." It was almost evening.

Nathan twisted the wet cloth into a tight knot. "Everything in me is crying to go after them. The fiends must have left a trail as wide as a herd of elephants. But I wouldn't get far enough for it to matter before the light gave out. I'll ask Kadar to follow the tracks as far as he can, so we can start from there at dawn."

Rhoda's lip wobbled. "My Mary ought to be here. It's not right. She should be here for her father's burial."

Nathan felt weary to the bone. "I'll go hire a wailing woman and the flutists, so we may bury Father." His voice caught. "You and Timothy will have to observe *Shiva* for all of us. Lord willing, Mary, Alexandra, and I will be home before the end of the seven days, to mourn with you."

He patted Rhoda's hand. "Rest assured those demons will pay for their sins." When Nathan caught up with the damnable madman and his conscienceless followers, he planned to annihilate every last one. Kill them for touching his wife and sister. Kill them for murdering his father. Kill them for not allowing Joseph of Rumah to be properly mourned.

Rhoda nodded. "Go quickly. There will barely be enough time for the people from Rumah to come and walk in the procession and to go home before dark."

"I can't believe my ears." Nathan's teeth gnashed. "You want to invite all of Rumah here? After the way they treated Father?"

A sad smile crossed Rhoda's careworn face. "I don't like the idea any more than you do. But what would your father want?" She pressed her fingers to her lips. "Look at him. My Joseph is as happy and peaceful in death as he was in life."

She spoke true. Joseph wore a serene smile. He would want his neighbors to attend his funeral. And he would want Nathan to forgive the men who killed him.

The rage burning in Nathan's stomach backed up and stung in his throat. He picked up his father's lifeless hand. *I wish I possessed your love and forgiveness, Father. But all I feel is hate and rage.*

CHAPTER 24

Huddled in the corner of the damp cave, Alexandra stared into the blackest darkness she'd ever known. The rebels had hustled her and the others into the rocky hole moments after they'd arrived in the camp. Two guards watched over the entrance. The rest of raiders lay fast asleep.

"Alexandra," Mary whispered.

"What do you need, dear?" The girl's head was pillowed on Alexandra's lap. She would have given Mary a comforting touch, but James was tucked under one of her arms and Sapphira under the other. Her cousin Elizabeth, not quite as needy as the others, slept stretched out on the floor beside Sapphira.

Mary nuzzled closer. "I am glad you are here."

The awfulness of their situation reared its ugly head. Again. Alexandra stifled a moan. "Try to go to sleep, sweet lamb."

Lex flexed her stiff back against the cold cave wall. *This is a mere inconvenience. Come what may, the Lord will see us through.* The faithful saying conjured up the memory of Joseph's still face. She prayed for the thousandth time that her father-in-law still lived. If only

James hadn't panicked. Terrified of the bandits, James was like a small, frightened bird, ready to burst from the brush at the first sign of danger. She'd have to keep a close watch on him. Any more of his rashness, and they could all end up dead.

A shiver went through her. She'd give anything to be in her husband's arms. Nathan would be home by now and wild with worry. He was coming to rescue them. She knew it. But it could be weeks and weeks before he tracked them down. After all, Lydia had been a captive for five months.

What has Judas done to you, my dear, dear Lydia? Alexandra rested her head against the hard stone and squeezed her eyes closed. She'd clearly need to proceed with caution where her sister was concerned. Lydia hadn't even acknowledged Lex or the others when they'd arrived in the camp. Instead she'd run into the zealot's arms and disappeared into the back of the cave with him.

The cold seeped deeper into Alexandra's bones. *Help me, Lord. Give me the courage and strength to do whatever it takes to keep us safe and whole until Nathan arrives.*

Lex woke with a start. A shaft of morning light cut across the craggy opening of the cave. The thin, long-faced raider who continually stared at her stood over her with his legs spread wide, his leering eyes wandering over her body. A sour taste filled her mouth. Then Mary and Sapphira stirred and the raider moved on. Alexandra woke her brood and coaxed them out of the gloomy den.

Men moved slowly about the campsite. Lydia was kneeling next to a small fire, stirring a steaming pot. Lex pushed the girls and James toward the warm flames. Lydia looked up. Her brow furrowed.

Alexandra offered her an encouraging smile. "Lydia. I've missed you terribly. How are you?"

Her sister ducked her head and moved the wooden spoon through the kettle with added vigor. "I wish Father had heeded my messages," her soft whisper barely reached Alexandra.

Lydia had always been so lively and full of fun and ready to laugh. The jittery, cowering woman across from Alexandra was a stranger. Lex's heart broke. She leaned forward and spoke gently, "What messages, dear?"

Lydia's shoulders dropped. "The ones telling him to stop searching for me."

A black hole opened up inside of Alexandra. "You can't mean that."

Judas stepped up behind Lydia and put his long, narrow hand on her head. Her sister flinched.

Fright careened through Lex. Judas' dark eyes bore down on her. "Lydia is my wife. Say otherwise and you will force me to teach you a lesson."

Alexandra swallowed and nodded.

"I am happy with my husband," Lydia rushed to assure her.

Husband? Alexandra couldn't believe her ears. Her lively, caring, loving sister couldn't actually consider the violent zealot a true husband, could she?

Tears clouded Alexandra's vision as she thought of Nathan. If Lydia had spent time with a man as kind and good as Nathan, she would know better. Of course, Alexandra's expectations for marriage had also been abysmal. It made sad sense, given the fact that the only example of a man they knew was that of their joyless, sharp-tongued father.

"It's time for the morning prayers," a deep, steady voice said.

All eyes turned to the thin, long-faced raider, who stood next to the mouth of the cave.

"I know," Judas said tightly. He clapped his hands. Prayer mats were brought forth.

The men gathered around Judas. Facing Jerusalem, they went down on their knees. The raider named Silas stared at her for a long moment before putting his head down to pray.

Alexandra leaned forward and pressed her face into the ground. She wanted to pray but her strength deserted her. Tears welled. Her body shook. The time of prayer ended too soon. Gathering back her courage, she sat up.

The men stayed on their mats. The raider next to Judas removed a small scroll from a cloth bag. Handling the sacred text with extreme care, the man passed the rolled scroll over to Judas. The dour zealot unfurled the parchment, cleared his throat, and read the words of the prophet Daniel. "*Now therefore, O our God, hear the prayer of thy servant, and his supplication, and cause thy face to shine upon thy sanctuary that is desolate.*"

Judas recited a long portion, then began to preach. He spoke eloquently about the beauty of the Lord's Temple, raged with righteous indignation against Rome, lamented the sinful practices of the Sadducees and High Priest John Hyrcanus. Enthralled, Judas's men nodded and said amen. Lydia divided her attention between the preaching and watching over a steaming kettle. Alexandra wished she could denounce Judas's teachings as vile or foolish, except she agreed with much that he said.

Finally the scroll was put away. The rebel leader and his followers fell to eating and talking. Some of the men suggested breaking up camp and moving higher into the hills, but then someone would ask Judas a question or say something that didn't sit right with the rebel leader, and he would launch into another lengthy speech.

Alexandra and her stoic cousin, Elizabeth, took turns comforting Mary, James, and Sapphira. Alexandra watched for an opportunity to speak to Lydia again, but her sister stayed close to Judas. Around midmorning the man the girls called Bear approached Alexandra carrying a skin of water and two wheat loaves.

The large, hairy man squatted on his haunches next to her. "Pay attention. I'm only saying this once. Some of us are not happy about the raid on your husband's farm. We plan to part ways with Judas. My friend..." Bear nodded in the direction of the cave entrance. The thin, long-faced raider stood framed in the black, craggy entrance. "...sent me to invite you to escape with us."

Alexandra's heart sped up. A revolt was afoot in the rebel camp. How appropriate. "You should all be ashamed of yourselves," she lectured.

Bear blinked and turned red-faced.

In no position to be picky over where help came from, she asked, "How do you plan to get us past Judas?"

"Leave that to us," Bear said.

"Will you take us back to the farm?"

"I'm afraid not."

"We will be nothing but trouble for you," she

warned.

The hairy man smiled sheepishly and shrugged. "We need wives. So we'll risk it."

"Wives?" Her loud cry earned a scowl from Bear. She lowered her voice. "Sapphira and Mary are too young to marry. And my cousin and I are already married."

"We don't mind."

She ground her teeth together. "We mind."

"You better get used to the idea. Judas plans to give these plump doves..." he pointed at Mary, Elizabeth, and Sapphira "...to his right-hand men." Then jabbed his thumb in her direction. "Our greedy leader plans to make you as his second wife." Bear wiggled his bushy brows. "So will it be us? Or them?"

Lex glanced between Judas and the thin, long-faced man and groaned.

Bear stood. "Decide quickly. We go tonight." With that he lumbered off.

Hands trembling, Alexandra broke up the wheat loaf and passed out pieces to the girls. She made James sit up. "Eat. You need your strength." She nibbled at the stale crust and watched Lydia go about her work.

Her sister lifted the cover off a steaming pot and the earthy smell of cooked lentils drifted through the campsite. She poured the small, brown beans into a bowl and brought it to Judas. Tall and willowy, Lydia moved with an ease and grace Alexandra had always envied. Then she noticed a small round bump showing beneath her sister's tunic. Lydia was with child. Alexandra flinched. Father had said so, but the sight of her sister's distended belly brought the awful truth home.

Lex pressed her hands to her flat stomach. What if Nathan came too late and Judas married her and forced himself on her? Her skin crawled. She'd rather die than have that happen. The thin, long-faced raider walked past. What if the menacing man forced her go with him when he made his escape, and then took her for his wife, and put his dirty, groping hands all over her? She shuddered.

A commotion arose as two raiders arrived in the camp leading a pair of donkeys burdened with giant jars. The other men whooped for joy and crowded around the sway-backed beasts. A mesh sack filled with clay cups, passed hands. The covers came off the pottery jars. "Judas. Judas," the men chanted.

The rebel leader stood a short way off. Lydia had a hold of his sleeve, urging him to listen to her. Alexandra wasn't close enough to hear what her sister was saying, but the alarm on Lydia's face was edging toward panic.

"Enough, woman," Judas barked, shaking off Lydia's hand. "No more of your nagging." The color drained from her face, and she sank to the ground and hid her face in her lap. Judas joined his companions, grabbed two cups, and banged them together until the men quieted. "I promised you wine for the weddings. Come and drink." The men cheered.

Alexandra broke out in a cold sweat. She wanted to jump to her feet and race away and never stop running.

Bear elbowed his way to the donkeys. "Hold up," he roared good-naturedly. "I have a wager to make." He dipped his cup into one of the jars and lifted it high. Wine sloshed over the rim. He opened his mouth and poured. Wine splashed against his tongue and dribbled down bushy beard. Draining the cup, he took a mug away from the man standing next to him, filled both cups, held them aloft, and waggled his brows. "I'll kiss the feet of the man who can guzzle half the wine I can. Do I have any takers?" Nearly every raider raised a hand. Bear laughed raucously. "Drink up friends! Drink up."

A blast of cold air ruffled Alexandra's tunic. She shivered and rubbed her arms.

Several sets of dice appeared. The men tossed the ivory cubes at the base of boulders, calling out bets before the die crashed to a stop.

James moved closer to Alexandra. The scar crossing his pale face pulsed. "What if they make me throw the dice again? What if someone suffers a horrible fate because of me? What if they make you cut me again?" He gagged. "I can't do it again. I can't."

Wine flowed like rain from a black sky.

Dice mashed against stone.

The demon named Judas danced about the camp.

CHAPTER 25

The clean smell of the dried myrtle and olive flower covering the burial cloth followed Nathan out of the tent. He blinked against the harsh sunlight and walked toward the well where Kadar and Timothy were drawing water for the horses.

Royal spotted him and nickered. Nathan stopped in front of his warhorse. "There's a good fellow." He patted the soft muzzle brushing against his chest. "You'd ride your heart out if I asked, wouldn't you?" He squeezed his eyes shut. Lex and Mary were suffering unthinkable atrocities and yet, here he was, talking to his horse. The good Lord knew he wanted to be off after them, running Royal and himself into the ground.

Timothy hugged Nathan around the waist and looked up at him with red-rimmed eyes. "Even though she's too bossy, I...I miss Mary." He buried his face in Nathan's tunic and cried silently, his little shoulders shaking.

Nathan gritted his teeth and patted the boy's head. Forget the funeral! Forget waiting until morning! Forget level-headedness! Reality grabbed him by the throat. His only chance of finding Judas quickly was to follow his tracks. But since Nathan couldn't make the sun stay in the sky, he had no choice but to wait.

Kadar set the water pitcher on the lip of the well. "I doubt it will make you feel any better, but some good might come from the wait. There's an excellent chance Herod and his company will reach us before nightfall, giving us more men for the hunt."

Nathan gave Kadar a hard look. "Come morning I'm leaving, whether Herod's here or not."

"I'll be right beside you."

Nathan pinched the bridge of his nose to stem the headache threatening to blow his skull open. "We can leave well before sunup, if..."

"...if I follow Judas' tracks." Kadar finished for him. "Go take care of your father and leave me to worry about everything else."

Nathan nodded and repeated one of his father's favorite precepts. "Let tomorrow take care of tomorrow." There'd be no more gentle advice from his father, the next day, or the day after that. Or ever. He exhaled heavily.

Kadar squeezed his shoulder. "Your father was a good man."

"There was none better," Nathan agreed. A man of prayer who loved his Lord and his people. One couldn't ask for a more faithful and loving husband and father. He lifted Timothy into his arms.

Kadar frowned. "And here comes one of the most worthless men ever born."

Simeon Onias stopped a few paces away. Nose swollen to three times its normal size, it was stuck high in the air. "Stop jabbering with this heathen swine and tell me your plan for rescuing my son."

Nathan narrowed his eyes at the hateful man. "Insult my friend again, and I will break more than your nose."

Simeon swiped his hands through the air. "Save your bluster for the outlaws." He pointed to his red snout. "I suppose I have to expect this sort of animal behavior from a man called the angel of death."

"You are on very dangerous ground," Nathan growled.

Simeon plucked at his costly robe. "I will overlook the brutish attack if you will reconsider commanding my army." He cocked his thumb at Kadar. "I'll give Hercules here twice what Antipater pays him to become my man."

Nathan and Kadar advanced on Simeon.

The Pharisee held up his hands. "Wait, wait, wait." He pedaled backwards. "Do as I say, or I promise to take you to court and see that you receive a public lashing."

Kadar's boom of laughter filled the yard. "What a strange little man you are. Running away like a chicken and squawking threats as you go."

Nathan stuck his finger in his father-in-law's face. "Seal your wicked lips and listen to me, very, very carefully. You will leave my home and go into Rumah and offer half your wealth for news of Judas's whereabouts. After that, you will go through the rest of Galilee making the same offer."

Simeon's scowl deepened. "You disappoint me. I had such high hopes for you."

Nathan hefted Timothy higher. "Go...before you tempt me to do something that will give the court a legitimate reason to try me."

"You will pay for your impertinence," Simeon warned.

Nathan raised a brow. "My father is dead. My wife and sister are captives to a madman. What more could you do to me?"

The wicked man's eyes flicked to Timothy.

Nathan patted his brother's back. "You want threats? I'll give you a threat. If you don't do everything in your power to find Judas, I promise there won't be enough locks or doors or strong walls in the world to save you from me."

The funeral arrangements made, Nathan, Timothy, and Rhoda sat in the main tent, sitting *Shiva* over Joseph's linen-wrapped body. The cries of the wailing woman rose and fell. Nathan rubbed his burning eyes. How were Lex and Mary? Were they cold and hungry? Or sick, or injured?

The tent flap opened. Rumah's town elders filed inside. Bartholomew, Old Zeb, and Thomas the Younger kneeled down beside Joseph's cold body.

Nathan's fist balled. These men hadn't killed his father, but their encouragement and approval of Judas and Hezekiah's raids on Roman sympathizers made them guilty in Nathan's eyes. His nod was stiff and formal. "How good of you to come and help put Father into the grave."

Bartholomew reached his hand to Nathan's arm. "Now, Nathan, you and your father brought this on yourselves."

Nathan glared at the fat fingers circling his arm and then at the elder's jowly face. "This is not the time or the place."

Bartholomew snatched his hand back. "Of course. By

all means. I meant no disrespect."

Old Zeb spoke up, "We came to do what is right."

Nathan saw red. "Do right? You bar my father from synagogue. Excuse his death to my face. Do you call that right?"

The wailing woman's undulating keening grew frenzied.

Rhoda stood. "The time grows late. We ought to begin." She looked to have aged ten years.

Nathan scrubbed his face. What was he doing? His father would expect better. He removed his sandals and took his place beside his father. The elders took off their sandals. At Nathan's signal, the four men lifted the bedroll turned funeral bier. Timothy walked at his side. Rhoda and the wailing woman led them outside.

Rocks dug into Nathan's feet. A stiff breeze buffeted the bed. Somber-faced guests filled the yard. Duty called for everyone to drop what they were doing to accompany the dead to their last resting place. Most of Rumah was here. Rot them and their feckless friendship.

A pair of flutists joined the wailing woman. Hiring them had taken the last of the family's money. Oftentimes professional mourners and musicians offered their services for free, out of respect or liking for the deceased. Did any of them step forward for Joseph? No. Curse them.

The women and the musicians went ahead of the bier, the men went behind it. Rumah's womenfolk kept their distance from Rhoda. Curse them. Surrounded by her four sisters and scads of nieces, his stepmother did not want for company, although Mary's absence from her mother's side proved as jarring as the orange flare of the dying sun.

The procession moved a short distance. Bartholomew waved it to a stop. He and the two other elders stood back, making way for the next bier bearers. His father's cousin, Potiphar, slithered into place and took hold of the bedroll. Nathan shook with outrage. Potiphar refused to speak up for Nathan and Joseph when they were thrown out of Rumah, but had the audacity to offer his help, after it wasn't needed? What a hypocrite.

The parade lurched on. Someone took up the funeral dirge. *"He that dwells in the secret place of the most high shall abide under the shadow of the Almighty. I will say of the Lord, he is my refuge and my fortress: my God, in him will I trust."*

The rest of the mourners joined in. The words stuck in Nathan's throat.

The ninety-first Psalm was repeated many times over, and the parade stopped at regular intervals to allow more and more men the *honor* of carrying Joseph's body—the hypocrites. They reached the cave turned crypt. Nathan took a deep breath. Pinhas rushed forward and grabbed a corner of the bedroll. Nathan glared at his old friend.

Hypocrite, hypocrite, hypocrite.

The bier moved forward. Dark walls closed around Nathan. He lowered the bedroll to the ground one last time. The others left. Nathan knelt by his father's side. He touched the white linen shroud. He ought to say a prayer. Recite a piece of scripture. A loud roaring filled his head. "You already seem so far away from me, Father. Why can't I sense your presence?" He squeezed his eyes closed. "I'll never forgive them for this. Never."

He stumbled blindly out of the cave. The stone closing the grave slid into place. Bartholomew recited the first line of the sanctification prayer, *"May His great name grow exalted and sanctified in the world that He created as He willed."* The mourners joined their voices to his. *"May He give reign to His kingship in your lifetimes and in your days."*

Nathan stared at the people, watched their mouths move—the same mouths that had remained silent when he and his family were run out of Rumah, and when Judas attacked his family.

The prayer ended. The congregation parted into two lines. Nathan remained rooted in place. Rhoda and Timothy took hold of his elbows and steered him toward the aisle formed by his neighbors.

Bartholomew and his wife were first in line. They stared at a point below Nathan's chin and offered the traditional words of comfort, "May God console you, together with all those who mourn." Here was the time for the couple to say something kind or thoughtful about Joseph. They sealed their lips shut.

Sick to death of the pompous bore, Nathan moved on to Old Zeb and his wife. The couple studied their feet and mumbled, "May God console you, together with all those who mourn." Though they'd known Rhoda since she was born, they didn't spare a single encouragement for the grieving widow.

Nathan gave a low growl.

Rhoda patted his hand. "It's all right." She pulled him ahead.

Pinhas and Martha were next in line. Pinhas stared past Nathan's shoulder. "May God console you..."

Nathan shook free of Rhoda and shoved Pinhas. The

solid stonemason fell back a step. Nathan followed. "Liar! You're nothing but a filthy liar."

Pinhas' face turned bright red.

Nathan whirled around and scowled at his neighbors. "Listen to you and your lying tongues," he accused. "Where were you when I begged you to turn Judas over the authorities? Where were you when Judas left Rumah and headed here? Where were you when Judas killed my father and kidnapped my wife and sister?" He pointed to the trail leading to Rumah. "Go. You weren't here when we needed you. We don't want you now. Go!" he thundered. "Go."

A child started to cry.

Nathan charged at Bartholomew. The startled man turned and fled. The others scattered.

Nathan righted his tunic. Timothy leaned against his mother. Rhoda circled her arms about her son. They watched in silence until the last person slipped out of sight.

It was black as pitch inside the tent. Nathan lay wide awake, waiting for the endless night to pass. Timothy still clung to him after having cried himself to sleep. At least Rhoda's breathing came low and steady now. Kadar had commandeered the small tent after booting Simeon Onias off the farm. The big man had followed Judas's tracks north to the foot of Mount Meron, so they would head out to Mount Meron a few hours before dawn and start tracking Judas from there.

They'd received no word from Herod.

Nathan touched Timothy's head. Nathan had decided that once this was over he would leave Rumah.

With his father gone, there was no good reason to stay. He didn't want to live side by side with the people responsible for Joseph's death. Nathan planned to pledge his loyalty to Herod, a man who'd proved a true friend.

A distinctive noise had Nathan sitting up. *Splat. Splat.* More rain pelted the tent. *Why? Why? Why?* his mind screamed. He scrambled to his feet, dislodging Timothy. The boy woke up whimpering.

"What's the matter?" Rhoda asked her voice anxious.

Nathan took two steps in the dark and tripped. "Job's bones!" he complained, kicking his sandals out of the way. He felt his way to the tent opening and threw back the flap. Fat raindrops hit his face. "Pray, Rhoda," he yelled. "Pray it doesn't rain at Mount Meron and wash the tracks away."

Lex and Mary would be in Judas's power that much longer.

He fell to his knees and turned his face up. *Dear God, have mercy.*

A loud roar rent the dark. Water poured out of the sky.

CHAPTER 26

Drunken men yelled and cursed and staggered about on wobbly legs. Bear sat next to a sputtering fire doling out slurred insults and roars of laughter as he steadily coaxed wine into his companions.

The chill breeze shifted and pushed billowing smoke into Alexandra's face. Her nose and throat filled and burned, making her cough. James, Mary, Sapphira, and Elizabeth huddled against her. They were all a miserable mess, wiping at watery eyes and runny noses.

A young man with a beak nose approached Sapphira. He was one of the few raiders still sober. About seventeen or eighteen years old, he had been tasked with standing guard. Lex's best guess was that he was part of the group planning to desert Judas.

"How are you, Sapphira?" the young man stammered. "I hope you are not angry with me."

Sapphira's lip quivered. "I'm afraid. And I want to go home." Tears slipped down her face. "Take me home, Barjesus. Please say you will take me home."

Alexandra raised a brow at Mary.

Mary leaned over and whispered, "Barjesus's family

lives to the north of Rumah. I think he is sweet on Sapphira."

The young man looked across the camp toward Judas. The wild-eyed man continued to throw the dice. Barjesus turned back to them and held out his hand to Sapphira. "Come with me. We need to talk."

Sapphira gave her hand to Barjesus and let him lead her away.

Lex rubbed at her aching temple. "Should we go after her?"

"No. Barjesus will take care of her." Mary sounded wistful. "I think he is going to try to convince Sapphira to escape with him."

Lex wished the girl well. "The rest of you ought to go with Barjesus." She patted Mary's arm. "You and Sapphira might be able to persuade him to take you home."

The breeze stiffened, ruffling Mary's hair. "Come with us," she pleaded.

Lex shook her head. "I can't."

"I want to go home," Mary's voice quavered.

Lex wrapped her arms about the girl and kissed her forehead. "I know, sweet lamb. But I can't leave without Lydia."

Mary hugged her like she was never going to let go.

James circled his arms around his drawn up knees. "I won't go without you and Lydia." His grumpy look dared her to disagree.

Surprised and pleased, Lex managed a small smile. "That is very brave of you."

James bristled. "You and I both know I'm a sniveling coward."

Lex ached for him. "I'm afraid, too."

"Yes, but you keep your wits about you." He put his

head on his knees.

Mary pushed away from Lex. "I want to stay with you and James."

"Nathan will be here soon," Lex assured the girl, hoping to heaven it was true. She turned to Elizabeth. "You don't have to stay. You can go with Sapphira, if you'd rather."

Her cousin shrugged her petite shoulders. "It doesn't matter to me."

"You are holding up very well," Lex said, liking the unflappable girl all the more for her quiet courage. "Are you a born stoic?"

"Heavens, no." Elizabeth's smile held a secret. "But it would be a sin to complain after my prayers have been answered."

Mary frowned. "Prayers? I don't understand."

Elizabeth grinned. "I'm deliriously happy to have been abducted."

Mary gasped. "You can't mean it."

"I most certainly do. Because it means Simeon Onias will divorce me." Elizabeth lifted her face toward heaven. "Praise the Lord."

Young Mary looked between Elizabeth and Alexandra. "I don't understand."

"The Law says a priest must divorce a wife who has been assaulted," Lex explained.

A horrified look crossed the young girl's face. "Nathan won't have to divorce you, will he?"

Alexandra patted Mary's hand. "No. The law applies only to priests whose bloodlines must remain pure and above suspicion." Lex turned to her cousin. "Abduction is not the same as assault."

Her cousin waved a dismissive hand. "It won't matter to your priggish father. He will blame me, call me a whore, and divorce me. My reputation will be ruined." Her smile turned fragile. "But disgrace seems a less horrifying prospect than living one more day with my revolting husband."

Alexandra wondered about Lydia. Did her sister view life with Judas as better than living with their unhappy, serpent-tongued father?

Lex patted Elizabeth's knee. "Don't give up on marriage. It can be truly wonderful."

"Don't worry about me." Elizabeth's eyes sparkled with mischief. "My first trip to Galilee has been instructive. I can't wait to see the look of surprise on my father's face when I tell him I want to marry an olive farmer. Do you know where I can find a farmer as good and handsome as your Nathan?"

Lydia drifted past them, claiming Lex's attention.

Her sister stopped outside the cave entrance and stooped down to tidy the food supplies. Lex took a look around. Judas was still engrossed in his game of dice. The rest of the outlaws were busy drinking themselves blind.

"I'll be right back," Lex told the others, slowly pushing up from the ground.

Lydia saw her coming. Fear flicked through her large doe eyes.

Lex rushed the rest of the way. She wrapped her fingers around Lydia's wrist. "Come with me." Lex pulled her unresisting sister behind a large boulder. "How are you, dear?"

"Don't do anything to antagonize Judas," Lydia begged. "He is mean when he drinks."

Lex ran her hands over Lydia's arms. They felt so

thin. Lex choked back tears. "Has he hurt you?"

Footsteps crunched behind her. Lex spun around. She put her hand to her heart. "James, you scared me half to death."

Her brother frowned. "What are you up to?"

A fat raindrop struck her forehead. Lex wiped it away. "I wanted to assure Lydia that help is on the way."

James's nose wrinkled. "Nathan has been hunting for Judas for months with nothing to show for it. And Father would rather spend his money on an army than waste it on a ransom."

Lydia blinked repeatedly. "Has Father found someone to lead his army?"

"Not that I know of," Lex answered. "He wanted my husband to do it, but Nathan refused. Emphatically." She wanted to tell Lydia all about Nathan. The sweet communion of pouring their hearts out, sister to sister, had always been a source of solace and strength to them both. A vast chasm yawned between them now. Sadness wrapped itself around Alexandra's heart.

The full moon disappeared behind black-rimmed clouds. Light rain fell around them.

Lydia gripped her arm. "We have to get a message to Father. Convince him Judas is the right man to head his army. Convince him to talk to Judas again."

Alexandra blinked. "What do you mean...talk to Judas, again?" The truth dawned as sickeningly as maggots blooming on rotting flesh. Father hadn't come to Galilee those many months ago to secure a religious artifact. No. He'd come to make a deal with Judas the Zealot. Her stomach soured. *How could you, Father? How could you?*

James slapped the boulder. "Rot him! Rot him! He

slapped the huge rock again. "Father tried to make a bargain with Satan. Am I right?" He scowled at Lydia. "But then Father came to Galilee, met Judas, realized he was dealing with a madman, and took back the offer. And, with his usual arrogance, Father insulted a crazed man. Of course, Judas, who is as unhinged as they get, took offense and attacked us." His voice grew louder and more hysterical. "Hasn't Father done enough damage? Apparently not, because here he is running around Galilee stirring up more trouble, while we sit here waiting for a demented zealot to defile Lex and to slice me into pieces!"

Alexandra's toes curled in her sandals and she shivered with dread. The moon parted the clouds. Lydia moaned and closed her eyes.

Judas came charging around the boulder.

Lex and James jumped back.

"You sneaky dogs!" Judas yelled. He shoved Lydia in the direction of the cave. "Go ready yourself for the strap."

Lex grabbed onto Judas's tunic. "Punish me," she begged, sick that she'd gotten her sister into trouble.

Judas twisted around, fisted his hand in her hair and forced her to her knees. "Go!" He bellowed at Lydia. "Go to the cave and stay there. Disobey me and I will beat you twice over."

"Leave her alone," Alexandra cried.

Lydia cast her a sorrowful look and fled to the cave.

Judas yanked Alexandra up by the hair. She clasped her stinging scalp. "Let go!"

He dragged her against his chest and jerked her head back. He reeked of wine and sweat. His wiry beard raked her neck. "Silence, woman!"

Gagging on her fear, she said, "Nathan will hunt you down and kill you if you hurt any of us."

"Do not speak his name!" Judas roared. "You are mine now."

She fought to remain calm. "I have a husband."

"Nathan of Rumah has forsaken his people and committed adultery with Rome. He is not worthy to call a daughter of Israel his wife." His voice turned pious. "The spirit of the Lord is upon me, moving me to claim the daughters of Simeon Onias. I must obey his call."

Alexandra suppressed an hysterical laugh. Moved by the spirit? Judas was a madman that's what he was. "What about the wedding contract?" she asked, desperate to distract the drunken man. "You will need to speak with my father."

Judas yanked her head back. "Contracts are Roman gibberish. Adam did not need a contract to marry Eve. The Lord commanded him to leave his mother and father, and to cleave unto his wife, and they shall be one flesh."

Lex's skin crawled at the thought of this man touching her as Nathan did. She blurt out a lie. "I'm with child."

Judas let go of her hair, grabbed her by the shoulders, and turned her to face him. What if she was carrying Nathan's child and didn't know it? She shuddered.

Judas' hot, sour breath spilled over her. "When the bastard comes it will be sold into slavery."

"Moses' Law forbids it," she argued, and immediately knew it was a mistake. Judas backhanded her across the face. Her eyes watered.

He smiled nastily. "I see you need a lesson in obedience."

The hair on the back of her neck stood up.

Judas saw her fear and laughed. "When I speak, you are to say 'as you will, husband.' And nothing else." He raised his brows expectantly.

She sealed her lips tight together. She couldn't call him husband. She wouldn't. The flat of his hand smacked her face. Her head snapped to the side. "Say it!" he yelled.

She clutched her burning cheek.

"Let her be," someone ordered.

Judas dragged her against his chest. "Stay away," he warned.

Lex glanced around. Judas's men had formed a circled around them. They parted, and the long-faced raider named Silas walked toward them. Lex didn't know whether to feel relieved or afraid.

Silas pulled a knife.

Judas shoved her.

She crashed into the dour raider, knocking his knife from his hand as she fell face-first into the dirt. Confused shouts came from all directions. Caked in mud, she rolled over and sat up.

Silas's body landed on her lap. She recoiled with a strangled cry. Blood foamed from his mouth. He gasped once and went limp.

Judas pulled the dead man off of her and dragged her to her feet. She swayed on unsteady legs. Judas pointed with the bloody knife. "Go down on your knees, wife, and say 'as you will, husband.'"

Sweet angels in heaven, he'd just killed a man, yet he meant to keep tormenting her? She shook her head.

Judas slashed the air with the bloody knife. A violent tremble rocked her. His mouth curved with a smile.

"We'll see how brave you are, wife, when I make your brother throw the dice."

She glanced over at James. He sat next to the big boulder, hugging his knees and rocking. "Do as he says, Alexandra. Do as he says," he pleaded. Elizabeth's arms were circled about Mary. Tears poured down their frightened faces.

Judas lunged for her. She jumped backwards, tripped, and fell. He seized her sandal and dragged her behind him. Her tunic rode up, exposing her bare legs. She pushed frantically at her skirt while her head and bottom bumped and scraped over sharp rocks.

Raving drunkenly, Judas continued to pull her toward one of the blazing campfires.

"Lord, save me," she prayed, writhing and kicking.

Two men came leaping over the fire.

CHAPTER 27

Alexandra shook with relief as Nathan tackled Judas to the ground.

Kadar drew his sword. His blond hair flying and his massive arms bulging, he fought off a half dozen men.

She scrambled to her feet and jumped back. Judas's knife lay in her path, like a snake ready to strike. She hesitated. *Stop acting like a frightened, old woman. Just pick it up!* She took a deep breath, grabbed up the wicked weapon, and raced to the cave.

Welcomed with hugs and tears, she gathered her brood around her. Men shouted and cried out to one another. A scream pierced the dark. Kadar pulled his bloody sword out of a man's chest, and using two hands, slashed the blade through another's man neck. The bodies dropped one behind the other.

Nathan and Judas rolled through the cook fire. Yellow embers shot upwards, crackled and popped. Lex cried out and leaped forward. They broke apart, jumped to their feet, and beat at their smoldering tunics. She froze in place.

Nathan drew his sword. His chest heaved. Hate lined

his face. Judas held his hands up in surrender. Lex's mind screamed. *Kill him. Kill him. Kill him.*

The raiders clashing with Kadar fell back. The giant shook his head. Sweat flew from his blond hair. "Should I spare the rest?"

The muscles in Nathan's jaw and neck flexed. His dark, intent eyes flicked over the men and came to a rest on her.

Lex shivered.

"Wife," Nathan said. "Did they harm you or the girls?"

"No...We...we weren't defiled."

"Nathan, watch out!" Mary screamed.

Lex's heart lodged in her throat. Judas held a knife high over his head. What? How could that be? She glanced down at the weapon in her hand. The knife had belonged to Silas, not Judas. A blood-curdling roar stopped her breath. Judas plunged the knife down. Nathan jerked to the side. The blade slid past his chest and buried in his shoulder. His sleeve turned red.

Kadar dove for Judas and tackled him flat.

Lex cried out and ran toward Nathan. One of the raiders grabbed her and she jabbed her elbow at him. "Let go!"

The raider wrapped her in his arms. Cold metal pressed against her throat. "I'll kill her," he bellowed.

Nathan banged Kadar's arm. "Whoa...whoa..."

The giant rolled off of Judas and jumped up.

Judas climbed to his feet. "Throw down your weapons," he ordered.

"Don't do it," Alexandra said. "Judas wants to kill you." Her stomach roiled at the thought of death stilling her beautiful, strong husband.

The raider shook her. "Silence woman."

Nathan pointed his sword at her attacker. "Harm her and I promise you'll be dead before you hit the dirt."

The raider slackened his hold on her and shifted in place.

"Alexandra," Nathan soothed. "Leave me to deal with Judas. Can you do that?" Though his eyes were red-rimmed from lack of sleep and he still had a knife sticking out of his shoulder, her warrior husband exuded confidence and ability.

She nodded.

"Throw down your weapons," Judas repeated.

Nathan pulled the bloody blade out of his arm as casually as removing a loose hair and tossed it at Judas' feet. His sword and knife followed. "Do as he says, Kadar."

The big man snarled, but surrendered his arms to a smiling raider.

Judas walked over to Alexandra. His dry, rough hand clamped onto her wrist. He narrowed his eyes at Nathan "You should have joined us, olive farmer. We could have the Romans on the run by now."

"I'd sooner lick Julius Caesar's feet," Nathan said.

Judas crowed. "You are an amusing fellow, Nathan."

Lex ground her teeth and clenched her fists. The fingers of her right hand curled tighter around smooth steel. Her breath caught. She still had the knife. She'd forgotten all about it in the confusion. She pressed the blade deeper into the folds of her skirt.

Judas's smile faded. He snapped his fingers. Over a dozen raiders surrounded Kadar and Nathan. Judas yanked her up against his side. His hot breath spilled down her neck. "As you take your last breath, olive

farmer, know that I will be taking my new wife to bed."
She struggled against him.

Nathan's eyes flashed like lightening. "You devil," he
roared, plowing through the man directly in front of
him while Kadar knocked down the men to either side
of him.

Lex drew her arm back. Using all her strength, she
drove the knife into Judas' belly. The blade sliced
through cloth and flesh more easily than she would
have supposed. Wet warmth oozed over her knuckles.

Judas sucked in his gut and doubled over, ripping the
dagger from her hand.

Nathan knocked the rebel leader over and pulled her
to his chest. Before she had time to hug him back, he
turned her around and gave her a firm shove. "Go watch
over the others."

The smell of blood following her, she ran back to
Lydia, James, Mary, and Elizabeth. Spinning around, she
pushed her hair out of her face.

Judas gained his feet and slashed at Nathan with his
knife. Kadar tossed a sword to Nathan. He caught it,
swung it in a wide arc, and struck Judas. The outlaw's
guts spilled out and he fell over dead.

Lydia collapsed. Alexandra hurried to her side, knelt
and held her sisters hand, and stroked her hair.

Outraged raiders swarmed Nathan. Alexandra's
heart slammed against her chest. It was all she could do
not to run to him.

Blades flashed and metal clanged. Nathan's sword appeared and disappeared again and again. Kadar slashed
his way toward Nathan. Meeting in the middle, the two
warriors fought back to back. Cast in the orange glow
from the firelight, they shone like avenging spirits sent

from the throne of God.

Nathan moved with ease and grace, belying the bloody nature of his work. Though he'd insisted he was a natural-born warrior, Alexandra hadn't believed it because he was ashamed of it. But he'd never looked more magnificent.

Men screamed and dropped dead until finally the remaining bandits fell back. Nathan's eyes flicked toward her.

She put her hand to her constricted throat. "We're safe," she said, and heard a crazed cry. A handful of raiders charged past Nathan. Hate-filled faces closed in on her. She moaned and leaned over Lydia, covering her sister's back.

She caught glimpses of Nathan behind the sea of grimy tunics rushing toward her. Nathan raised his sword over his head and chopped down. Blood spurted from the mouth of a raider, and the man went down. Sword gone, Nathan unsheathed his knife, grabbed the next raider around the chest, slit the man's throat. Eye blazing and mouth hard, Nathan charged ahead—the angel of death in all his wrathful glory.

The raiders closed on her and she braced for the worst and focused on Nathan, wanting his face to be the last thing she saw in this life.

Nathan dove headfirst, upending one of the men.

Then a loud roar sounded, and the big raider named Bear came out of nowhere and cut down two of his fellow outlaws. Lex hadn't recovered from her shock when Kadar came leaping over a dead body. The giant puffed out his chest and stood between Nathan and a pair raiders regaining their feet. The men looked Kadar up and down, shook their heads, and turned and fled.

Lex sat up.

Nathan and the last raider wrestled in the dirt, rolling over and over. They came to a stop at her knees, kicking and spraying dirt.

Molars grinding over grit, she fisted her hands in the raider's coarse tunic and tugged and tugged. Her effort allowed the man room to work his knife free from his belt. She cried out in dismay and let go of his tunic.

Before she could go after the knife, Nathan flipped the man to his belly, locked his arm around the man's head and pulled back. The raider's neck broke with a loud snap, and Nathan released his hold and rolled to his feet.

The dead man's face hit the ground with a thud and lay canted grotesquely to one side. Lex's stomach pitched and she twisted away and vomited. Sickened by the thick smell of blood and her own rank fear, she heaved and gagged long after her belly was empty. Weary to the bone and shaking, she wiped her mouth on her sleeve and looked up.

Nathan's hands were braced on his knees. He was heaving for breath and watching her out of dark and haunted eyes. She ached for him. He hated his past. Hated that he had killed his fellow Israelites. Hated the name angel of death. And now more blood stained his hands—blood belonging to his neighbors and men he'd called friends.

Lex exhaled and rose on shaky legs. She stepped toward Nathan, needing and wanting the closeness of him.

He stopped her with an upraised hand.

"Nathan?" she whispered.

"Go take care of James and Mary."

His cold voice broke her heart.

CHAPTER 28

Nathan walked about the decimated rebel camp in a daze. Although he was the one who had ordered the surviving raiders to move the dead into the cave, he still felt it was a better burial than they deserved. Mark the Younger's lifeless eyes stared up at him. They used to be fairly good friends. Now Mark's head was canted at an unnatural angle because Nathan had snapped his neck, a vicious act Lex had witnessed close up. One that had sickened her.

He couldn't glance her way without remembering the look of revulsion that had crossed her face as she stared up at him after he'd killed Mark. Then she'd proceeded to vomit her stomach up. How was he supposed to meet her eyes again?

Nathan moved to the edge of the camp and called Mary over.

She rushed to him and hugged him. "I knew you would find a way to save us."

He patted her back. "I have a favor to ask of you, sweet lamb."

"I'll do anything. I'm so glad you are here." His sister hugged him again.

"Alexandra will want to wash before we leave." Judas the Zealot's blood stained his wife's hands. Some of the blood might be her own, from having been dragged over the ground by the mad man. Her lip was split. Bruises circled her neck. The injuries made Nathan want to kill the crazed man all over again.

He uncurled his fisted fingers and squeezed Mary's shoulder. "Could you find some water and a rag and take them to Alexandra?"

The raider named Bear approached. Unusually somber, the bushy-bearded man pulled on his collar and cleared his throat. "Nathan. May I ask after your father?"

The blood drained from Nathan's head.

Mary burst into tears. "Father is dead, isn't he?" She buried her face in his chest.

Nathan's anger boiled to the surface.

Bear looked completely shaken.

Nathan saw Lex hurrying toward them. He squeezed his eyes closed.

His wife arrived breathless. "What's the matter, dear?"

Nathan felt Lex's eyes on him. He looked at the boulder beyond her. "My father never woke up. I buried—" his voice broke.

Mary's sobs turned violent.

Lex's hand settled on his arm. "I'm so sorry,"

Another blast of fury surged through him. "Mary needs you," he said through gritted teeth. Not wanting his hate to sully Lex more than it already had, he left Mary to her care and walked away, taking Bear with him. They joined the others in moving the last of the dead bodies into the cave.

◆ ◆ ◆

They left the rebel camp behind and walked through the rain and the dark for an hour before stopping for the night. Alexandra couldn't remember ever feeling so tired. Nathan volunteered to take the first watch. She offered to join him, but he walked away without acknowledging her. Shivering under a thin blanket, she fought to stay awake, but sleep quickly claimed her. Rising at dawn to cloudy skies, they pushed on. The trip home ought to have held a measure of joy, but the news of Joseph's death and the blood and violence behind them had left everyone quiet and subdued. Early afternoon found them resting beside a brook.

Alexandra stayed with Nathan and the horses as the others went to refresh themselves downstream.

Nathan's eyes clouded. He looked away. "Go wash. I'll take care of Royal and Satan."

She reached for him. "Nathan."

His frown deepened. "I'm not fit for company. Go." He turned his back to her.

Her throat closed and tears sprang to her eyes. She spun away and made her way blindly to the others, knelt down on a flat stone, dipped her hands in the cool water, and dabbed her fingers to her flushed face and neck. The cheerful splashing of the brook offered no comfort.

She longed to hold Nathan and ached to be in his arms. *Show me how to help him, Lord.*

Kadar squatted next to her and wet a small rag in the stream. The giant soldier had appointed himself Lydia's nursemaid.

Lex offered him a weak smile. "Thank you for caring

for Lydia. I—"

He waved his Hercules-sized hand. "It's no bother."

Lex pushed her tangled hair away from her face. "Has she said anything yet?" Lydia remained glassy-eyed and unresponsive, making James's angry grumbling and Mary's sorrowful weeping seem pleasant.

Kadar's visage darkened. "Judas can thank his maker he is dead."

"His death was too easy," she agreed, and released a shuddering breath. "I hope I can find a way to make Nathan believe it."

"Has your stomach settled?"

Her face heated, remembering her disgraceful display. "I'm better, thank you. It was the smell of the blood...it didn't agree with me." It was only half the truth. Seeing Nathan snap a man's neck had shaken her more deeply than she liked to admit.

"Don't be too hard on yourself." Kadar grunted and smiled. "I've seen men hardier than you vomit on their sandals after viewing the carnage of battle."

She pressed a hand to her stomach. "Nathan hates that he killed his fellow Israelites."

Kadar's mouth twisted with distaste. "He shouldn't. You might have noticed his fellow Jews showed great enthusiasm in trying to kill him."

"Hmm...I hadn't thought about it that way." She looked over at Nathan. Misery marred his face. She sighed. "Convincing Nathan won't be easy. He takes all the blame on himself."

"Herod told me about Nathan in battle. Now I've seen it for myself—" Kadar glanced at Nathan as well.

Lex eyes snapped back to Kadar. "What did Herod say?"

The giant soldier rubbed the back of his neck as he considered her request. "Herod could tell the story better than me."

She leaned forward. "I want to hear it from you."

Kadar exhaled a resigned breath.

Her toes curled in her sandals. Lord help her, she wanted to know, but she didn't.

Alexandra walked beside Nathan on the hard-packed path. He led Royal by the bridle while Mary and Elizabeth shared the warhorse's saddle. Up ahead, James trudged beside Kadar's black stallion. Lydia sat behind Kadar, resting her face against the giant's back. Alexandra continued to mull over what she'd learned from Kadar.

The iron-gray clouds slowly parted, giving way to patches of bright, blue sky and the buffeting wind gradually mellowed to a soft breeze. Small clumps of white flowers dotted the hillsides. Alexandra inhaled the sweet smell settling about her.

"We'll be in Rumah soon," Nathan told the girls. "You're limping," he said to her, a hint of tenderness in his voice.

Her heart beat faster. "Am I?" She yearned for his touch, for his kisses.

His fingers brushed her upper arm. Her breath caught.

Nathan pulled her to a stop. "We should stop and have a look." He knelt and lifted her foot. His strong, callused fingers closed around her ankle. She swallowed. His warm breath moved over her skin. "You have a blister, and a bad one at that."

"A blister?" The nearness of him made her numb to everything but him. She glanced at the swollen, red skin on the side of her foot where her sandal had rubbed. "It's nothing."

Nathan raised a brow. "Nothing?"

She waved off his concern. "A mere inconvenience. I will—"

Nathan flinched.

Her head swirled sickeningly. She clutched her stomach. Could she be any more thoughtless, repeating one of her father-in-law's favorite sayings? "I'm sorry. Forgive me. I—" she fumbled for the right words.

The angry wall came up. Nathan dropped her foot. He stood and stepped back.

Her chest constricted. What if Nathan's wounds were too deep to heal? What if he never stopped pushing her away? What if things were never right between them again?

The tears she'd been fighting all day began to flow. She buried her face in her hands.

Nathan's arms came around her. "Lex." The tender way he said her name made her cry all the harder. His lips moved against her ear. "Lex, what's wrong?"

Her breath hitched. "I was beginning to fear you'd never hold me again."

James led Royal away. Kadar moved off as well, leaving them alone.

Nathan's fingers pressed harder against her back. "I tried to stay away, but I saw you limping and I couldn't stop myself."

Laughter burbled up. "If I'd known that, I would have started hobbling sooner." She pushed closer to him. "I missed you."

"You aren't revolted by me?"

She gasped. "Revolted? No, never."

"You can't want my bloody hands on you."

She cupped his hand and kissed the tender skin above his thumb. "Your hands are beautiful." She laid her cheek against his open palm. "Your touch makes me come alive."

His thumb brushed her swollen lip. "The sight of your bruises and bloodstained clothes makes me want to go on killing. The depth of my rage frightens me." Pain shadowed his eyes. "I'm afraid I will soil you with my hate."

"You are being too hard on yourself." She drew his hands to her waist. "You killed to protect me."

His brow furrowed. "My blood sang as I slaughtered them. And I rejoiced in it. Where was the good in that?" He tried to pull away.

She tightened her grip. "Listen to me!"

"Lex..."

"Your father would have listened."

Nathan narrowed his eyes at her, but he stilled.

Her mouth went dry. "Judas and his men gave you no choice but to kill them. You fought them with the same hard determination as Kadar. But then some of the men turned to attack me, and it wasn't until that moment that you turned blind to everything except killing."

Nathan continued to frown.

She licked her lips. "Kadar said he heard you fought the same way when Herod fell in battle and was swarmed by enemy soldiers. They said you fought with the strength of ten soldiers, single-handedly rescuing Herod."

Nathan spoke through gritted teeth. "I earned the

name angel of death that day."

She clasped his rigid hands. "I think the only times your blood sings is when someone you love or care for is threatened."

He laughed without humor. "I'll give you leave to believe it. Because I'm that desperate to keep your love." He pulled his hands free and tapped his chest. "But, I know what's in here."

A tremble shook her. "I don't care if you are the angel of death. I still love you." She held her arms out. He remained rooted in place. Her heart ached for him. For herself.

Kadar circled back on his horse. "I hate to bother you, but..." he jerked his thumb over his shoulder "...look who just came over the hill."

Alexandra forced her eyes away from Nathan.

Sapphira and Barjesus hurried toward them, holding hands.

CHAPTER 29

Nathan pinched the bridge of his nose. "You want to get married?" he repeated.

Sapphira pressed closer to Barjesus. The young outlaw lifted his chin. "We'd like to travel the rest of the way to Rumah with you. For Sapphira's sake, I'd ask you not to mention that she spent a bit of time separated from everyone."

Nathan arched his brow at Sapphira. Her reputation would suffer if people found out she'd spent a day and night alone with Barjesus.

She blushed prettily. "Barjesus didn't force me to go with him. I wanted to."

Nathan turned to a rapt Alexandra, Mary, James, and Elizabeth. "Did the boy do harm to any of you?"

They shook their heads. Alexandra wet her split lip. "Barjesus stood guard at the camp." An ugly purple bruise marred her soft, lovely cheek. Nathan's hand curled around the cold metal of his sword.

Forgive him. Lex's beautiful, gray eyes begged. Though bloodshot, they spoke to him as clearly as words.

Forgive? How was he supposed to forgive? He peeled

his fingers off his sword, squared his shoulders and pointed at Barjesus. "If I catch you raiding with Hezekiah or the others, you're a dead man. Do you understand?"

The young rebel's face turned white as the belly of a fish.

Sapphira clasped the boy's hand. "Barjesus promised me he would go back to farming." She shook Barjesus's arm. "Tell him."

The boy wiped at the sweat beading his forehead. "I am done with raiding. I swear it on the name of the Lord."

Nathan lowered his arm. "See that you are. In turn, I promise I won't tell Sapphira's parents the two of you spent the night alone." Their faces reddened and they began studying their feet, confirming Nathan's suspicions regarding the breakneck speed of their courtship.

The sun disappeared behind a cloud. Nathan rubbed the back of his neck. "We best get going."

Alexandra took a couple of limping steps, saw him watching her and frowned. "Perhaps we could move more quickly if I were to ride on Royal?"

"Maybe? You need to be kinder to yourself, wife." Glad for an excuse to touch her, he scooped her up in his arms.

Her lips brushed his ear. "Where's a deserted olive orchard when you need one?"

His belly warmed and his loins tightened. Disgusted with himself, he quickly placed her on the saddle.

Lex grabbed her side. "Ouch, that hurts."

He pushed her hand aside and pressed his fingers against her belly. "Does it hurt anywhere else?"

She winced. "My ribs are the worst."

His hands balled, and he relished the burn and heaviness throbbing through his sword arm. What was he doing pretending to be an olive farmer? He expelled a heavy breath. "You should have told me. I could have bound them."

She made a face. "I just want to get home."

He clicked his tongue and Royal moved forward. "I want to stop in Rumah before going home." Lex glanced down at him. He touched her bruised cheek and his blood heated. "I want them to see what Judas did to you."

Her brow furrowed.

"I know. I hate to put you through it," he said. "But, I want Bartholomew and the other elders to see with their own eyes the evil you suffered."

"Will it help heal the rift between us and them?"

He rolled his knotted shoulders. "Pinhas, for one, has had a change of heart. He came out to the farm in the middle of the night, in the pouring rain, to tell me where Judas was hiding. It's how I found you so quickly."

"Did he?" Lex smiled weakly. "Bless him. It's a good start." She raised her brows, looking for him to agree.

Nathan sealed his lips shut.

They arrived in Rumah with an hour of light to spare and trod boldly down the narrow thoroughfare to Sapphira's home. Door after door opened. Families stepped outside. Frowning, angry faces followed them. Voices murmured against them. Thick hostility consumed the breathable air.

Nathan's hand went to his sword. "Something's wrong."

"I don't like it up here," Lex said through gritted

teeth.

Nathan helped her off the horse. She was trembling. His muscles tightened. She had to be close to the breaking point, yet she called Mary and Elizabeth to her and circled her arms around them.

Old Zeke left his doorstep and marched toward them. "What are you going to do about Herod?"

Nathan looked around. Where were Bartholomew and the other elders? Half of the men were absent. A ball of ice formed in his stomach. "What happened?"

"Herod charged into Rumah like a raging bull and dragged Hezekiah away from his dinner table and paraded him up and down the road, announcing he was taking Hezekiah to his fortress in Sepphoris to try and execute him." Zeke's wrinkled face was purple with rage. Spittle flew from his puckered mouth. "Herod threatened us. Told us we'd face the same fate, if we didn't return home and live in peace."

Nathan wanted to strangle Herod. "What's been done about it?"

"Bartholomew and Thomas and most of the other men followed Herod to Sepphoris to try to put a stop to it." Old Zeke wiped his sleeve across his beard. "Pinhas and John dashed off to Jerusalem to complain to Antipater and John Hyrcanus."

"Hezekiah should be brought before the high court in Jerusalem," Nathan said.

Old Zeke pointed a gnarled finger. "Go tell that to Herod."

They reached the farm at sundown. The tent, barn, and the new, stone house stood as gray shadows against the leaden sky. Alexandra ought to feel joy at returning home, but the stop in Rumah had been a disaster, causing the black anger filling Nathan to come boiling back to life.

Timothy tumbled out of the main tent and ran toward them with Rhoda close behind him. Mary raced into her mother's embrace, and they cried and hugged.

Nathan joined them, and he and his stepmother shared some quiet words.

A lump rose in Alexandra's throat. She wanted to go to them, but she felt like an intruder. James and Elizabeth stopped on either side of her.

James's elbow touched hers. "Do you think Father will be as happy to see us?"

Alexandra scanned the yard. Her father was nowhere to be seen. Praise heaven. She wasn't ready to face his harsh tongue. And considering Nathan's present mood, it was probably for the best.

Kadar's large black stallion filled her view. "Where should I take your sister?" he asked, glancing back at Lydia. Her sister's arms were still wrapped around the giant's waist, her head resting against his broad back.

Chilled, Alexandra rubbed her arms. "Take her to the small tent."

Kadar coaxed his horse forward. Alexandra glanced back over at Nathan in time to see him moving off to tend to the animals and Rhoda coming toward her. The tall woman threw her thin arms around Alexandra. "Bless you, my dear girl, for watching over my Mary. Bless you."

Startled, Alexandra laughed, then tears spilled down her face. "I'm so sorry you lost Joseph."

Rhoda patted her back. "I'll try not to be a burden to

you and Nathan."

Alexandra gasped. "Burden? We *need* you," she rushed to assure the widow. All Joseph's possessions now belonged to Nathan. Rhoda was at his mercy, and by extension, Alexandra's. "Please don't go back to your family," Alexandra said. "I know it's your right, but I'd miss your help and your company."

Her mother-in-law straightened. "I'll stay and teach you all I know. But if you change your mind—"

Alexandra grabbed up the older woman's chapped hand. "I won't change my mind. I love you. And I love Timothy and Mary. You are as dear to me as Lydia and James."

Rhoda dabbed at Alexandra's tears with the rag clutched in her hand. "You must take after your mother. I don't see a hint of your infernal father in you, I'm happy to say."

Alexandra took a deep breath. She supposed it couldn't be put off any longer. "Where is my father?"

Rhoda scowled. "Kadar had a *word* with the jackass, and that was the last we saw of him. And good riddance too."

Alexandra bit her lip. "I'm sorry for the misery he caused."

"Your father is the one who should apologize." The older woman's face softened. "Come inside. I'll get some wash water and fresh clothes for you and your sister."

A short while later Alexandra had Lydia settled on a bedroll. Lex tucked a blanket under her sister's chin. "I'm going to get you something to eat."

Lydia stared sightlessly up at the tent's ceiling. Alexandra squeezed her eyes closed. Lydia had always bubbled with life and joy. "I missed you so much, dear. Please come back to me."

Kadar entered the tent carrying a plate of food.

Alexandra reached for the plate. "You read my mind."

The big man nodded at the tent door. "Go join your family. I'll care for your sister."

Alexandra frowned apologetically. "I can't leave her alone with you. It wouldn't be proper."

Lydia stirred. "Kadar?" Her sister pulled her thin, frail arm out from under the cover and reached for the giant.

Kadar moved to Lydia and knelt beside her. "I'm here."

Her sister sighed and closed her eyes. "Stay with me."

"I will," Kadar said. "But you have to promise me you will eat the food I've brought." Lydia was dangerously thin. The baby swelling her belly only served to emphasize it.

Lydia nodded and struggled to sit up. Kadar propped pillows behind her. Then, picking up the plate of food, he gave Alexandra a pointed look. *Her reputation is already ruined*, it said. *Let's concentrate on saving her life.* Turning back to Lydia, he held a piece of bread to her mouth. Her sister nibbled at it.

Alexandra slipped out of the small tent and entered the large, lamp-lit tent. She joined the family around the reed table. Timothy was unusually subdued. James and Elizabeth picked at their food. Nathan stared at the tent wall, his face hard and unmoving. The silence lengthened. Mary pillowed her head on Rhoda's lap and fell fast asleep. Alexandra's eyes kept going back to Joseph's empty spot, and her heart grew heavier and heavier.

"I'm going to sell the farm," Nathan announced, shattering the silence.

Alexandra's brow knotted. "Sell the farm?"

Nathan shoved his plate back. "I can't stay in Rumah. Nothing good will come of it."

Alexandra sat up on her knees and leaned toward him. "You don't have to do it for me. I—"

"It has nothing to do with you," Nathan snapped.

Alexandra sagged back onto her heels. She lifted her hand to her face. Judas' fists had landed like sweet kisses compared to the painful punch of Nathan's anger.

Nathan touched her knee. "Forgive me."

She hugged her arms. "I don't understand. I thought you loved the farm." She wanted to live the rest of her days here and she'd believed he did, too.

He scrubbed his face. "My father was an olive farmer. I've tried, but—"

"Where will we go?" Rhoda demanded.

Nathan stood. "I plan to rejoin the army. Herod will give us rooms in one of his fortresses."

Rhoda's jaw dropped. "You want my Mary and Timothy to live with that dog?"

Timothy smiled ear-to-ear. "Will I get to wear a sword?"

"Quiet, monkey," Nathan said.

Timothy's lower lip wobbled. Mary woke with a start, looked around, and burst into tears.

The color drained from Nathan's face. He backed away from the table.

Alexandra jumped to her feet. Her heart beat hard against her chest. She moved toward Nathan. "Stay. Talk to us."

Misery marred his face. "There's nothing to talk

about. I will kill someone if I stay in Rumah." His eyes met hers. "You saw what I'm capable of."

The image of her husband snapping a man's neck flashed through her mind. She swallowed.

Pain flared in the brown eyes she loved so well. Nathan turned his back to her and disappeared out the door.

Alexandra looked at Rhoda.

"Go. Go." The older woman shooed her on. "He needs you."

"Thank you." Alexandra wrapped a shawl about her shoulders and slipped out into the night.

Nathan had disappeared, but she could guess where he'd gone. She crossed the yard and headed up the moonlit trail leading to her father-in-law's tomb. Though she hated the idea of leaving the farm, she'd do it with a smile for Nathan's sake. His rejoining the army and Herod was another matter. But that wasn't why she was going to her husband.

She found Nathan sitting on his haunches, his back pressed against the stone used to cover the entrance to the grave.

The moon passed behind a cloud. Cold air sliced through her tunic. She pulled her shawl tighter about her arms. "Nathan," her voice trembled. "Take me to the orchard. Make love to me."

He groaned and his head dropped back against the rock. "I can't, Lex. I won't touch you while this black hate is eating me up."

"I don't mind." She took a step toward him.

"Lex, don't," he ground out the words. "Go. Just go."

Tears stung her eyes. "I want to comfort you."

"Go!" Nathan barked.

Her throat closed and her heart broke into thousands of pieces. She turned and fled blindly down the dark path.

Nathan woke early the next day. Leaving the farm behind, he rode south and arrived in Sepphoris about midday. The city hummed with nervous excitement, reminding him of a Roman stadium anticipating the start of a chariot race. He left Royal at the stables and went straight to Herod's private quarters.

A stoop-backed slave opened the heavy, wood door and waved Nathan inside. "Fortune smiles on you." The slave grinned, revealing a row of rotten teeth. "You made it in time for the execution."

Nathan pushed past the slave and crossed to Herod. "You are going to kill Hezekiah? Do you want to start a full-out revolt?"

Herod stood by a bed as austere as the rest of the chamber. The remains of the morning meal were strewn over a rickety table. "Olive farmer," he said congenially, cinching his sword belt tight. "Why aren't you out in the hills chasing Judas?"

Nathan flinched. Had Herod betrayed him? Nathan's eyes narrowed. "You knew Judas had kidnapped Alexandra and Mary and you didn't come to help?"

"Hold on." Herod put his hands up. "When I arrived in Rumah, I discovered Hezekiah and arrested him. I sent my men out to hunt for Judas before returning to Sepphoris with my prisoner."

"You can call off the hounds. Judas is dead."

Herod studied him for a moment and grinned. "Yes, I expect he is."

Not in the mood to be humored, Nathan got to the point. "What's this nonsense about executing Hezekiah?"

"I gave him a fair trial."

Nathan gritted his teeth. "You don't have the authority to try anyone, never mind execute them."

Herod plucked up an apple from the table and shined it up on his tunic. "The Sanhedrin has enough fickle women in its ranks to fill a Persian harem. Our spineless leaders will slap Hezekiah's hand and send him home. Rome wants an end to the looting and killing. I mean to quiet the raiders for good."

"Killing Hezekiah will lead to more trouble."

"Ha. You're one to talk. You killed Judas."

His conscience still raw over the matter, Nathan couldn't meet Herod's eye. "Judas didn't give me any choice."

Herod crunched into the apple. "Stop worrying about me and go home to your family."

Nathan crossed his arms and braced his legs. "I'm not going anywhere until you promise to send Hezekiah to Jerusalem."

Herod flung the apple down onto the table, sending plates and bowls clinking and clattering together. "I can't believe you are taking sides with those killing, thieving scoundrels."

Nathan blew out a frustrated breath. "I'm not taking sides with anybody. I want an end to the upheaval."

"Tell that to Judas." Herod gave him a pointed look. "Or maybe, the attack on your family is giving you second thoughts about aligning with me?"

Nathan closed his eyes and saw Lex's mottled bruises and his father's lifeless body. His hand curled around his sword. "My loyalty belongs to you and Antipater."

Herod thumped him on the back. "If you grow bored growing olives, my house is open to you."

Nathan shifted in place. "How soon can you take us in?"

Herod's smile was wicked. "So, you've come to your senses, have you?"

Nathan hitched a shoulder. "You're the only friend I have left."

Herod grunted. "You always were too truthful for your own good." His eyes turned calculating. "Do you think Hezekiah and his followers will give up their cause?"

Nathan shook his head. "They won't be bowing the knee to Rome anytime soon."

"I agree," Herod said. "And I believe the quickest way to convince the Galilean rebels to lay down their weapons is to make an example of Hezekiah."

Nathan looked Herod square in the eye. "Kill Hezekiah and all of Galilee will riot."

"I'll squash it."

Nathan threw his hands up. "Wonderful! Furnish your father's enemies with new darts to throw at him. Give them more ways to discredit him."

Herod growled low in his throat. "You go too far." Questioning the notoriously touchy man about his loyalty to his family was a good way to end up hurt or dead.

Herod headed to the door.

Nathan bolted past him and blocked his path. "Don't do this."

Herod's eyes narrowed. "I've made up my mind. Now, get out of my way or I'll go through you."

Nathan pulled the door open and sent it crashing into the wall. Herod marched past him.

Nathan followed. Malchus and Obodas pushed away from the wall where they'd been waiting. Spotting Nathan, they raised their brows.

He walked past them without a second look and they fell in line. Herod led them up a series of stairways and out on the rooftop, into the blinding sun. Guards marched Hezekiah to the weather-worn parapet.

Silence descended. Hezekiah's eyes met Nathan's. The rebel leader shook his head in disgust.

Nathan flinched. He had a soft spot in his heart for the barrel-chested, affable man. Hezekiah had a young wife and three children.

The executioner tied Hezekiah's hand behind his back.

A familiar voice rang out from below, "Traitor! Traitor!" Nathan searched the sea of angry faces and found Bartholomew and Thomas and the rest of his neighbors, raising their fists at him. They were so quick to judge. *Rot them!*

The guards forced Hezekiah down onto his knees. The executioner raised his sword with two hands. The blade whooshed down. Hezekiah's head fell from his shoulders.

Nathan squeezed his eyes closed.

CHAPTER 30

The family sat in mourning for Joseph for one week, then left for Jerusalem. The Holy City seemed smaller than Alexandra remembered. And the Mount of Olives was pleasant enough, but it couldn't compare to the wild beauty of her Galilean orchard. When would she see it again?

They'd arrived six days ago and had given James, Lydia, and Elizabeth over to her father.

Alexandra and Nathan stood in the entry hall of her father's home, waiting to see if he would see them. They'd come four days in a row to visit and been turned away each time.

She fiddled with her cumbersome veil. She'd forgotten how uncomfortable the layers of heavy cloth were. "My father divorced Elizabeth as quickly as she said he would. She wasn't with Father for a full day before he sent her home." Alexandra imagined her cousin had left this house with a wide smile on her face, bless her.

Nathan merely nodded.

Her father's bald eunuch returned.

Alexandra held her breath.

"Your father doesn't want to see you. He won't allow

you to visit Lydia." Goda folded his hands and smiled smugly. "He says to stop coming."

Alexandra swallowed back her grief. Nathan patted her back. She held out two small bags filled with honeyed nuts." Please give these to Lydia and James and tell them I tried to visit."

Goda took the bags, then leaned closer. "Your brother is gone."

Alexandra blinked. "Gone? Gone where?"

The slave shrugged. "He left in the middle of the night and hasn't been seen since."

Nathan frowned. "How long has he been missing?"

"Two days."

Alexandra imagined the worst. "I hope he's not hurt or in danger."

Nathan ran his hand down her arm. "What's being done to find the boy?"

"Master Simeon has men looking for him." The brow over Goda's right eye began to tick—a sign he was being less than truthful.

"You know something." Alexandra turned to Nathan. "He knows more."

Nathan arched a brow at Goda. "Well?"

The eunuch smiled and tossed the bags of nuts back-and-forth between his hands. "A few coins will loosen my lips."

Nathan knocked Goda's hand aside. "Leave us, you greedy cretin."

Goda stuffed the sacks of nuts into his pocket. "A fellow has got to make money if he's going to buy his way out of slavery."

Nathan stabbed the air with his finger. "Go."

The slave's lips curled with a mocking smile. "You

know where to find me if you change your mind."

Alexandra clasped Nathan's hand. He looked down at her, and his eyes softened. "I'll find James."

She frowned. Married for five months now, and here they were back in Jerusalem, with Nathan promising to help her find a sibling. Again.

He squeezed her fingers. "I know what you are thinking. This is not the same as Lydia. James is missing because he wants to be missing. Jerusalem is too small for him to remain hidden for long." He opened the front door. "I'll take you back to camp, and then I'll see if I can find him."

She sighed. "You must regret the day you met me."

He tugged on her veil. "I regret this ugly garment. I wish you'd stop wearing it."

She wrinkled her nose. "I hate it, too. Let's build a big fire tonight, and we can toss in the veil and watch it burn."

"Timothy will love that," Nathan said.

They laughed for the first time in weeks. It felt good. Leaving her father's house, they headed back to the Mount of Olives.

"Would you mind taking the road that goes by the Temple?" Alexandra asked. "It won't take any longer than cutting through the alleys. I want to see the Temple before the *Pesach* pilgrims overrun the city."

Nathan rolled his shoulders. "Trust me. You don't want to go near the place."

A wave of dread rolled through her. "Why not?"

Nathan exhaled heavily. "Judas and Hezekiah's mothers have been demonstrating at the Temple daily, demanding justice for their sons."

Alexandra's stomach knotted. This couldn't be good.

"Why didn't you tell me?"

"I didn't want you to worry." Nathan kicked at the road with his sandal. "I'm going to accept Herod's offer and move the family into the Hasmonean Palace."

Alexandra frowned. "I know it's probably for the best, but—"

Nathan stopped her with a look. "The Mount of Olives is going to fill with people who hate us. The men who abducted you and killed my father will be there. I don't want them anywhere near you."

Alexandra opened her mouth.

"Don't fight me on this, Lex," Nathan warned.

Anger, fear, misery, roiled her insides. "I guess you must have just been doing it to please your father."

Nathan's brow furrowed. "Doing what?"

"One of the things that amazed me when we married was how you and your father discussed matters with Rhoda and me before making decisions." The words soured in her mouth. "But that died with your father, didn't it?"

He blanched. "Lex."

She halted and fisted her hands in her tunic. "You are selling the farm, rejoining the army, and moving the family into Herod's home, all without talking it over with us. It's your right. But...but." What could she say to get through to him? The wall between them grew thicker and thicker with each passing day. The depth of Nathan's anger frightened her.

She spotted Kadar coming toward them. She sniffed back her tears, wiped her runny nose on the veil, and smiled despite herself. The giant man searched them out daily, always working his way around to asking about Lydia.

Grim-faced, Kadar skipped the usual greetings and addressed Nathan, "Antipater sent me. The Sanhedrin has summoned you and Herod to appear before the court, to answer for killing Hezekiah and Judas."

Alexandra groaned.

"How bad is it?" Nathan asked, the muscle in his jaw ticking.

Kadar shook his head. "Not good. All of Galilee is up in arms over Hezekiah and Judas's deaths. The Sanhedrin is outraged they were bypassed. Antipater tried to stop it, but—" The giant shrugged. "Herod's bald ambition makes people nervous. There's talk of wanting to cut off the head of the snake before it circles back to bite." Kadar's frown deepened. "The charge isn't for insubordination. It's for murder."

Alexandra's knees buckled. Nathan's strong arms came around her. If convicted, he would be put to death. The complaint forming on her lips died. Her husband's beautiful brown eyes had gone hard as flint. He wasn't going down without a fight.

Nathan righted his ragged tunic. The garment was torn at the neck, and his hair was uncombed. He felt ridiculous, but there was no help for it. Defendants were expected to show humility and remorse.

Kadar clapped Nathan on the back. "Trust Antipater. He'll bring you out of this alive. The Sanhedrin's real target is Herod."

Nathan nodded, but he wasn't convinced. Antipater's tireless work behind the scenes and generous bribes might not be enough to counteract the daily protests, headed by Hezekiah and Judas's mothers.

Nathan followed Antipater and Herod's three brothers out the door. The Temple was a short walk away. Onlookers crowded the wide streets, loudly jeering and booing. Nathan lowered his face and kept walking. They entered the Temple grounds and pushed past hordes of curious spectators.

Lex and Rhoda stood beside the entrance to the Women's Court, clinging to each other, worry furrowing their faces. He'd pleaded with them to stay at the camp since they couldn't even watch the trial, but they'd insisted on coming. He looked back at them and smiled encouragingly. *Dear God, let me leave this place alive. Please let me return to my family.*

The white walls of the Temple glistened in the sun. A puff of smoke drifted past them, carrying the scent of sweet incense and burnt offerings. Nathan caught glimpses of the priests attending to the sacrifices. The Hall of Hewn Stones, where the Sanhedrin held court, loomed large. A favorite teacher of the Lord sat in the shade of the lumbering building, ringed by his dedicated disciples.

Encircled by the sacred sites, Nathan was suddenly glad he was wearing the clothes of a penitent man.

A loud commotion broke out and the crowd parted. Nathan blinked. Herod strode toward them, leading a one hundred and fifty-man army. Was he mad? Marching soldiers into Jerusalem was wicked enough. Bringing them onto Temple grounds bordered on blasphemy.

Nathan reversed course. *Of all the arrogant, insensitive, ill-advised moves.*

He stopped short of Herod. "What in the name of Beelzebub are you doing?"

Herod grinned. "I'm saving your hide, olive farmer."

"Would it kill you to show a little humility?" Nathan growled.

Immaculately groomed, without a hair out of place, Herod wore a purple robe. *Royal* purple, rot him.

Herod's eyes turned reptilian. "Why should I bow and grovel before those overblown bores? I won't give them the satisfaction." Herod pointed around the compound. "All of Jerusalem abuses me and my family behind our backs, but look at them now."

A mix of fear and caution showed on the faces trained on them. People began to slip away. Herod grunted his approval. "This trial is a farce, and you know it. I've been found guilty before setting a foot in court. I brought my soldiers along to balance the scales. Those sour old men will think twice before convicting us now."

Nathan glanced ahead at Antipater and Herod's brothers. "Your father told you to bring a band of bodyguards. He didn't mean a whole army."

Herod's smile faltered. "My father isn't pleased, but he has confidence in me. I know what I'm doing. I'm asking you to trust me."

Nathan watched a small family dressed in their finest and bringing a lamb and turtledoves as offering to the Lord for the newborn babe cradled in the mother's arm hurry across the courtyard, moving away from the trouble. The show of force would probably work, but at a cost of offending most of his fellow Jews. It was bad enough all of Galilee had turned against him. If he threw his support behind Herod, all of Judea would hate him too.

Nathan's eyes went back to Lex and Rhoda. "My wife and stepmother are here. I don't want them to get caught in the middle of a fight."

"Trust me," Herod repeated.

Nathan looked past his friend's gaudy clothes. Herod had offered up his home and help to Nathan. Whereas men he counted as brothers, Pinhas and Bartholomew and Hezekiah, had proved faithless. Nathan blew out a long breath. Loyalty deserved loyalty. "All right, you strutting peacock...we'll do it your way."

Herod clapped him on the back. "You are a good man. Let's go get this over with."

The temple guard escorted Nathan and Herod into the inner sanctum of the Hall of Hewn Stone. The seventy-one members of the Sanhedrin sat on stone benches arranged in a semicircle. Clerks stood off to one side, ready to record the proceedings. Three rows of scholars were on hand to give expert opinions on the Law. Nathan had always wondered what the hall looked like. If things went badly, he'd have the comfort of knowing the hideous, gray walls and worn, cedar floors were uglier than sin.

The witnesses against Nathan and Herod entered the hall through a side door. Bartholomew and Pinhas and a few other men from Rumah filed past Nathan. His Galilean neighbors were too busy gawking at the men of wealth and prestige sitting as judges to notice the dirty look he gave them.

High priest Hyrcanus, looking more tired and bedraggled than usual, opened the proceedings by addressing the witnesses, reminding them of their duty to speak the truth.

"I'm going to kill the little weasel," Herod grumbled.

"Hyrcanus is caught between Antipater and the elders," Nathan whispered.

Herod's lips curled with disgust.

Nathan scanned the faces of the judges, searching for his father-in-law. Simeon Onias sat at the far end of a bench. The mean-hearted coward wore a self-satisfied smile. Nathan planned to have a word with the gutless man, once the proceedings were over.

Herod swiped his hand through the air. "Sextus Caesar sent Hyrcanus a letter warning him against trying me. But the sniveling coward sided with my enemies."

Nathan arched a brow. "Hyrcanus has his own enemies to worry about." As the letter more than likely contained a threat of death, the timid high priest earned a measure of respect from Nathan.

"I'll make him pay for betraying me," Herod hissed.

The pain and rage they carried between them ought to set the place on fire.

John Hyrcanus called the court to order. Silence descended. The high priest coughed and righted his tunic. "Nathan of Rumah's accuser will present his charges."

Simeon Onias stood. A loud buzzing filled the chamber.

Nathan's hands fisted. His conniving, hypocrite of a father-in-law was going to use the Law to do his dirty work.

Simeon Onias raised his hands. The room quieted. The fastidious man smoothed the folds of his expensive robe. "Friends and brethren, I understand your surprise. Yes, Nathan of Rumah rescued my son and daughter. But Judas's death was unnecessary. I put a large ransom into my son-in-law's hands and instructed him to give the money to Judas. What happened, you ask yourselves?"

Simeon gave Nathan a pitying look. Nathan gripped

the edge of the stone bench, resisting the urge to go strangle the rotten liar.

"Nathan of Rumah and I had a falling out over the terms of the marriage contract," Simeon confided. "My son-in-law became angry when he learned I wasn't going to give him any more money." The pious man smirked. "You might find it interesting to know the soldiers in Antipater's army call Nathan the angel of death because he excels at killing. I think my son-in-law murdered Judas and kept the ransom."

The room erupted with noisy speculation.

Blood rushed to Nathan's head. He narrowed his eyes at Simeon. His father-in-law blanched and glanced toward the witnesses. Others would be called to back up his pack of lies. Pinhas and Bartholomew squirmed in place. They must have accepted bribes. Rot them! The traitors better hope the court reached a verdict of guilt, otherwise they were dead men.

Simeon tilted his nose up and sat down.

Chief Priest Hyrcanus called for Herod's accusers to stand.

Herod crossed his arms and puffed out his chest.

Silence reigned.

The members of the Sanhedrin shared uncomfortable looks and shifted in their seats, their hesitance, no doubt, due to the small army outside the Hall Of Hewn Stones. A word from Herod and the soldiers would wreak havoc on Jerusalem.

Nervous coughs echoed off the walls.

Finally, one man rose. Shemaiah. The elderly man was well-respected and principled.

Shemaiah frowned at his fellow elders. "We have before us two men accused of murder. I will address

Nathan of Rumah's case first. Have you seen his wife's bruises?"

Caught by surprise, Nathan moaned out loud. The type of feral cry he had to stifle each time he looked at Lex's injuries.

Anguish filled Shemaiah's kind eyes. "Forgive me, son. Your wife strikes me as a strong woman. I assume she won't mind me speaking of these things to save you."

Nathan's chest tightened. Of course Lex wouldn't mind. He marveled at her inner strength. She'd already forgiven those who had wronged her.

Shemaiah cleared his throat. "If someone beat my wife, I would kill the fiend and feed the worthless man's remains to my dogs."

Audible gasps circled the room. Old and sprightly, Shemaiah fit everyone's ideal of the kind-hearted grandfather. He narrowed his eyes at his fellow elders. "A man may kill, but it doesn't make him a killer. Nathan of Rumah did what any of us would."

Nathan thought of his father. Though the gentlest of men, Joseph of Rumah would undoubtedly have acted brutally on behalf of his wife and children. But nobody would make the mistake of calling him a murderer.

Lex's words came back to him. *The only times your blood sings is when someone you love or care for is in danger.* Would he have spared Judas if the rebel had surrendered? Yes. Yes, he would have. It was Judas who refused to back down. It was kill or be killed. Nathan exhaled. He hated the title angel of death, and probably always would, but he needed to stop running from it. It might actually be for the good—others would think twice before lifting a hand to his loved ones.

His chest tightened. What a fool he had been for refusing to touch Lex. If the Sanhedrin found him guilty, he'd be put to death immediately. *Let me live, Lord. I want to hold my wife in my arms again.*

Shemaiah's eyes shifted and turned frosty. "Herod of Idumea's case is altogether different. He murdered a man to gain favor with Rome."

Herod jumped up and jabbed his finger at the elder. "You would have slapped Hezekiah's hand and sent him home."

"Sit down," Nathan said through gritted teeth.

Shemaiah didn't flinch. "Thanks to your high-handedness, we will never know what we might have done, will we?"

"Ignorant fools," Herod said, glaring around the hall. "Sextus Caesar praised my action. Rome sent a rousing commendation."

Nathan flinched. Shemaiah spoke true. Herod cared more about pleasing Rome than securing the trust and respect of his countrymen.

Shemaiah stood taller. "If we let this ox intimidate us, there will be no stopping him. Herod is far too ambitious. Let him go today, and he will come back someday as king and slay us."

"Amen. Amen," several voices sang out.

Emboldened, Shemaiah turned to High Priest Hyrcanus. "Call the witnesses, and we will put the matter to a vote."

A rumble of approval went up.

Red-faced, Herod looked ready to explode.

Like a battlefield on the brink of war, the air was thick with tension. Nathan's breathing slowed. His eyes scanned the room. His fingers curled, itching to grip a sword. What if the soldiers waiting in the courtyard of the Temple started to cut people down? Lex and Rhoda were in the middle of that crowd.

Truth be told, he wasn't sure what he'd do if matters turned violent. The situation was impossible. The thought of drawing the sword against either the rulers of Israel or Herod made him sick.

High Priest Hyrcanus stood and held up his chubby hands. "This session is hereby adjourned. We will take the matter up again tomorrow." A loud uproar rocked the hall. Men jumped to their feet. The rotund priest beat a hasty path for the door. Passing Herod, he paused. "This delay is the best I can do. I advise you to use the reprieve to leave the country."

"Why, you—" Herod growled, but the high priest was already scurrying away.

Bodies packed the aisles leading to the exit. The immediate danger over, Nathan rolled his tight shoulders. He and Herod fell into line.

"What are you going to do?" Nathan asked.

Herod cast a hate-filled look about the hall. "I'm going to Syria. Sextus Caesar will put these windbags in their place." He laid a hand on Nathan's shoulder. "Come with me."

Nathan massaged his forehead. He didn't want to see his good friend put to death. But Herod was going about this all wrong. "Give me time to think about it," Nathan said, stalling. Actually, he wanted to talk the matter over with Lex and Rhoda.

His gut twisted, remembering the sad look on Lex's face when she asked him if he'd consulted her just to please his father. What a selfish idiot he'd become.

Herod's black eyes met Nathan's. "I'm counting on

you."

"You'll hear from me soon."

A hand gripped Nathan's elbow, holding him back. Simeon Onais's bald-headed slave shoved a folded note into Nathan's hand and fled.

Nathan looked around. Was the message from Simeon or the slave? Sure he wasn't going to like the contents, no matter the author, Nathan shoved the letter into his pocket. It could wait. All he cared about was finding Lex.

CHAPTER 31

A slave woman belonging to Antipater came to Rhoda and Lex after court was dismissed with a message from Nathan, instructing them to return to camp, and he would meet them there.

Tight-lipped the whole walk back to the Mount of Olives, Rhoda continued to show her displeasure with Nathan by banging and clanging her way through the preparations for the evening meal. Thinking it best to stay out of the way, Alexandra sat under the ancient olive tree shading the tents, entertaining Mary and Timothy with a made-up game that involved tossing olive pits into a clay cup.

The amusement required a minimum of her attention, which was good, as she couldn't stop worrying over Nathan.

"Lex."

She turned at the sound of the breathless voice. Nathan jogged toward her. His face was flushed and intent. She stood. Her hand went to her throat. Was he bringing good news or bad news?

He raced the last of the way, caught her up in his arms, and buried his face in her neck. His warm lips moved against her flesh. "Lex, forgive me. Please forgive me."

She shuddered and rubbed his back. "What happened? What's the matter?"

His hot breath filled her ear. "I need you. I ache to lie with you."

Her pulse quickened and heat rushed through her. It had been weeks since they slept together as man and wife. She was starved for him.

Rhoda announced her presence with several noisy coughs. "Come along, Mary and Timothy. I have some friends I want to visit before your brother drags us off to live in Antipater's *grand home*. We will have our dinner elsewhere." Her voice was purposely loud." We won't be back until dark."

Nathan's low laugh curled through Alexandra.

The older woman cleared her throat. "Be good to my Alexandra, or I will have something to say about it."

"I've been a fool," Nathan confessed to his stepmother. "A mistake I hope to correct very soon." His hands slid up and down Alexandra's waist. "If you will have me," he whispered, his voice thick.

She pushed closer to him. "Always and forever."

He scooped her off her feet and crossed the camp with long, powerful strides. The small tent went dark as he closed the flap. Nathan's desire filled the air. He laid her down, and his body covered her, pressing her into the ground. His hungry mouth devoured her mouth. Her blood heated. He'd never come to her like this. So desperate. So needy. His teeth nipped into her lower lip. Her insides contracted. She cried out.

Nathan pulled back. He was panting. "I'm sorry."

"Don't stop." She reached for him. "Please don't

stop."

Concern and yearning warred on his face. "I am burning up for you. I'm afraid I'll hurt you."

She licked her swollen lip. "Come. Come lose yourself in me."

His brown eyes flared and his full weight crashed down on her. "I love you, Lex."

She wrapped her arms tight around him.

Sparkling sunlight danced over the tent entrance. A gentle breeze caressed Alexandra's arms. "I've missed this," she whispered.

Nathan wound a lock of her hair around his finger. "I didn't think it was possible to love you more than I already did. You are too good to me. Especially after the way I treated you."

Gloriously content, she traced her finger over his bare chest. "What happened to bring on this...ah...change?"

She felt a tremble go through him. "I died a thousand times while Judas held you captive, imagining I'd lost you. I died a thousand more deaths this morning, thinking I might never get to hold you in my arms again."

She touched his face. "I wept for joy when I heard the charges against you had been dropped."

His fingers stroked the sensitive skin along her jaw. "All I could think about when I left the Hall of Hewn Stones was getting to you. But I knew if I saw you, I wouldn't be able to keep my hands off of you, so I sent the slave woman to tell you to go without me and I went to the bazaars to give you and Rhoda time to reach the camp. I bought you a gift."

She smiled. "You did?"

He stretched out his free arm, grabbed his tunic and pulled an ivory-colored scarf from one pocket. Something else dropped out. Nathan draped the cloth over her head. "To replace the one we plan to burn."

Her breath caught. "It's beautiful." Short and light, the scalloped edge of the linen head cover was decorated with the finest embroidery she'd ever seen. "I thought you forgot."

"No, but I did forget about this." He held a folded note between his fingers.

"Where did you get that?"

"Goda gave it to me."

She frowned. "What does it say?"

"I don't know. I didn't read it."

She helped him open the note.

"Twenty silver pieces will buy you free passage into a hated Pharisee's home," Nathan read.

Her inside turned cold. She was tired of hate, death, and revenge. "I know my father deserves to be punished, but—"

Nathan placed his finger to her lips. "Shh, you don't have to worry. Your father is safe from me. I sat in court this morning, watching Herod's rage turn him into something ugly. Disgusted with him and with myself, my anger burst like rotten fruit under a boot. I realized what a fool I had been for wasting my time hating, when I could use it to love you."

She took Goda's letter from him, tossed it aside, and drew his hands to her stomach. "You'll soon have more reason to choose love. I am with child." She'd been waiting for a good time to tell him. She held her breath.

Nathan's face lit up. "Lex." He sat up and pulled her

onto his lap. His smile faltered. "How are you? Have you been sick?"

"No. Well, I'm tired, but otherwise I feel good." She sighed. "Are you happy about the baby? Truly happy?"

Nathan pulled her to his chest and stroked her hair. "Aside from our wedding night, this is the happiest day of my life."

Joy bubbled through her.

"I am going to move you to Antipater's house, today," Nathan said. "You deserve a real home. A real bed."

Her elation waned, Alexandra squeezed her eyes closed. "Whenever I imagine our child. I see us sitting under the shade of an olive tree with the baby. I see the farm."

Nathan's hand stilled. "It's a hard life."

He hadn't said no. She took it as a good sign. "Are you determined to sell the farm and rejoin the army?"

Nathan kissed her forehead. "No. I'd like to talk it over with you and Rhoda and decide together what's best for the family."

She hugged him. "You are going to make a wonderful father."

Come nightfall Nathan and Lex sat holding hands by a small fire. Rhoda had returned to the campsite a short time earlier with Mary and Timothy. They hadn't stopped smiling since hearing about the baby. Their happy chatter soothed Nathan's raw soul. Anger and hatred lingered, shouting to be fed and nurtured, but he was determined to master it for the sake of his family, wife, and child. He wanted them to know the love of a good, kind, wise father.

Lex released his hand. "I'll be right back," she said, getting to her feet. She went inside the small tent and came back out carrying the heavy, ugly veil they hated. A beautiful smile lit her face as she balled up the long garment and tossed it into the fire.

Rhoda and Mary's eyes went wide.

Timothy's brows shot up. "Job's bones, Alexandra. Why'd you do that?"

Nathan smiled. They were coming more easily, no longer feeling quite so foreign on his face.

Alexandra wiped her hands and sat back down beside Nathan. The ivory scarf Nathan bought for her held back her long brown hair, a perfect counterpoint to her creamy, smooth skin and rose-tinged cheeks. Her gray eyes met his. "The veil belongs to an old life that is over and done with. My place is with you, wherever that leads."

Her entrance into his life was the greatest gift he'd ever received. Humbled, Nathan took her hand and squeezed her fingers. "You'd follow me to the other side of the world, if I asked, wouldn't you?"

A smile lit her face. She nodded.

He tried to imagine her living in a hulking fortress surrounded by an army. A foul taste arose. He swallowed. Another image arose—Alexandra kissing him under the leaves of the young olives trees they'd planted beside the ancient olive orchard she loved.

Taking her from the farm to live as a soldier's wife would just be exchanging one hard life for another. He was deceiving himself to think otherwise. His reasons for running away from the farm had all been selfish ones.

He cleared his throat. "I've been having second

thoughts about selling the farm and rejoining the army."

"Praise heaven," Rhoda said in her straightforward way.

Mary and Timothy clapped and spoke over one another.

Lex's brow creased. "But you will have to live beside your enemies."

Nathan kissed her fingers. "With you showing me the way, I hope I can learn to be as forgiving as you. I want to be able to walk through Rumah again. I want to work beside Pinhas. I want to attend synagogue. To pray and read from the precious scrolls I have known and loved since I was a boy." He studied the flames licking the sky. "But, we need to be ready to accept the fact our neighbors might never welcome us back into their midst."

Rhoda reached over and patted Nathan's knee. "I would like to try to live in peace with them. I'm praying my Joseph's death shook some sense into them."

He turned to Lex.

She nodded. "I agree with Rhoda."

"It's decided, then," Nathan said. "We will keep the farm."

Lex, Rhoda, and Mary shared happy smiles

Timothy sighed loudly. "I probably wouldn't have liked living in a fort."

Mary put her arm around Timothy. "Nathan will finish the stone house, and you will forget all about forts."

The boy propped his chin in his hands dejectedly.

"Cheer up, monkey," Nathan said. "I'll take you to visit High Priest Hyrcanus's palace fortress tomorrow, and we can take Royal out for a ride while we're there."

Timothy smiled wide and nodded enthusiastically.

Lex leaned against Nathan. "Herod won't like it when you tell him you're not joining the army. He'll press you hard to ride as one of his men."

"Trust me to deal with Herod. I have plenty of practice saying no to him." Nathan recalled the hate-filled look on Herod's face after the trial, and his threats against the Sanhedrin. "I think Herod and I would have soon parted ways even if I had decided to join the army."

Lex rubbed his arm. "Thank you for doing this for us."

"I'm doing it for myself, as well." He kissed the top of her head. "I don't want to find myself in another war, lifting a sword against my brethren."

"Will you sell your sword?" Rhoda asked.

He shook his head. "No. But I vow I will never raise my sword in battle, unless it is to protect my family."

By the end of the week the Mount of Olives filled with those arriving to observe *Pesach*.

Nathan and Timothy sat on a blanket outside the main tent under a bright, blue sky. The boy lined up his newest collection of rocks, shining up a speckled stone with a wet rag. Nathan stroked the blade of his knife over the oiled sharpening stone, lifted the knife to the sun, and inspected it.

Pinhas and Bartholomew accompanied Barjesus and Sapphira into the camp.

Nathan's joints tightened. The villagers from Rumah had been settling into the campsites around them, but until now none of them had gone out of their way to pick a fight. He longed to be at one with his neighbors again, but he'd settle for an end to the open hostility. He set the knife aside and stood. "Go get the others," he instructed Timothy. The boy raced inside the tent. Lex, Rhoda, and Mary followed him back out.

"*Shalom*, neighbors," Bartholomew called out.

Nathan nodded. "Peace to you." They were off to a good start.

Pinhas wore a hesitant look. "We've come to offer our apologies."

The tension knotting Nathan's shoulders eased. He offered his friend a smile. "You don't know how good it is to hear you say that."

"So, you've finally come to your senses," Rhoda said. "What happened?" Leave it to his practical-minded stepmother to come to the point.

Bartholomew pointed at Barjesus and Sapphira. "These two refuse to be quiet. They've gone near and far telling everyone of Judas's evils."

"We told them how brave you were, Alexandra," Sapphira added, her face beaming.

Lex blushed at the praise, but she didn't duck her head as she used to when finding herself the center of attention. She reached out for Sapphira's hand and squeezed it. "We wish you a happy marriage."

Dewy-eyed and pink-cheeked, the former slave maid appeared very much in love. "Bless you all for your kindness," Sapphira said. "Will you come to our wedding? Please say you will."

Nathan gave Bartholomew a direct look. "Will we be welcomed?" Nathan held his breath.

The elder's corpulent face sagged. "I did you and your family a great wrong. Will you ever be able to forgive me?"

Lex, Rhoda, and Mary spoke over one another. "Yes. Of course. Indeed."

A heavy weight fell off Nathan's back. Thick emotion filled his chest and throat. "I already forgave you. I did it for my father's sake, and for my family, and for myself. But it is good to be able to say it to you." The sweetness of forgiveness tasted better in his mouth than the sour remains of revenge. He didn't know if he'd ever achieve the utter serenity his father had worn like a second skin. But, if he got even halfway there, he was sure to be the happiest man in Galilee.

Timothy pushed his way forward. "Does this mean I'll be able to play with Matthias again?"

Pinhas kneeled down in front of Timothy. "Matthias told me to tell you that even though I wouldn't allow him to see you he is still your friend. He would like you to climb the crooked tree with him. He's there now."

Timothy swiveled his head around. "Can I go?" he asked, his eyes bright.

Nathan squeezed the boy's small shoulder. "Make sure you are back by dinner."

Timothy gave a loud whoop and galloped off.

Everybody laughed. Everyone except Pinhas. The stonecutter climbed to his feet as though weighed down by a load of the stones he so skillfully cut. His pained eyes met Nathan's. "If I had known Judas was going to the farm, I would have found a way to stop him. He told us he was taking his men deeper into the mountains. I cared for Joseph like he was my own father. I hate that he died so senselessly."

The confession washed over Nathan like a refreshing rain. He patted Pinhas' arm. "Father never stopped loving you or believing the best about you. I'm glad you were there to help me put Father into the grave. It would have pleased him."

Pinhas' face flushed red. "I should have stood by you." He stabbed at the dirt with his sandal. "You probably won't believe me, but Bartholomew and I were at your trial to testify to your innocence."

Nathan winced. He'd been angry with his neighbors for rushing to believe the worst about him, yet he'd done the same in return. He touched Pinhas's sleeve. They looked each other in the eye. "I thought my father-in-law had bribed you to tell lies about me," Nathan said. "I was thinking some very unkind things about you that day. We've both said and done things we wish we hadn't. I'm ready to put it all in the past. Know you will be welcomed back into my home with open arms, if you so choose."

Pinhas sagged in place. "Martha and I would like to share the *Pesach* supper with you." He turned red again and shook his head with vigor. "I know. That's too much to ask."

Nathan wanted to whoop like Timothy had. He hadn't allowed himself to hope for this much. The two families had always celebrated *Pesach* together. He laughed. "Nothing could make us happier."

Pinhas pinched the corners of his eyes, staunching his tears. "May the Lord strike me dead if I turn my back on you again, my friend."

Nathan's chest tightened. He embraced the stonecutter and gave him a kiss on both cheeks. "The Lord strike me dead if I ever lift a sword against my friends."

They thumped each other's backs and stepped apart, Pinhas grinning as foolishly as Nathan.

"My Joseph said you two would reconcile," Rhoda

said sobbing. She dabbed her eyes on the washrag clutched in her hand. "I wish he could be here to see it."

Alexandra put her arm around Rhoda's thin shoulders. Their growing friendship pleased Nathan.

Bartholomew shifted his bulk from one foot to the other. "If there is anything I can do for you, name it."

There was another matter Nathan hoped to settle for Lex's peace of mind. "My wife's brother is missing. We'd appreciate it if you would ask around about the boy."

"Bartholomew! Pinhas!" A breathless voice called out. Old Zeke hobbled toward. He came to a wheezing stop. "Trouble's coming. Herod is marching an army on Jerusalem."

Nathan stomach soured, recalling the look in Herod's eye when he left the Hall of Hewn Stones.

Bartholomew's jowls shook. "What's this?"

Pinhas frowned. "Where'd you hear that wild rumor?"

Old Zeke pointed up at the city. "A messenger returning from Egypt came across the soldiers this morning. The temple guard is out in full force. High Priest Hyrcanus and most of the Sanhedrin are locked inside the Temple, and the markets are crowded with people buying up all the food and wine."

Nathan asked, "Do you know who the messenger rides for? The messenger might be riling everyone up for nothing. A couple hundred men is a far cry from an army."

Old Zeke frowned. "The man was Antipater's messenger."

Nathan exhaled heavily. "Antipater's man would know a legion when he saw one. Herod went to Syria. He must have convinced Sextus Caesar to give him a small army."

Lex pressed against Nathan. "Do you think Herod would actually attack Jerusalem?"

Nathan dragged his hand over his face. "He was angry and making threats. And a man doesn't march an army across the land on a whim."

"Do you think Antipater put Herod up to it?" Bartholomew asked.

"No," Nathan replied. "Herod's style is to strike out. Antipater is more subtle than that. I doubt he knows what Herod is up to." Nathan scanned the campsites dotting the orchard, then looked back at his friends. "We can't stay here. Go pack up your families and take them inside the city walls."

Bartholomew 's pudgy face fell. "Surely Antipater will stop Herod,"

Mind filling with tasks to be done, Nathan shook his head. "Antipater is in Idumea. Herod's brothers are away as well. By the time they get word, it might be too late for them to act."

Bartholomew pointed. "You ought to ride out to Herod. Try to talk some sense into him."

Lex inhaled sharply.

Nathan touched his hand to her elbow. "I can't leave my family unprotected." Memories of Roman soldiers swarming through Jerusalem came flooding back. Priests cut down as they performed their sacred duties. The blood of his fellow Jews pooling in the streets.

Pinhas straightened. "I'll watch over Rhoda and Alexandra for you."

Nathan smiled tightly. "I appreciate the offer, but—"

"But, nothing," Bartholomew said.

Bile rose in Nathan's throat. "Herod won't listen. I

begged him not to kill Hezekiah. But it didn't help."
He pictured Hezekiah's head dropping to the ground. A
great ache filled his heart. His eyes moved between Bartholomew, Pinhas, and Old Zeke. "I tried to save Hezekiah. I truly tried."

Bartholomew's eyes softened. "I believe you, son."
Pinhas and Zeke nodded in agreement.

Nathan swallowed. "I hate what happened."

"So do we," Bartholomew said. The corners of
his mouth turned downward. "After all you've been
through, I can understand why you don't want to be
apart from your family. But you must try to stop
Herod."

Nathan turned to Lex. "What do you think?" He'd already asked so much of her.

She linked her fingers with his. "Herod is our friend.
We can't turn our backs on him." Outwardly she was a
picture of calm. But Nathan felt the rapid beat of her
blood rushing through her wrist.

Amazed again by her strength and her loving heart,
he squeezed her hand. "Very well, I'll go."

Showered with blessing from his family and friends,
Nathan headed for the stables. One question drummed
in his mind. How was he supposed to turn back the
army bearing down on Jerusalem?

CHAPTER 32

P inhas escorted Lex and the rest of the family to her father's home shortly after Nathan rode out of Jerusalem. They'd arrived a few hours ago to find her father missing and the house closed up. They learned from the neighbors that Simeon had fled to Egypt taking Lydia and the slaves with him. Alexandra assumed her father was afraid Herod would kill him for even thinking about raising his own army.

She hoped rather than believed the change would be good for Lydia.

A knock sounded at the door. Alexandra hurried across the open-air courtyard, half expecting it to be one of her Galilean neighbors. She'd offered shelter to anyone who didn't have a place to go. Most had relatives in Jerusalem, but Sapphira and Barjesus's families had come, as well as few others.

Pinhas greeted her with a weak smile.

Lex's hand went to her throat. *Please don't let anything have happened to Nathan.*

"No, it's not Nathan," Pinhas hastened to assure her.

She resumed breathing. "What then?"

Pinhas offered her a weak smile. "I would like to

bring my family here so I can watch over you and Rhoda in case the worst happens."

"What about Antipater's men?"

Nathan had asked Pinhas to round up able men to stand guard over them.

"They are on their way." Pinhas shrugged. "I want to be here for Nathan. And for you. Not many people would have acted as selflessly as you have, sending your husband off with an army approaching."

Embarrassed, Lex ducked her head. She hadn't watched Nathan go with a brave smile because she was courageous or insensible to the danger. She'd done it for Nathan. For all the things she loved about him, his loyalty, devotion, and goodness. She might as well cut his heart out as ask him to turn away from his responsibilities. He'd married her out of duty, hadn't he? The sacrifice of her peace of mind seemed a minor price to pay for all she gained. She certainly shouldn't be praised for it.

Pinhas cleared his throat. "I also came to tell you I found your brother."

Her head snapped up. She blinked repeatedly. "James? Did you speak to him?"

"No. I was afraid of scaring him off. I can take you to him, if you like."

Mind whirling, Lex nodded. "I'll go tell Rhoda and we can leave."

A few moments later Pinhas was leading Alexandra and Mary through Jerusalem's jammed streets. News that Herod was marching on Jerusalem had sent the festival pilgrims and the people who lived outside the city walls streaming into the city. People scurried here and there on urgent business or stood in small circles outside their homes, somberly speculating over Herod and his Roman army. Children peeked out from the safety of their doorways, eyes wide with fear or excitement.

Mary clung to Alexandra's hand. They'd brought her along to close the mouths of the gossips, but given the current tumult, a man and woman would have to be practicing adultery openly in the street for anyone to notice.

They left the upper city behind and entered the Mishneh District. They came upon a small work party patching a tumble-down section of the city wall.

"Most of the men have gone home." Pinhas raised his voice to be heard over the ping of hammer on stone. "The young men without families volunteered to stay and continue the work."

Lex nodded and smiled.

Pinhas went to have a word with the stonecutters.

Mary pressed closer to her. "James didn't go far from home."

Lex peered down the nearby alleys. "I didn't know James and Father had friends in this part of the city."

"Lex."

Alexandra turned at the sound of her brother's voice. A young stonecutter stood before her. The boy's clothes were stained with dirt and sweat. His face was beet-red from exertion, almost hiding the purple scar crossing one cheek.

Lex's lips went numb. "James?"

Her brother actually smiled. "It's me."

"How? What?" Lex touched James's grimy sleeve, trying to make sense of what she was seeing. "Did you have a fight with Father?"

James's smile vanished. "I despise the man. I want

nothing more to do with him."

"You can come live with me and Nathan." She didn't know what else to say.

James shook his head. "I'm staying here."

Lex recognized the stubborn tone. "You can go home. Father has taken Lydia to Egypt. I think it will be a very long time before we see them again."

"They left?" James asked astonished. "Do you know what this means?" A hateful smile crossed his grimy face. "He will miss *Pesach*."

She stared blankly at James.

He rubbed his hands together. "He's never missed the required feasts. Not ever."

Lex's eyes filled with tears. She didn't know what made her sadder—James's utter glee over this sad fact or that he kept calling Father *he*.

James stepped closer. Her brother smelled of the dirt and hard work. "Don't cry over me, Sister." He wiped away a tear. "I'm not worth it." Hands that had been soft and smooth were now rough and dry.

His sad eyes broke her heart. She threw her arms around him. "You *are* worth it. Come home, James. I promise things will be better."

He freed himself and set her at arm's length. "I'm staying with the stonecutters."

She choked back tears. "Why?"

"You wouldn't understand." He glanced at Pinhas and then back at her, a mask of grim determination in place. "Don't waste time worrying about me. I'm with good people, doing good work." He patted her arm. "Go be happy, Alexandra. You deserve it."

Then he turned and walked back to the wall. Gripping a heavy hammer, he swung it up and down, matching the slow, steady rhythm of the other stonecutters. His shoulders rolled with easy grace. She'd been used to seeing them hunched up around his ears. He looked older. Stronger. Different.

A small smile crossed her face. If he could hear her, he'd get that sour look on his face he always got when he was unhappy. Or would he? Maybe this change was for the best.

Mary took hold of Lex's hand. "We should go back."

Pinhas waved goodbye to his stonecutter friends. "I'll keep an eye on him," he promised.

Lex nodded. "Thank you." She put her head down and walked away. The sound of hammer on stone grew dimmer and dimmer. Reaching the Fish Gate, she slowed and looked back one more time at her brother. *God go with you, James.*

She released a shuddering breath. A new family had been given into her keeping. They needed her. And she needed them. She lifted her chin and strode through the gate.

The cloud of dust had been visible for the last hour. The air was gritty with it now. The slap of hobnailed sandals pounding on stone grew louder and louder.

Royal loped up a small hill, and Nathan pulled the horse to a stop. Heavily armed soldiers marched six abreast up the straight, narrow road. It wasn't a full Roman legion. Even so, a thousand well-trained soldiers could slice through an undefended city as easily as a knife slipping through olive oil. At their present rate, the Roman army would reach the gates of Jerusalem by nightfall.

Nathan had ridden out of Jerusalem alone. It couldn't be helped. He was one of the few men who owned a horse, and he was also one of the few men Herod might listen to. Messengers had been sent to Antipater and his sons, alerting them to the looming disaster. Nathan needed to find a way to slow Herod down until help arrived.

Royal shifted nervously under him. Nathan flicked the reins clutched in his hand and descended toward the mouth of the lion.

Herod left the vanguard behind and crossed the valley to meet him. The sun glinted off his black, woolly hair as his sleek white stallion pranced to a stop in front of Nathan.

"Olive farmer," Herod said, his black eyes guarded. "I don't suppose you've come to join me?"

Nathan hated that things had come to this. "I won't take up arms against my people. I've had enough of that."

Herod nodded. "Jerusalem is safe from me. I swear it. My fight is with the Sanhedrin."

"No Israelite will see it that way."

Herod's face darkened. "I'm as Jewish as you are."

Nathan leaned forward in his saddle. "Prove it. Turn your army around."

"Prove you are a man," Herod spit back. "Join me. Or maybe you like groveling at the feet of those old leeches."

"I hate the corruption. That doesn't mean I want to see the members of the Sanhedrin killed. There has to be another way."

Herod was his own worst enemy. Couldn't he see that, choosing Rome over the Lord God of Israel would prove his critics correct?

Herod slashed his hand through the air. "Coddling the Sanhedrin hasn't worked. The rot is too deep. The seat of power needs to be gutted and rebuilt." He wagged his thick brows. "Your father-in-law can be the first to die."

Nathan hesitated.

"Ha!" Herod pointed, triumphant. "You're tempted. Don't deny it."

Nathan held onto his calm. "This is the Lord's business."

"I've made it my business."

Nathan lifted a brow. "Why?"

Herod's lips firmed.

Nathan slapped his palm to his forehead. "You aren't satisfied with being Governor of Galilee. You want more."

Herod's chest swelled. "I want to give my father a kingdom. What's wrong with that? High Priest Hyrcanus wants to grow richer and fatter. And Simeon Onias wants to be high priest. The difference is that my ambition is naked. I am not hiding it behind priestly robes and false piety."

Nathan scrubbed his face. He thought Herod ten times a better man than Judea's present elders. He was a learned man, a natural soldier, and a skilled leader. He had the talent to create gardens as beautiful as Solomon's, and the vision to build cities as great as David's. But Antipater couldn't be king, and neither could Herod. And all the money and armies in the world wouldn't change that immovable truth.

Nathan strove to sound reasonable. "The people will never accept a king who doesn't come from the line of

David."

"They can complain all they want, as long as they bend the knee to my father."

Herod's stallion nipped at Royal. Nathan clicked his tongue and Royal backed up. Nathan shot Herod a skeptical look. "I've never heard Antipater say he wanted to be king."

"I don't know how Father tolerates bowing to that weasel Hyrcanus." Herod uncorked his water pouch and took a long drink. Wiping his mouth, he smiled with grim satisfaction. "Let's see how brave our high priest is when he finds a Roman army on his doorstep. I will enjoy making him kiss my feet."

Nathan's jaw clenched. "This isn't about your father. This is about your overblown pride." For all Herod's strengths, they weren't balanced with humility and godliness. Nathan knew it and loved his friend despite it. He'd had always feared Herod's pride would be his undoing. Still, the magnitude of Herod's ambition, the blatant disregard for the decrees of God, and the depth of his contempt for the people of God stunned.

"I'm surprised Sextus Caesar went along with you," Nathan said. It went against the Roman policy of *Pax Romana*, the marrying of peace and prosperity. The rebel trouble in Galilee would pale compared to the uprising that would explode if Herod butchered the members of the Sanhedrin.

"The bribe helped." Herod grunted and laughed. "Bribes always help."

Nathan shook his head in disgust.

Herod looked away. "Support me on this, Nathan, and Simeon Onias's wealth is yours. Think of the good you can do. Think—"

"Don't," Nathan said viciously. "Would you try to bribe your brothers?"

Herod's head snapped back around. "Don't get self-righteous with me. You like money as well as any man."

"This isn't about me. This is about you being a pig-headed bully."

Herod turned his stallion into Royal with a hard bump. Royal stumbled and neighed loudly.

"Job's bones!" Nathan complained, pulling back on his reins. The startled war horse regained his footing.

Herod wheeled his horse about. He locked eyes with Nathan. "I'm asking you as a friend to stand by me."

Nathan gasped as though absorbing a punch. He'd take on Rome or Persia, or the pits of hell, if Herod asked. But he couldn't ride into Jerusalem and cut down his fellow Jews. Not again. And Herod knew it better than anyone.

"Beelzebub take you," Nathan said, more disappointed than angry. He didn't want Herod going down that path, either. Their friendship wouldn't survive. It was dying as they spoke. Nathan exhaled heavily and looked away.

Riders streamed over the hill—Antipater, Herod's three brothers, Kadar, a handful of soldiers. Thank the Lord. Maybe one of them could talk some sense into Herod.

Horses and men came to a halt. Fresh dust swirled up.

Herod's white teeth flashed. "Sextus Caesar sends his greetings." He jerked his thumb at the approaching army. "Not bad, huh?"

His brothers and Kadar shifted uncomfortably in their saddles. Antipater frowned. "Sextus Caesar ordered you to attack Jerusalem?"

Herod's smile faded. "Not in so many words. But Sextus was none too happy to hear how I was treated. He's not going to sit back and let the Sanhedrin execute me."

"Sextus loaned you an army so you could protect yourself," Antipater pointed out, then shook his head. "Having an army camped out in Galilee would have caused plenty of outrage. But this..." He waved in the direction of the invading soldiers. "How am I supposed to explain this?"

Herod's face darkened. He punched his fist into his palm. "Kill the pompous fools and you won't have to answer to anybody."

Disappointment washed through Nathan. He shook his head sadly.

"Have some patience, son," Antipater soothed. "There is a right time to fight, and this isn't one of them."

"I can't turn back now. I'll look like a fool." Herod's lips firmed. "I've started this, and I mean to finish it."

His bothers winced. Nathan frowned.

Antipater blew out an impatient breath. "If you go, you are on your own. You won't get any help from me."

"Own my own?" Herod repeated, a note of hesitation in his voice.

"I've spent years wooing men and building alliances." Antipater remained rock calm. "Go ahead and wreck the careful web I've constructed. Your brothers and I will go back home and leave you to figure out how to put everything right afterward."

Nathan flinched. He hated witnessing Herod get put in his place, no matter how much his hard-headed friend needed it.

Black eyes churning like a storm-tossed sea, Herod

bit down on his words. "Very well. I will return to Galilee and await word from you."

Antipater urged his horse forward, until he was even with his son's white stallion. "Send Sextus's army back home with my thanks." He patted Herod's arm. "I'll send word when it's safe for you to return to Jerusalem."

Herod gave a curt nod and wheeled his horse around. "Ha," he called out. The stallion bolted forward, and man and beast disappeared behind a curtain of dust.

A heaviness filled Nathan's chest, watching the dust cloud grow smaller and smaller. *Goodbye, friend. May the Lord's mercy go with you.*

CHAPTER 33

A lexandra fluffed up the soft pillow. She set it beside the others on her childhood bed. A week and a half had passed since Nathan had faced down Herod. The festival celebrations had come to a close. Eager to return to the farm, she'd come to her father's home to bid goodbye to the room she and Lydia had shared. Dappled sunlight fell across the mosaic-tiled floor and danced over the floral mural covering the walls. The room spoke of wealth and privilege, but its grand opulence didn't begin to compare with the wild beauty of Galilee's rolling hills, or the simple pleasures of the olive farm.

She tiptoed to the middle of the room and ran her hand over the smooth, wooden backs of the chairs she and Lydia had sat in for hour upon hour. Her fingers came away covered with dust. Smothered by memories of the relentless quiet and endless monotony of her former life, she moved to the lattice-covered window. Inhaling the fresh air, she peered through the diamond-shaped openings.

Familiar sights greeted her. Benjamin and Banna, cherub-faced boys and future priests, wrestled on the ground in a nearby courtyard. A dozen black-clad, long-bearded Pharisees moved in a solemn procession down the main road. The white columns of Phillip Peter's house. A woman looked out the second-story window —Phillip Peter's new bride, Martha.

Lex waved. Martha lifted her hand.

Alexandra could be sitting there now as Peter's wife, but then Nathan had come charging over that Galilean hill and into her life.

Nathan didn't just save her from the rebels that day. He rescued her from sitting at a window, watching life pass her by. Most marvelous of all, he'd saved her from a safe, dull marriage, and blessed her with one filled with happiness and love.

She pressed her hands to her belly, where their baby grew. *Praise you, Lord, for your grace and goodness to us.*

Excited chatter broke out below. She saw the reason for the commotion and smiled. Her beautiful husband was walking toward the house. He was coming for her, coming to take her home.

Pinhas and a few other men from Rumah accompanied Nathan, as did Sapphira and Barjesus. One by one their Galilean neighbors had been stopping by the campsite to offer their apologies and to ask for forgiveness. It did Alexandra's heart good to see Nathan talking and laughing with them.

The black-clad Pharisees swarmed around Nathan. Men came out of nearby houses. They clapped Nathan on the back, offering him blessings and thanks. Sapphira and Barjesus stood off to the side, smiling their approval. The newly married couple sang Nathan and Alexandra's praises wherever they went, and Lex knew they had helped Nathan's reinstatement into the community tremendously.

Lex and Sapphira liked each other better now, but she didn't think they would ever be good friends. Lex couldn't quite find it in her heart to forgive the slave maiden for trying to steal her splendid husband.

Nathan spotted Lex in the window and smiled. Her breath hitched. She waved, spun around and crossed the room. Closing the door of her childhood room, she rushed down the stairs to join him.

A short time later they found themselves alone, walking down the winding road leading to the Mount of Olives. A warm breeze helped them on their way. Purple lilies poked out of rocky crevices.

Alexandra pushed closer to Nathan. "How did your meeting with Antipater go?" An official summons had arrived that morning.

"He thanked me for killing Judas. He asked if there was anything we needed."

"That was kind of him."

The wind ruffled Nathan's dark curls. "Antipater is many things, but kind is not one of them. He wants me to keep my eyes and ears open and tell him if anyone rises up to replace Hezekiah."

Her insides tensed. "Do you think that will happen?"

Nathan's fingers brushed against hers. "No. Hezekiah's death has had a chilling effect. Everyone just wants to return home and get on with their own business. Herod predicted that's what would happen."

She sighed. "Poor Herod. I imagine he would love to tell his critics 'I told you so.' And he'd be more than a little annoyed that you are being praised while he is being called every foul name there is."

Nathan ducked his head.

She bit her lip. Nathan was taking Herod's disgrace hard. "Will you go see him and try to mend your friendship?"

"No." Nathan's hand circled hers. "He'd take my head off if I tried."

"Are you sure he won't get over it?"

"I'm sure. I know him. He thinks I should be in Sepphoris with him, sharing his misery and outrage. "

She squeezed Nathan's hand. "Life on the farm will be hard for the next year or two without Herod's help."

Nathan pulled a leather pouch out of his pocket and dangled it in front of her. "Hold out your hand." She blinked. "It's heavy," Nathan warned, setting the bulging bag on her open palm.

Her fingers closed around soft leather. Coins clinked together. Her brows rose.

Nathan laughed. "Antipater gave me a reward."

She threw her arms around him. "Rhoda will be thrilled."

They grinned like children at each other, knowing what a feat it was to get a smile out of the no-nonsense woman.

Nathan smoothed his hand over her back. "We will be able to pay Pinhas to finish building the house. I won't have to hire out my labor to others, and I can immediately begin doubling the size of our orchard."

Excitement welling, Lex hugged Nathan and clutched the folds of his tunic. "Oh, and we can invite Barjesus and Sapphira and her parents to come and live and work on the farm like we talked about! And we can hire tutors for Timothy. And put aside a generous dowry for Mary." She went up on her toes and gave Nathan a long kiss.

His warm laugh curled around her. "What happened to the shy woman I married?"

She pulled her arms into her chest and stepped back. "Whoops," she said, looking around to see if anybody had been watching. A family was walking ahead of them, but their backs were to Alexandra and Nathan. She tried not to smile. "I can't wait to get back home."

Nathan's eyes darkened. "We will pitch our tent in the orchard."

She swallowed. "I would like that."

He gathered her close. "I thought you would."

"I never knew it could be this wonderful," she whispered.

"What?" He wiped a tear from the corner of her eye.

She pressed her hands to his chest. His heart beat strong against her palms. "This. Marriage. I didn't know it could be this full of love and happiness."

He took her hand and lifted it to his mouth. Warm lips brushed over her fingers. "I have some more good news for you." His beautiful eyes met hers. "We've only just started, my love. We've only just started."

HISTORICAL NOTE

The books in The Herod Chronicles series are a dramatization of historical events. My intentions are to present an overview of the events, while staying true to the spirit of the time.

The idea for The Warrior, and ultimately the series, came about while I was doing research for another book, and I read a short blurb about Herod the Great starting his career as the governor of Galilee. To please the Romans Herod killed Hezekiah, a man characterized as a bandit or a rebel, depending on your sympathies. Herod was put on trial for murder. Shemaiah was the only member of the Sanhedrin to speak up against Herod, prompting Herod to march on Jerusalem with a Roman army. These were the handful of facts I worked. The rest of the particulars of the story were all my invention.

Though they live in my heart and mind, Nathan and Alexandra, Simeon Onias, Judas the Zealot, and their extended families are entirely fictional.

To avoid confusion, I changed Antigonus's (The nephew of the High Priest John Hyrcanus.) name to Hasmond, as it was too similar to Antipater (Herod's father). I changed the time of Julius Caesar's visit to Antioch from summer to the previous winter. I did it for my own pleasure—I loved the idea of the maiden's dance and wanted it to play a part in Nathan and Alexandra's romance.

AUTHOR NOTE

Thank you for reading **The Warrior**! If you are so inclined, I'd love a review of The Warrior. Reviews can be hard to come by. You, the reader, have the power to make or break a book.

For more information about my books please visit my website: www.WandaAnnThomas.com

All the best,
Wanda Ann Thomas

WANDA ANN THOMAS'
BOOKS

THE HEROD CHRONICLES

The Warrior (Book 1)
The Barbarian (Book 2)
Warring Desires (Book 3)
Apostate Priest (Book 4)

Inspirational Ancient World Romance

Faithful Daughter of Israel

BRIDES OF SWEET CREEK RANCH

The Mail-Order Bride Carries a Gun (Book 1)
Gunslingers Don't Die (Book 2)
The Cowboy Refuses to Lose (Book 3)
The Cattle Rustler and the Runaway Bride (Book 4)
The Cowboy Takes A Gamble (Book 5)

ACKNOWLEDGEMENTS

Hugs and gratitude to my critique partners Megan, Michelle, Judi, and Deb. I can't thank you enough for sharing your advice and knowledge and for your tough, honest, insightful assessment of my writing. You girls are the best!

A big shout out to Romance Writers of America and my MERWA friends, great organizations lending assistance and education to aspiring and published authors.

Much appreciation to my editor Faith Freewoman who was a joy to work with. Her expertise and eye for detail added the shine to the manuscript. The beautiful book cover was created by Dar Albert of Wicked Smart Designs.

ABOUT THE AUTHOR

Wanda Ann Thomas is the author of Sweet Historical Western Romances and Ancient World Christian Romance. The common bond is my delight in LOVE stories. And creating stories is my happy place. After juggling a career as a dental hygienist and raising a family, I was ready for a new challenge. Twelve years and ten books later I am more enthralled with writing than ever.

Penning historical romances set among the tumultuous perils of the ancient world was inspired by my reading the works of the historian Josephus. The inspiration for THE HEROD CHRONICLES series came about while doing research for another project and learning the particulars of Herod the Great's career. A fascinating complicated man, Herod's larger-than-life exploits seemed made for fiction. Detailing the life and times of Herod also allowed me to explore my interest in the Roman world and my passion for heart-wrenching love stories, featuring warrior heroes and courageous heroines who will brave any danger for loved ones and struggle against overwhelming obstacles to win their happily ever after.

I'm blessed to be living my own happily ever after with

my high school sweetheart turned husband. Our three beautiful children and their spouses and the grandchildren are the light of our lives. When not at my desk writing I enjoy playing a round of golf, or sitting by the pool, or watching my flower gardens bloom. Road trips are a favorite recreation. There nothing more I relish than the excitement of traveling to new places and touring museums and historic homes or exploring cities or visiting national parks. And refreshed and brimming with vivid sights, sounds, and images, I am just as eager to return home and plunge back into writing the next story.

14602457R00225